NOLAN

Nolan: Western Promises Series, Book 1
© 2019 J.B. Richard
ISBN-Paperback: 978-0-9991553-1-8
ISBN-Ebook: 978-0-9991553-2-5

 Published by:
Fig Publishing
www.jbrichard.com

Editorial services by: Anne Victory, Editing and Gathering Leaves Editing
Cover and interior design by TLC Book Design, *TLCBookDesign.com*
Cover: Tamara Dever; Interior: Monica Thomas
Cowboy on horse ©okiepony/depsitphotos.com

Printed in the United States of America

WESTERN PROMISES
BOOK 1

NOLAN

J.B. RICHARD

FIG PUBLISHING

CHAPTER 1

SMOKE ROSE THICK in the sky, overcasting the valley. Nolan was sick to death of tracking this bunch.

"Dammit." He cursed under his breath.

Planting another burned-out homestead family was not how he wanted to start his morning. Stiffness had set into his achy bones from too many nights of sleeping on the ground. The thought of hot coffee and a fire to warm himself by appealed more to his raw senses. But all that was going to have to wait.

He kicked the bay gelding into a trot. His hand rested easy on his hip just above his pistol, ready for trouble if it came. He would have no pause in putting to death the sons of bitches that did this evil. Lawless men who took the lives of innocent folks and stole as they pleased needed killing. That had been Nolan's way of thinking even before Mary and Matthew were gunned down.

He gave a quick wave to Captain Farnsworth. The bluecoat soldiers were spread out along the tree line. Some of the army mounts pranced nervously in wait. Every gun was drawn and ready to follow Nolan's lead into another day of hell. God only knew what they would find. Nolan's mind was filled with the bloody picture of the butchering that had been done to the last four families he'd found while trailing this murdering bunch.

He'd blistered his hands while digging graves, along with the soldiers, to put each and every poor soul to rest. Children had been left where they'd fallen to rot in the heat of the day. And all the men had been scalped. It wasn't really a surprise. Some of the tracks they were following couldn't be mistaken as white men. It'd been an easy path to track. An unshod horse was a telling sign of dogging an Indian.

It wasn't often white men rode with red fellas, but that didn't appear to be the case this time. Crow—Nolan would bet for this neck of the woods—and Crow warriors were known to hack up the bodies of their victims. Nolan, unfortunately, had seen too much of that along this bloody trail. White men, even lawless ones, weren't usually savvy to that kind of savagery. A bullet point-blank between the eyes wasn't any less brutal, though perhaps quicker. There'd been a few homesteaders killed that way too, and that wasn't usually the way of an Indian. Nolan scratched his head. No matter. He would tree all those scumbags for Captain Farnsworth.

A hound dog was exactly what Nolan had been called by many. His tracking skills were matched only by Bill Hickok, who'd taught Nolan to read sign. His reputation of always treeing his man had been precisely why the army had sought him out to scout for Captain Farnsworth. They would catch this bunch of murdering thieves, but when?

So here he was, living off army bean slop, way the hell out in the middle of nowhere. Couldn't blame anyone but himself. He'd agreed to be scout for this shit. He must be addlebrained. Trailing after death and seeing nothing good in his days—he was growing mighty tired of it. At least the soldier boys had been smart enough to sign their names and get paid to suffer.

Nolan pulled up on the reins and sat his horse. He was sickened by what he saw. The inferno blazed above the treetops and warmed the morning chill. Of late, the buzz of swarming flies always seemed to be thick in his ears. He covered his mouth with his shirt to keep from choking. The suffocating black smoke billowed up from what was left of the log home still engulfed in flames. Another poor settler family snuffed out by the lawless breed the army was hunting. What a senseless loss of life.

Arrows stuck out of a man's chest, and the poor fella's hair had been lifted just like the other men they'd buried along this trail. Hell of a way to die. Poor nester most likely had been walking to the barn, thinking of hitching oxen to plow to begin a hard day's work. It wasn't an easy life, but it was honest.

A day would come when Nolan would rejoice in waking without being witness to death's misery. The bloody body, eyes wide and dully staring, lay on the open ground between the burning house and what was left of the barn. It, too, was being eaten by the strong appetite of the raging fire. The awful stench of the stock animals left inside to burn badly fouled the air and turned Nolan's stomach. By God, the thick stink would probably never leave his nostrils.

Red, white—didn't make any difference to Nolan. Lawless was lawless. These bastards he was trailing for the captain, hell, Nolan would enjoy watching them hang. Even if he had to unofficially throw down the hammer himself. Judgment would fall on every murdering one of the sons of bitches for what they'd done. Nolan and the soldiers had laid too many families in the ground. He might as well set up shop as an undertaker, rather than scouting. The dreaded chore of digging graves was one he was becoming far too familiar with, and he hated every back-aching minute of it. Each child he threw dirt on brought back memories of his son.

Why had he let Mary and Matthew step into that stagecoach?

Maybe, had he done things differently, the bleak gray sky of death wouldn't be always clouding over him. Instead of scouting, he would be working on the ranch he and Mary had bought after moving farther west. It'd been a nice, friendly little town they'd settled just outside of. Mary had been pleased that there was a schoolhouse and at least a circuit preacher. But that wasn't where Nolan's mind had been focused.

They'd creaked along the coach road in the wagon, and his eyes had taken in the sprawling acres of green prairie grass. That and a good source of water had been exactly what he'd needed to grow their small breeding stock of horses into many. After losing Mary and Matthew, Nolan had sold it all for a little bit of nothing.

If things hadn't changed in his life, maybe he would have sold a dozen head of horses to Captain Farnsworth. The army mounts were looking run-down. As were the captain's weary men from the long hours spent in the saddle over the past weeks of trailing this bunch. These thoughts of what Nolan's old life would be like in the present were foolish. Those dreams were as dead as Mary and Matthew and needed to stay buried.

Seeing no other bodies but the one man, Nolan figured if the nester had himself any young ones, they must have burned up inside the house. Maybe his woman too, if she hadn't been taken. Now there was no way of telling if there had been a woman here.

Besides being killers, the men they were trailing were stealing women. The bodies they'd buried from the other homesteads had all been men and children. Not one woman had been found alive or dead thus far. That sat funny with Nolan because Crow warriors weren't ever known to take a white woman captive. Thundercloud, a Crow scout for the army, had told Nolan months back that the Crow looked down on the whites as a filthy race. Crow bucks didn't breed with white women.

"Bury the dead!" It was the same order Captain Farnsworth had shouted at the past four burned-out homesteads.

Nolan pushed his hair under his hat and let out a deep sigh. His saddle creaked as he shifted his weight, and he yanked the reins and turned his horse. With fresh memories of Mary and Matthew in his mind, he wasn't picking up a spade to do any burying. He nudged the bay to walk away.

What good did he have in his life?

His thoughts drifted from the death all around him to Kate. It wasn't hard to picture the white picket fence, fresh-hung linens flapping on the line, and the smell of her good cooking wafting from the kitchen window. There was nothing prettier than the way her wavy strawberry hair always fell in messy rings over her shoulders. How long had it been—three, maybe four months—since he'd seen her last? Her beautiful smile was always welcoming, and she smelled as sweet as honeysuckle. Whew... he could almost feel his arms wrapped around her soft, slender frame. The thought made him lonely for her tender touch. If he didn't get himself killed, the first thing Nolan was going to do after catching this band of renegades was visit Kate. But who knew how long it would be until he could press his lips against hers?

Choosing to be a scout meant his days all ran together. Nolan rubbed a hand over his face.

Damn, his head was thumping. Gathering his wits was what he needed to do. He had a job to get done for the army. And that was exactly where his focus needed to be, or he'd end up catching lead or arrows.

"Over here." Nolan gave a wave to Captain Farnsworth, then nodded toward the mixed tracks of unshod and shod horses. Nolan's hunch had to be right about that lot being a mix of white trash and red vermin. The hoofprints pretty much spelled it out. He pointed and followed the trail with his finger for the captain to see. Northwest toward the mountains was where the killers were headed.

With the house still burning and its owner planted six feet under, Nolan and the bluecoat soldiers rode fast after the saddle trash who'd done this purely evil deed.

CHAPTER 2

"NATHANIAL...WHERE ARE YOU?" Jenny was the only one in her family who would take time to fetch Nate for supper—or anything else for that matter.

Now that they were traveling with a wagon train, Nate was treated about half decent by Jenny's folks. She had called it all "a heart-wrenching shame." Nate didn't know anything about that sap. In his seven years of living, Jenny so far had been the only one willing to receive his awkward efforts at love.

Hells bells, he hadn't been wanted from day one. His ma had been a dirty saloon whore who insisted that Nate call her by name—Lucinda. By the age of two, he knew how to play poker, and for his third birthday, the saloon keeper, Wally, had let Nate start slinging drinks for customers, earning his first few bits for a week's work. Nate had hated every minute of that life. Too bad Jenny wasn't old enough to be his mama.

"Nathanial, answer me!"

He wished Jenny would stop her damn yelling. Surely she'd eventually find him. Then she would see why he couldn't give a holler back. From where he lay under the brush, he saw her pick up a small, round, smooth stone. She flicked her wrist, and the pebble skipped four times across the top of the water before sinking. Nate had shown her that earlier in the day.

Jenny waded through the knee-high stream, her arms stretched out like wings, as if that were going to keep her from falling. She was as wobbly as a newborn colt trying to stand, and all at once she slipped, sank in, and got a face full of water.

Nate snickered quietly, and Jenny climbed the bank on hands and knees. Only, she didn't know he was finding her grunting efforts funny. She stood on the bank, straightened her drippy dress, then looked about for him. Mud had to be squishing up between her toes as she took a step and kept searching. As quick as a wink, Jenny slipped again and was flat on her back with feet above head. She rolled down the slick, mud-covered bank before landing in a clump of high, grassy brush.

This time there was no hiding Nate's giggle. Jenny quickly sat up, and her eyes shifted, searching until she saw him hidden in the weeds under a thorny bush.

She crawled through the thick grass to where he lay, and Nate smirked at her the whole time.

Jenny stuck her tongue out at him. "What're you looking at?"

Nate pulled a glob of thick mud out of Jenny's yellow hair. "You look like a pig that's been rolling around in slop."

"Why didn't you answer me?" Jenny scolded him like a big sister, though they weren't kin. She did often call him "little brother," even after her pa, Mr. Harper, had slapped her mouth hard for doing so.

"Hush." Nate squashed a finger to Jenny's lips, then nodded at a clump of grass. "See that hole yonder. A big ol' fat rabbit is down there hidin'. I aim to catch 'im."

"With what?" she whispered as they stared at the hole. "How do you know it ain't a whistle-pig burrow?"

Did Jenny really think him to be that dumb? He rolled his eyes. He wasn't going to fall for her teasing. "Could you shut up, please?"

Catching that rabbit was important to Nate. There was one ongoing matter that he and Jenny didn't talk much about. She knew though, and tears had come to her eyes that morning at breakfast. Her pa expected Nate to help sustain the family, even though he wasn't considered one of them and never was allowed to partake in the bounty. Something as stupid as squirrel meat had sometimes kept Mr. Harper from pounding on his hide.

This morning, Nate had tried not to walk stiff and give away his sore back. He would have liked some of the mush that Jenny and her sisters were eating, but Mr. Harper hadn't allowed it. He'd sent Nate off to gather wood. Likely because the day before, he hadn't caught any fish when Mr. Harper had told him to, so there'd been no meat for supper. Maybe if Nate could bring something noticeable to the skillet, Jenny's pa wouldn't drag him from his blanket tonight and beat on him. Rabbit was a fine meal.

Jenny huffed and playfully punched Nate's arm. "Don't tell me to be quiet." Not once had she raised a mean hand to hit Nate.

He was nothing to the other Harpers but their little bastard farmhand, or so they liked to call him. Mrs. Harper and Jenny's three older sisters all had turned a blind eye and deaf ear to the cruelty that the man of the house dealt out.

"Who showed you how to make that?" Jenny's tone was serious as she took a look at his rabbit trap.

Nate shrugged because he didn't really have an answer. He'd thought of it himself. Jenny's eyes roamed over the contraption, and she shook her head in disbelief. Aw, Nate didn't see that it was much. He'd twisted sapling branches together, letting the leaves fall in place. Then he'd threaded ground pine as netting through the spaces between the branches. The bait was a yummy carrot, which he'd snitched from the wagon, right out from under Mrs. Harper's stuck-up nose. Slick and sticky fingers was a means of survival taught to him by his pa and the others in the gang.

"Will it work?" Jenny grinned and nudged him a couple of times.

"It's pretty simple really. I just have to wait and then drop this string when that dumb bunny comes out to eat." Not too far up, Nate had suspended the trap to hover over the bait by a length of thin rope.

"You're so smart, little brother. I wish Ma and Pa would let you go to school. If you had the right book learning, I don't imagine there's anything you couldn't do." Jenny pinched Nate's cheeks, and he pushed her away.

They both knew attending school was nothing more than a dream for Nate. Even though his pa was far away and locked up in jail, Nate would never find himself welcomed into any house, town, or community. Newspapers and dime novels had made sure of that. Those awful stories had spread across the country like wildfire. Though most of what had been said about Pa and the gang was true.

Another truth was that Mr. Harper was damn lucky Pa was behind bars, because he would have plugged a bullet in the pig and made him squeal for treating his boy so badly. No one but Pa or one of the gang was allowed to hit Nate. Harper was just someone he got dumped with because no one else had even considered taking him.

Nate and Jenny were both still staring at the rabbit hole.

"Ma said to fetch ya. It's time to eat."

Jenny's ma barely served Nate enough to live on. There were three other families in the wagon train, and everyone took their meals together, including Nate. Though no one had ever spoken up to question his measly portion, he'd thought maybe Mrs. Harper would have shown him some kindness in front of the others.

Nate wiped at his eyes, hoping Jenny hadn't seen. Back on the Harpers' farm, he had been fed the family's leftover scraps. After they'd eaten in the house, he was then slopped like a hog in the barn, and that chore had fallen to Jenny. Their friendship had been born out of the shriveling stomach of starvation.

"Dammit, Jenny. I just know that rabbit's gonna stick its head up outta that hole any minute now. I gotta stay and catch him. Please…with a cherry on top?" Why Nate felt the need to beg, he didn't know. One bat of his baby-blue eyes and Jenny usually awed all over him. The awful part was Pa had taught Nate to use his cute, innocent face against people, and he did. But he would never do it to hurt Jenny.

"If Ma hears that language, you'll get your mouth washed out with soap." Jenny wasn't fibbing. One day, Mrs. Harper had grabbed Nate by the scruff for throwing down a streak of curses. She'd nearly drowned him while she scrubbed his mouth out with foul-smelling lye.

Nate put on a smile. "Old sourpuss face ain't here now, is she?"

Besides, he could outrun Mrs. Harper, the fat ass. That was if she even bothered to come after him. So at the moment, he wasn't worried. He was well aware that his grin was as sweet as honey and, at times, as rotten ornery as the filthy words that spilled through his lips. Would Jenny fall for it and give in?

"All right. I'll tell Ma I couldn't find you." Jenny smiled.

"Thanks, sis." When they were alone, Nate called her that. Jenny stood, brushed grass from her dress, then walked back toward the creek.

Nate kept a tight grip on the string and thought about what he and Jenny had planned for themselves. Three weeks was all they had yet to endure with the wagon train. Jenny had overheard talk of all the wagons stopping at the next town to buy supplies. She had come up with the brilliant idea for the two of them to hide somewhere in that town and stay behind after the wagon train moved on. Then they could run away to wherever they wanted, just the two of them.

It was Nate's hope and Jenny's wish to get him away from her pa. Fingers crossed, their future was looking bright.

Nate turned back to watch the bunny hole as Jenny disappeared over the grassy bank on her way across the creek. A few silent minutes passed as he waited for the furry critter to appear. "Where are you, ya stupid rabbit?"

A gun boomed, and a repeat of rifle fire rang in Nate's ears. Then more gunfire thundered through the air. Nate twisted around fast, forgetting about where he was, and nearly poked his eyes out on the thorns of the thick bushes. He ducked his head, scurried out, and sat up on his knees, looking toward the creek. He had dropped the string and sprung the trap. Forgotten was the rabbit.

What in blazes was going on? Nate's heart was pounding. Jenny had just gone through the water, and she was on the other side of the bank where the gunfire was coming from. Was she okay?

"Breathe," he told himself.

Who would be doing all that shooting? The gunfire was too close to be one of the men from the wagon train out hunting. Besides, who wasted that many bullets to kill a deer or antelope? Maybe bandits had come to loot the wagons. Nate had experience with that, only on the thieving end of things.

Another volley of gunfire pounded his ears. This time it was followed by the pitched screams of pain. There was but one person Nate was thinking of—Jenny. He scrambled through the weeds as fast as he could until he was at the highest point of the bank and could see across the creek to the wagons. What he saw gripped him so the wind was squeezed from his lungs.

Nate quickly crouched in the high grass, too afraid to cross the creek.

Fear had frozen him. There were so many of them, and he recognized their kind. The dusty trail-covered men were the type cut from the same cloth as Nate's pa.

Guns boomed. Men fell to their deaths. Women and children screamed. Where the hell was Jenny? She'd just a minute ago crossed through the blessed stream.

Nate quickly searched around each wagon amid the fighting. Renegade Indians with their faces painted and wearing mostly white men's clothing yelled their war cries. Horses were wheeled every which direction. Some of those Indians were aiming shotguns like the white fellas fighting alongside them. Others pulled their bowstrings. A crossfire of bullets ripped apart the camp. The few horses that had been left yoked to the wagons lay dead.

Had Jenny gotten to a safe place? *God, please be protecting her.* Nate hadn't ever been much for praying, but there were times when he needed someone a whole lot stronger than himself.

The thunderous pound of running horses, a shout, a scream, the boom of rifles, and the crack of pistols—it all deafened Nate. An arrow cut through the air, sinking deep into Mr. Collins's chest. He dropped to the ground and held the piercing shaft that stuck out of him. Mrs. Collins was being carried off kicking and screaming. She flailed in an effort to reach out to her husband, who was dead and couldn't save her.

Blood stained the ground everywhere. Not three feet from where they all should have been sitting and eating supper lay the hacked-up, bloody body of a man named June. Nate cried. June had been nice to him.

Before he could wipe his eyes, a bullet blew a hole through Mr. Harper's chest. The man dropped to his knees as another lead ball twisted him by the shoulder. Then a third bullet hit him square between the eyes, blowing off the back of his head.

Holy shit. Jenny's pa was dead.

Mrs. Harper clawed and kicked as she was dragged off into the trees just like Mrs. Collins. The three daughters were also pulled along against their will, every one of them screaming toward heaven for mercy.

As far as Nate could tell, Jenny hadn't been taken. "Please stay safe. Wherever you're at."

His eyes darted around in search of her. Had she been killed back in those trees where he couldn't see?

The Harpers' wagon was on fire, as were two of the three others. The wind twirled the smoke in a different direction, and in the midst of the smoke, Jenny appeared, hand over her mouth, coughing. Nate blinked twice, making sure it was her. Sure enough, there she was, running for her life straight toward him.

"Run faster, Jenny!" Nate couldn't have yelled any louder.

Ten stretching steps and Jenny would be into the creek. Nate waved her to him with both hands. Running headlong, she tripped on the hem of her dress. Thank God she hadn't fallen, but her pace had slowed.

"Get outta here, Nathanial!" Tears streamed down her face.

Nate wiped at his eyes. No way could he leave Jenny. His life wasn't worth as much as hers. She was a good person, but he'd been born with bad blood running through his veins.

Nate's legs all of a sudden worked, and he sprang to his feet. He hurried down over the bank toward Jenny, hitting the creek with a splash. Water flew up in his face and soaked his clothes. She was almost to the creek, directly across from him. She just needed to splash through as fast as she could, get to Nate, and then they could run.

An arrow spiraled through the air toward Jenny. It speared her arm and threw her sprawling across the rocky dirt.

"No!" Nate didn't want to believe it. Jenny just couldn't be hurt.

He grabbed and yanked at his ears to muffle the sound of her painful screams. Red gushed from her arm. Nate couldn't breathe, his heart pounding agonizingly.

"I'm coming, Jenny!" He barely choked out the words. Tears ran down his face. What if she bled out?

"Run, little brother!" Jenny waved him away.

Wearing a yellow streak a mile wide, Nate turned and rushed from the water. He scrambled in retreat over the tall grassy bank.

Jenny's scream twisted him around once again, and he faced the creek. One of the red devil sons of bitches was off his horse and loomed over Jenny in less time than it took for Nate to draw a single breath.

The long crow-black hair was braided along one side of the Indian's face, hawk feathers dangling from the end. Yellow and red spots mixed with stripes of paint, masking the heathen's face. Those markings matched the painted symbols on the buckskin shirt. A pistol was strapped to the warrior's hip.

Jenny was jerked to her feet. The shooting all around them stopped. To blink would mean that Nate's watery eyes would miss seeing her for a second. Why wasn't his tongue working to yell for her to be let go?

A man in a fancy blue coat, with a short-brimmed hat and slick curled mustache, pranced his bold white horse toward Jenny. "What have you done?" The fancy man belted the Indian across the face with the backside of his hand.

The heathen spit blood.

"She's no good to me now with only one arm. Damn shame…She's very pretty and young. She would have brought a handsome price." This evil, sneering dandy reached from where he sat atop his horse and ran his fingers through Jenny's yellow hair.

Nate had never shot anything more than a rabbit. But just then, he wished he had a full load of buckshot at the ready, because he would've blown that fancy bastard off his horse. He had unfortunately witnessed some of the members of Pa's gang using women in a bad way. Before Nate could finish the thought that these slimy pricks could use Jenny in that same way, the fancy man drew a Smith & Wesson pocket pistol, aimed, and fired. Jenny's body crumpled and hit the dirt, her life spilling out all over the ground in a great puddle of dark red.

"You bastard!" Nate's voice cracked like a whip, and he instantly realized his mistake.

"Kill that kid!" The dandy son of a bitch shouted the order.

A bullet from the pocket gun zinged past him. The Indian drew his .45 as Nate twisted around and took off running. He flew through the brush and trees as fast as his feet would carry him. Where could he hide? He couldn't outrun them. They had horses. The brush was thick though. They would have to track Nate down on foot. And he was much smaller. He could crawl in under thorny places that neither the fancy man nor the Indian would fit. But a bullet didn't need much space.

The rabbit hole. Nate was tiny enough to hide under the trap. It was the perfect blending cover.

He buried his eyes in the fold of his arms and fought his hardest not to sob. Every footstep of the two men searching the brush grew louder in his ears. They seemed to be closing in on him. Sweat had popped up all over Nate, and he was trying not to breathe too loud. If he peeked just one wink, he might panic. Jumping up and running like a scared rabbit would get him shot down for sure. Though the loud thumping of his heart might give him away too. No doubt, the dandy-dressed killer would blow a hole through Nate if he were heard.

Too many times, Pa had told him not to cry, not to be weak. So why was he sniveling? Nate lifted his head just a little and glared at the murdering bastard as he walked back toward the creek. Pa would have shot the fancy man in the back. Nate would never forget that handsomely slick face. He aimed to end Jenny's killer and make Pa proud.

The fancy man and the red devil disappeared over the grassy bank and seemed to have finally given up on finding Nate. Maybe he was no longer worth the bother of getting scratched to hell inside the thorn patch. Or perhaps their leave was false and they were attempting to lure him out of hiding. He knew the tricks those kinds of men used. He'd seen them played out when he'd ridden with Pa and the gang. Nate could hear the splashing steps of one man. Curled up under the trap, he couldn't see over the grass to the water. Had the Indian stayed on this side of the bank to creep like a fox and slyly hunt Nate?

Slowly he slithered out from under the camouflage, careful not to snag his clothing. Breathing was good. He just needed to calm the pace before he passed out. He kept himself flat on the ground and eyed every prickly thicket and pocket of tall grass between himself and the creek bank. Pa had been a leery man, always watching for trouble, and Nate had been taught early in life to do the same.

A bird landed on a branch not far from him and closer to the water. That chirping little windbag was a good sign no one was hiding close by. If there was danger, like a man that shouldn't have been there, that twittering music maker would have hidden itself by hushing its beak. Nate had been hunkered down in one spot long enough that as far as the sparrow was concerned, he had become part of the surroundings, so he was no longer noticed as a threat. Plus the rabbit from earlier hopped out and away from its hole, then nibbled on some blades of grass.

Nate crawled with careful steps, one at a time, so as not to rustle the grass or snap a twig under his weight, slowly making his way toward the creek.

Jenny's dead body had been left in a blood-soaked heap. The fancy man and the Indian were both on their horses. They trotted into the trees where Mrs. Harper and the daughters had been dragged off.

Nate slipped over the bank and then hurried through the rippling calf-high water. He dropped to his knees next to Jenny's still body, her eyes staring dully into the sky. Tears streamed down his face, and once again, he could hardly breathe. Why had this happened? He and Jenny were to be together. That had been the plan.

Gently Nate lifted her head. With the slightest touch, he closed her blank green eyes. Though hugging Jenny to him for hours did nothing to console him, he couldn't seem to stop rocking her. Nothing but seeing her smiling face come to life could have halted his sobs. If only he could will her back to him. Sis had been the only good to ever touch Nate's life. Now she was gone. There would be no more secrets between them. No laughter. No silly play. He would never again hear the gentleness of her voice. He'd been robbed of her love.

An ache unlike any he'd ever felt ripped through him. "Please wake up, Jenny." Nate choked on his sobs. Somewhere in his mind, he knew she would never open her eyes again. He just didn't want to believe she was dead.

Without her, Nate had nothing worth living for. No one had ever cared about him, so the deep grief that racked his body was unfamiliar.

Seeing the things he had when he'd ridden with Pa, Nate knew what sad thing needed done next. He had to think to force his arms and legs to work. Being close to nine years older than himself, Jenny was much bigger. He did his best to carry her away from her death place but ended up having to drag her.

Near the smoldering wagons, he placed Jenny down for the moment. Wiping his eyes roughly, he searched about the ground until he found a shovel. All the while, Nate tried his damnedest not to look at the other dead souls. He sobbed, unable to recall in all his days on this earth shedding more tears than he was today.

With the first shovelful of dirt thrown from Jenny's grave, Nate swallowed down his sick stomach. Three more scoops and he was covered in sweat. He'd been drained of strength before picking up the spade. Sorrow did that to a body. Unfortunately, that was a lesson Nate was learning.

The grim work was coming along slowly. A numbness had settled into him. He no longer felt like a living person but more like a thing just moving along through time. There was no quit in him though. Jenny would have a fine funeral. It didn't matter that he would be the only loved one standing over her grave.

Nate dropped the shovel and looked at his blistered hands, but he didn't care about himself. He looked over at Jenny lying in the grass where he'd left her.

He went and lovingly kissed her forehead. Already his lips felt she was growing cold. The once bright, smiling face was now turning grayish. By luck, Mrs. Harper had hung some linens out to air, and those pieces hadn't burned up in the wagon. Nate fetched Jenny's quilt, then wrapped her up tight. Decorated with tiny pink and yellow flowers, it had only been scorched a little near the edges.

Jenny hadn't deserved this. Maybe this was the awful price Nate had to pay since he'd gone along with so many horrible evils Pa had committed. If that were true, then why hadn't God slaughtered him instead? For some reason he was alive and Jenny wasn't. But crying over her like a damn baby wouldn't get her laid to rest. Nate wiped his dirty sleeve across his wet eyes, then took a deep breath.

One, two, three... He rolled Jenny into her grave, and the thump of her body hitting the ground below sickened Nate. It wasn't fair, his tiny size. Couldn't one thing in life ever work out right for him? Why couldn't he be bigger? Then he could have placed Jenny gently in her grave. For fear of not being able to get himself out, her plot was only as deep as Nate was tall. He hoped no animal would dig her up.

Tears streamed down Nate's face, and he let out a scream. He hated the fancy man. He hated that Jenny was dead. He hated everything. He fell to the ground and sobbed. That dandy son of a bitch would pay for what he'd done.

Another thought came to him. Were the other girls and women still alive? Had the fancy man killed them all and Nate would find Mrs. Harper and the other three daughters back in those trees? He reckoned he'd best go look.

Lots of hoofprints was all he found. He now knew the direction that murdering bunch was headed. First he would finish what needed doing there. He picked up the shovel. It didn't take long until his back ached and his hands were sore. After throwing down the shovel, he wiped his blood on his pants.

One of the wagons had been flipped over and smashed during the attack, but not burned. Some of those boards hadn't been ruined. It gave Nate an idea. He tugged until, at last, a short board worked loose. Yanking the second piece loose wasn't as hard as the first. It took him some time to rummage through the mess and find a usable length of rope. His mind flooded with loving thoughts of Jenny as he twisted the twine to hold the cross section in place. He reached into his pants pocket and pulled out his flip knife. Would he even be able to carve her name onto the cross with his hands shaking so badly?

JENY HARPR. A GOOD SISTR.

The epitaph wasn't fancy words, but the sentiment was true.

Nate stood at the head of Jenny's grave and looked toward heaven. No doubt, Jenny was up there.

"God is good. God is great. Let us thank him for our food. By his hands, we are fed. Give us, Lord, our daily bread. Amen." It was the only real prayer Nate knew. Jenny had taught him the blessing to say before he ate. Thanking God for this heartache just seemed wrong, but Jenny would like it.

Night fell around Nate. Exhaustion took hold of him, his eyes fluttered heavily, and he dropped down beside the freshly dug dirt. There wasn't an ounce of strength left in him.

Could he ever forgive himself for not saving Jenny? Maybe if he caught the fancy man that had killed her. And to do that, he needed to stop being a crybaby little boy and become a man.

Nate woke to sprinkling rain wetting his face. Flashes of what had befallen Jenny and the whole attack on the wagon train flashed in his tired mind. He sobbed, and he'd just opened his eyes. Why not just lie there and shrivel up?

A rumble of thunder sounded in the distance. Nate's life had always been one big gray sky hovering over him, and it didn't look to be going anywhere. There was one ray of hope that could give him some peace. He could catch Jenny's killer.

Nate pushed himself up to sit, then rested a hand on the fresh, loose heap of dirt covering Jenny. It was a good thing Pa couldn't see him right this minute. He would have called Nate a worthless, sniveling crybaby, along with a few choice words for added belittling. Nate wiped his sleeve across his teary eyes, then picked up his shovel. Trying to become a man was hard. Nate could do it though. He had to for Jenny.

He hardly took notice of the drizzling rain that dampened his clothes throughout the day. He was soaked to the bone. Somehow he didn't seem to feel it, though he was shivering. Hunger never once panged him. Working without rest, he dug graves for Mr. Harper and the others that he hadn't buried yesterday. He bawled as he dropped the Collins baby into the ground. His hands shook while contemplating the best spot to push on Mrs. Peterson, who'd been with child. Trying hard to avoid her rounded belly, he rolled her into her grave. Before he had them all covered, the cloudy gray day had faded into a wet black night. Still, he worked into the wee hours.

Drenched with the cold rain, exhausted, and sick to his stomach, Nate fell next to Jenny's grave. His eyes closed, though sleep didn't come easy and he was restless. Jenny's frantic screams echoed over and over in his head until the nightmare startled him awake again. Her pale face haunted him. Repeatedly, Nate's mind pictured her running from the arrow that would every time mark her for death. A few times he woke right before the fancy man had pulled the trigger. It all scared him, and he wished he wasn't alone.

Nate's eyes were slow to open on another damn day. Pink streaks of morning light lit the sky. Pink had been Jenny's favorite color.

Nate rolled over in the grass, stiff from the cold. He stared at the cross with Jenny's name on it. He didn't want to leave her, but the longer he waited, the harder it would be to trail her killer. The rain might have already washed away the hoofprints, but that alone wouldn't stop him from finding the fancy man. Nate had the rest of his life to bring down Jenny's killer.

He forced himself to stand, then went off in search of flowers. He wouldn't go without leaving her a beautiful bunch. Daisies were her favorite, and Nate hoped he could find some. Once again, he found himself wiping tears from his eyes. What he picked weren't white and yellow daisies, but the wildflowers were colorful. He thought the bouquet was pretty, like Jenny, and the flowers smelled pleasant. Nate sneezed after breathing in the sweet fragrance. He would miss Jenny Harper dearly.

"I love you." He whispered his goodbye.

Walking away from Jenny's grave was much harder than digging it. Nate would settle with the fancy man for this. What bullets he had found on the ground around the wagons, he'd shoved into his pockets. The Henry rifle he carried might have belonged to Mr. Collins, but it didn't matter now since the man was dead. There wasn't anything else Nate needed.

He stopped atop a small hill and looked one last time over his shoulder at Jenny's grave. He sniffed and wiped the tears from his eyes. He would never forget Jenny or the face of the man who had killed her.

"I promise. I won't stop till I git him for ya, Jenny."

CHAPTER 3

NOLAN WALKED HIS HORSE around the burned wagons. It was the same lawless bunch that had burned out the homesteaders. He was seeing the same mixture of shod and unshod hoofprints spread all over the ground. But where were the bodies? It couldn't have been a wagon train full of only women.

"Sir, you need to see this." One of blue boys fetched Nolan to a little meadow not far from sight of the burned wagons. Shaded by dogwood trees and cradled by a trickling creek, Nolan thought the patch of green grass to be a right pretty spot except for the nine fresh graves.

The captain rode up next to him. "What do you make of this?"

Nolan shook his head and nudged his horse forward for a better look. One of the graves had a marker. He read the girl's name to himself. Huh. There had been no female bodies left before this girl. Why? He stepped down from his horse and placed his foot next to the much smaller boot track alongside the girl's grave.

"A child. A little boy. Young. That's a tiny boot that made that print." Nolan looked to the captain, who was studying the track.

It didn't make sense though. No one had been left alive so far. The kid had obviously gotten lucky and must have been hiding somewhere during the attack. Nolan turned from the captain and looked around at the other graves. Whoever the youngster was, he'd cared enough to bury the dead and specially mark this girl's resting place. Strong willed. The kid had grit to have done the work of digging graves and pitching dirt on those he'd felt tender about. It was no easy chore for anyone. The hardest thing Nolan had ever done was bury Mary and Matthew.

Nolan swung a leg over the saddle. He felt a need to find the youngster, though why, he didn't know. The small boot print was maybe a day old. Depending on how quickly the boy was walking, Nolan reckoned they would ride up on the kid maybe five or six miles ahead of them.

Nolan spurred the bay, leading the captain and his soldiers riding over a hill, and followed the boot tracks. Most likely, the youngster was frightened and had wandered to find help.

After four or five miles, it was clear the half-pint was following after whoever had slaughtered his people. The dumb kid would get himself killed. Nolan stretched his eyeglass. No one in sight as far as he could see. Not that he was worried, but he did hope they would catch up with the boy before nightfall.

Matthew had always stuck close to Nolan's side when there'd been barn chores to be done after dark. Kids could get scared for no reason, but this boy had definite cause to be shaking in his boots. There wasn't a doubt in Nolan's mind that the youngster had witnessed a brutal attack and should, by all accounts, be terrified of those he was trailing after. Though that didn't appear to be true. The kid's path was straight and easy to read.

Did the little grasshopper even have the know-how to start a fire to keep warm? When the sun went down, it sometimes brought about a chill in the air. If the boy was capable and built too big a flame, then he might be spotted. This bad bunch that the army was hunting likely would be watching their back trail. If the boy wasn't extrasmart and was closing in on those murderers, he would be dead before morning. Nolan didn't know a whole lot about kids, but he knew people. When they were emotional, as he suspected this kid was, people didn't always behave too smart.

Nolan let out a deep sigh. Catching up with those no-accounts was taking more time than he had ever wanted to spend. One of two things needed to happen—and quick. He needed to get the boy out of trouble's path or find the bunch responsible for causing the kid's heartache and deal with them before the boy got hurt. He glanced up at the sun directly overhead, trying to ignore his piercing headache. There were plenty of hours left in the day for looking. He touched spurs to the bay.

The shadow of fading daylight followed the group west until the sun topped the mountain. Captain Farnsworth put up a hand, halting the soldiers to make camp.

Peace was what Nolan desired, and to get it, he needed the quiet of wide-open prairie. He nudged his horse forward. Not once in his time of scouting for the captain had Nolan been questioned about riding off on his own to camp. He didn't offer many words toward being friendly with the army men. That was just not his way. He was their scout and no more.

A coyote howled far off in the distance as Nolan rode under the moonlight. Stars speckled the sky, and the air was cooling some. If he had found the boy, it might have turned out to be a nice night for once. He reined in, then stepped down out of the saddle. His mind wasn't on scouting as he untied his bedroll. The little fool wasn't lost, and the boy was far too young to be going at trouble alone. The kid had to be weighed down and aching bad inside. Nolan understood that kind of crushing pain.

The soft crackling of the fire relaxed him some as he fed sticks to the flame. Coffee might soothe him. He fetched the fixings from his saddlebags, then set the pot to boil. Listening to the bay chewing grass and the humming of various night bugs, Nolan stretched out his tired bones on his ground blanket. It was hard to let his mind drift to thoughts of Matthew after trailing this other boy all damn day.

Matthew hadn't been a tiny youngster like the grasshopper Nolan was tracking. From infancy to the day he had been shot down, he'd carried a sturdy build that modeled his father's. The boot print from the youngster belonging to the wagon train barely made a dent in the mud. The little fella must have been a featherweight.

Lying on his back, Nolan stared up at the stars as they winked at him. If only he could go back to that day and stop his wife and son from stepping foot on that stagecoach. Oh hell, wishes were for children and fools. The best he could do was maybe keep the half-pint from finding trouble too big for the pup to handle. As small as that boot print was, Nolan should have found the kid curled up and hiding somewhere, crying for his mama. Not this little cuss.

Was he on the prowl for those who'd murdered his people? It certainly seemed that way, given that the little boots were following the trail of the mismatched hoofprints. Just as Nolan had ridden after the lawless men who'd shot up the stagecoach and killed Mary and Matthew while attempting to rob a bank.

Happiness was something he no longer knew. Matthew had been shot down by a no-good son of a bitch like the one Nolan was trailing for the captain.

He shook off the thoughts as dawn crested the horizon, secured his bedroll, then swung into the saddle. Before meeting with the captain, he wanted to scout ahead but wasn't seeing any more of the kid's tracks. Hopefully, the half-pint hadn't gotten himself lost on the prairie or killed.

Another night and day passed, and other than an occasional small boot track, Nolan saw no sign of the little boy. It had been a week since they'd come upon the burned wagons, and the fool-headed brat was still on the trail. Nolan was, however, impressed with the speed with which the kid was traveling by foot. Maybe he didn't stop to sleep. What was the youngster eating? The past two nights had been cold. Was the half-pint staying warm enough?

Captain Farnsworth reined in next to Nolan. "We'll make camp here. Men, dismount."

What the captain had just said was only half heard by Nolan. His mind was stuck on the little boy. He barely noticed that the captain had gotten off his horse and stood facing him.

"Nolan…Nolan…I want to start out early tomorrow." Captain Farnsworth snapped his fingers and finally got his attention.

"Oh yeah…yes, sir, Captain." Nolan had been caught with his mind twenty miles away. Maybe with some rest, he could keep his focus on the true reason he was there. Tracking down an orphaned boy wasn't his job.

Nolan stepped down off the bay and then untied his blanket roll for another night. Before he knew it, he found himself repeating the reverse process the following morning.

They rode fast as the sun rose overhead. Now the youngster's tracks were fresh. Nolan saw a mark in the dirt alongside the step of the little boy's right foot. Hopping down off the bay, Nolan fingered the groove in the ground. The half-pint was carrying something. A gun? The half-moon mark was part of the barrel. The tracks implicated that the boy was leaning on it like a crutch. Was he hurt or maybe just tired? Nolan reckoned the little boy wasn't heavy enough to push the whole of the rifle barrel deep enough into the dirt to show the full circle. How old was this kid?

Touching the groove again, Nolan's mind drifted far away to a place he hadn't been in a long time.

"Steady that gun," he whispered to Matthew. The small-caliber rifle was propped atop a fallen log. His son was ready to fire at Nolan's say-so.

A deer stopped its feeding and lifted its head to look. The smoke of the cracking gun filled their nostrils. The button buck dropped to the ground.

"Nice shot, son." He ruffled Matthew's hair, the proud father.

"Did you find something?" Captain Farnsworth's demanding voice quickly brought Nolan back from his far-off place. He glanced up at the captain, who was looking over his shoulder at the slight gun barrel mark.

"No." Nolan straightened, then stepped up and swung a leg over the saddle and sank spurs to the bay.

As much as he wanted to, there was simply no outrunning his memories.

Please let me find the boy before the dumb kid collides with those he's hunting. The trail of that murdering bunch was also getting fresher. The little fool wouldn't win the battle he was aiming to fight. Buzzard food was what he'd end up.

If Nolan figured right, the men he was trailing would soon turn direction and head into the mountains. The outlaws were traveling with women, which would be easier on open ground but risky. The chance of being seen would be greater on the lowland, and that could mean a fight or maybe getting caught. The mountain, on the other hand, would provide much cover and was only hours from where the murdering bunch had last made camp. If Nolan were them, he would head up and over the mountain rather than riding around. Time wise, the shortcut would shave days off their effort. That was if Nolan's hunch was correct. He would bet that this bunch was making their way toward Montana, then farther north to cross the border into Canada to sell the women.

Nolan wheeled the bay and headed back to find Captain Farnsworth. His hunch was worth talking through with the captain. If they rode fast enough, maybe they could cut off this bunch before they reached the mountain. It was much harder to take a defensive stance on open ground.

Nolan rode out of a patch of trees and saw army men making a noon camp. The captain was unsaddling his horse. Nolan trotted the bay up next to the man, then stepped down. "Captain, I got an idea."

"Let me get some coffee first. Then I'll listen to whatever it is you have to say." The captain was throwing his brass around, and Nolan didn't think much of it. He'd led the army this far. The captain's disrespectful tone was not appreciated.

"Captain, we need to move now if this is gonna work." Nolan wasn't going to beg the man to get off his ass and fight. Captain Farnsworth knew his duty and his orders. Nolan had read the paperwork himself before he'd agreed to assist with this mission.

"My men are tired, and our horses need rest. Whatever your grand idea, it can wait." The captain sure knew how to rub Nolan the wrong way. What a bunch of bullshit.

Nolan was feeling generous. He kept his mouth shut and didn't shove the captain's excuses down his gullet. *The hell with this.* He'd go look for himself and search for the boy along the way.

"Salute me before you walk away." The captain's tone was sharp, and it pissed Nolan off all the more.

Nolan's brow furrowed, and he turned and glared at Captain Farnsworth. "I ain't wearing blue. So whatever it is that has your ass chapped, you don't speak to me that way."

After trailing death for so long, they were all growing weary with one another. They hadn't even so much as seen a glimpse of the killers. Hoofprints were the only identifier. Nolan understood the captain's frustration, but the man had best get off his back.

"As a scout, you have to abide by my orders."

It took everything for Nolan not to smirk at the captain, who sounded like a whiny brat who hadn't gotten his way. "I accept your instructions and do my job, but I ain't here to puff up your pride. So, Captain, sir, you can go salute yourself." Nolan grinned, tipped his hat, and then walked away toward the fire.

Uniformed men sat around jawing and eating slop. By God, if Nolan had to look at another pot of beans, he was going to be sick. He poured himself a tin of coffee, then took a long swig. It was hot. That was all he could say about the mud. He pitched the remains, then tossed the tin to the ground. Was it truly that hard to make a good cup of coffee?

Aw shit, it wasn't the thick black mud that had him stirred up or even the captain's off remarks.

Finding that addlebrained kid before something bad happened was what Nolan itched to do. Now that he had a little something hot in him, he wasn't going to stand around like a dummy. He'd passed through this area before and recalled that the mountain range stretched as far and wide as the eye could see. The path the half-pint was trailing wouldn't be so easily followed over hard, rocky ground. Underbrush and just the backbone of the mountain soil would help mask any sign left behind by the outlaws. Any youngster could get lost real easy.

Why couldn't Nolan just forget the kid? The little boy wasn't anything to him.

He swung into the saddle. The sun passed overhead, and the bright rays felt too warm on his shoulders. He'd hoped for once that there'd be a cool wind flowing down out of the mountains and across the plains, but the air seemed to be sitting still. It had just been miserably hot lately.

A few hours later, Nolan pulled up on the reins, lifted his canteen, and drank. That big orange ball in the sky was still throwing the heat. He wiped the sweat from his brow, then pushed his hat back down onto his head to shade his eyes.

Twisting in the saddle, Nolan fetched the spyglass from his saddlebags. The captain and his blue boys were riding up from behind in their formed lines. Nolan turned while pulling the end to lengthen the scope. He pressed the lens to his eye and studied the ground between himself and the tree line of the mountain. Natural waves and dips in the landscape could hide something on open prairie, but his eyes were trained to search carefully.

Back and forth he swept the hand glass across the landscape, looking for any sign of trouble—Indian, outlaw, or otherwise. Squinting, he strained his eyes to look closer. What was he seeing? A lump in the grass, partially hidden by a crop of rocks. A movement. Small, but his eye had caught it. The little boy maybe? Nolan couldn't tell from that distance, but he aimed to find out.

CHAPTER 4

A S NOLAN RODE CLOSER, the lump in the grass began to take shape in the small form of a child. A shadow passed over him from above, and he looked up into the sky and saw the vultures for the first time. At that moment, the stench of maggot-infested meat hit his nostrils, and his stomach turned.

He slowed the bay to a walk. Not dead, but holy shit, the towhead was far too young to be on his own. The tiny babe wasn't too many years off the tit. The child kept looking over at something behind that cropping of rocks. Nolan stood in the stirrups and stretched his neck. A body, half-naked and painted in dried blood, lay not four feet from the kid—the source of the rotten odor. Maybe the boy's mama? Nolan flopped back down into the saddle and took a deep breath.

He wanted the scruffy-looking little boy to see him before he rode up too close and maybe put a fright into the child. Hunched over and sitting on his knees, the youngster's back was to him. The tot was wearing a raggedy coat four sizes too big. Nolan could see exactly what the little boy was doing. Digging a grave.

Nolan reined in and sat his horse a few yards from the kid. The creak of the saddle as he shifted his weight seemed unusually loud.

Had the boy even noticed him? He hadn't looked up from his work.

"Howdy." Nolan waited for the half-pint to say something but was greeted with silence. He doubted the filthy kid was deaf, just playing dumb most likely. Matthew had never been a backward child but at times had been too unguarded. This boy didn't know him. Maybe the kid was scared to speak up without first trusting a person. That wasn't entirely a bad thing.

Nolan stepped down off his horse and carried the reins, slowly walking toward the boy. Whoever the dead woman was—most likely kin—the tot was scratching away at the dirt with a pocketknife. That was a hell of a way to dig a six-foot hole.

"Need some help?"

The little tomcat twisted around faster than a rattler strikes. A Henry rifle was cocked in the twiggy arms, far outweighing the half-pint, and it showed as the boy struggled to hold the big gun aimed straight. It would only take a slight breeze and the half-pint would topple over. A few of the uniformed men drew their guns in a panic, aiming at the little boy.

"Take it easy." Nolan threw his hands up in a sign of peace but kept his eyes on the youngster's gun. "Captain, have your men put their guns away before someone gets shot." He took another step toward the little boy.

"Git the hell away from me, mister, or I'll blow a hole through your gut the size of that horse!"

Nolan cracked a half grin at the tough little tomcat. He almost wanted to laugh, if it weren't for the rifle pointed at his middle. "Look, son, I ain't gonna hurt ya. I'm offerin' to help."

"I ain't your son!" The boy's teeth were gritted.

"Fair enough. You got a name?" Nolan braved another step.

The little boy again was playing deaf to Nolan's question. After being alone for nearly a week, why wasn't this little fella happy to see help arrive or crying about what all had happened to him? Tightlipped and as sober-faced as a preacher on Sunday morning was the picture of this boy.

"Anyone got a shovel?" Nolan hollered out while keeping his eyes on the gun pointed at him. A short-handled spade was tossed on the ground next to him. "I'm gonna pick that up, and you're gonna let me." He bent forward, not looking at the shovel but searching the snippet's eyes. Nolan didn't like what he saw. This ornery little cuss wasn't afraid to face a grown man. No longer did he doubt the brat would pull the trigger.

Slowly, so as not to startle the boy into squeezing off a shot, Nolan dropped to his knees and began to shovel dirt. With his baby blues, the babe gawked at him strangely. It'd been some time since the boy had last been around people. Maybe the kid hadn't expected help to come.

The soft lines of the boy's face slowly turned into a wrinkled-up nose and mean little scowl. Did this kid truly think he could go at it all alone? Digging a grave for the dead woman was only one barrier stacked in front of him. Yeah, the boy had left proof of his grit at the wagon train. Seeing the size of the grasshopper, Nolan was surprised he had the strength to dig nine graves and do the burying.

The squinting little glare was a plain enough truth that he did not want Nolan there helping. "No!" the boy unexpectedly shouted.

Nolan stopped his shoveling and eyed the kid. Dressed in nothing more than rags and dirty from head to heels, he would bet this little boy was used to standing alone. "Son, why don't you lower your aim, put the rifle aside, and I'll hand you the shovel?"

All twitchy like, the boy looked over his shoulder. Then he glanced about at the soldiers here and there working to set up camp. "Why ain't you wearing a uniform? Ain't you a blue belly?"

If Nolan closed his eyes, he'd swear he was listening to a full-grown man. The words didn't fit with the tot that stood knee-high in front of him. Tenderness, Nolan would bet, was something he had never brushed up against. He and Mary had argued a few times about her coddling Matthew. This boy must have had a rough few years of living.

"I'm a scout."

The boy's eyes went to the pistol strapped on Nolan's hip. "So you're not a soldier? You fight, don't ya?"

"I draw my gun when I have to." Nolan was honest.

"I've always been told that the bluecoats were no damn good and I wasn't to trust a one of 'em. Do the ciphering…I can only trust myself. So you can go." The boy sharply waved the barrel of the gun for Nolan to git.

The few times Nolan had spanked Matthew, his son had bawled like a baby before he even bent the child over. This boy was trying to stand far too tall for his small boots and seemed to see himself as a man instead of the child that he was. Nolan wouldn't have minded giving the tot a good lick for keeping that gun pointed at him, but if he were to dare grab at that rifle, he'd likely get shot. He had a different thought on how to take the boy's aim off him.

Nolan straightened from digging, then extended a hand as if handing the spade to the boy. The youngster took the bait and lowered his aim. Nolan's hand quickly grabbed the rifle away from the brazen kid.

"That's my gun! Give it back!" The ornery cuss kicked at the dirt but made no move to try to grab at the gun in Nolan's hand.

The snippet's eyes weren't focused on the rifle. Nolan's free hand was being keenly watched, and the boy had backed off a step or two. It was Nolan's experience that a scared pup would eventually bite. The kid wasn't trusting. That was for sure.

"You ain't big enough to handle a rifle this size. Had you squeezed the trigger, it would have blown you back twenty paces."

"I can shoot a pistol real good. We can trade—my Henry for the Colt on your hip." This boy was no quitter.

Nolan couldn't help but laugh. "How old are you, son... five?" The first time Nolan had taken him hunting, Matthew was eight, and the rifle hadn't been a double-barreled Henry.

"Seven. What's that matter?" The boy's lippy mouth was quickly growing old.

"The only thing you're getting from me is this here." Nolan handed the boy the shovel, and the brat grabbed it from his hand. "Who is she?" Clearly the youngster knew the woman. He was, after all, digging a grave for her.

"Mrs. Harper." The kid gave a quick answer. The snow-capped head was facedown, and he was digging with a fury.

Nolan recalled the grave at the wagons, the one with the cross that had read Jenny Harper. "Did you know Jenny?"

The boy's head snapped up, and he glared at Nolan, blue eyes ablaze with anger. The painful hate Nolan saw was a mirror image of his own after he'd lost Mary and Matthew.

"We're tracking down the men who did this. We came across what was left of the wagon train." How explaining it was going to make the boy feel any better, Nolan didn't know. But for some reason he thought he should tell the truth of seeing Jenny's grave.

The little tomcat threw another shovelful of dirt with a vengeance. "She was my sister." The small voice was barely a whisper.

Nolan shook his head. What? So this woman was the little boy's ma? A youngster that age should be mighty upset at the death of his mama. This little tot wasn't crying or clingy. He was going about his work, digging like a man. Only he wasn't a man. He was pint-sized, actually less. It didn't make sense.

The sight of the dead Mrs. Harper was enough to sicken any fighting man. A swarm of flies buzzed about, and maggots crawled around her large, open gut wound. Nolan barely could stomach looking her over.

She'd been dragged behind a horse. Cuts and scrapes covered every exposed part of her body. Nolan touched his hand to the dark marks on her neck. She'd been choked, and to finish her, she'd suffered a long slice across her midsection. Her guts were slopping through her shredded clothing.

A gruesome example to frighten the other girls and women so they wouldn't give a fight or try to run. That was what this woman's brutal death was: a warning. Why did the boy think himself man enough to stand up against the type of men who would do such as this?

Nolan looked over at the half-pint. No tears. Only anger. He looked again at the dead Mrs. Harper. This woman wasn't the little boy's mama. Nolan would bet on that.

He faced the boy just as the loose soil slipped away under the slight weight of the small boot and he fell into the hole. It was maybe a foot and a half to two feet in depth at the most.

The little fella wasn't crying or whining, so Nolan reckoned the boy hadn't fallen far enough to hurt himself. He brushed himself off, then went to work. Dirt piled up quick. When he was done, the grave had been dug too deep for the half-pint to climb out on his own. He extended a hand, but the little tomcat glared. There was no intention of accepting help in those piercing blue eyes. What had been done to this child to make one so young that distrustful?

"Don't touch me! I can climb out of this damn stupid hole myself!"

Nolan was tempted to grab the foul-talking brat and give him a good hard shake to knock it off. If he had a bar of lye soap, he'd be using it to scrub the brat's dirty mouth clean. Who had raised this boy to talk in such a way?

Mary had once caught Matthew spitting out a bad word after sinking a fishing hook into his finger. Whoo-wee, she'd been none too happy. She'd marched their son by the arm into the house. Matthew had been made to memorize scripture that shut the door on using profane words. Nolan, too, had caught the devil from Mary for not correcting the boy quickly enough.

He knew with every breath this little boy drew, he was hating the world. Nolan had felt that way himself for a long time after burying Mary and Matthew. It was a sad thing the boy had experienced at the wagon train, but at the same time, this brat needed straightened out.

"Stop your cussing or shut your mouth."

"Mister, you can go make house with the devil. Don't tell me what to do." The brat glared up out of the hole.

Nolan couldn't fault the boy for the awful heartache he must have been suffering. But the smart-ass lip needed to end real damn quick. "You talk to me like that again, I'm gonna tan your backside."

Their eyes locked on one another. Unbelievable. Even under the threat of a spanking, the boy wasn't afraid to challenge Nolan. This brazen little heathen was more than a handful. No fighting words were fired back out of the boy's mouth, but the glaring baby blues weren't backing down.

Fine, Nolan thought. If the kid wanted to get out of the hole himself, then Nolan would let the little piss pot have at it. He straightened and decided to watch the show. Only, this boy's brassiness wasn't so entertaining.

Nolan didn't give a word of instruction as the half-pint tried a second time to find a toehold on the dirt wall and failed to hoist himself out of the grave. The boy brushed the dirt from his raggedy pants, then tried a knee to lift himself. It was becoming obvious that the half-pint was not willing to give up. He was now jumping up, trying to catch hold of the dirt shelf that made up the rim of the hole. He slipped and fell to his knees. Time after time, the kid failed. When would this boy quit?

Wait a minute. Maybe Nolan was seeing it all wrong. Letting the brat try to fail had been a good thing. Surely the boy was getting tired of being stuck down in that hole.

Nolan reached out and offered his hand a second time. "Come on. You're just wasting time." If the little tomcat took hold, then it was a small start to trusting Nolan.

His thought struck him. Why did he want this boy's trust?

The ornery cuss didn't want to, and it showed on the scowling little face. But he did slowly give his hand. There was something about the feel of the boy's small fingers held tight in Nolan's that both bothered him and captured his attention. He was gentle, and no effort was needed to lift the grasshopper out of the shallow grave.

"You can let go of me now." The boy stared, and Nolan jolted. He hadn't realized he'd kept hold of the kid.

What the boy did next was mighty thoughtful. Having no ground blanket to wrap the dead woman in, the boy shucked the old, tattered coat and gently covered the woman's face.

"Git out of my way." The tender moment hadn't lasted long, and the brat was talking way too tough for being a runt. But Nolan stepped back, giving the feisty little beast space. Was this teeny fella honestly going to try to lift this woman of sizable girth into her grave? The kid had sand but no damn sense.

It nearly made Nolan sick to watch. How god-awful long would he have to endure watching the boy fail before the brat would accept some help? He had tried every angle possible to get the woman in her grave and hadn't budged her an inch. What was the half-pint thinking? He didn't own a quarter of the strength needed to get the man-sized chore done. Mrs. Harper wasn't a small-boned woman.

Nolan had enough of watching the boy struggle. His mind was seeing Mary's and Matthew's caskets being lowered into the ground. That had been a day from hell. Whoever this woman was to the boy, he was working hard to see her properly buried. That meant something.

One step was all Nolan had taken, and the boy was opening his mouth. "I don't want your help."

"Well, you're gonna git it anyway." Nolan gently pushed the half-pint aside.

"I can do it myself." The brat crossed his arms and was welcome to stomp his feet all he wanted. Nolan didn't care about a little tantrum. He turned off his ears to the little brat's whining.

Nolan got his arms under the Harper woman, then gently lifted her. He could feel the boy's eyes on him as he carried her a few steps, then lowered her easylike into the earth. The half-pint stood by with shovel in hand and wore a far-off stare. Maybe it was Jenny that the kid was thinking about. Nolan had touched a nerve when he'd spoken the name. If it were Mrs. Harper that the tot's mind was stuck on, then he should have been a sobbing mess. That wasn't what Nolan was seeing. The little boy's thoughts were somewhere else.

One stretching step and Nolan was out of the grave. He stood next to the kid. The half-pint looked up at Nolan, and the shine of fresh tears was there. He sniffled, then wiped a dirty sleeve across his eyes. The little tomcat fought to keep from crying. This child wasn't going to let his guard down for anything. Why so tough?

"I can't look at their faces when I'm pitching dirt on them." With head hanging low and shoulders drooped, the half-pint sank the spade into the freshly dug dirt. The boy then tossed the first scoop onto Mrs. Harper.

That initial bail was the hardest. Nolan had learned that hard, awful truth himself. He'd sat next to Mary's and Matthew's graves for hours before pitching that one shovelful to mound them over. It meant saying goodbye forever, and that wasn't an easy thing.

Nolan walked away and left the half-pint alone to do what needed doing. Companionship hadn't been what he wanted when mourning the loss of his wife and son. Maybe that hadn't been the best way for him to grieve. He'd wallowed in the quiet of having no one, picking up the bottle. Thank God the boy was far too young to learn that lesson.

Nolan was curious though. The boy had obviously learned something of life from someone. Brave beyond his years. What would become of the little fella now? Maybe the kid had kin besides those killed at the wagon train that could take him in.

Nolan needed to speak to the captain. Perhaps the half-pint could clue the army to who exactly was leaving all the carnage behind. He spotted the captain, who was walking away from the fire with a steaming tin of coffee in his hands.

"Captain, sir, I'd like to have a word with ya about the boy." Nolan hustled over and then quickly spelled out his thoughts, especially the ones about the kid maybe being a witness.

Captain Farnsworth rolled his eyes in a staunch manner that conveyed his annoyance. "I say we leave the boy to wander till he finds a settler family to take him in. He was probably hiding someplace, didn't see much of anything, and the fact that he's a babe makes him unreliable—if he witnessed anything at all. Kids get things mixed up when they're upset, and that little one's obviously angry. Do I have to remind ya he had a gun pointed at you? He can't be of any help to us. Besides, he don't look to be worth much. If he has any living kin, I doubt they'll care that he's been found."

There was nothing about the captain's sharp words that Nolan liked. A dirt-streaked face and shabby clothing didn't make the kid's life worthless. "We're trailing stolen women to git them back and send them home. What makes that boy any different?"

The captain's eyes narrowed, and he glared at Nolan. It was obvious proof that he didn't like being questioned.

He glanced with disgust at the child. "As far as we know, this boy is now an orphan. Look at that filthy runt... Who would want him?"

There were orphanages that the boy could be sent to, but that wasn't where Nolan's mind was. "I'm telling ya the boy might be of help to us." He stressed the fact again.

"How?" Captain Farnsworth sneered as if what Nolan had just said was absolute foolishness.

"The boy was with that wagon train and probably had seen the men who did this." How many different ways did he have to say it before it sank into the captain's brain? It was an important fact that Nolan couldn't overlook. It would certainly be an advantage to be able to put a face or name with whom they were chasing after.

The captain spat a string of tobacco juice close to Nolan's feet. "We know who slaughtered those people and that poor woman buried yonder. We don't need the kid to tell us it was Indians. He's useless."

It wasn't just what the captain did that pissed Nolan off but also the attitude shown toward the little boy. This child was not insignificant.

Nolan threw a quick glance over his shoulder. The half-pint had been cradling himself a few minutes ago but was now on his feet, standing next to the grave. He wiped at his red eyes. Nolan would quit his duty as scout before leaving the youngster to his own means.

He looked back at the captain and pointed a finger. "I told you there were shod horses in that bunch. Indians don't shoe their ponies."

"Then the horses were most likely stolen. I don't believe we're hunting white men."

Captain Farnsworth just wasn't willing to see it any other way. Nolan was ready to be done with the fool. Their ways of thinking were too different at times. But he'd give convincing the captain one more try. "When Indians steal a horse that's shod, they don't leave the shoes on very long. They pull it off. We can settle this matter by asking the boy what he saw."

Nolan looked over his shoulder, and the half-pint was gone. Had the boy walked off?

He quickly twisted in all directions and searched everywhere around the camp. "Dammit!" He ran toward the horses. The little brat was throwing a leg over Nolan's bay gelding. He should have known not to take his eyes off the ornery little cuss. "Hey, stop right there!"

The boy kicked the bay, and instantly the horse lunged forward, knocking Nolan aside. He threw his hands out and grabbed the rotten, thieving brat's ankle before they both tumbled and hit the ground with a heavy thud. Nolan lost his hold on the boy, rolled quickly, and reached with both hands as the errant imp tried scrambling away. They grappled across the ground as Nolan fought to settle the heathen's flailing arms and legs. Holy shit. This was worse than trying to catch a greased pig.

Teeth sank into Nolan's hand, and pain shot through his arm. Without thought, he jerked away from the small but feisty open mouth coming at him a second time. The little coyote quickly twisted around and tried to bite his other hand. Nolan swung a hand up and grabbed the brat by the scruff.

"Let go of me!" the boy howled.

Was this kid afraid of anything? Because fighting a grown man and stealing a horse definitely weren't on that list. Matthew had mostly done whatever was asked of him. Not once had Nolan's son ever thrown a fighting fit such as this after being caught doing something he shouldn't have in the first place.

It was a struggle, but Nolan managed to get to his feet as the little fighting cat twisted around to break free from his grip. At arm's length, he held the brat until the heathen quit squirming and kicking.

Nolan had broken a damn sweat. "Are you done?"

There was nothing right about the boy's hateful glare aimed at him. A beaten-down pup would grow up to be a biting dog, and this boy was already showing his mean teeth. But Nolan didn't feel pity toward the kid.

Damn. His hand was thumping something awful, and he was seeing red. Matthew would have gotten his hide torn off.

Nolan marched the ornery cuss to fireside, then forced the brat down to sit. "If you know what's good for ya, don't move from that spot."

The brat actually stuck his tongue out at him. Unbelievable. Had Nolan lost his damn mind? What was he doing with this kid?

He pulled in a deep breath and stomped away, picking up his hat off the ground and dusting the dirt from the brim. Then he caught sight of the amused I-told-you-so laughter from the captain.

CHAPTER 5

AS HE WALKED TOWARD HIM, Nolan wanted to wipe that smug smile off Farnsworth's face.

The captain put a hand up before he could say a word. "I didn't become a soldier to play wet nurse. Now let me alone. I'm busy." Farnsworth tossed his saddle onto his horse's back. "Mount up, men!"

Was he really going to start this bullshit again?

Nolan grabbed the captain's shoulder and spun the man away from cinching the saddle strap. "I ain't leavin' the boy behind."

The half-pint owned lots of fighting spirit and most likely would be trouble until they could get him somewhere he could be taken care of. But the nearest town was weeks away. No doubt, the youngster would die if left without their help.

"I ain't asking your permission. I'm bringing the boy with us. Me telling you is nothing more than a courtesy." There was nothing friendly in Nolan's tone.

The captain sneered. "Then I guess you can be the one to ride double through the mountain with him."

Nolan laughed at the captain's fool words. "You said it yourself, Captain. That boy's a runt. My saddle's heavier than he is." Nolan walked away to where the kid was standing next to the smoldering ashes, watching the packing of camp. "Come on. You'll ride with me, and if you try stealing my horse again, I'll leave ya out there for the coyotes to eat."

The boy eyed Nolan for a minute, then followed slowly.

Maybe he had truly thought that he would be left behind. The smartest thing the kid could do was just keep his distance from the captain.

Nolan glanced down at the half-pint walking a step behind him. There was nothing like a full belly to make one want to nap. His baby blues were drooping heavily with drowsiness. Nolan had seen the army doc hand the boy a heaping plate of beans. The kid had drowned his face in the slop, lapping it up. He doubted the boy had even tasted the food. He probably hadn't had much to eat in the past seven days all alone out on the prairie. He had seen the boy pick the crumbs from the hardtack off his shirt, then lick his fingers.

Nolan stepped up, swinging a leg over the saddle, then reached out for the boy's arm. Just that quick, the half-pint flinched. Shoulders hunched, he turned away to guard his grimacing face. Someone's hand had made this boy awful twitchy.

"Give me your hand."

The half-pint slowly opened himself up but kept his eyes on his boots. And his face was flushed red. Perhaps the best thing was to dump the boy with the next settler family they came across. It was looking as if he had too many scars not to be a big headache.

The small hand slowly reached for Nolan's, and he lifted the kid into the saddle. There was that something again, like when the boy had taken his hand to get out of the Harper woman's grave. In a strange way, it bothered Nolan to feel the shy, tender touch of one much weaker than himself. He hadn't been a father in a long time.

Should he sit the grasshopper in the saddle in front of him? Not carrying much weight on the little bones, if the boy fell off the back of the bay, Nolan might not notice. Though he doubted the kid even trusted him enough to rest his tired eyes. He decided to leave the half-pint sitting behind him and spurred the bay.

The soldiers were strung out in a long line. Nolan led them winding through the trees up and across the mountainside. The surrounding foliage was full and green, a natural canopy that shaded the group from the sun. A slight breeze stirred the stuffy air enough so Nolan could breathe without choking. Sweat trickled down his back and soaked the front of his shirt. The kid had to be sweltering behind him too, and Nolan doubted he'd taken much time for bathing lately.

"I could go for a cool swim. How about you?" He looked over his shoulder just as the half-pint's slight weight fell against him. The youngster was asleep.

At this age, how many times had Matthew begged to go with Nolan? Didn't matter where he was off to, his son had always wanted to be in his back pocket. Usually, until they'd gotten home, Matthew had been slumped in the crook of Nolan's arm, fast asleep in the saddle.

He turned from the child and looked forward to search the ground for a sign of the outlaws. Whoever the killers were, they were careless or didn't care that they were being dogged. Why wouldn't men on the run with stolen women try to hide their trail? Maybe it was the amount of firepower that made this bunch so confident.

By Nolan's count, there were at least twenty-five horses. How many of those were carrying women? He couldn't rightly guess.

There were fifteen soldiers, and the captain made sixteen. Nolan counted as one more fighting man. The boy would just need to be kept out of the way somewhere safe if any shooting started. They were outnumbered in guns but not in skill.

What he followed was no more than a deer path leading them deeper into the hills. Nolan pulled up on the reins in a little clearing and studied the ground. He then walked the bay in a widening circle. He felt a small stirring nudge against his back, and he figured the kid was waking. He didn't bother to look over his shoulder to see for certain. Hours had passed, and he'd nearly forgotten the boy was behind him. The kid was a distraction, something Nolan didn't need. What was important were the signs he was trying to follow.

CHAPTER 6

NATE STRETCHED AND YAWNED. Where was he? How many miles had he crossed with the soldiers? Was he getting any closer to the fancy man who'd killed Jenny? Nate wanted to ask, but who would ever listen to him? Tipsy, one of the no-accounts that had ridden in Pa's gang, had once threatened to cut out Nate's tongue if he didn't shut his jib from asking so many questions.

This man that he was riding with now hadn't hit him yet. Maybe the scout was different than the other men he had known. Nate's ears were good, and he'd heard most of what the captain had said about leaving him. For some reason the army scout had stuck up for him. But that didn't make them friends. If they would have been friendly, then Nate would definitely be asking what the hell they were doing walking about in tight circles on this horse, spinning around this way and that while the man looked at the ground.

Nate was getting about half-dizzy while the soldiers were all just sitting on their mounts, watching.

Nate stretched his neck and squinted to see what it was on the ground that the scout seemed so interested in. He didn't see anything. He leaned and stretched as far as he could for a better look. Why wasn't he seeing it? There weren't no dead bodies … thank the Lord. Dirt, grass, and a few rocks was all he saw. He shifted his weight a little more to stretch a hair farther. He could almost see what was ahead and dared a bit more, but he slipped.

Aw shit.

The scout's muscular arm shot out from the broad shoulder and caught Nate before he fell.

His face flushed a deep red, and he hoped the man would see Nate was sorry. He hadn't meant to be trouble. Nate shrank back at the cold, hard glare of the dark blue eyes. This was no easy man. He figured his time was up. The captain didn't want him there, and with this bit of trouble, well … Nate wouldn't blame the scout for dropping him off the horse and leaving him behind for being no good.

Maybe if Nate dared to open his mouth and explain. Or would that just anger the man and then Nate would be left behind for sure? He didn't want to be alone in the mountains. If he voiced that weakness, he would look to be a coward. He couldn't help it though. The woods were dark and scary after the sun went down. One night out on the prairie, with the stars twinkling over him and no moon or fire to cast light on what surrounded him in the pitch black, his hair had stood on end when his ears had caught hold of a rabbit squealing for its life. Some critter bigger than that bunny had itself a meal, and the shrieking had been abruptly cut off.

What did Nate have to lose by speaking up? He'd been slapped before for talking when he shouldn't have. This man would probably get rid of Nate the first chance that showed itself. So what was Nate so worried about?

"I wanted to see what you were looking at."

Without pause, the man pointed to a white scrape. "That's what happens when a horse's hoof hits a rock."

Nate hadn't expected the scout to explain anything to him or even really talk to him. Something inside him lit up, and he wanted to know more. He'd seen marks like that before but hadn't known the cause.

The scout twisted in the saddle and pointed to a similar mark, only in a different place. "The problem is over there."

Nate turned and looked at another white scrape. "How could they go in two directions?"

"They separated." The man hadn't stopped studying the ground and seemed to be reading something no one else could, including Nate.

He'd sure like to know how it was done. "Why?" Nate was curious. No one but Jenny ever had time for him, but this man had spared a few minutes to show and teach him something new. If Nate simply grinned, he might jinx the small happiness.

"I ain't sure why." The man rubbed at the dark stubble on his chin while he seemed to be thinking things over. Nate sat quiet, and the scout waved for the captain.

The army man trotted his horse up next to the bay. "What is it?"

Nate didn't like the captain's bossiness. Why was the scout tolerating it? Earlier, he'd told the captain how it was going to be, and that was the very reason Nate was there, riding with the scout. Now, all of a sudden, the scout didn't even seem to hear the irritation in the other man's voice.

"Three riders split off from the bunch and went that way. They might double around and come at us." What the scout had said made sense to Nate, but did the captain agree?

"So which way is the main bunch headed?" The captain seemed confused as he looked about at all those horse prints on the ground.

The scout turned and pointed to the second trail that led away from the clearing.

"We should follow the main bunch." The captain didn't really seem to be asking, and he was nodding in agreement with himself.

Nate didn't like the idea and started to open his mouth to say it might be a trap. Then he stopped himself because of the look the captain was giving him. He sensed that the captain wanted to wring Nate's neck for some reason.

The scout didn't even seem to notice, not that Nate expected him to care, and he went on with his thoughts. "Three men rode off from that bunch. It will only take one man with a good rifle aim to pick quite a few of us off before we ever git close to the women. We don't know where those three went. It could be an ambush."

What? Had Nate heard the scout right? Jenny's sisters might be alive? Nate had figured, after finding Mrs. Harper the way he had, that the daughters were all dead and he just hadn't come across their bodies. If what the scout said was true, Nate would do his best to save Nancy, Susanna, and... What was the other one's name? Barely a one of them had ever breathed in Nate's direction, but this would be for Jenny. It was the same reason he'd seen to it that Mrs. Harper had been buried proper. He'd done more for that fat pig in the time it took to dig her grave than she'd ever done for him. It was all for Jenny. Nate hadn't been able to save her, and that pained him.

"Answer me, boy!" The captain grabbed him by the side of his shirt, pinching a bit of skin too.

Tears sprang to Nate's eyes, but before he could jerk away, the scout shoved the captain's hand off and swung the bay so he could no longer reach Nate.

"Don't touch the boy again." The scout glanced between the captain and the soldiers waiting at the tree line for their orders. "Captain Farnsworth, you're in charge here, and those are your men. Don't force me to set you straight in front of them. 'Cause after you gotta be picked up off the ground, they won't follow you so easily."

Nate was trying to calm his breathing as his heart pounded. He found himself clinging to the back of the scout's shirt.

What had just happened? This man had stuck up for him in a way that no one ever had, not even Jenny. Why? What did the scout want from him?

The captain didn't say a word to argue, and Nate just stayed quiet as well.

"I can move quicker and more quietly on my own. I would suggest, Captain, that you have your men make an early camp. I'll scout this trail first." The scout pointed off down the trail where the three had split away. "When I find something to report, I'll be back."

Captain Farnsworth nodded. The scout then turned in the saddle and gently took Nate by the arm. He was being slightly lifted to slide down easy from the saddle. No way. Nate didn't want to stay with the captain. He held tight as the man reached toward the ground with him, drawing his feet up from touching the dirt and dangling on the end of the scout's arm.

"What … are you doing?" The man grinned.

"Let me go with you. I can help … Please, please, please." Nate wasn't above begging. The captain would probably send him off into the mountain all alone or something worse. He would swing on the scout's arm for an hour if that's what it took to convince the man to take him along.

"I must be crazy." The scout began to lift Nate onto the saddle once again.

The captain started laughing, but it wasn't funny to Nate. He turned with a glare. Captain Jackass was about to find out that he could go live with the devil. So far, the scout hadn't let the bluecoat hurt Nate. But a firm hand clamped down over his mouth and cut off any words from flying off his tongue.

Captain Farnsworth laughed harder. "Nolan, something tells me you're going to regret being lured in by that rotten kid." He turned his horse and trotted away.

Nate was, without warning, plopped down just behind the saddle horn. The scout's face was red, and Nate pictured steam pouring from the man's ears. He pointed a finger at Nate. "No more lip. Especially where Captain Farnsworth is concerned. You stay away from him. Do ya hear me?"

Nate nodded that he understood, sort of. "You told him what you were thinking, so why can't I?" Honestly, he wanted to know. There was no difference that he saw.

"Boy, you got some growing to do before you can stand tall in man-size boots. If you keep talking the way you do, you might find yourself in a heap of trouble that you can't git out of."

Nate seeing himself as a man was just a comforting lie. If he could trick his mind into believing that he was big enough to take care of himself, then maybe he wouldn't be so scared to be on his own. He was alone in this world and had no choice other than to give up boyhood.

"We've been jawing long enough. Turn around and stay quiet and still." The scout moved his canteen to a strap on the back and helped Nate get situated.

The bay was nudged forward, and Nate did as he'd been told. He wasn't going to say a single word.

They'd gone about three miles when the scout pointed out the end of a snapped branch. "That break is too high off the ground to be a deer or large animal that done it." The man had kept his voice low, and he reined in next to the broken piece. "See how it's shoulder height with me?"

Nate nodded and pictured the fancy man as he might have passed. He wanted to know more. And just like that, without begging or pleading, the man opened up to teach him further.

"There ain't no leaves falling at this time of year to hide prints on the ground. So you wanna look for any spot of dirt that might be a little softer to hold a good horseshoe print. Then you study it. That way, if you come across a place where others have ridden, then you won't lose your wanted man's trail. That mark is as good as a fingerprint, unless your man is tricky enough to switch horses. But most ain't. They find a good, solid horse and stick with that animal."

Nate took in every word and rolled it around in his mind. Pa had sure been lucky. How many posses had they slipped away from? If this man had been riding with the law at any of those times, Pa would have been sent to prison long before that day in Northfield.

Nate looked about the ground as the gelding began to walk again. Streaks of sun filtered through the many thick branches of leaves and touched the ground, making the mountainside appear golden. A whistling bird sang for its mate, who repeated the love song.

It was hot but starting to cool off with the birth of the evening shadows, and Nate's sharp eyes spotted something. Keeping quiet, he nudged the man behind him, then pointed to a small swath of dirt between two rocks. A partial horse print was pressed into the ground. The man grinned, turned the bay, and followed the trail down the backside of the mountain.

From the corner of Nate's eye, he caught a quick movement to the right of them in the brush. The scout had seen it too, because he grabbed up his rifle and took aim. Was it the fancy man? Nate's heart took to pounding. A deer jumped from the thicket with its white tail flickering high in the air. He let out a grateful sigh that they hadn't just sprung a trap.

Pa had always watched his back trail, for good reason. It seemed that being the hunter instead of the hunted could be just as dangerous, but Nate kind of liked looking forward rather than always worrying about being bird-dogged.

They played their game of finding sign while tracking the three riders. The scout would pull up on the reins without saying a word and then would wait while Nate searched quickly. Five of ten times so far, Nate had been right on the mark. Was the scout enjoying their game? It was hard to tell by the sober face and watchful eyes that seemed to be searching in every direction.

On one hand, Nate could count the number of times he'd had what Jenny referred to as fun. While it lasted, this was number six.

A coyote called out in the distance, rousing Nate from his thoughts. He caught a whiff of smoke. "You smell that?" His gut tightened, and he shifted his weight and slid quickly out of the saddle just in front of the man swiping a miss at catching hold of him. Nate ducked under the gelding, emerging on the other side.

"That burning wood smell might be coming from a campfire," Nate said more to himself than to the scout. Maybe the fancy man was warming up supper without a worry that anyone was coming for him.

The air all of a sudden felt chilly, and his skin grew clammy. Three against two, the odds were not in his favor. That alone wasn't going to stop him. He could maybe run off their horses, then steal a gun. After Nate caught them, he would march the fancy man and the other two back to the captain to deal out what was coming to the murderers. Yup, he was man enough to face down the dandy killer.

***

Nolan left the bay standing, and he followed after the kid on foot. He, too, now smelled the smoke. The half-pint stopped midstep and quietly pointed. The shack was dug into the side of the mountain. It was fronted with stacked stone that leaned heavy to one side. A deerskin flap served as a door. Someone was home. The chimney was pouring out a thick line of gray.

"Stay here." Nolan didn't know who or how many might be in there or if they were friendly. If things went bad for him. The boy, at this distance, could be on the bay and gone before anyone from the cabin could catch hold of him.

"I ain't afraid to walk up to that cabin." The boy puffed out his little chest.

The captain's words about regret rang in Nolan's ears. "Git yourself covered behind a tree." He could clearly see the boy's pissing little temper as he kicked at the dirt two or three times. He didn't like to be told what to do. What a surprise. Had Nolan truly expected anything with this child to go easy?

The brat stood his ground, mumbling under his breath. Nolan couldn't hear what for certain the kid was griping about, but he would guess it was full of curses. He should have left the imp back at the soldiers' camp. Didn't the boy understand the danger of the situation? "Do as you're told, 'cause if you don't and I unbuckle my belt, you'll git your ass whupped. If something bad starts happening, you get on that horse and ride fast back to camp for help. Can't risk none of these men gettin' away."

The rascal stepped behind a tree with his arms folded tight across his chest and his little face all wrinkled up mean. Nolan would give the boy a good talking to later.

Slowly he crept toward the filthy shack with his pistol ready. A cougar skin was stretched tight to dry between two trees. Fox, skunk, and beaver pelts were draped in a heap over a fallen log.

A water bucket sat on a stump. The ground near it was wet where the water had been sloshed out and hadn't yet dried in the sun. Someone had been there not long ago, if they weren't still there.

Reaching with his pistol while keeping to one side of the doorframe, Nolan shoved aside the skin flap and peered inside. The room was no more than a dirt floor and four rickety standing walls made of log and stone packed together with mud. Sky peeked through the thatched roof. A table and two chairs were pushed far back in a corner. Nolan stepped inside.

An unmade cot sat at the other end of the room. The fire was stoked hot. Where was the person who had fed the flames?

Maybe whoever lived there had seen or heard them coming and decided to hide. Judging by all the furs, the man was a trapper. Not getting to town around folks too often, mountain men could be strange around people. Nolan should check on the half-pint.

He'd turned to walk back out the door when a faint rustle of clothing caught his ears. He instantly spun on his heel, his aim directed under the table. "Show yourself!"

Was that a soft whimper he heard? Keeping his gun aimed, he slowly leaned down and peered beneath the tabletop. A frightened young woman cowered in the corner. Her eyes were wild with fear like a trapped animal. There was blood on her wrists where the leather strap that bound her hands was twisted awful tight. The dress she was wearing had been torn and was dirty. But the goods she wore looked to be made of fine threads, not homespun. Store-bought, Nolan would bet. This was no mountain woman traded from one man to another. Was she one of the stolen women they were searching for? There was one way to find out.

"Miss."

She let out a god-awful shriek. Nolan quickly holstered his pistol and hurried to pull the table away from her. Whoever had taken her might hear her screaming and come shooting. Nolan needed to quiet her down quick.

She dragged herself across the floor to escape him. Her one leg seemed to be dead weight, bent in a funny way right below the knee.

Nolan stepped toward her, keeping his hands where she could see them. "Take it easy, miss."

Her eyes were wide, and the tears were flowing. She visibly shook from head to toe. Nolan could imagine what had been done to her.

"I'm gonna pull my knife and cut your hands free." Slowly he hunkered down, then slit the rope. She rubbed at her raw wrists. "Captain Farnsworth and his army are camped about six miles from here. I'm gonna take you there. He'll git you home."

"My leg's broken." She grimaced in pain.

The poor thing, Nolan thought. Her hair was matted with dried blood from the gash above her eye. She would probably end up with a scar where her top lip was busted open and swollen fat. Nolan reckoned this young lady was lucky to be alive.

He helped her gently to her feet, shouldering most of her weight because of the bum leg. She sniffled back fresh tears of pain with each gimping step as they hobbled together from the house.

"You best git your hands off that gal." The gruff voice came from behind Nolan.

He slowly turned while lowering the girl to the ground. The trapper was a grizzly of a man wearing a coon hat. A trophy necklace of claws and teeth hung loose around the big man's neck. It drooped along the buckskin shirt and nearly touched the thick-waisted rawhide belt. This was no green sapling that would bend easily. Judging by the scars on the man's face, some large animal must have clawed at him, proving this big fella had weathered a few storms. Nolan's gut sensed he wasn't going to talk his way out of this.

"I got me a bill of sale for that gal. But I'm willing to trade. I got me something I think you'll want." The big fella sneered.

Nolan quickly glanced to where he'd left the boy. A familiar meanness rose up in him. No one had ever laid a hand on Matthew. He hadn't recognized the feeling when he'd backed down the captain from taking hold of the kid.

Out of nowhere, the burly trapper had a tight grip on the half-pint and held him dangling off the ground by his tiny neck. The little boy squirmed, kicked, and was trying to suck air into his lungs. He clawed with his small hands at the trapper's big paw. The boy was shaken limp to stop fighting. Nolan was seeing red.

The kid was then squeezed tight in one arm and held to the front of the big man. The trapper had drawn a seven-inch blade that shone in the fading sun, and he pressed the tip of the knife under the boy's chin. One slip and the youngster would be dead, as Nolan suspected was the trapper's plan all along. Nolan wasn't going to let that happen.

"I don't think you're gonna trade." Nolan's jaw tightened and his eyes narrowed.

The old fighting bear stood there and laughed at the truth. The little boy's teeth were gnashed together, holding back a muffled whimper. A trickle of blood oozed down the tip of the blade.

"You're right. I ain't in the mood to trade. I'm gonna skin your boy."

The Colt cracked in Nolan's hand. He didn't remember even drawing his pistol. The gritty old trapper dropped to his knees, then fell on his face. In the same instant, the boy had been dropped and hit the ground. The girl's screams echoed through the mountain. Nolan ran to the half-pint and scooped him off the ground to stand. A bit of blood dripped from his chin, and the little boy's legs were shaking so badly that Nolan kept hold of him so he wouldn't fall over.

"Tilt your head back and let me have a look." Nolan squinted to examine the cut. The tip only scratched into the flesh. The boy might end up with a small scar. Maybe now Nolan's heart would slow down. "You okay?" He eased the boy down to sit and catch his breath.

The half-pint touched at his neck. "I will be once you shut her up."

It was true. The girl's screams were ringing in their ears.

Nolan cracked a grin and ruffled the tough little pup's hair. By all rights, this youngster should have been sobbing worse than the girl. Why was he keeping himself all bottled up? Maybe the kid's tears didn't come easy to him with someone he didn't know too well watching over him.

Nolan stood then and walked away to tend to the crying girl.

"I'm Nathanial."

Nolan stopped and looked over his shoulder at the half-pint, who was wiping the blood off his neck across the raggedy shirtsleeve.

"Nolan Crosson."

There was just something about this knee-high peck of trouble that Nolan liked.

CHAPTER 7

NOLAN CAREFULLY LIFTED the girl to sit on the bay. She grimaced and tears welled up in her eyes. Her leg must have hurt like the devil. The sun would be down within the hour. They wouldn't make it back to the army camp before nightfall. She would have to somehow handle her pain through the wee hours before Doc could set the leg tomorrow. If it was even worth saving. Nolan couldn't tell. It was badly swollen, nearly double in size, and the bone looked to be pushing out but hadn't torn through the skin. This sure would slow their pace, and Nolan would have to walk through the mountain, leading the bay.

He lifted Nathanial to sit on the saddle behind the girl.

This certainly would be a bad time to come across the two men who had brought the girl there to sell. Most likely, those men had ridden on through the trapper's camp after doing their business and had gone to meet up with the main bunch. There was still the possibility of an ambush though. Nolan wouldn't leave the ailing young lady and the half-pint for even a short time to go scout around. It would be too dangerous for them to be without protection. If those men had heard the pistol shot, they might return that way. Or they could be hiding in wait somewhere to hear or see if any other ruckus broke out. A shootout wasn't what Nolan needed right now. Maybe a shot of whiskey.

They started off up the mountain, and not one of them spoke a word about anything. The girl was softly crying, but the little boy didn't whimper a sound. He just stared off somewhere far away from this hell. Nolan tried to keep his eyes and ears open for trouble as they made the climb up the mountainside. It wasn't easy to do. His thoughts kept drifting to how different Matthew had been at this age compared to Nathanial. If Nolan didn't get a grip on his mind, he could end up walking the three of them right into a deadly trap.

They crested the mountaintop as darkness fell all around them. Nolan stopped, lifted his hat, and wiped the sweat from his head. "We'll camp here and go on in the morning."

The girl was red-eyed from crying a constant stream of tears after facing death, and Nathanial had gone straight-faced sober after the event. Nolan didn't understand. The half-pint slid off the bay, then walked off into the darkness, disappearing without a word. It wasn't just Nathanial's lack of emotion that bothered Nolan. This kid was stirring up memories of Matthew that he had all but pushed away. Most days were made easier by not remembering his loss, but after what he'd experienced with Nathanial today, the memory of his son had jumped right into Nolan's head.

An innocent-enough hunting trip had brought him and Matthew into a run-in with Indians. No one, including himself, had seemed interested in a fight. Nolan had given a short wave, and they'd nodded. That was the end of it.

Then he'd looked at his son. Matthew's eyes were wide and teary. Nolan had taken his reins and led him home. A week of coaxing had been what it took to get Matthew to leave the house and go hunting again. Facing what could have very easily been a fight to the death had the child in tears for days.

Nathanial didn't seem the least bit bothered and had proved it by walking off into the dark by himself. Nolan turned away from watching after the kid. Those days of teaching his son were … something special. Nolan shouldn't want to forget.

He untied then laid out his saddle blanket to make the girl as comfortable as he could. She winced in pain with any little movement. Purple bruising had spread like a rash from her ankle up over her knee. "Miss, I got some whiskey in my saddlebags if you'd like a nip to take the edge off."

Nathanial returned just then with an arm full of sticks and must have overheard what was said. "You want me to fetch the bottle for ya?"

Manners … So the boy had been keeping them hidden. The offer was kind and nice to see. However, the bay was still saddled, and Nolan didn't trust this little coyote not to steal the horse. "Thanks, but I'll git it. Can you git a fire a-working with those branches?"

Nathanial rolled his eyes and huffed loudly. "Hell yes, I can start a fire."

Nolan's eyes narrowed. "What did I tell you about that mouth?"

The boy shrank back. "Yes, sir, I can start a fire. Is that better?"

The respect of the word sir caught Nolan off guard, though the last few words had been spoken with some sass. Was this Nathanial's way of warming up to him? If so, then Nolan wanted to build on it. He worked together with the boy and fixed a fire. The flames soon danced, and both young people seemed comforted.

Nolan left them then to unsaddle the bay and fetch the whiskey. He uncorked the bottle, then handed it to the young lady. She hadn't quit her crying yet. Nathanial had sat himself on the blanket next to her and was staring at the ugly leg. Nolan nudged the boy with his boot to knock it off. The little tomcat looked up and scowled for a breath or two, then turned back to the girl. She took another swallow from the bottle.

"Miss, you'd best take it easy with that, or come tomorrow morning, your head will be feeling more pain than what you are right now."

Nolan wasn't sure if Nathanial was speaking from his own experience of what he'd seen. He reached, and she handed him the bottle. He sat then and placed the whiskey aside. "Do you know any names of the men who done this to you?"

She nodded and began to sob into her hands. This would be important information for the army, and Nolan would need to report it as soon as he could.

"Well, who was it?"

Nolan felt a small kick to his boot. Nathanial was frowning at him. Okay, the boy was right. His manners had been blunt. The young lady had been through quite a lot today, and only she knew what all she'd suffered since being taken captive.

Nathanial slowly reached out and stroked her hair, an odd turn from his earlier gruffness. The kind gesture produced a small smile on her face, and Nolan thought back on the grave with Jenny's name on it. Women were taken from that camp. Nolan watched the pair to see if they knew each other, but that didn't seem to be the case.

His eyes had never left the two, and still he wasn't sure how it had happened. The young woman had pulled Nathanial onto her lap and cradled him. She clung to the little boy and cried as she rocked them both. Nathanial's eyes were wide, and his gaze met Nolan's. The boy didn't seem to know what to make of the woman's behavior either.

Nolan hesitantly reached over and awkwardly patted the girl's shoulder. "I apologize, miss. My intention wasn't to upset ya. The army's been trying to get their hands on this bunch. It would be easier if we knew who it is that we're hunting." He hoped she wouldn't be afraid to speak up. She might lock it all away somewhere in her mind, and the army would get no answers.

She sat up straight, sniffed, and wiped at her eyes with her raggedy dress. "My horse spooked and threw me. Deegan Jones said I wasn't any good to him with a broken leg. He'd aimed his pistol and was about to shoot me when one of his men said I could still be worth a little profit." Fresh tears sprang to the lady's eyes.

Nolan wasn't thinking of the hurt girl. Deegan Jones was a ruthless killer, wanted throughout the territory. An ex-Confederate officer who had built up wealth by smuggling. His trade had started during the war and had now grown considerably. Being a leader of soldiers, Jones knew how to successfully execute a mission and move a large number in his rank without being seen. It was no wonder the army was always one step behind this bunch. Deegan Jones was a deviously clever man and typically never left a witness alive. He probably figured that no one would find the girl way the hell out there in the mountains. And if by chance someone did, her mind would be so far gone from suffering at the hands of that trapper, who would believe her story?

Nolan eyed Nathanial. The half-pint had somehow slipped through Jones's fingers and escaped death.

The woman let go from holding Nathanial and laid herself on the blanket. She stared off into the flames. The boy came and sat close to Nolan, which was unexpected.

Nathanial didn't seem interested in him. Instead, he studied the girl for a long minute. He fidgeted with a string on his shirt and bit at his lip as if he wanted to say something but wasn't sure he should. "Did you fall in with any girls by the name of Harper?"

The boy scooted a little closer yet to Nolan and seemed to be afraid of the answer. The tot was quivering from head to toe. Nolan could hear fear in his frail, shaky voice, but the big blue and teary eyes were all over the girl.

"Are any of them still alive?" Nathanial hadn't waited for the girl to answer the first question and looked as if he were going to cry any second now.

The girl wiped at her eyes and didn't look away from the flames. "They were … but I don't know now."

Nathanial inched a smidgen closer and would soon be sitting in Nolan's pocket. The boy looked up at him. "Can a person run out of tears?"

Nolan grinned and shook his head. Nathanial glanced again at the girl. Nolan touched lightly under his chin and turned him. "Why don't you try to get some sleep?"

Tears sprang to the little tomcat's eyes, and he fiercely shook his head. "I don't wanna close my eyes."

Nolan quickly recalled that he'd been awakened on occasion to find Matthew standing at the edge of the bed and staring. *"Pa, I had a bad dream. I wanna sleep with you and Ma."* Matthew had been able to close his eyes and sleep after being tucked safely between Nolan and Mary.

The poor girl was a pitiful sight, one that Nolan himself wouldn't forget. Hate marks discolored her face and arms. Her clothing probably hid other bruises. The boy most likely would have nightmares. Nolan would deal with that shortly.

"Miss, how many women does Jones have in his possession?"

"Ten, including me." She closed her eyes. It was an easily read sign. She was done talking.

Nolan looked at Nathanial. "If we're going to catch these men, I need to know everything you've seen." He listened intently as Nate described what he saw and did. His fists tightened with the description of this fancy man that he knew to be Deegan Jones.

Nolan stood to go fetch his saddle from where he'd dropped it before he'd handed the whiskey to the girl, and he rolled around in his mind what both young people had said.

Nathanial popped up off the ground. "Where're you going? Are you leaving us out here and going back to the army?" The tough little pup's tears teetered on the rim of spilling, and the girl sprang up to sit. Her eyes were wide, and tears streamed down her face.

"Son, I ain't going nowhere. I'm just getting my saddle to bring closer to the fire so I can stretch out and prop my head on it. But if it would make ya feel better, you can use it as a pillow." Nolan took a few steps, bent, and picked up the saddle. He could feel the boy's eyes on him the whole time. Slowly Nathanial began to sit back down and gave a slight nod, and the girl laid herself to the ground once again.

Nolan dropped his saddle next to where the towhead sat warming his hands at the fire. The mountain breeze had cooled to a slight chill. The girl had herself wrapped in the ground blanket and looked to be sleeping. Nolan hunkered down and untied his heavy wool-lined coat from the back of the saddle. He dropped it over the boy's head, tipping the runt over in the dirt. "Now git some shut-eye."

A patch of snowy hair and a pair of blue eyes peeked out from under the coat. A thankful grin came to life on the little face. Nolan stretched out and rested back against a tree. He chuckled to himself. The half-pint was tiny enough to completely tent himself inside the coat and had curled up tight against Nolan's saddle.

Nolan didn't even remember closing his eyes, but he woke, stretching long. The fire had gone out. The girl was still asleep. He didn't see the little boy, and his saddle was gone. He jumped to his feet with the thought that he would skin that brat when he got his hands on him. How would he get the girl to the soldiers' camp without a horse? Carrying her more than three miles didn't exactly appeal to him. It was then the sleeping cobwebs pulled out of Nolan's mind. Even heavier than carrying that girl was carrying his saddle. It was no light tack.

Turning about, he spotted the trail where the kid had worked to drag it. The trail led Nolan right to the little culprit, standing next to the bay. The half-pint was trying to lift the saddle bigger than himself onto the horse's back.

"You trying to steal my horse again?"

"No." The kid was quick to answer. "I just thought…Never mind. You probably wouldn't believe me anyhow." Nathanial dropped the saddle, and his shoulders drooped.

"Try me." Nolan was willing to hear out the pout-faced kid.

"I…I wanted to…be helpful." Nathanial couldn't seem to find the right words to explain himself.

The boy's gaze was downcast, and his little face reddened into a flush. Was he ashamed that he'd gotten caught trying to do something nice?

"Dammit!" The boy kicked at the dirt, then looked square at Nolan. "Wouldn't it have been good to have the bay saddled and ready for when you and the girl woke? You did save my life."

The half-pint was a powder keg. Nolan hadn't expected the outburst. Nathanial was all fussed up and teary-eyed.

"Son, you don't owe me anything for saving your life. I would have done the same for anyone." Nolan no longer believed that he had been trying to steal the horse. He picked up the saddle, then set the leather on the horse's back. "Pull the cinch."

The little boy eyed Nolan for a minute before going to work, and his pout quickly faded.

CHAPTER 8

AYLIGHT WAS BREAKING over the mountaintop as Nolan walked into the camp with Nathanial and the girl sitting in tow on the bay.

Captain Farnsworth hustled toward the three of them. "Who is she? Where'd you find her?"

The captain's questions would have to wait. The girl's leg was swollen up bigger than yesterday, and she could barely move it without bursting into tears.

Nolan helped her slide real easy off the horse. "Doc!"

Two others came running. They shouldered the girl's weight, one on each side, and carried her toward the tent Doc had just stepped out of.

Now that she was being taken care of, Nolan could give report. He looked over at the captain. "We're hunting for Mr. Deegan Jones."

At the mention of the killer's name, the captain took a step back and nearly gasped. "I've never known Jones to work with filthy redskins. Are you sure?" The captain knew better than to think Nolan would fabricate the story.

"The girl has seen Jones and so has Nathanial. They both can confirm what I'm telling ya. Deegan Jones is our man."

Nolan threw a quick glance around and saw that Nathanial

was off the bay. The boy was being led toward the fire by a soldier who was holding out a plate of beans. The captain just stood silent and seemed to be thinking over the information.

He turned his gaze toward the girl who was being helped to stretch out on a ground blanket under a canopy. "Excuse me, Captain."

Nolan fetched his bottle of whiskey to give to the ailing girl before he joined Doc and the others. They were hovered over the poor crying girl.

Doc looked up at all of them from where he was hunkered down next to the girl, examining her injury. "I think it might be broken in more than one place."

He took the bottle from Nolan's hand, pulled the cork, and gave it to the bawling young woman. She drew a long swallow, then coughed for a spell before throwing back another gulp. No one was going to fault her for it. Sweat beaded her brow, and pain seemed to wrinkle up her pale, gray face. Had she been a horse, they would have already put her out of her misery.

Doc shook his head and looked a little bewildered for a minute before gesturing at two soldiers. "You and you...I need two good-size straight sticks so long by wide."

Nolan threw a quick glance over his shoulder at Nathanial licking the plate of beans clean. The kid was out of the way for now. Maybe the half-pint would eat more and stay put across camp. He didn't want the boy to see Doc doing the grim work of setting the girl's leg.

"Someone take that whiskey from her before she guzzles it all down. Darlin', you're gonna want to save some of that for when you wake. This will hurt, and it ain't gonna feel much better once I'm done." Doc had been brutally honest with her.

Nolan reached for the bottle, but the girl pushed his hands away. She sucked down another long swallow before he was able to get it wrenched from her fingers. She had to be close to drunk. Nearly half the bottle was gone.

He threw another glance over his shoulder. The half-pint must have had his fill of beans and was walking toward Nolan. *Aw shit.* "Git. I don't want you under foot."

The little brat turned a deaf ear and brazenly walked right up and stood next to Nolan as though he belonged there. Nathanial's eyes were all over the withering girl. It was hard not to feel sick when watching someone suffer in that much pain. So why didn't Nolan see tears in the little boy's eyes? His tight gut was telling him this tot wasn't scared of what he was about to witness.

Doc looked up from where he sat on his knees in the dirt. He met the gaze of every man and seemed to be saying that if any one of them couldn't stomach it, this was their chance to go. "I'm ready, boys, when you all are." Doc settled himself in close to do his work.

The girl began to wildly shake her head. The sticks had been brought and quickly trimmed to Doc's liking. The two even pieces of wood—to hold the leg once it was set—lay close to his hands. At least it didn't look like she was going to lose the leg, though Nolan might just be wishing she would.

He gently pushed aside the half-pint. "I told you to go on and git." Hunkering down the same as Doc, he rested his hands over the girl's shoulders. At Doc's nod, Nolan pressed his weight down, pinning the girl to the ground. He could feel her shaking with fear of what was to come. The captain and another soldier both had dropped to their knees and helped hold her down.

Nolan then realized Nathanial hadn't left his side. "Mind what I say and run along. You don't need to be part of this." If his hands hadn't been busy at the moment, he would have liked to open the brat's ears with a good, hard ass tanning.

It wasn't surprising that the boy ignored him.

"Wait!" The half-pint grabbed Doc's arms. "Just give me a minute."

Nathanial hunted about the ground, then picked up a thick stick. One crack over the boy's knee and the stick broke in two. Nolan knew what he was about to do. Where'd the youngster learn that trick?

"Bite down when it hurts," Nathanial instructed the ailing girl as if familiar with the procedure. The kid slipped the hunk of wood into her mouth.

Nolan's eyes narrowed as he studied this little boy. Most youngsters wouldn't have known to do what the boy just did. What troubled Nolan was there were really only two causes to use that tactic. One, a man might need to be quiet while being patched up along the trail so he didn't attract unwanted attention, say from a posse. The other Nolan had experienced himself. Biting down hard had helped him to handle the pain of getting a bullet dug out of his leg during the war.

Did Nathanial understand pain, or had the little boy ever been on the run like a wanted man and seen it happen? It was a stretch to think that way. But the youngster didn't act in accordance with Nolan's memory of Matthew or any of his son's friends at that age. He sure would like to know this kid's backstory.

"What?" Nathanial brazenly gawked at Nolan for staring while trying to figure him out. "I've seen worse," the boy admitted too proudly.

Nolan somehow knew that Nathanial wasn't talking about Mrs. Harper or the grizzly trapper. It was a sure bet that this babe had seen some awful bad things in his few years of living.

"On the count of three, gentlemen." Doc's instructions roused Nolan from his thoughts.

Everyone nodded their understanding of what was going to happen.

"One, two, three." Doc pushed the bone straight.

The girl screamed out, nearly choking on the chunk of wood, and sweat beads popped out all over her. Tears streamed down her face and dripped off her chin, and she was a pale green. Nolan reckoned the poor thing would have lost her stomach had she been holding anything in it.

Doc's hands worked mighty fast to set the two sticks in place with the little boy's help to hold one on each side of her busted leg. Doc whipped the bandage around and wrapped all as one, tight together, as fast as counting to five.

The pain must have been too much, and the girl passed out. Nolan eased off from holding her down. He was glad that was done.

"Did I do good helping ya to set the stick straight?" Why did Nathanial think everything he did was bad?

Nathanial had asked Nolan just this morning if having the bay saddled for him would have been good. Now the boy was asking Doc something similar. Who had taught the boy that? As tough as the pup showed himself to be, Nathanial seemed fairly insecure.

Doc chuckled. "Why…you did so well that I oughta talk to Captain Farnsworth about hiring you on as my assistant."

Nolan had never seen Nathanial smile before.

The boy was hunkered down and watching Doc sponge at the girl's face. "Is she dead?" He poked at her once, then twice with his tiny finger.

"No." Doc scowled. "She blacked out is all. She'll come to shortly."

The half-pint suspiciously eyed Doc. Nolan reckoned maybe Nathanial didn't wholly trust what he had said. He straightened to stand and was glad that Nathanial seemed to have found himself a friend. Good. It was a small start to trusting people.

Nolan walked away, needing some fresh air. He stopped after a few steps and helped himself to a long swallow from the bottle. A little tug on his shirt made him look down to see Nathanial grinning. The boy's eyes flashed toward the bottle, and Nolan laughed. It seemed like the brazen child wanted a shot of whiskey.

"No way in hell. Now git."

Nathanial took off running, maybe to find Doc. That ornery little cuss was full of piss and vinegar.

CHAPTER 9

NOLAN LED THE SOLDIERS, following the other set of tracks, twisting and turning down the mountain. He'd gotten a strange look from the kid when he'd sat Nathanial on the front of the saddle instead of behind him. Maybe the kid was used to being ignored rather than noticed. Another disturbing thing Nolan had seen that morning had been the scowl he'd given the captain all while Captain Farnsworth shouted orders to his men.

Pecking orders in the army didn't often change unless someone was killed or promoted, and the former usually brought about the latter. It made Nolan wonder more about how Nathanial knew when to use a chunk of stick to help the girl. Had the boy witnessed a pecking order of a different kind? Whereas the army had rules and consequences in place for disorder, scuffles could easily break out between men who owned strong opinions of their skills, like a gang of wanted men.

No...Nolan normally had a good sense of a person before he actually learned any facts about them. This was a little boy, not a grown man. His gut feeling had to be wrong concerning Nathanial and why maybe this tot knew things that other boys his age wouldn't have the faintest clue about. How the hell could a little blue-eyed babe seem so familiar with and carry traits of those who often fought the law?

Nolan got a nudge to his gut with a little bony elbow. It roused him from his thoughts, and Nathanial quickly pointed to a horse track. The boy was proving himself to have a sharp mind for learning. Not everyone could read sign or seemed so aware of their surroundings. This boy had a watchful eye on his back trail. Nolan reckoned that wasn't a good thing. A habit like that came from running away from something or someone.

"Look there." Nathanial pointed again. The white stub of a rubbed-out cigarette lay on the ground.

"Quiet." Nolan hushed the boy. He knew Nathanial had just been excited to share the find. He reined in, then stepped down out of the saddle. He left Nathanial sitting the bay, and he walked over and picked up the stub.

Nolan fingered the end. It no longer held warmth and had a hard, stale feel to it. The cigarette had been tossed hours ago. One of the men they were trailing was a careless smoker, making the path of Deegan Jones much clearer for him to follow.

He stepped back into the saddle, and Nathanial handed him the reins. They rode out of the trees and across a long stretch of open grass. The sun overhead was blistering hot, which was unusual for barely being June. Maybe the man upstairs wasn't paying attention, because it'd been awful damn parching lately. Sometimes they got a little relief at night when the sun wasn't up and the air seemed to cool off, especially when they were in the mountains. The goofy weather was just one more doggone thing that Nolan and the soldiers had to deal with.

Scarce patches of trees teased them with a touch of shade. Every man's head was beaded with sweat, and the air wasn't moving to cool them even a little. All that could be heard by any of them was the ongoing moan of the girl about her busted leg. Being jostled on horseback across the miles seemed to be nearly killing her. Nolan would have liked to plug his ears with mud. The sweaty, sticky half-pint fidgeting around in the saddle wasn't helping his mood either. His mouth was dry, and the blasted heat was shriveling him up.

The water in his canteen was flat and half-warm, but Nolan took a long swallow and wet his throat.

"Hey." Nathanial, with his nose all wrinkled up, nudged Nolan's gut. "You gonna be a hog and drink all the water yourself?"

Nolan handed over the canteen. The little hellcat quickly gulped a swallow, then, just as fast, spit the water out. "That's warm as piss." The boy's face was wrinkled up even worse than when he'd thought he wasn't getting any water.

"I don't recall forcing you to drink it." Nolan took back the canteen, capped the top, then nudged the bay into a trot.

According to the sun, only an hour had passed since they'd last appreciated a little rest in the shade. Nolan would have sworn that time was standing still as they wearily plodded along under the scorching heat. Sweat burned his eyes. Up ahead, he could see a thick patch of trees. Was it heaven? *Please, let there be water.* They were all in desperate need, including the horses.

They rode into the shade. Red embers on the ground caught Nolan's eyes. He ripped the boy around to the back of the saddle for safety, then pulled his rifle. How stupid of him not to have foreseen it. The army men followed suit with their weapons, and the girl cried louder. Captain Farnsworth waved two men to skirt the trees and look for any of Jones's men who might be hiding in wait to ambush them.

They had one ailing woman whining in their ears and giving Nolan a damn headache. Jones had nine females to look after in this heat. This spot of trees was situated like an island in a sea of grass, easily defended, a smart place to rest a group of stolen women for a spell. And there was a small spring to drink from. The captain's men all could have been shot to pieces while crossing that stretch of flat prairie toward these trees. Nolan needed to be smarter or they would stay one step behind Jones—or worse … dead.

"All is clear, Captain." The two soldiers had quickly reported back.

Nolan slipped his rifle back into the leather scabbard. "Captain, I'd like to scout ahead. Being that there's hot coals in that fire, I don't think the women are too far ahead of us." He wiped the sweat from his brow.

The captain glanced at his tired men and the girl who was being helped off her horse. "The girl has to rest. I could send a few of my men with you." He had never before offered Nolan help in his duties, but in the blasted heat, everyone was floundering, including Nolan.

"No, sir, I'll go alone."

"Okay then. We'll catch up as soon as the young lady can handle her pain."

Nolan nodded to confirm that he understood. He turned the bay and followed the tracks of Deegan Jones's army, then quickly jerked up on the reins. He twisted around and looked at Nathanial, who was sitting silent behind him. He'd almost forgotten the boy was there.

As red as those embers were, there was a good chance that Nolan could ride up on Jones and be captured. Being a youngster wouldn't save Nathanial from a bullet. Maybe Doc would keep an eye on his boy.

Nolan's thought struck him. Nathanial wasn't Matthew. His mind was just tired from the heat. He had meant *the* boy, not *his* boy.

"Don't make me stay. I know you'll keep me safe." Nathanial's words were spoken with such soft, pure honesty that Nolan couldn't deny him. He grinned, left the kid sitting behind him, and nudged the bay to walk out of the trees.

They rode a few miles, and the view of the hills and mountains in the distance ahead were a grand display of creation. It
almost made Nolan forget about how damn hot it was. They
dipped down off a butte and rode into a little valley. The dirt
there was softer than out on the grassy prairie. Nolan pulled
up on the reins, then shifted Nathanial around to sit in front
of him.

"Do you see what I see?" Nolan gave the boy a wink because
it was obvious. Nathanial would have to have been blind to
miss it.

The babe's face lit up with a wide grin, and he nodded. The
dirt, not being hard, had been torn up where the many horses
had passed through the countryside, so the trail of that son of
a bitch Jones would be easily followed. They rode the rim of
a canyon, then made their way down onto a flat that dropped
into a long valley.

Easing his bay to a stop, Nolan stepped down out of the
saddle, then looked at Nathanial. "Git down."

Nathanial slid off the bay and stood staring at him as if to
say *What next?*

Nolan hunkered down and touched at a groove in the dirt.
"Mr. Jones is only an hour ahead of us, maybe not even that far."

The boy squatted next to Nolan and studied the groove.
"How can you tell that by looking at hoofprints?" There were
doubtful wrinkles across his nose. He touched the print the
same as Nolan had.

Nolan pointed out the edging of the shod hoofprints.
"These prints ain't square-edged like a fresh track would be,
nor is the edge rounded or dusted over. Those things are signs
of an aged print. Back about a mile, we passed horse droppings
that weren't yet stiff from too many hours of baking in the hot
sun. Everything around ya will tell you something if you're
smart enough to look and listen."

Nathanial was quiet and seemed to be thinking over all Nolan had shared.

"Tell me what you hear right now," Nolan prompted to see if the boy had really understood.

The boy perked his ears.

Nolan thought he might burst something from straining to hear. "You're trying too hard. Relax … I'll show ya. In those trees, I can hear birds chirping. If you're hungry, that's a meal, or if those birds suddenly git quiet, then that's a warning they don't like something that's close by. So you best be leery."

"I already knew that," the boy boasted.

"Okay, smarty-pants, how about this?" Nolan lightly brushed at the side of his whiskered face. "The air is beginning to move, pushed from the west. If the leaves turn over belly up, there's rain coming. You don't wanna be caught out in the open during a lightning storm."

"My turn. I hear water trickling over rocks. That means I can refresh our canteen and water the bay." Nathanial smiled wide and seemed proud of himself.

"That's right. I hear it too." Without thought, Nolan ruffled Nathanial's snowy hair. "So what are ya waiting for? Go let our horse drink." He handed Nathanial the reins, and the boy walked off into the trees with the bay.

Nolan straightened and glanced at their back trail. A strung-out line of horses caught his eye as he noticed the army had caught up to them. He winced at what he saw though. The blue coats of the uniformed men riding along the rim of the canyon were unmistakable.

Nolan palmed his pistol and ducked into the tree line. Had Jones and his men seen him and Nathanial from this view? Could be that Jones had a man watching them right this minute. Thus far, Jones hadn't been covering his trail. Why wasn't the man worried about having followers? That advantage might allow the army to overtake the unhurried Mr. Jones.

If someone from Jones's camp was watching, then Nolan and Nathanial together, just the two of them, might not raise suspicion. A father and son out hunting. But once they were joined by the captain, that misinterpretation would be recognized, and that someone who might be out there could decide to pick off a few who were following.

The half-pint returned from his chore, smiling and seeming happy. He handed Nolan the reins, and the boy didn't bat an eye at his pulled pistol.

"We'll rest in the shade and give the bay a good breather till the captain and his men git here. If you wanna go cool off and soak your feet in the creek for a little while, you can. But stay where I can see ya."

Tears sprang up in the boy's eyes. Why? Nothing Nolan had said should have upset the kid.

"Are you trying to lose me? I know how it works. I go back there out of sight, and then when the captain gets here, you leave without me. I was wrong. I thought maybe I could trust you." The boy wiped at the stream of tears that streaked his dirty little face.

"Nathanial, that ain't true. Why would you think that? I just told ya to stay where I could keep an eye on ya." Nolan took one step toward the youngster, but Nathanial sprang away. Whatever trust Nolan had built with this kid was crashing down.

He sensed what Nathanial's next move was going to be by his wildly searching eyes. He reached out and grabbed at him but missed. The boy spun on his heel and ran away into the trees, and Nolan tore off after him. This pup was fast, and Nolan was getting winded. Nathanial ducked a low-hanging branch that slowed Nolan's running pace. Darting between the trees, he was able to keep Nolan from catching hold of him. With a running leap, Nathanial flew feet first into the middle of the creek. The boy hurriedly splashed at a run to the other side and was scrambling up the bank.

In one stretching stride, Nolan jumped the creek. He landed no more than an arm's length behind Nathanial. He pitched himself and tackled the boy to the ground.

"Let me go!" Nathanial repeatedly hollered through his tears.

For once, the boy wasn't kicking and squirming to fight Nolan. He rolled over and sat up while keeping Nathanial held tight to him. He wasn't going to be fooled and let loose for the boy to run again.

"Listen to me, Nathanial." Nolan tilted the boy's small chin up and forced him to look at him. Nathanial kept his red eyes looking down. "I will not leave you behind... Do you hear me, son? If I wanted rid of ya, I could've left you along the trail before now. But I wouldn't ever do that to you."

Nolan felt the kid's tense muscles slowly ease up, and he began to loosen his hold, expecting the youngster to roll off his lap and distance himself by at least a few feet. But that wasn't at all what the boy did. He stayed planted with Nolan, and they sat there on the ground for a while, neither of them talking. The half-pint didn't completely relax, but he hadn't shied away. Nolan sensed that the kid was thinking about him, and he, too, had some questions for Nathanial.

"Nolan, what's going on? Is it Jones?"

Nolan twisted around and saw the captain and several of the soldiers standing on the opposite side of the creek.

"No, sir. We'll be right there." He'd lost his quiet chance to ask who it was that had put such a frightened distrust of people into the boy. The Harpers maybe? Nathanial had mentioned his pa not liking the bluecoats. Who else was there?

Nolan kept hold of Nathanial's arm as they waded back through the water and toward the bay.

As a tight group, they rode out of the valley and over rolling hills of long grass. They crossed a shallow creek, then traveled through several stands of trees. Neither he nor the boy spoke of what had happened. But Nolan did want answers. This was just not the time. They could ride up on Jones and find themselves in a fight real damn fast.

By nightfall, they'd not made as many miles as Nolan or the captain would have liked. They found a place to camp that would give them all some cover if attacked. It was a possibility that Jones's army could come riding in and shoot up the camp. Captain Farnsworth always posted a soldier as a night guard, but that didn't mean any of them were completely safe.

Jones was known to be a sneaky bastard, and that worried Nolan. He'd heard rumor of the Georgia port night raid executed by Jones during the war. He and his men had attacked a small fleet of three cargo ships. The sailors had been taken by surprise in the wee hours. They'd been gutted, then were hung on display along the ship's mast. Jones had made off with the other two ships for his own trade use.

Nolan looked down at Nathanial, and he felt that protective meanness stir up in him. He needed to know if Jones was out there in the night, waiting for the chance to kill them all.

"Don't you run off." Nolan took the boy's arm and helped him slide off the saddle. "You stay with Doc and git something into your belly. I'll be back."

The boy nodded. It had been too stifling hot at noonday for any of them to eat anything. Nathanial had gone since breakfast without a bite.

Nolan turned his horse and trotted off. He didn't reckon Jones knew that the captain was getting closer, or the killer would have tried to cover his tracks. Though perhaps the unspoiled trail they'd been following was a trick. Nolan hunted through the darkness and found nothing of an ambush, then returned to camp.

The smell of beans turned his stomach, but he was hungry. Scooping a slopping spoonful onto a tin plate, Nolan thought of Kate's fine cooking. Fried chicken, potatoes, corn, whatever was fresh from her garden—he could taste it all. He had a growing appetite for both Kate and her cooking.

Nolan sat down with his plate next to Doc. He looked about and realized Nathanial wasn't anywhere he could see. "Where's the boy?"

Doc pointed, and Nolan tilted his head back and looked up into the tree branches above him. Nathanial grinned and waved.

Before Nolan could ask, Doc must have read his mind. "Captain Farnsworth chased him up there. It was a hell of a sight to see." He chuckled, but Nolan wasn't laughing. Doc rubbed a hand over his mouth. "I ain't sure what exactly the boy did. I seen him come flying out of the captain's tent with shaving cream smeared all over himself. Captain Farnsworth was red-faced and hot on the boy's heels."

Some of the soldiers sitting around the fire nodded in agreement. They'd seen it too. Their smirks and chuckles told of the camp's amusement. Nolan didn't find Nathanial's poor behavior entertaining.

Doc playfully nudged him. "Did you know Nathanial can climb a tree as quick as any squirrel?" He couldn't seem to stop chuckling, and all that did was irritate Nolan more. Doc looked about, then leaned in close so only Nolan could hear. "The captain stood at the bottom of that tree like a barking hound that had lost its coon." He straightened, and his grin told of his tickled delight. "The kid ain't come down since. Ain't that right, boys?" Doc looked at his fellow soldiers sitting around the fire, and all were wearing the same amused grin. "I think the captain might string that boy up. You've got your hands full with that little wildcat." He gave Nolan a friendly slap on the back.

Nolan finished his tasteless grub while thinking about what he'd have done if it had been Matthew who'd riled the captain's anger. He needed to forget it. Nathanial wasn't Nolan's to be overly concerned about.

He tossed his plate to the ground, stood, and walked from camp. The dark sky held a number of glittering stars that he couldn't even begin to guess. He leaned back against a tree, then lit a cigar, staring out over the prairie at the endless world. A low murmuring of voices carried from around the fire. Nolan figured staying close to the soldiers' camp would be wise. Now that the army was toting a little boy and a hurt young woman, if a fight did come, his gun would be needed.

One star twinkled brighter than the others, and Nolan recalled how his son liked to look at the night sky. He thought back to the last day he'd heard his son's voice and felt Mary's warm touch. He'd kissed her before helping her into the coach. Matthew had begged and pouted to stay with Nolan. He had promised right then that the very hour Matthew and his ma got home ... well, they would have a picnic and go fishing.

The sun never rose on that day.

A rustling in the grass caught Nolan's ears, and he turned to see Nathanial walking toward him. "You finally come down off that branch, huh?"

The little boy straddled a dead fallen tree and sat, swinging his legs. It was the first true childlike behavior he had seen from this kid.

"You ever been fishing?" Nolan ground the end of his cigar out with his boot heel.

"No, sir." There was that respect from Nathanial again. It showed up when Nolan least expected it. This boy wasn't easy to figure out.

"When this is over, you and me, we're going fishing." Sitting in the dark, Nolan couldn't see it, but he could feel the boy's wide smile. Perched together on the fallen log, they quietly took in the peacefulness of the night. Nolan didn't know why he'd promised to take Nathanial fishing. What did he truly even know about this little boy? The loss of Nolan's family was what he was struggling with. Maybe burying all the homesteaders' children had stirred up something inside him. And then seeing how no one seemed to care about this poor kid...Nolan missed hearing himself called Pa.

Playing father to some orphaned brat, though, wasn't the reason Nolan was there in the middle of nowhere. He had a job to do. "Go on back to the fire and git some sleep."

Nolan was honestly more miffed at himself than the half-pint. One minute he dreamed of being a father again, and then in the next breath, he threw the notion out of his mind.

"I ain't no baby. I don't have a bedtime. I can go to sleep when I want." By God, Nathanial was lippy.

It wasn't helping Nolan's mood. "Do as you're told."

"What if I don't?" The sassy little shit punched his hands to his hips. Would this boy ever be easy to handle?

Nolan had enough of the back talk. "Do you really wanna find out?" He reached and unbuckled his belt.

The little tomcat jumped to his feet, and in the pale moonlight, Nolan could just make out the boy's glare. Oh, this brat was something else. Nathanial had walked just out of his reach, then turned around and stuck his tongue out. Nolan stood, and the boy must have known what was coming next because he took off running. Nolan sat, and Nathanial immediately slowed his pace. The ornery cuss was pushing at him by strolling along like it was a Sunday walk.

"Nathanial, git your ass to bed."

The boy huffed loudly and marched off. Nolan sat alone for a short time after he had disappeared among the tents. Nolan reckoned he'd best go make sure the little troublemaker had gone to sleep and wasn't up irritating the captain in any way. To his surprise, the little rascal had actually done what he'd been told.

Thinking there weren't enough eyes and ears to keep a lookout for Jones's men through the night, Nolan didn't sleep so much as took to a bit of nodding off. The early morning air carried a slight chill. Rain was coming. He pulled his coat up over Nathanial's shoulders and lightly touched at the crown of his head. The fair hair that Nolan smoothed between his fingers was soft, like the white duck fluff stuffed in pillows.

Thunder rumbled overhead, and he looked up to a sunless morning. The sky was blackening rather than lighting up to start the day. A cold breeze kicked up and turned the leaves on the trees belly side up. With a sudden boom of thunder, a drizzle of rain began to fall.

CHAPTER 10

STRUNG OUT IN A LINE, they rode into a wide river valley as the rain grew heavier. Thunder cracked. Lightning flashed.

Nolan felt the boy tremble behind him in the saddle. "You scared?" He looked over his shoulder at the half-pint.

Nathanial shook his head, wearing a little wrinkled scowl on his face. "Hell no. I ain't afraid of no storm. I took a chill."

Nolan quickly recalled that Nathanial had buried his coat with the Harper woman. Nursing a sick kid would just be more trouble than any of them needed. Listening to the girl crying about her leg every minute of the day was bad enough. He lifted the little boy around and sat him on the saddle in front. His slicker fit loose, so he pulled the open ends around and covered Nathanial as best he could. It would be some protection to keep the kid from getting soaked to the bone.

Nudging the bay to walk forward, Nolan looked down at Nathanial and grinned. The half-pint had somehow fixed his tiny body in a way that he was able to button himself inside the slicker to stay nearly completely dry. Huh, smart kid. Nathanial rested back against Nolan while peeking through the gap between two buttons. It was nice to see the boy showing his true age.

What wasn't so pleasant was the damn thick slop that covered the ground. The horses' hooves sank deep into the mud. The cavalry men and Nolan were all soaking wet and miserable. The woman wasn't helping anyone's mood with her moaning about the chilly weather, besides her aching leg.

Nolan led them through a stretch of trees into a clearing, then back under the trees to save them from the driving rain. His ears were sick of hearing the bawling woman. None of the rest of them were in love with the damn drenching wetness, but this was what they had to deal with. Crying about it wasn't going to make their moving forward any easier. Yet the little boy hadn't complained once.

"Captain, why don't you set up your tent and make that girl comfortable for a while? Maybe then she'll shut up." Nolan wasn't being funny, though the captain grinned.

Captain Farnsworth twisted in the saddle and eyed the shivering girl. "I hate to stop now. I don't believe Mr. Jones had time to cross the river before the storm hit." The captain blew into his gloved hands for some warmth. "If that killer is on this side of the river, I'd sure like to catch him and string him up. But with all the noise she's making, he's sure to hear us coming."

Nolan waited for a decision to be made, rain dripping steadily off the rim of his hat. The captain seemed to be contemplating their next move. The girl rubbed at her bandaged leg, then wiped at her red eyes. The line of soldiers was all wrapped in their slickers, and their mounts were covered up over the knees in mud.

The captain nodded to himself. "We'll camp here. You scout ahead for Jones. Don't make a move against him, not alone."

"Yes, sir." The pelting rain wouldn't be enough to stop Nolan's effort to end this battle. His motive was purely selfish. Once the captain captured Jones and the women were rescued,

Nolan would be freed in a sense. The thought of riding to see Kate lifted his spirits.

Short-lived was his happiness as he tried to tug open his coat while the boy fought him by holding the buttons shut. It was clear that Nathanial did not want to stay there in the army camp. Nolan wasn't in the mood to argue with the little cuss, so he left him tucked inside his coat. He spurred the bay, and the boy sat still with the gelding's forward steps. They rode with the rain dumping down on them as far as the river. The rising water rushed by, carrying debris from upstream.

"Can we cross that?" Nathanial, all wide-eyed, looked up at Nolan. Every part of him except his little face and a tuft of white hair was tucked inside the slicker.

"No." They couldn't cross the river, but neither could Mr. Jones. Nolan liked that thought.

As quickly as the wind and rain had stirred up, he doubted the killer had beat the storm to cross the river. What Nolan needed to figure out was which direction along this bank had Jones gone with the missing women. The downpour washed away any kind of tracks. Nolan could only guess which way to search. He turned the bay, and they slowly weaved through the trees along the sloppy, muddy bank.

If Nolan happened to ride up on Jones's camp, he didn't want Nathanial with him. There might be shooting trouble, and the boy would be caught right in the middle of it. In hindsight, he could now see his stupidity for not making the boy stay at the soldiers' camp. He would keep Nathanial as safe as he could, and that meant doing something he didn't want to.

He left the little boy wrapped inside the slicker, sitting under a big tree for some shelter from the thunderous rain. It was the best spot Nolan could see. He didn't like that it was only a few short steps from the edge of the raging white current. If the youngster got bored and took to messing around, it would take but one wrong step to fall in and be swept away.

"I'll be gone for a while." Nolan wagged a finger at Nathanial. "You stay away from that flood." Nolan pulled a piece of jerky from his pocket and handed it to Nathanial. "Don't you move from this spot. I'll be back for ya."

"Yes, sir," the little tomcat grumbled. Nolan could hear by the lippy tone that Nathanial had returned to thinking he knew what was best for himself.

Nolan stepped into the saddle. There was something he hadn't thought of until just now. What if Jones's men were also on the move? Nathanial could be found.

He watched the boy for a minute, getting settled inside the slicker. "If you see anyone, hide yourself till I come for ya."

"Okay." Nathanial chewed off a piece of jerky.

The boy's casual shrug implied no worry. What had changed? A few days ago, the half-pint had burst into tears, believing he was going to be deserted. Now Nathanial seemed comfortable being left on his own, and Nolan didn't like it. Not that he wanted the boy worrying over being abandoned. Maybe instead, Nathanial was starting to trust his word.

He turned and walked the bay away upriver.

Several hours he'd ridden. Even with the rain pouring down, Nolan figured some sign of Jones should have been found by now. Nothing but slopping mud. He must have ridden in the wrong direction. Wheeling the gelding, he started back to fetch Nathanial.

A single shot rang out not a mile away. Nolan quickly yanked on the reins and spun his horse. He kicked the bay, rushing toward the sound of a second shot. A high-pitched scream cut through the falling rain. A rifle boomed close by. Nolan jerked up the reins and palmed his pistol. Dammit. Where was the shooter?

A black mop of something in the river caught Nolan's eye. The rest of her sprang up from under the rushing current. Her scream was choked off by a slap of white water. She floundered to keep her head up, tossed by the thrashing tide. The only good was she was being carried closer to him. He quickly holstered his gun as she was dragged under. She reemerged, spitting water, ten yards nearer.

Nolan grabbed his rope, jumped off the bay, and ran knee-deep into the swift flow. He tossed the line and got lucky. The wind hadn't blown aside his aim. The rope end splashed the water within an inch of the woman. She wildly reached but missed it and disappeared under the current.

Nolan quickly worked and dragged in the line. This time he wouldn't throw the rope to her and chance her missing a second swipe at it. It had been a long time since he'd done any roping. He drew back, circling his line. If he missed, then she would be carried past him. There wouldn't be another chance at saving her. *God, let my hand be steady.* He pitched the lasso.

Nolan had snagged her. *Amen.* The swift, choppy water played tug-of-war with him. He hung on tight to the rope and fought against being cast in himself. His boots rooted into the mud, and he heaved to pull her soggy body through the rough current toward the shore. The falling rain muffled the sound of the pounding hooves charging at them.

Nolan saw the gunman out of the corner of his eye, and he yanked the woman to her feet. "Run!" He half dragged her as they ran through the thick slop of mud that covered every inch of the ground. There was no doubt in his mind that the horsemen charging up fast behind them were Jones's men coming for the woman. They hoofed it faster through the puddles toward his horse. A boom cracked like thunder, and a bullet cut through the sheet of rain that was between Nolan and the woman. Shit, that was close.

All at once, she tripped on the soaked and torn hem of her dress. She hit the slopping ground, and her hand ripped from Nolan's grasp. He jerked her onto her feet. She just stared toward the charging gunman and seemed to be frozen. Nolan grabbed her and tossed her over his shoulder. He ran the last few steps, and without pause, he threw her onto the bay.

He quickly pulled his rifle and swung the barrel around. He aimed, squeezed the trigger, and one of Jones's men twisted in the saddle. The gunman grabbed for his gut and fell off his horse, thudding against the hard, soaked ground.

A bullet nipped Nolan's sleeve. He pulled back on the trigger. Another of Jones's men fell, flipping backward off his horse and splashing into a puddle.

Swinging quickly into the saddle, Nolan fired his gun before kicking the gelding into a run. A rifle boomed, returning a shot. He twisted in the saddle, squeezing the trigger on the run. The woman held tight to him to keep from falling off the horse. The bay raced across an open field, and rain stung at their faces. In the same instant that the crack of the rifle hit Nolan's ears, the woman behind him screamed. She tumbled off the bay, and Nolan missed a grab for her outstretched hand.

Spinning the gelding around sharply, he charged past her, going straight at Jones's man. Nolan's rifle boomed, and the bullet drilled into the man's chest. He flew out of the saddle and hit the mud facedown. Nolan jerked the reins and hurried to where the woman lay. Her wide, teary eyes were full of fear as she stared at the bleeding hole in her shoulder.

Doc would patch her up. Nolan stepped down from the saddle. She didn't fight him when he picked her up and sat her on his horse.

Sinking spurs into the gelding, Nolan ran the horse fast toward camp. When Jones's men didn't return with the woman, others would be sent to search. Depending on how far downriver they hunted, Nathanial would be found. Why hadn't he made the boy stay behind with the soldiers? That camp, as far as protection, would have been the safest place for Nathanial. Nothing the captain would have done could compare with what Jones's men would inflict upon the youngster.

"Captain!" Nolan raced the bay in close to the tents, then jerked up the reins. Two soldiers quickly helped the woman down from his horse and hurried her off into Doc's tent.

"Did you encounter Jones?" The captain was standing in the rain next to the bay. Nolan shook his head. "Just a few of his men. If I ain't back by morning, Jones's camp is upriver."

Nolan didn't know in what shape he might find Nathanial. He wheeled the bay.

"Nolan, wait." The captain grabbed at the bay's bridle, and Nolan pulled up on the reins. "Where the hell are you going? You ain't going back after Jones alone."

"No, sir. I need to find Nathanial." He sank spurs, pushed past the captain, and raced the bay toward the river.

CHAPTER 11

CHILL AND STIFFNESS had made its home in Nate's bones from being hunkered down in the wet weather for so many hours. Tucked deep inside the coat, he rubbed his hands together for heat. A warm fire was what he was wishing for, and eating beans at the soldiers' camp wouldn't be so bad either. The jerky Nolan had given him wasn't keeping his belly from rumbling. Most of the day had passed. Where was Nolan? He'd said he would only be gone a few hours. Maybe he got himself shot down by the fancy man.

A whistling noise carried from somewhere nearby. What was that? Maybe it was just the roar of the river. Nate strained his ears to hear clearly through the rain. Murmured voices. Who was out there? Nolan? Or was it Jenny's killer?

Rising mist seeped out of the ground all around him. That and the falling rain blurred even his short sight. He squinted to see better. The damp, gray coldness of the fading day gave him the willies. Maybe he'd been alone too long and was simply hearing voices that weren't truly there.

Ghosts aren't real. Nate repeated it over in his mind. If bad spirits didn't exist, then what in the devil was taking shape out of the thick gray mist right before his eyes?

Three men on horseback, maybe twenty feet away, glowered at Nate.

No! Dear God, it just couldn't be true. Tears sprang into Nate's eyes, and his heart thumped wildly. It was them. The outlaws that had killed Mr. Harper and the other men in the wagon train. One of the evil bastards grinned. Maybe he'd gotten a glimpse of Nate that day of the attack and recognized him.

Nate jumped to his feet, tripped on the long slicker, and fell face-first into the mud. He yanked up the coat like Jenny had held up her dress to run from the fancy man. His boots slipped every which direction, treading in place. The only thing racing away was his heart. And if these men caught Nate, then all racing would abruptly come to an end.

Nate scrambled fast on all fours, splashing through the puddles. His boots finally got a toehold, and he popped off the ground running. With a frantic glance over his shoulder, he saw that the horsemen had closed in on him fast and they were only a short horse length from being on top of him. It was too late to hide. Nate ducked a swipe from one rider. Then another grabbed at him, and that near miss pulled some of his hair. No way could he outrun them on horses. What was he going to do? Nolan wasn't there to save him.

Nate slipped and fell again, and that saved him from being snagged. He hurried like hell and plucked himself out of the mud. The thunder of the circling horses shook the ground under him as he ran.

Oh my God, I'm gonna die in a mud puddle. No way. He wasn't giving up yet. The damn slicker was keeping him from running faster.

Tough luck was one running horse stride from falling hard over Nate. He wanted Nolan. If he were there, then Nate wouldn't be sweating for his life. Tears streamed down his face, masked by the falling rain.

A big hand reached down and grabbed a fist of the giant coat at the scruff of Nate's neck. Lifted with a jerk up off the ground, he wildly kicked to free himself. The light had come to him purely by accident. When he ducked his head inside the coat collar, his tiny body slid out of the slicker and the man's grasp.

Nate's ass hit the slopping mud with a hard plop, but there was no worrying about his aching backside at the moment. He hurriedly pushed up onto his feet, and in no more than one misstep, he rolled his ankle and fell to his knees, splashing mud in his eyes. The man who'd lost his grip wheeled his horse and came back. Nate wiped at his face and ducked the grab at him while the other two riders nearly treaded over him.

Nate twisted out of the way and pitched himself rolling. He turned over in a deep puddle, covered from head to heels in mud, and quickly hopped to his feet. Nolan's image flashed into his mind. If there was a god, Nolan would hurry and save him.

The ground washed away under his feet, and Nate tumbled, swiftly carried away by the mudslide. *Aw shit.* Down the sloped bank he slid, thrown into the thrashing white current. He was lost to Jones's men, and they disappeared in a blink as Nate was rolled under the water.

Tossed back up, he gulped for air, swallowing what felt like a bucket of river. His arms flailed and he tried to kick, but he was helpless to swim. Without warning, his head was dunked. Then just as quick and unexpected, he broke free above the surface.

The water beat on him harder than any fist he'd ever felt. Sucking in air was all Nate could do to help himself. A splash of water dove into his lungs, and he coughed without stop. In a flash, the thought of opening his mouth to call out for help crossed Nate's mind. Only there was no one to save him. Nolan was gone, for whatever reason.

If Nate were swallowed up and sank to the belly of the river, there wasn't a living person who would miss him. His floundering to kick, to stay atop the water, was quickly slowing. His breathing was ragged, and he couldn't hold up much longer. Fresh tears covered those already in his eyes.

Something below the water hit Nate's legs, and he was twisted, then dragged under. A streak of pain tore through him, and his mouth instantly opened to scream. His belly filled with water as he lost his fight to hold his breath. Flipped again by the crashing water, his head broke the surface, and he gasped for air. It was too much effort to keep trying to spit out the constant downpour of splashing water.

The river before him whirled with debris. The whole of a tree popped up out of the water within Nate's grasp. He saw little hope in those branches, but something inside him pushed him not to quit. He swung an arm like a lumberjack would throw an ax. Grabbing a handful of leaves and twigs, Nate held on for dear life. But the white water was stronger than him, ripping his hand loose. Wildly he grabbed at whatever he could, and by pure luck, he caught hold of a single branch with both hands.

The floating tree must have been caught on rocks under the swift current. It wasn't being carried farther downriver. The root end had somehow been washed up onto the shore and was braced there against the thick base of an upright standing evergreen. Nate held tight with what little strength he had left. The water pounded at him to break his grip.

Slowly he pulled himself to the thickness of the tree trunk where he could do no more than give up. The last of his strength had been torn from his battered carcass by the strong current. His beat-up and exhausted body fell limp. He had no will over it. His head dangled over the roundness of the rough tree bark. Water gushed over and around him. Ended was his fight to try to breathe air as the angry river overtook him in a quiet darkness.

Nolan jerked up the reins, and his eyes went straight to the mud-trampled slicker. The many hoofprints told of what happened to Nathanial.

"Nathanial!" He heard no answer.

The damn falling rain wasn't helping his cause any. Fear squeezed his chest so he had to think to breathe. He wouldn't believe the kid drowned until he found the little body. Nolan nudged his horse forward. His trained eyes searched every inch of the river's choppy white water and along its edges.

"Nathanial!" Nolan was nearly hoarse, and his ears ached to hear that boy's voice.

Better than a mile he'd ridden when he spotted the small body. Nathanial lay hooked over a tree and appeared lifeless. The swift current could sweep the boy away at any minute. Nolan grabbed his rope and jumped off his horse. Quickly he tied an end around his waist, then secured the rope to his saddle horn.

He sank a foot into the water and held himself steady a minute before risking another step against the jerky current. In any breath, Nolan could be swept away if his legs were not securely planted under him. The water's pull was much stronger than he'd thought as he inched closer to getting his hands on Nathanial.

It hurt, but Nolan used all ten fingers like claws to hook into the bark and branches as he stepped alongside the tree trunk toward the kid. The pounding water fought him every inch of the way. He quickly grabbed and tossed Nathanial over his shoulder. He couldn't tell if the boy was breathing, but now wasn't the time to check. If he was spotted in this position by any of Jones's men, it would be over for both Nolan and Nathanial. Steadying his steps in the river was a solitary battle that would not be won if he was flanked by any other source of trouble.

Carefully he secured each handhold on the tree and slowly pulled himself along the branches until he reached the water's edge. His boots sank in the mud as he climbed the sloppy bank. And all the while, Nolan held to the half-pint dangling over his shoulder.

He laid the gray-faced boy out on the ground. If there was a rise and fall of life to Nathanial's chest, Nolan wasn't seeing it. "Wake up." He rubbed hard at his breastbone. He wanted more than anything for this boy to live.

Nate's eyes fluttered open. He quickly rolled onto all fours, gagging water out of his lungs. Then he flopped over onto his back and stared up at the gray clouds, sprinkles of rain splattering his face.

Nolan had come for him. Had Nate's body held any strength, he would have smiled. His head lagged to the side, and his eyes held to Nolan's happy grin. *Must be the rain getting in his eyes*, Nate thought, seeing wetness there.

"I'm sick of the damn rain," Nate whined, and he didn't understand Nolan's chuckle. What humor was there in the stormy weather? He didn't see anything to laugh about. "It ain't funny." He barely jerked his head up in time to retch more river water.

"Come on … Let's git you back to camp." Nolan hauled Nate to his feet, but his legs were too weak and his knees buckled. Nolan's fast hands kept him from falling.

All that was being asked of him was to walk a short ten feet to the bay. Nolan had saved him from drowning, and Nate wanted to please him in the worst way. But his body just wasn't doing as it was told.

Nate burst out crying. "I'm too tired to go anywhere." His arms were too heavy for him to wipe away his tears. "Please just let me sleep."

He wanted to lie down, but Nolan was still holding him up to stand. Nate's pitiful whining didn't seem to be enough to anger him. He could see that in the soft lines of the man's face. The stare that he was getting was the same tender look Jenny had comforted him with after her pa had beat on him. Could it be true that someone other than Jenny actually cared about him? That maybe Nolan saving him all those times had been more than just performing the duties of an army scout.

Nate was afraid to believe something so wonderful could happen for a second time in his life. Due to this man's kindness, the warmness he'd felt when he'd been with Jenny was now stirring up inside him. More tears than he knew he had began to flow down his cheeks.

How could he be sure Nolan's friendship was true? That he honestly had been looking after Nate and not just doing his job? His mind was too exhausted to think about it all. He cried harder. It was all he could do.

Nolan picked Nate up and carried him. Not like a soggy sack of goods. Nolan *held* him. He rested his bobbing head to the man's shoulder and felt at home there. Not one harsh look or growling word was cursed at him for being a crybaby. Pa would have left him at the river's edge until he picked himself up, but Nolan didn't seem upset with him at all. He turned his face into the collar of Nolan's coat and sobbed. Nate wasn't used to the firm but gentle touch that now smoothed his wet hair. Until this moment, he'd believed that all men hit.

Nate wrapped his arms around Nolan's neck and held tight as he tugged on the horn and pulled them both into the saddle. Before the bay took a step forward, Nate had been wrapped in Nolan's ground blanket and rested back while sitting across the man's lap. His shivering didn't come from being too cold, though he was soaked. It was all the overwhelming things that had happened to him lately that shook him to his core. He buried his face and clung to Nolan's coat, quivering and crying.

It hurt Nate that this man, for whatever reason, was honestly showing him affection. He barely recognized it. Pa's love—the same as Mr. Harper's—could be seen in the number of bruises he'd kept hidden under his clothing.

Nate was so sorry. He'd been nothing but ornery since he'd met the scout, so why was Nolan drawn to him? Looking back to that first day and forward, Nolan had been trying to be nice to him, but he'd been blind to it.

The bay began to trot. A strong arm wrapped around him and snugged him tight. For the first time, he felt truly safe. He didn't want to lose that, ever. Did he even know how to be good so someone would want to keep him?

Nate peeked through his tears and out over the blanket to see the darkness of night falling around them. His tired eyes didn't want to stay open as his head bobbed to his chest. Would he wake to find he'd only dreamed of Nolan's attachment toward him?

———◆————————◆———

Nate was startled awake in a sweat and breathing heavy. His nightmare had been too real. The fancy man had stood on the far side of the river, watching Nate flounder a mere breath away from drowning. On the other bank had stood Nolan. But the man's hand had been just out of reach to save him.

"You okay?" Nolan was sitting next to him, drinking a tin cup of steaming hot coffee.

Nate looked about to make sure where he was. The fancy man couldn't possibly be anywhere around or Nolan wouldn't be lounging. They were inside a mud-splattered tent, and some of the bluecoat soldiers were there, along with the girl with the broken leg. All of them were sleeping. The small indoor fire felt warm to Nate's skin, as did Nolan's big coat that blanketed him. There was no sound of sprinkling rain tapping on the outside of the canvas. The storm must have moved off.

Nate pulled himself up and sat, inching a bit closer to Nolan. He liked the safe feeling of being at this man's side, and he was able to calm his breathing. "You mad at me?"

Nolan raised a brow and grinned. "Why would you ask me that?"

"You said to not go near the river." Nate didn't understand why Nolan burst out with an amused chuckle. "I'm serious." He sat up a little straighter and stared Nolan straight in the eyes.

"I don't think you jumped in that water on purpose." Nolan reached, and Nate didn't shy away from the touch to ruffle his hair.

"No, sir. I slipped."

Nolan nodded. "Son, the signs were all there for me to read. I know how you fell in the river. There ain't no need for you to explain and relive it. I'm just sorry I wasn't there to stop it."

"But you did save me." Nate grinned because of what Nolan had just said. It was proof that their friendship had to be true.

"Here." Nolan pulled a dry spare shirt from the saddlebags and handed it to him. "Shuck your damp clothes. You can wear this till yours's dry."

Nolan stood then and left Nate to change. From inside the tent, he could see the scout standing next to the fire outside, already talking with a few soldiers. If he had anything to bet, he would throw down every penny on the hunch that Nolan would be a good pa to have. His chance of that wish being granted would be about as likely as Nate sprouting angelic wings. He grew from bad seed. That meant no good man would want to keep Nate. He and Nolan were just together because he was found by the army. Their time would end when they caught the fancy man. But it sure was nice to think about Nolan being his pa.

Nate pulled the big man-size shirt over his head. It hung loose off his shoulder and down over his feet. Oh well. It was dry and felt good against his goose-pimpled skin.

He wrapped the ground blanket around himself, then went and stood with Nolan next to the fire. His legs still felt weak. The cold river had soaked into his bones, leaving him with a deep chill. He yawned, and his eyes drooped. A few hours of sleep hadn't taken all the tiredness out of him. Nate rested his head against Nolan's hip, and to help hold himself up, he leaned his weight against the length of his leg. A firm hand came to rest on his shoulder, and he looked up at Nolan.

"What are you doing out here? Git your hide back in that tent and go to sleep." Nolan started to turn him, but he jerked away.

"I want some coffee to warm my insides." Was it wrong for Nate to want coffee? No one had sent Nolan to bed, and he was drinking hot coffee. Nate was sort of his own boss, though he didn't want to piss Nolan off and say so. He wanted his friendship with this man to grow.

Nolan hunkered down in front of him. Both the man's hands were now resting on each of Nate's shoulders so they were squarely facing one another. "I'll let you have a few shots of mine just this once. Then you'll do as you were told."

There was something—not meanness, but firmness—in Nolan's stare. Nate sensed that he would lose the battle if he tried to argue otherwise. "Yes, sir."

He was handed a tin cup with only a swallow or two left at the bottom. It wasn't exactly like getting his own way, but it was a little something warm in his belly.

"Go on now." Nolan nodded toward the tent.

Nate handed back the cup, pouted a little, then walked off. He pulled the tent flap closed, then found a dry spot on the ground to lie.

A big part of him trusted Nolan, but was Nate just a bother to the man? It seemed like it minutes ago at the fire. Friendship wasn't something he had much experience with to know if it was put on or not. Was he just fooling himself into thinking that maybe Nolan cared about him a little bit? What value could Nate bring to the man? Pa had only wanted him around when he'd served a purpose. Nate had always been a good decoy during robberies and had been the gang's lookout a few times too. He'd never failed them.

Nolan wouldn't need any such help as that. Nate had already learned lots about his trade as a scout, and he would be willing to be taught more.

Who was Nate trying to fool? No one, including Nolan, would ever see past the Younger name and give him a chance. He needed to stop thinking Nolan was looking at him differently than any other man had.

CHAPTER 12

NOLAN LIFTED NATHANIAL to sit on the saddle in front of him. He'd considered leaving him with the soldiers where it would be safer, but if a fight broke out, Nolan knew the cavalry would be caught up in fighting and might overlook him. He also knew he couldn't focus if he spent his whole day worrying if Nathanial was okay.

Nathanial had weathered through the river just as well as he had all his other near-death stuff, but there was no missing the pout on the kid's face. Maybe it came from still being tired. Matthew had been that way sometimes.

They rode out from camp, and Nolan chose to look past the half-pint's grumpiness. Perhaps after a mile or two of steady riding, Nathanial would nod off and nap for a time. A few hours of extra sleep might just change his disposition. Until then, there was lots the boy could learn.

"Most times after a heavy rain, any sign of a man's trail will have been washed away. But trackers as good as we are … I'm betting you can find some small mark for us to follow."

The boy looked up and grinned at Nolan. It seemed that whatever was eating at Nathanial slowly began to leave. They rode toward the river with more gray clouds hanging over their heads. Everything around them was soaked from yesterday's downpour. There was no place to put more rain. It brought to the skin a miserable chill. Nolan was wearing the spare shirt as an extra layer of warmth and had his coat draped around Nathanial. He worried about the kid getting sick after being waterlogged for so long last evening.

They rode out of the trees, and there was the roaring beast. The river stretched long and wide before them. Nolan pulled up on the reins a few horse lengths from the overflowing bank.

Nathanial shrank back against him. "I don't wanna go across that." His voice was all choked up.

The current was swiftly making its course. The river maybe wasn't as choppy as when he had fished Nathanial from the water. But it was certainly a force that Nolan had no mind to tangle with. Nathanial was so quiet. The half-pint's eyes were wide and teary.

Nolan lifted the little chin. "Don't pay no mind to that old river. It can bellow all it wants. I ain't gonna let it take ya."

Nathanial unexpectedly twisted around in the saddle and hugged Nolan around the middle. It happened so fast that he was already turned back around and stared once again at the deep water. It was out of character for the youngster to show a hardy liking for anything. Nolan didn't know what to say. He tucked an arm around Nathanial and snugged him tight. The kid had slept in the crook of his arm nearly all the way back to camp after being pulled from the river. If Nathanial hadn't felt safe there, he wouldn't have been able to close his eyes.

Nolan turned the bay and walked the horse along the river's edge to the spot where he'd sighted the woman in the water. His keen eyes searched both ahead of them for danger and the ground for tracks to guide them.

Turning his horse up through the trees, he skirted around where the river's bank had washed out. They climbed a steep tree-covered hillside that opened onto a level stretch scattered with pines. There was an overlook that allowed for Nolan to see across the river. There were miles of tree-covered hills. The expanse of wild country made him lonely, and he thought of Kate.

"Look," Nathanial hurriedly whispered.

The unshod print on the ground wasn't too old. Nolan pulled his rifle, then turned the bay, walking down a long slope and into the trees. They hadn't ridden more than fifty yards when Nolan jerked up the reins and quickly cupped a hand over the boy's mouth. Not far in front of them, a line of smoke rose from a clearing next to the river's edge. Through the trees, Nolan could see five of the women. A man with a rifle stood guard over the ladies. More men, at least a dozen and some Indian, sat around a fire. There were others that Nolan could hear shouting back and forth, but their positions were unseen. Several women worked over the fire, cooking.

Nolan tugged gently on the reins, and the gelding stepped slowly backward. He then wheeled the horse and rode back up the slope and onto the flat above the camp. He pulled up on the reins and stepped down out of the saddle, handing the reins to Nathanial. "If any shooting starts, you git yourself back to Captain Farnsworth." Nolan kept his voice low so it wouldn't carry down the hillside and alert Jones's men.

The half-pint shook his head.

"Nathanial, I ain't asking ya. You best do as I say."

Nolan pulled the spyglass from his pocket, then walked in a crouch toward the rim of the downslope. Getting down flat on his belly, he inched forward right to the very edge of the hillside. He pressed the lens to his eye and closely studied Jones's camp. Nolan's thinking was such that the water was far too high and the current too swift to risk crossing with a passel of women. A natural block to keep Jones from a retreat across the river. Nolan and Nathanial had to ride around the washed-out bank a short way downriver. Jones couldn't run that direction either, thanks to the washout.

The way Nolan figured it, the captain and his men could surround Jones on the two remaining sides, one of which would be the hilltop Nolan was spying from. It wasn't easy to shoot up a hillside with good aim. The number of advantages in the captain's favor were stacking up. Jones could be hanged long before nightfall. This was going to be a good day.

A slight stir in the muddy grass distracted Nolan enough that he turned his head from his work. Nathanial was on his belly, peeking over the rim of the downslope.

Nolan threw a glance over his shoulder. The bay's reins dangled to the ground. "I told you to watch the horse." Why couldn't this boy just once do as he was told? "If the gelding spooks and runs off for any reason, it will put us afoot. And if we're noticed, Jones's men will easily run down the two of us. My one gun won't be no match for twenty armed men."

If Nolan and Nathanial weren't seen, then it would be a long walk back to the camp, and the chance to catch Jones might slip by. At a time like this, did he really have to explain that? Nolan was anything but pleased.

The brazen boy met his glare. "I don't have to listen to you, and I wanna see if the fancy man is down there. Besides, your horse ain't gonna run off. He's grazing."

Thank God, Nathanial had the sense to keep his voice low. The boy had a bright mind and was always curious. He took to being taught, but this was not the time for playing school.

"You're lucky I have to keep my hands free to maybe use my gun, or you wouldn't sit for a week. Now git back to that horse before I change my mind and whup ya."

Nolan's narrowed eyes were fixed on Nathanial as he crawled back a few steps before standing, then walked with shoulders slumped and picked up the reins.

Nolan turned back to spying on Jones's camp. A more accurate count of the firepower down there was important so the captain could plan the best strategy for attack. If he wasn't mistaken. Tanner Brown and a few other big-name gunslingers who hired out their skills were among those in Jones's army. Nolan needed to get Nathanial out of there fast.

They rode in the direction in which Nolan knew to find the captain following behind. No more than an hour outside Jones's camp, he spotted the bluecoats riding down off a ridge. He spurred the bay, not wanting to waste any time in getting the captain and going back after Deegan Jones.

A smile spread across his face as he trotted the bay up next to Captain Farnsworth. "We're about to git our man. I'll explain as we ride."

The captain nodded and looked pleased. They were all ready to end this fight. This day had been a longtime coming. The captain settled his gaze on Nathanial, and his cat-who-caught-the-mouse expression dissolved into something fiercely different. What had changed? Whatever the reason for the quick flip in mood, the captain's glare was aimed directly at Nathanial, and Nolan didn't like it. He, too, was still unhappy with the boy, but he had reason. Nathanial had done nothing this time to provoke the captain, other than being in sight.

"Doc, you and Smitty stay behind with the women and the brat." Captain Farnsworth had no sooner shouted the order than Nathanial's head shot up.

The boy threw a scowling look at Nolan. "I'm going too."

Nolan didn't want to hear any lip from him. He also didn't think the captain was wrong in figuring that Nathanial should stay behind, away from the fight. Tanner Brown and his famed .38 had, without the help of his brothers, killed a posse of seven good men to escape justice.

"No." It was all Nolan was going to say about this matter. He lowered the little hellcat from the saddle to stand on the ground. Nolan didn't care. The boy could stomp at the dirt all he wanted.

"I wanna go. You're mean … Why can't you take me? You're no different than that rotten son of a bitch." Nathanial waved a quick hand at the captain and glared.

Nolan had his fill of the brat's brazen temperament. He jumped off his horse, took hold of the boy, and threw Nathanial over his knee. He spanked the foulmouthed youngster good and hard, then jerked him to his feet to stand. "Stop your cussin'. A boy your age shouldn't be talking that way. You will stay here. I can't trust you out there to do as I say. Now you think on that." Nolan threw a leg over the saddle. "Captain, I'm ready to ride."

He put spurs to the bay, then glanced back once at Nathanial's tear-streaked face. Nolan wasn't feeling bad for the little boy. Nathanial needed to learn a lesson.

CHAPTER 13

"DAMMIT." Nolan handed his eyeglass to Captain Farnsworth. Jones's camp was empty, and the women were gone.

Nolan walked his horse down the slope into the middle of where the camp had stood. The ashes of the fire still glowed red. Why would they have left? Jones was known for standing his ground, and so far as Nolan could tell, Jones only knew about him tracking them and couldn't know about the captain and his men too.

After Jones's men never returned from getting the girl out of the river, Jones would have sent others to find them, and there they'd have found the ones Nolan had killed. If the rain hadn't washed away the bay's trail yet, then Jones's men would have found Nolan's tracks when they found their gunned-down buddies. It would have appeared that he had been working alone to rescue the girl, and that report would have been given to Jones. He doubted Jones's scout, if he had one, would have been able to trace the bay through the mess of slopping rain far enough to discover the presence of the bluecoats.

So why did they wrap up camp so fast? It didn't make sense. Jones wouldn't back away from one rider with a gun. Why hadn't some of his men come hunting the woman? Even under the soaking grime of the river that she'd been covered in, Nolan and every other man had been able to see she was a fine-looking woman with a nice shapely figure. She, in particular, would have fetched a high price if sold. That meant she was extremely valuable. Mr. Jones had control of plenty of guns to get the job of killing one man done.

Of course, all that was on the speculation that the soldiers' camp hadn't been found and Jones believed Nolan had entirely acted as one man.

Either way, a greedy son of a bitch didn't just walk away from what would be a definite profit.

There was something else that didn't make sense. When Nolan had been spying, he hadn't seen a guard posted to cover Jones's camp. There'd only been one man with a rifle, standing next to the women, keeping watch on just them. Why? At that point, Nolan had taken something of great value away from Jones. The hillside Nolan and the boy had watched from would have been a perfect spot to position a guard to watch over the entire camp. What was Jones up to? Nolan didn't believe for a minute that Deegan Jones was that reckless. Did he want to be seen and followed?

The tracks of those who'd left the camp were headed north, following along the riverbank. There'd been no effort to cover the trail. It didn't sit well with Nolan. Jones, that sneaky bastard, was planning something.

Nolan ran the bay. Captain Farnsworth matched the pace and led the lines of soldiers in pursuit of Deegan Jones. They rode for better than an hour. The muddy hoofprints they followed were growing fresher. Something about the slowed pace of those they chased bothered Nolan more every minute. It was as if Jones wanted them to see each step and keep following. Were they being lured into a trap? There were plenty of good hiding places for an ambush.

Nolan slowed the pace and got a sideways glance from Farnsworth. "Why are we backing off?" the captain snapped and couldn't have looked any more annoyed.

"I got a bad feeling. I think we're making a mistake by running up on Jones's heels." The tracks Nolan was seeing were maybe fifteen minutes old. He slowed their pace even more. An ambush might come any minute.

Farnsworth looked over his shoulder at his men, and Nolan assumed the captain was seeing the same thing he was. All the soldiers bunched together, tighter than fish in a barrel. It would take but a few minutes for every one of them to be killed if there was any ambush up ahead.

"What do you suggest we do? I don't want to lose Jones. We're too close to ending this." Captain Farnsworth rubbed a hand over the back of his neck.

Nolan pointed to a bald knob three-quarters of a mile up the ridge side, which followed along the river. "You take half your men and ride parallel to the river. If Jones has men waiting for us, they won't be sitting high on the ridge side. Likely, they'll be much closer, making sure they don't miss us. Up there on that knob, you should be behind Jones's men. I'll lead the other half of your men following straight after him. If you hear any shots, then come a-running. At least we won't all get shot to hell, and you might get Jones."

Not that Nolan had to look hard, but he'd found where Jones chanced crossing the high-flowing river with the women. The killer had gambled that no one would be fool enough to follow. The swift current could be deadly. One wrong step and both a horse and rider might easily be carried away. It seemed that Jones was letting nature take care of the captain and his men.

Nolan's gut tightened. He didn't believe it. Jones had picked this path for a reason. Why? It had to be more than just the danger of crossing the river.

Farnsworth rode down off the ridge side with his men following in a line, and he glared at Nolan. He could rightly guess that the captain was cursing in his head that splitting his ranks at Nolan's say had been a waste of time since there'd been no ambush and Jones had escaped across the river.

"We'll cross here, men!" The captain shouted the order.

They were on the heels of Mr. Jones, and this was the closest they'd been to capturing the killer. Really, all they'd done in the past some-odd weeks while chasing after the madman was bury the tragedy. Nolan's thoughts quickly went to Nathanial. He wasn't crossing the river without the little boy. No one but Nolan would carry him through the rushing current.

"Captain, I think it would be safer to cross as a group with the women and boy." Nolan didn't say it to the captain, but Jones could wait. They weren't going to lose the trail. If his hunch was right, then Jones might be waiting for them.

"It irks me to let Jones get farther ahead of us, but you're right. Soldier, ride back and fetch the others." Captain Farnsworth shook his head and wiped the sweat from under the brim of his hat. The mountain air wasn't all that warm, so the captain must've been hot around the collar about Jones possibly escaping.

Nolan understood the frustration, though he was mighty glad the captain was in agreement. Otherwise, it might have turned real unfriendly when Nolan refused to go forward without Nathanial.

The soldiers dismounted, and they all waited for what seemed like hours. It was a relief to finally see the small group arrive. Nolan stepped the bay up to stand alongside Doc's horse. Before he even had a chance to reach out and pull Nathanial over into the saddle, the half-pint took a flying leap into his arms. He could see by the little boy's teary wide eyes that Nathanial was scared nearly to death of that water. He didn't fault the youngster none. The boy had come too close to drowning.

Nathanial shrank back against him. Nolan nudged the bay to walk closer to the water's edge. The half-pint twisted around and practically climbed into Nolan's shirt pocket. Tears were flowing, and Nathanial clung to him with quite a strong grip. He couldn't be trying to settle Nathanial to sit still in the saddle and guide the bay through the rough current. They both might end up drowned.

Nolan jerked up the reins before the bay stepped into the river. "Son, look at me."

The half-pint kept his face buried in the front of Nolan's shirt. "No. Leave me here. I don't wanna go." He shook his head and cried harder.

"Trust me, son. What did I already tell you once? You don't belong to that river."

Nathanial looked up and nodded just a bit. Nolan helped to get him turned around and settled in the saddle.

"I want you to hold on tight to the horn. The horse will do all the work." With one hand, Nolan grasped the pommel over the boy's hands. Then he wrapped an arm around Nathanial's middle and snugged him tight.

He nudged the bay to step into the water. Losing his footing, the bay sidestepped a few feet downriver. Nathanial whimpered, and his small white-knuckled grip tightened under Nolan's hand.

Nolan spurred the bay forward. The gelding gained strength and stepped steadily to break through the rippling current. Tree branches and other debris were carried past them in the water. Nolan hoped there were no such things hidden under the surface to take out the horse's feet or, worse, break one of the animal's legs. They would be washed away, and there would be no saving either of them.

Nathanial held on tight just as Nolan had told the boy to do. He was wet almost up to his knees when the bay at last climbed the muddy bank. The half-pint blew out a deep breath and seemed to finally be breathing easy. The bay, too, had done a fine job. Nolan reached and patted the gelding's neck for work well done. Nathanial did the same as Nolan stepped down to look over the horse's legs for any injury.

"Nolan." Nathanial caught his arm, and the kid squirmed a little in the saddle. "Thanks." The boy stared at his dripping boots.

Nolan leaned forward to look into Nathanial's eyes. "For what…gittin' you across the river?"

Nathanial wiped at his eyes. "For not being bitter. I ain't ever been spanked. Pa could hold a grudge though, even against me."

"Well, you deserved a good ass tanning, and you'll get another one if you ever talk to me like that again. I think you know though. I ain't the kind of man who holds hard feelings against a boy."

Nolan turned and rubbed his hand down over one of the bay's legs. This was the first the boy had mentioned kin. He had assumed Nathanial's father had been laid in one of the graves near the burned wagon train. The kid didn't act like anyone should be looking for him, so Nolan must've been right.

He finished his inspection, then stepped into the saddle. The soldiers, mostly in pairs, made their way slowly across the river. The women, too, had made it through the current safely.

As a tight group, they rode fast down out of the mountains on the trail of Deegan Jones. Their clothes cooked dry as the sun had decided to part the clouds and show its warm rays. There was but one thing on everyone's mind, and it kept them all quiet. Jones would not go down without a hell of a fight. Men, and maybe others, would be killed in the battle.

Nolan pulled a piece of jerky from his shirt pocket, handing the dried meat to the boy as they rode. Neither Nolan nor the captain had it in mind to stop. Not even to allow the women to find comfort and rest for a short time. The army would have Jones this day.

"What will the soldiers do to the fancy man when they catch him? Will the fancy man be hauled off to jail?" Nathanial looked up and was chewing on a bite of jerky.

Nolan hadn't expected the question. The choices a man made sometimes came with brutal consequences. Had Matthew lived, Nolan would have taught his son the truth of that. Nathanial had faced lots of hard things on this trail so far. Nolan reckoned it wouldn't hurt the boy to hear what would probably become of Jones. "If he fights, we will kill him. If he don't, he'll have his day before a judge, then most likely hang."

"I want the dandy, with his curled mustache, to hang for killing Jenny." The boy's face wrinkled up. It was the cutest mean thing Nolan ever did see. Nathanial's wish, though, wasn't so sweet for a youngster that age.

"You ever seen a man hang?" Nolan doubted Nathanial ever did, or the boy wouldn't have been so expectant.

"No," the babe admitted and shrugged.

"It ain't like payday, son. It's not a pleasant thing to sit a man on his horse with the intention of watching that man strangle. Even if the fella at the end of the rope does deserve it."

"At Jenny's grave, I promised I'd stop her killer. I aim to keep my word. You always seem to keep yours." Nathanial was still seeing himself as too much of a man.

"Son, you're biting off a lot to chew. The captain and the soldiers will see that justice comes to Deegan Jones. Ain't no reason for a youngster like yourself to be part of it."

"Ain't I already tangled up in this trouble?" Nathanial rolled his eyes.

Nolan wanted to give the boy a good, hard shake. "You got a smart-mouthed answer for everything, don't ya?"

The little tomcat smirked.

They rode without a word spoken between them. Nolan could tell by how Nathanial was staring off that the boy was figuring things out in his mind. It wasn't right that a kid so young should be so full of hate. Hurting, yes. Nathanial had seen too much killing that it would have been impossible for him not to have a fair share of aching inside. But for a little boy to want revenge in seeing a grown man hang…it truly bothered Nolan. What Nathanial really needed was to awaken to the fact that he was just a little boy. Maybe then he wouldn't try being so darn tough and could just be a child.

Nolan came back from his faraway thoughts as they rode out of the trees and into an open meadow. He jerked his horse to a halt. The men behind him followed suit. Nolan's mind snapped alert and his gut tightened. Something wasn't right. The stretch of grass was too quiet. There wasn't a bird chirping or squirrel chattering. This was a widespread meadow of lush green grass surrounded by a forest of thick trees. Why wasn't there any game feeding there? Nolan didn't so much as see a cottontail nibbling on a clover.

"Nolan," Nathanial whispered and had stiffened, then shrank back against him. Like he had thought before, Nathanial was smarter in some ways than most boys that age. He reckoned they were both feeling the trouble that seemed to be all around them. It had to be Jones. The many hoofprints before them told a story that Deegan Jones had crossed this very meadow, and by doing so, the killer was now leading the captain to do likewise.

"Captain, ready your men." Nolan sensed that Jones was about to strike like a rattler hidden out of sight. He had been bitten once. He'd sucked the poison out of his arm, then cut the head off that serpent.

"What is it?" The captain fought to gain control of his nervously prancing mount. The bay, too, was stepping anxiously.

"I ain't sure, but I don't like the feel of this meadow." Nolan figured he should dismount and use the tall grass as cover. He could crawl out there and have a good look ahead of them for any trouble, rather than riding right into what might be a slaughter pen.

"That's the same bullshit excuse you used back at the river, and we lost time while Jones slipped across. We probably could've captured him back there if I wouldn't have listened to you." Captain Farnsworth huffed. "And don't give me any of that splitting-the-ranks crap either. We are riding straight across that field after Jones, and that's an order."

Nolan pointed a finger at Farnsworth. "If you're so convinced it ain't a trap, then you ride across first. When you're safe on the other side, call out, and the rest of us will come over."

"Piss on you, Nolan. My men will go wherever I tell them to. Bickering is just wasting time, and Jones is probably miles ahead by now." Captain Farnsworth nudged his horse to walk forward, and the soldiers began to follow.

Nolan could hang back and watch how it all played out, but he wasn't a coward. If Jones came at them, then he wanted to be up front to have a clear shot at Jones. But he also had Nathanial to think about and needed to do everything he could to keep the boy safe. He wouldn't leave him behind with no protection even if only for a few minutes while the army crossed the field. He wouldn't risk Nathanial maybe getting captured or gunned down.

Nolan spurred the bay and fell into pace next to the captain. He kept Nathanial pulled close as they all rode in a group farther out onto the open meadow. His eyes carefully watched the tree line. He saw no sign of what might be waiting for them, but his gut was still feeling awful uneasy. They were nearly halfway across the field when the whistle of an arrow cut through the air. A painful groan filled every ear. Nolan wheeled his horse to find a soldier sprawled on the ground with a feathered shaft stuck out of his chest.

He latched onto Nathanial and pitched them both to the dirt. Arrows flew from somewhere inside the tree line. Panic spread through the ranks. Men rushed to pull their weapons. Others fought the reins to calm their spooked mounts. One of the women screamed as if being scalped. The captain was flat on the ground, propped on his elbows with his rifle aimed toward the tree line.

A second soldier burst out with a dying moan, then toppled off his horse. Nolan jumped to his feet and ran the few steps to the bay. He grabbed his rifle, then pushed the gelding to move. Nolan quickly glanced over his shoulder. Nathanial was hugging the grassy earth right where he'd left him.

A painful scream from one of the army men turned his eyes. He dropped where he stood to flatten himself into the dirt. An arrow had lanced the soldier's shoulder, but the young man was still alive. This time the attack had come from the far side of the tree line. *Dammit.* They were caught in the open, and there was no cover within running distance. Jones had baited the captain in without much effort, and then Nolan had followed along like a fool.

He quickly searched every brush patch and tree to get an eye on their enemy. The cavalry men were scattered across the ground with guns readied for an attack.

No more arrows sliced through the air. Just the crying women and the paining soldier could be heard.

Nolan couldn't catch a glimpse of their attackers. "Captain, you see anyone?"

He thought it might just be only two Indians, one hidden among the trees on each side of the field. Otherwise, he and the bluecoats would have all been dead by now. The stronghold of Jones's force must have been kept with the women as protection for Jones's assets. It would take some time, but the army, including Nathanial, could still be picked off one by one. The way they were lying out in the open field made them all fairly easy targets.

"No, I can't pin down where they're hiding." Captain Farnsworth rolled just as an arrow stuck into the ground where he'd been. Another arrow flew and dug into the dirt near the woman with the broken leg. She screamed out crazy over and over. They couldn't shoot if they didn't have a target. Jones might be expecting them to waste lead and deplete their supply. They couldn't afford to be fools twice.

Nate wasn't blindsided by the trouble they were in. He'd gotten out of tighter spots. There was one outcropping of rocks that stood twenty yards off. That cluster wasn't large enough for all of them to hide behind. He'd aimed to sneak down between them, but a white horse stepped from the tree line beyond the rocks at the far end of the field. It was the son of a bitch that killed Jenny. He was watching his handiwork.

Flashes of the wagon train attack spun Nate's mind in a ring. The arrow that had sliced Jenny's arm, it might have been pitched from one of the bows that was aimed at the bluecoats right this minute.

There was a way of drawing out these cowards. Nate had done it for Pa. Nolan, Captain Farnsworth, and the other soldiers needed to see where to shoot. Nate would turn those redskins into targets. For Jenny, he would be brave. The fancy man would not win this battle.

Nate jumped to his feet at a run and charged full stride at the fancy man. "I'm coming for you!"

An arrow sliced through Nate's pants, cutting open the top of his leg. A scream burst out of him, and he grabbed where his leg was bleeding. Tripping, he then hit the ground rolling.

"Nathanial, stay down!" Nolan sounded mad.

Nate couldn't just stay facedown in the dirt. It wouldn't help anyone but the fancy man get his way. Today Nate was a soldier. He needed to charge forward. He jumped to his feet again and felt warm blood streaking inside his pant leg. A trail of arrows stuck in the dirt, nipping at his running heels. A salute of gunfire echoed in his ears. He dove behind the cropping of rocks with his heart pounding and sweat beading his head. Holy crow feathers, that had been close.

Nate sighed a deep breath, then looked at his leg. "Eww." Blood stained the thigh of his pants, and it was speedily growing. His stomach flopped. Tears streaked down his cheeks. Was Doc going to be able to stop all that red from flowing out of him?

"Nathanial!" That was Nolan calling him.

Nate wiped tears from his eyes and peered around the rocks. Nolan was hoofing it toward him. Behind him, Captain Farnsworth ran toward his horse.

"Men, mount up. Doc, tend to the wounded." Soldiers everywhere scrambled to follow orders. The captain was on his horse and held the reins of the bay. "Nolan, let's go. It's Jones."

Nolan skidded to a halt and looked back at the captain, then glanced at Nate. Their eyes met, and he instantly sensed that Nolan was torn between duty and not wanting to leave him. He knew they would all be safer if Jones was caught.

"I'll be okay with Doc." Nate waved at Nolan to go, and he turned back and took off toward the captain and the bay.

Nate watched as all the soldiers but Doc charged after the fancy man. He hoped that rotten bastard was shot down, executed like Jones had ended Jenny's life.

"Let me see that leg." Doc had walked up from behind, and Nate jumped. Doc looked over his bloody thigh. "You're gonna have to drop your drawers. I won't be able to roll up your pants that far, and I need to have a good look-see at that wound."

He had to be joking. Nate threw a glance at the women.

Doc chuckled. "Come on. Nobody's gonna peek at ya."

Nate dropped his pants. There was so much red. His stomach churned, and his head felt woozy. Oh yeah, he was going to retch. He just knew it. Nate swallowed hard and silently pleaded with his stomach to stay put as Doc eyed the nasty cut.

"You're gonna need some stitches." Doc reached into his medic bag.

Nate jerked up his pants and had his trousers buttoned in less time than it took for him to draw breath. "No, sir. You ain't touching me with a needle and thread. It'll hurt."

"I ain't gonna lie to ya. Getting stitched up is gonna hurt something awful, but you need it done." Doc threaded the needle.

Nate took a gimpy step back and grimaced. "I told ya, sawbones, I ain't gittin' sewn together."

"Sarah, come here. I need your help to hold this sissy down." Doc was just being mean.

"I ain't yellow." No woman was going to sit on Nate. He looked past Doc. Sarah hurried toward them.

"Then drop your drawers and let me fix you up." Doc tied off the knot on the end of thread.

"Look, I'm fine." Nate lied through his teeth. "It ain't bleeding much, and it hardly pains at all. See, I can walk." He tried his hardest not to limp. A stab shot through his leg, so much so that he saw stars for a minute and sweat broke out all over him. Fresh tears blurred his eyes.

Doc took full advantage of his sudden weakness. He grabbed Nate and pulled him to the ground. Sarah was right there hovering.

Nate kicked and squirmed. "Let me go!"

His itty-bitty strength was no match for Doc. That didn't keep him from trying to free himself.

Doc was all but sitting on top of Nate, trying to keep him still. "Sarah, tug his pants down just far enough that I can start stitching. Dammit, Nathanial! Hold still, boy, or it'll hurt worse."

Doc and Sarah managed to get his pants down around his knees. Nate wailed as the needle jabbed through his skin. He stopped fighting and lay stiff as a board. Sarah took Nate's hand. He squeezed his eyes tight shut and bawled as Doc gave a sharp tug and pulled the string taut. When would it be over? Doc hadn't been lying. Being stitched hurt like the devil.

"Open your eyes. I'm done." Doc pulled Nate easy to his feet. "Twelve is what ya needed. That's a lucky number." He actually grinned and seemed happy.

"Uh-huh, sure it is, sawbones." Nate wiped his sleeve across his eyes. Doc had the nerve to chuckle.

Sarah put an arm around Nate's shoulder. He limped, but he was able to walk slowly on his own.

She helped ease him down to sit near the wounded soldier and the girl with the broken leg. She then sat down next to Nate. "I had a little boy at home. I would guess you to be Josiah's age. You're about the same size. We'd just celebrated his fifth birthday with a chocolate cake before all this happened."

Nate's face colored a little, hating his tiny size. Sarah's far-off stare and happy grin gave away that she was seeing her little boy's face. Maybe she was picturing the moment Josiah had blown out his candles or opened his present. Whatever grateful remembrance had been making her eyes twinkle and shine, Nate would bet it was worth more than gold to her.

"My husband was a prominent cattleman. We had a fine ranch. Tall green grass grew in every direction the eye looked. Josiah liked to play near the creek in a small patch of wildflowers. When those men came to take me, they hadn't cared that Josiah was practically a baby. They just shot him down in his favorite spot." Sarah wiped at her eyes.

Nate could picture how nice Sarah's life had been before the trash that was Deegan Jones stole her away.

She scooted a little closer to Nate, then reached out and hugged him tight. "I'm sorry you got hurt." Sarah kissed his head.

There was a warm softness to her. It was a different safe feeling than when Nate was close to Nolan. Josiah had been a lucky boy. Sarah seemed to be a real good mama. She made Nate wish he had a mother to love him. He'd known Lucinda only a few years before she'd died.

For a long while, neither he nor Sarah spoke a word. The only god-awful sound any one of them heard in that stretch of bloody meadow was Doc digging graves for the two fallen soldiers. It seemed like forever until he had the men mounded over.

Maybe Nolan and the captain were hanging that awful Deegan Jones right this minute. It gave Nate small pleasure to think so.

Sarah let go of him and stood. She straightened her dress, then looked straight at Doc. "I didn't know either of those men, but I will say a few words over their graves. Unless you, sir, would like to do so. You did, after all, soldier with them."

Doc shook his head.

Everyone went and stood at graveside with heads bowed. Sarah held on to Nate's hand real tight as if he were trying to get away. His heart pained at how badly she must have missed Josiah that she clung to a no-good brat like him.

"The Lord is my shepherd; I shall not want…" Sarah went on, and Nate looked around at the miserable faces. The ladies both wiped at their tears. Doc looked exhausted, as though he hadn't slept in a week. And the wounded soldier rubbed at his bandaged shoulder and stared at the graves as if one of them were his own. Sarah quoted more scripture from memory. Nate wasn't familiar with the words, but they did bring about a comfort. "Amen." Sarah ended her eulogy.

"Amen," everyone else repeated.

Doc built them a fire as evening came on. They had nothing to eat, but none of them complained of hunger pains. The hurt soldier was already asleep next to the fire. The young woman sat alone, staring off across the field and into the trees. Nate didn't know exactly what she was pondering. He could likely guess though. Would she or any of them survive this hell? And if they did, what kind of life would be waiting for them?

Doc dropped down and sat on the ground facing both Nate and Sarah. "How about a game of poker to lighten the mood? I'll teach you two how to play." He pulled a deck of cards out of a pair of saddlebags and began to deal them each five.

"I know how to play." Nate wasn't bragging.

"Why am I not surprised? No cheating." Doc winked at him.

It was the sawbones that proved himself to be quite a dirty dealer, winning the first five hands. Several times Nate caught Doc playfully shifting cards with a sleight of hand from the bottom.

"If I's bigger, I'd punch you for being a no-good cheat." Nate grinned, and Doc chuckled.

Sarah called and laid down a full house to win the next hand. Then two pair brought Nate victory.

"You little coyote. You learned from my bad ways and cheated to win, didn't ya?" Doc ruffled Nate's hair, and he knew Doc was just funning him.

Nate's own laughter sounded strange to his ears. Fun was something he knew little about. He could count on one hand the number of times he'd found pleasure in something that Jenny hadn't been a part of.

"It's your turn to deal, little man." Doc handed Nate the deck.

He was lost in dealing the cards as he counted to five in his head with each pass. He was just tossing down the final card when a boom split the night like thunder landed under his seat. He no more jumped when the sound came again, and this time Nate recognized it for what it was.

Gunfire.

A bullet split Sarah's head, and Nate screamed. Her blood had splattered his shirt and face, and she slumped over, falling on top of him.

"Doc! Git her off me!" He was pinned down. He squirmed and heaved to roll the dead weight off. A sickening warm flow of blood leaked from her and soaked his shirt. It sent an icy chill through his skin and straight into his bones.

Gunfire boomed. Nate's ears rang. Doc reloaded his rifle. *One, two, three…* Nate gritted his teeth and pushed at poor Sarah. It took all his might until her weight shifted enough that he quickly wiggled free. He just lay there in the grass next to her dead body and caught his breath for a minute. His heart pounded, and a new kind of pain struck his chest. It wasn't the hurting kind like getting beat. All at once, he couldn't breathe.

If these were Deegan Jones's men, then did that mean Nolan and the other soldiers were dead? Otherwise, Jones's men wouldn't have broken through the captain's rifle line.

Doc's gun boomed and shook Nate from being dumbstruck. He wiped at his tears. He'd lost Jenny and now maybe Nolan. If he didn't get focused on how to help Doc, they'd end up dead too.

He quickly sat up and looked about for an option other than dying. The wounded soldier was off the ground, running toward a saddled horse. He grabbed for a rifle in its sheath and was shot down. The young woman screamed to high heaven. It was just Doc now, fighting against the three horsemen.

Nate had been stuck in the middle of plenty of gun battles with Pa. Doc might not expect him to pull his weight in a fight as Pa always had. Nate would do what he knew until a bullet stopped him or Doc picked off the three. He only hoped God was with them.

Nate scrambled across the ground to where the dead soldier's rifle lay. He snatched up the gun, then jumped to his feet and gimped at a fast run. Pain nearly buckled his leg, but he fought off the fierce throb to keep going. If Doc had to repeatedly take time to reload, and with the odds not in their favor, they might all be shot down in only a few minutes.

Nate threw himself on the ground next to Doc, then quickly handed the loaded gun over. He hurriedly fed shells to reload the empty chambers of the other rifle. Doc didn't appear to be sweating the fight they were hunkered into.

Nate couldn't seem to take a deep breath. He didn't want to be splattered everywhere like poor Sarah.

"Nathanial, you git that girl and yourself on a horse. Ride fast for the captain. If you can't find him or you see that the army lost its battle, then you keep on riding. There's a town about three or so weeks that way. I can hold these men off for a while and give ya a good head start."

How could Doc expect him to just ride away? Nate wouldn't leave him there to fight alone. No way. He had a better plan. He'd learned long ago that it was wise not to ask permission. He could catch hell later.

Nate reloaded Doc's rifle, then scrambled to his feet and ran toward the young woman. Dammit, his leg burned with each step. He didn't want to look to see if it was bleeding again. If he passed out, he couldn't be any help to Doc. He grabbed the crying girl by the hand and half dragged her to the closest horse. It wasn't easy, given his small size. Though Nate did his best to push her up into the saddle without causing pain to her broken leg. She could have shut her mouth from bawling and helped a little. Holy Moses, Nate had thought she wanted to live. He certainly did. Not that he had much to live for, but he didn't want to die.

"Ride toward the sunset till you see the bluecoats." Nate pointed her in that direction, then slapped at the horse's backside. The mare jumped forward and shot off at a run with the crying woman barely hanging on. The dummy would most likely get herself lost. Well, that was better than being killed. Maybe she would get lucky and stumble across help.

Two of Jones's men were fool enough to try to follow her across the open field. Doc shot them both out of their saddles. The third man was smarter, staying out of rifle range. He'd given cover fire to the riders before Doc had killed the two. A bullet kicked up dirt close to Doc.

Keeping crouched low so as not to be a target, Nate hurriedly limped to where Doc was hunkered down behind a fallen tree. It was plainly understood that his deep-furrowed brow meant the man was not happy to see Nate there. A bullet smashed into the tree directly in front of them, and splinters of wood exploded into the air. Instinct took over, and they both ducked their heads as another piece of lead zinged past them. Nate quickly slapped his hands over his ears as Doc swung the rifle up, aimed, and squeezed the trigger.

A volley of gunfire echoed across the field. The cartridges in Doc's gun belt were getting low. Running out of bullets would be a sure way of dying. Nate crawled to where the dead soldier lay, then pulled the pistol out of the cavalry-stamped leather holster. It was six more shells to keep them breathing.

Quickly Nate took the gun to Doc. Then something in his mind triggered. That day when he and Nolan had been up on the hillside, spying on Jones's camp, Nate had let the reins of the bay dangle low, and Nolan had gotten himself awfully angry about it. He had scolded Nate that if the bay had spooked and run off, being caught afoot would mean they could easily be run down by a man on horse. That same lesson could be applied to his and Doc's situation.

Gunfire boomed. Nate ran as fast as he could while limping. He grabbed the reins of a cavalry mount. The animal had been standing in the open. Nate needed to get himself and the horse into the trees for cover. He pulled the horse and had gone a few feet when his ankle twisted in a sunken patch of ground.

Hitting the grass, he rolled. A bullet missed him by a wee foot, kicking up dirt in his face. Doc returned fire, giving Nate cover to get to his feet.

He grabbed the reins for a second time and tugged the animal until it trotted into the trees. Was he doing the right thing? When he'd ridden with Pa, Nate had always been on the wrong side of these kinds of battles. Back then, he'd only worried about saving himself from an untimely end. Doing good had never entered his mind.

Nate gave a whistle for Doc and got a nod. What if more of Deegan Jones's men showed up before they could get away? Maybe the girl had reached Nolan and the captain. Help might be on its way. God forbid she'd been captured and was the fancy man's prisoner once again. Nate and Doc just had to be smart. They could get out of this trouble with their hides intact ... maybe.

Doc fired on the run toward where Nate held the horse. Jones's horseman charged them. Nate's eyes stretched wide. The man's rifle was aimed at Doc's back. Nate feared he was about to meet his end. Being painted with Sarah's blood had been enough. He didn't want to see the doctor shot down right in front of him.

"Doc, git down!"

Doc pitched himself rolling into the tree line and came up on one knee. He fired off a quick shot. The man in the saddle twisted at the shoulder, and instantly there was blood. Though it hadn't slowed his charging pace.

Doc swung into the saddle. Nate was yanked from the ground and thrown on the horse behind him.

Doc spurred the animal into a run up the ridge side, and Nate held on tight. The horse ran as if unbridled, weaving its own path through the trees. Was Doc even holding the reins?

Doc ducked.

"Ouch!" Nate had been hit by the branch and nearly knocked out of the saddle.

The horse crashed through some brush that tore at his clothing. He threw a glance over his shoulder. There was some distance, but Jones's man was still coming at them quick.

"What the hell are you doing? Git this horse going straight! We ain't even running in the right direction to find the captain." Nate didn't want them to get caught or shot.

"We ain't running. We're leading him up into that mountain. I want him to get closer. I'm gonna let him think he has us on the run. When he's sure he's got us, I'll jump off the horse and wait somewhere in the brush while you keep leading him. He'll pass me by without a thought, and that's when I'll git him."

Nate liked Doc's plan as long as it worked, and it did.

A single shot was fired.

"Come on back!" Doc's call was the signal.

Nate turned the horse and returned along the same deer path through the trees. As he rode up to Doc, he tried not to look at the dead man lying in a puddle of blood.

Doc stepped up into the saddle. They rode quietly into the meadow that had been a battlefield most of the day. The sun was setting when Doc started to dig the graves for Sarah and the soldier named Bill.

With a pistol in his hands, Nate kept watch for any sign of more trouble while Doc worked on getting blisters. With the shadows of night creeping up on them, his heart took to pounding at every little noise inside the tree line. His nerves were raw, and he started to cry. He wished he could cover up and go to sleep under Nolan's big coat.

CHAPTER 14

NOLAN HELD THE WINCHESTER aimed in a standoff with a number of Jones's men. They'd exchanged lead, with some casualties, for the past few hours. Nolan swung his rifle. What he'd heard sounded like a horse charging up behind them, but he couldn't see anything through the trees. Had some of Jones's men slipped around to attack from the rear? The horse appeared through the haze of gun smoke, but the rider wasn't who Nolan expected to see. What in the hell was the woman doing there?

"Captain Farnsworth!" Nolan caught her as she dropped out of the saddle, pale, breathless, and shaking all over. "Where are the others? Is Nathanial alive?"

Gunfire boomed.

Her sobbing was doing nothing but rubbing him raw. He wanted answers, now. How was he to decipher her damn blubbering? If she didn't quickly stop her bawling, Nolan was going to take hold of her and shake out what he needed to know.

The captain must have read Nolan's thoughts because he stepped between him and the woman. "Miss, my men, where are they?" Captain Farnsworth pulled her behind a tree for safety as rifle fire echoed all around them.

The captain was much kinder in the way he'd asked, but the urgency was still there. She sniffled, trying to hold back her tears. Nolan's ears were straining to hear what she was about to say over the rifle blasts.

"Three men shot them all. There was so much gunfire. I'm sure everyone's dead." She broke down, sobbing into her hands.

The captain and Nolan exchanged blank stares. Maybe they were thinking the same thing. She had to be wrong. It seemed impossible that some of Jones's men were able to slip past the captain's rifle line during the engagement, which was still going on.

A repeat of rifle fire bounced between the ridges.

Nolan wouldn't allow himself to believe that Nathanial could be dead. "I'm goin' back to see if anyone's alive." The wily little cuss was too smart to hard living, and the woman was hysterical. He turned toward where the bay was tied.

Captain Farnsworth grabbed Nolan's shoulder. "I need you here. You're too good of a marksman to let go. I'll send two others."

Nolan shook his head, but before he could argue, the captain put up a hand. "Fine, I'll send three men back. I can't spare you. As you already know, most of my men are not seasoned fighters, expect for a few."

Nolan nodded and walked away to retake his position.

Night fell around them, and only a few shots had been exchanged in over an hour. Jones's men were holding them there so he could run with the women. Only, Nolan's mind wasn't on rescuing those women. That newly familiar meanness had risen up from deep inside him. Matthew had been shot down and now maybe Nathanial too.

Nolan hadn't slept, and still, Jones's men had slipped away sometime in the dead of night. He couldn't wait much longer for the soldiers to report back. Hopefully, Nathanial was with them.

He hadn't had a choice about leaving Nathanial behind when the army had ridden out of the meadow after Jones. The little ornery cuss had needed Doc's attention. Nolan hadn't known what trouble he might be riding into when he'd left. But now he had a personal reason to hunt down Deegan Jones.

Where was the captain? Nolan needed to find the man and talk. He marched toward the tents. Captain Farnsworth was pouring himself a cup of coffee at the fire.

"Captain, sir, I can't take any more waitin'. Your men ain't back, and they should've been by now. I'm riding to that meadow."

Farnsworth nodded. "Pick a few men to go with ya." The captain looked around at the scattering of moaning wounded. "The rest of us aren't going anywhere. I'm giving the injured and the woman time to rest. Jones's men were shot up just as badly. Both camps, I'm sure, will be on the mend today." Captain Farnsworth retreated into his tent and closed the flap. It seemed that for once, the captain wasn't worried about Jones, and that was just fine with Nolan because at the moment, he was only concerned about Nathanial.

Nolan grabbed his saddle off the ground and gave a wave for a couple of soldiers jawing nearby to join him. Maybe Nathanial had hidden like when Jones's men had attacked the wagon train. When he got to the meadow, he would search the brush while the soldiers properly buried the dead.

"Riders coming in ... There's Doc!" One of the posted soldiers hollered down the hillside into camp.

Nolan quickly turned to see. *Please let the boy be with Doc.* He hurried along with a few other soldiers toward the horses and their riders. Captain Farnsworth rushed from inside the tent and ran for Doc.

Nolan didn't see Nathanial in the front of the saddle. Doc looked to be the only rider.

He quickly saluted the captain. "Sir, they came at us out of nowhere."

Nolan didn't want to hear Doc telling about how the attack had played out, not now anyway. He stepped around his horse, and there was Nathanial. The youngster was turned backward in the saddle and sleeping soundly. Nathanial's arms and legs dangled around the back half of the horse's girth, his snow-patched head resting on the round rump. Had he been shot? Almost his whole shirt was stained with dried blood, and red freckled his face as well. The boy was pale and skinned up some. He didn't appear to be okay.

"Is he hurt?" Nolan looked to Doc for an answer.

"That's Sarah's blood he's wearing. The boy's fine. Tired is all." Doc reached behind him, rousing the half-pint.

Nathanial's eyes fluttered open. "Nolan."

He reached out for Nolan.

Matthew's face flashed in his mind. Why was he feeling the need to play father to this boy? It wasn't just that he merely missed his son. There was more than just a growing fondness in him for Nathanial. Had the boy reached out to any other man just then, it would have caused Nolan pain.

He lifted Nathanial off Doc's horse. The half-pint yawned and wavered on his feet for a minute.

"Come on. Let's git you cleaned up." Nolan led him next to the fire. Once the boy was sitting comfortably, Nolan hurried and fetched his bedroll off the bay. He also went to the creek and got some water. After he'd washed the dried blood off Nathanial's face and hands, he laid the blanket out on the ground next to the warm flames. He curled up, and Nolan tucked his coat around the boy. The child was asleep in no time.

Nolan was having too many thoughts about this boy. There was one man who could answer a few of his questions. He found Doc sitting and eating a tin plate full of beans with a biscuit. Nolan squatted next to the only other man there that Nathanial seemed to sort of trust.

"Nolan, I know what you're gonna ask, and I'll tell it to you straight. That boy is half an outlaw."

What was Doc talking about? Nolan looked across the fire at the peacefully sleeping youngster. The half-pint was more than a handful, yes, but outlaw? That was a strong word to describe a little boy. Nolan raised a brow and wondered what had made Doc say such a thing.

"He was nearly fearless when we faced Jones's men. When I stitched him up, that was entirely different. He cried like a little girl."

Nolan found what Doc said to be a small something to chuckle about.

"That ornery cuss knew how to draw those redskins out of hiding. That hadn't been no accident, him up and running. Now, Nolan, you ask yourself why that is." Doc took a bite of biscuit, giving him time to think.

"I've often wondered a few things about Nathanial and how he knows certain stuff. Some things that scare a man don't seem to rile him too much, and where does a little boy learn a thing like that?"

Nolan eyed Doc for an answer, and he shrugged. "Hell, I don't know. But Nathanial knew how to load both my rifle and pistol. He'd done that chore a hundred times before. I'd bet on it. That youngster has experienced life—and not in a good way. Nathanial's mind is set that he don't take orders. I tried to send him here with the woman. To be honest, I'm glad I had him with me. He done his part like a man, not a boy. Though if that youngster don't soon git a steady hand laid on him to guide him, I suspect he'll dangle at the end of a rope someday."

Nolan stood while rolling around in his head all that Doc had said. He'd heard, too, what he'd said without spitting out the words. Nolan could be that steady hand in the boy's life. Nathanial had mentioned his pa once and hadn't at any time confirmed that he was killed during the wagon train attack.

He had told Nolan that Mrs. Harper's husband had been among the dead, not his pa. If not dead, where else would the kid's father be besides out looking for him? And some time had passed. The kid's pa should've found him by now.

Maybe Nathanial was too heartsick to mention his pa had been killed. And the half-pint hadn't mentioned any other kinfolk than those killed in the wagon train attack. Even then, he had only ever talked of the girl, Jenny. There might be distant cousins or some relation somewhere that would be willing to take the boy in. That wasn't what Nolan wanted though.

When he got lonely and his mind strayed, family was exactly what he dreamed of. As of late, that meant Nathanial, and then Kate came to Nolan's mind. Then the unforgettable loss he'd suffered would hit him again. There were things in life that a man shouldn't have to do even once, but perchance twice ... burying a child was a hell Nolan couldn't fight his way through a second time. Thinking he'd lost Nathanial ... Well, no one else could see the fear with their eyes, but he'd been shaken up.

Nolan left Doc and dished out a plate of beans. Seeing Nathanial begin to stir, he heaped another scoop onto the plate, then walked over to the boy, handing him the food. The half-pint hungrily ate without manners, using his fingers. The spoon sat on the edge of the plate as decoration only.

A little outlaw, huh? Nolan wanted to know all about this kid. If he could get Nathanial to talk ... But so far, he'd been tightlipped about most of his past. "Let's go hunt something other than beans to eat."

Nathanial quickly lapped the plate clean, then tossed the tin on the ground. "I'm ready." The half-pint jumped to his feet. Nolan doubted the kid had ever sat at a proper table to take a meal.

"Wipe your mouth."

He wiped the bean smear off his lips onto his shirtsleeve.

They were on the bay and rode from camp. Fluffy white clouds dotted the blue sky. The trees around them were thick with life. Birds chirped, and they spotted a swarm of honeybees buzzing around a hive. Nolan believed them to be fairly safe from encountering any of Jones's men, but he'd been wrong before. His eyes searched both for sign of game and men on the ground ahead of them, though his mind was not on what he was seeing. Nathanial had him thinking too much on a change in the way he'd been living since losing Mary and Matthew.

"Before scouting, I at times had worn a badge. That wasn't how I'd typically made a living though. My wife and I had a nice ranch. I bred and traded horses. My son … he was a purdy fair rider." The words weren't easy for Nolan to say, but it was exactly the bait he needed to use.

Nathanial looked up with a raised brow and eyed Nolan. The boy was clearly thinking something. But would it get him speaking of kin?

"If you have family, then why ain't ya with them? Did they leave ya? Were you a mean daddy? 'Cause you always wear that grouchy look like ya have somethin' sour in your belly."

Nolan couldn't help but laugh. "I didn't always appear so gruff. And to answer your other question, I suspect if you'd have asked my son after getting spanked, then he would have said I was a mean father. But when I was teachin' him how to bend a horseshoe or fix a harness, then I do believe our time workin' together made us a close father and son."

"My pa would up and leave me for weeks, sometimes a month or more. I hate him for it. Mister, you should go back and say sorry to your son before he takes to feeling about you the way I wish I'd been born to someone else."

Nolan hadn't expected to see the strong watery eyes and quivering lip. This boy wasn't going to let himself cry though.

"I didn't abandon my wife and son. I do wish I could speak to my boy, but I won't ever hear Matthew's voice again."

Nathanial's face wrinkled up. "Why not? Where is he?"

"Mary and Matthew ain't here anymore. Just like Jenny, they were killed by an outlaw." Nolan and the boy were both quiet for a while.

"My pa, he got himself shot." Those were the first words Nathanial had offered about who he really was.

Nolan wanted to know more. "Mr. Harper?"

Nolan thought back to the woman he'd helped the half-pint plant and the nine graves at the wagon train. The marker of the girl had read Jenny Harper.

The little boy huffed, looking disgusted. "Mr. Harper... that hateful son of a... He weren't my pa." Nathanial had quickly changed his wording after he got a scowl from Nolan to stop the sharp tongue.

"Then how is it that Jenny's your sister?" Nolan seemed to have asked the wrong question because immediately the boy stopped talking.

Nolan didn't have patience for this. He wanted answers. "Okay then, who's your pa? If you have kin somewhere, Captain Farnsworth will see that you're sent to them just like he plans to do for the woman."

Nathanial's eyes narrowed, and he glared at Nolan. "I'm a bastard. That's all you need to know. If that ain't good enough for ya, you can go to hell." The little hellcat slid off the front of the saddle before Nolan could get a hand on him.

Nathanial gimped away at an angry run. Doc had been right. This boy wasn't a kid at all.

Nolan spurred the bay into a trot, close enough to scoop Nathanial up by the scruff of his shirt, kicking and hollering. He threw the brat lying over his lap, holding him there until Nathanial's fight left out. He pulled him up to sit, but neither of them spoke.

Nathanial kept his face down, tucked into his chest, hiding tears. What was so bad about the name this boy wore that the kid wasn't willing to openly share it? At Nathanial's age, Matthew had chattered to anyone who'd listen about what all Nolan and he had done on any day. Nathanial, on the other hand, held in everything about himself.

They rode in silence for a long time. Nolan pulled up on the reins, then eased to lift the rifle from its sheath. He lowered the gun slowly for Nathanial to take aim. His arms were around Nathanial's shoulders, helping to hold the Winchester steady. The kid was awful tiny to handle the big rifle, but this little boy needed a good lesson in life.

Nolan leaned close and whispered, "Aim at the shoulder of the deer. When you're ready, squeeze the trigger."

The rifle boomed. In a brief pause, the deer dropped to the ground. "That was some good shooting, son." Nolan ruffled his hair, and the half-pint was all smiles.

Nolan nudged the bay forward before pulling up on the reins next to the dead animal. He stepped from the saddle. Nathanial was already knelt in front of the deer. Nolan handed his knife to him. "You know what you're doin' with that? It ain't no toy. Now be careful." Nolan knelt next to Nathanial as the boy sliced the deer open and gagged a little at the bad smell.

"I ain't ever killed an animal as big as a deer. I'm good at huntin' rabbits and squirrel. Your son, did he have a fair aim?"

Was Nathanial trying to prove himself a better aim than Matthew? It was a silly thought, but it must have come to Nolan for a reason. If he was taken with Nolan, then there was little outward sign of it. There was also no trying to picture himself being a father to this boy. He was already doing the job. Nathanial was smiling and seemed happy about their father-and-son time. Could Nolan chance living out each day, perhaps waiting to lose another son?

"You're wearing that grumpy look again. I didn't cut the deer right, did I?" There was a definite pout on Nathanial's little face.

Nolan playfully tweaked the boy's nose. "You're doin' fine. Now roll up your sleeve, reach in there, and dig those guts out." He rolled his sleeve up to help while Nathanial happily did as he had been told. Nolan let the half-pint think he was helping lift the deer onto the back of the gelding, behind the saddle.

"Where did you learn to shoot like that? You have a steady eye. Your aim was right on." Nolan didn't really expect an answer. He was just talking, letting the half-pint know he was proud of him.

"My uncles Frank and—I can't remember my other uncle's name. They weren't really kin, just men close to my pa. They'd all ridden together in the war. Something Raiders had been the name they'd went by, or that's how Pa told me the story. Pa had to leave me for a spell with my uncles. They had a nice farm in Missouri. That's where I learned to shoot. Pa'd been real proud when he came to git me." Nathanial, for once, hadn't thought to hide his past.

Nolan couldn't believe what he'd just heard. Doc had been right. This boy had been born to and taught to be a little outlaw. Nolan felt a tug on his sleeve and woke from being profoundly dumbstruck.

"My shoulder hurts a little." Nathanial rubbed at the sore spot. "The Winchester has a fierce kick. I'm man enough to handle it though. So if you wanna take me hunting again, I'd go."

Nolan stepped into the saddle, then lifted Nathanial to sit in front of him. "I'm tellin' you right now git it out of your head that you're a man. You are a boy. Someday I'll git ya a gun that fits your small size, and we'll go hunting again."

They rode toward camp with plenty of daylight left in the sky, and Nolan listened as Nathanial hummed a happy tune. The bay was still walking when he let Nathanial slide out of the saddle.

The boy limped hurriedly to where Doc sat. "I shot a deer." Nolan could see that he still had some kid left in him.

Doc tossed Nathanial a crude whittled wooden figure of a horse. The boy smiled. "Thanks, Doc. Nolan, look." Nathanial twisted around and held up the gift for him to see. The boy plopped down in the dirt and began to play with the horse figure.

Nolan grinned. Nathanial behaving like a child was a good thing to see. He nodded a thank-you to Doc.

CHAPTER 15

THE DAY WAS SUN FILLED and sweaty hot. A swimming hole would be nice about now.

The half-pint squirmed around behind Nolan in the saddle. "Sit still before you fall off." He looked over his shoulder, wondering why Nathanial was fidgeting.

The boy had turned himself backward and was using the bay's rump as the running ground to play with the little wooden figure.

"If you fall off, I'm gonna leave ya for the buzzards." Nolan winked at the half-pint. Nathanial rolled his blue eyes, then turned back to playing.

Nolan found where Jones had made camp. They weren't far behind the women. Red ashes still glowed where the fire had been left to burn out. The hoofprints on the ground were no older than an hour.

"Nathanial, sit up. Keep an eye open."

The boy did quickly without any lippy fight. Nolan nudged the bay to walk. The captain was a step off his pace. The other soldiers followed in a row of doubles, rounding a bend in the trail where the woman's body, still swinging from the tree, was waiting for them.

"Aw shit."

The young woman dangled from the end of a rope. The tree

that held her feet from touching the ground had been chosen so the army would find her dead directly in their path. A warning from Mr. Jones that he would kill every woman before allowing the captain to save even one of them.

"Nancy," the half-pint said aloud to no one.

Nathanial shifted his weight to slide off the back of the bay. Nolan caught hold of the boy before the small feet hit the ground. He pulled Nathanial around to the front of the saddle, shielded the little boy's teary eyes with his hand, and turned Nathanial's face away from the sight of the blue-faced girl. She was a hideous sight with her wide, lifeless eyes blankly staring off.

"I should bury her." Nathanial's voice was meek, not tender.

"No. The soldiers will plant her. You're done digging graves. If you wanna say a few words over her, I'll let ya do that much but not till she's mounded over with dirt." Nolan was firm. The boy would not win this battle, no matter if he did get lippy.

"I don't have any kind words for Nancy Harper. She was nothin' but mean to me. I only want to see her laid to rest for Jenny." Nathanial had choked on his words, and tears slipped down his cheeks.

Nolan kept the half-pint's head turned away. He walked the bay off a way as the soldiers cut the girl down, dropping her in a heap to the ground. He waited with Nathanial until the girl was rolled into the grave and covered. The half-pint silently cried.

They rode after Jones then and fell off the pace a little.

The captain rode up next to Nolan. "I'm not sure what we should do. I don't want to see another of those women strung up or worse. The deaths of nine more women on my con-science…Jones is a sick bastard. Fretting about being killed off one by one…I can't imagine the angst those poor creatures are experiencing. Not to mention publicity like that will kill my military career more than just giving up and letting Jones get away to steal more women to sell." The captain dabbed a handkerchief across his sweaty brow.

Nate had only been half listening as the captain started talking. He was thinking of Pa. Pa had always gone straight for the throat when dealing with a man that was bucking him. Nate knew all too well the risk of being caught in a crossfire. Being placed in the middle of a fight without wanting to be, that was just how his life was. The women, if they hadn't already, would have to realize that hard truth. Maybe he just didn't know any better.

The ornery captain sounded like he was ready to give up, and Nate had come too close to getting Jenny's killer for that.

"We need to go straight after the fancy man. One, he won't be expecting it since we've backed off some after findin' the last woman. Two, and most importantly, I reckon those women and what they've been through … each one of 'em have probably wished at least once that they were already dead. They'd probably appreciate whatever risk it took that they might be rescued."

Nate saw the confounded look pass between the captain and Nolan. He shut up, but Nolan wasn't about to go silent. "What makes you say a thing like that?"

Nate held his tongue.

"Oh, I see. You're not gonna answer me 'cause you don't have to listen to me. You're dealing that card to me again, huh? How about I make ya walk till you feel like talkin'?" The scout's easy grin was giving away his playfulness.

"I don't believe you." What Nate did believe was that Nolan would never hurt him on purpose.

Nolan ruffled his hair. "I reckon you're right. I'd just end up waiting for ya."

They camped near a pond that shimmered with orange from the fading sun. Some of the soldiers sat around lazily fishing. Nate played at the water's edge until near dark when Nolan fetched him for supper. He ate his burned hunk of fish and beans without complaint. This wasn't exactly like having a family, though Nate was being taken care of.

"Time for you to git some sleep." Nolan laid the blanket out on the ground.

Nate curled up, ready for sleep to take him to a peaceful place. Every bone in him was tired, but he was a bit scared to close his eyes. After what he'd seen today, he might have a nightmare.

His dreams had mostly been haunted since as far back as he could remember. Lately it'd been worse. The little wooden horse figure was held tight in his hand. Jenny had given Nate an old teddy bear that'd been hers when she was little. Then her rotten pa had found it. Where the small comfort ended up, who knew?

If Nate closed his eyes, Nancy Harper's blue face hanging at the end of that rope would be there to steal his peace. Nancy and Jenny had looked so much alike. At times, he had almost mixed them up.

Nolan stretched out long on a blanket next to Nate. This man, like no other, made Nate feel secure. He stared at the scout for a long while. Why did this man watch over him? It was more than just that though. He was being guarded in a way he hadn't ever experienced. Pa wouldn't have turned his eyes from the dead girl hanging in the tree. Rather, he would have forced Nate to have a good look and said something stupid like... this was life, and if Nate didn't keep a watchful eye, matched with a quick hand on a gun when he grew older, then this could be his fate. Pa hadn't ever protected him from anything bad, not one time that he could recall.

Nolan was different than Pa. Nate had seen him kill, but not without cause. Pa hadn't been an upright man. Nate thought

Nolan was brave and good. So he just couldn't figure out why the scout wanted to have anything to do with him.

"Why are you friendly to me?"

The man slid his hat off his face and turned from where he rested back against his saddle. "Why shouldn't I be?"

Nate shrugged, thinking before he said too much. He'd thought a couple of times about sharing his secret with Nolan. "If you knew my full name, you wouldn't like me anymore. I ain't from good seed. Nobody cares a spit about me once they find out who I am." They stared each other down, trying to figure one another.

"Why don't you tell me? I bet we'll still be friends."

Nate rolled away onto his side so his back was facing Nolan. What he really wanted to do was scoot closer to his side. He doubted Nolan would laugh if he were to tell of the nightmare that he was afraid would be there as soon as he shut his lids. Tears welled up in his eyes. There was always the chance that Nolan would push him away.

Nate lay still as Nolan blanketed him with the same warm wool-lined coat that he had been allowed to cuddle up with for how many nights when the air held a chill. It smelled of Nolan. That scent made him feel safe and closer to the scout than the two or three feet that separated where they slept on the ground. Love was a word Nate didn't so much trust. Until just lately, Jenny had been the only person to stir this fuzzy feeling in him.

———————◆———————

The half-pint caught hold of Nolan's hand before he let go of the coat. The baby blues were full of tears. "I like you."

Nathanial pulled his hand away under the coat and closed his eyes tight. This child had crawled deep under Nolan's skin. He gently rested a hand to the fair hair and smoothed the crown of the small head. Tender words didn't come easy to him, even before Mary and Matthew had been killed. He didn't say it, but he liked the little boy too. Nolan pulled the coat up over Nathanial's tiny shoulders. What the boy had said was a small affection but had taken big guts, given his natural distrust.

Nolan rested his head back against his saddle to think. Doc was a father and a soldier. Being away for months at a time with the army was no way to raise a child. That wasn't what Nolan wanted. To do right by Nathanial, he would have to give up being a scout. Which was of no worry to him. The more time he spent with the child, the more he wanted to be a father to this boy. Fear of losing something he cared about wasn't going to get the best of him this time.

As soon as the army could replace him as scout, he and Nathanial would leave. They would ride for Kate's ranch. Nolan made an unspoken promise to be a good father, closed his eyes, and was ready to start a new life.

Having the half-pint in the saddle with Nolan was something he was growing mighty used to. He hardly noticed Nathanial sitting in front of him. Playing with the eye scope, the boy was good at entertaining himself.

"There's somethin' down there." Nathanial's eye was tight pressed to the lens. Buzzards circled overhead.

"Let me see that."

Nathanial handed Nolan the spyglass. He took a long look. There was nothing good going to come from this day. There was no closing Nathanial's eyes to this slaughter.

Nolan sat his horse, waiting for the captain and the others to join them. Captain Farnsworth pulled up on the reins next to him, and he handed the lens to the captain.

At least a dozen Indians lay dead, sprawled across the floor of the grassy valley. From the army's vantage on the rocky hilltop, it was the perfect place to put together what had happened.

Down off the hilltop and out into the openness of the valley, Nolan rode with the captain matching the pace. Their mounts balked at tramping through the scattering of rotting dead. Putrid was the smell of death surrounding them. A thick covering of flies buzzed around the bodies. What an awful, bloody sight.

Nolan reined in, studying the marks on the ground. Nathanial leaned forward to eye the tracks too. "Why would the fancy man kill his own men? Did he double-cross them?"

This boy's mind was too damn bright.

Nolan nodded. "I reckon so."

There were men in the captain's ranks that wouldn't have seen what happened as clearly as the half-pint did. There was a slight shift of weight in the saddle, but Nolan caught hold of Nathanial's arm before he slid to the ground.

"Where do ya think you're goin'?"

There was an odd groove in the dirt that the boy's gaze fell on. Nolan let Nathanial drop from the saddle.

"We don't have time for this." Captain Farnsworth's eyes narrowed.

Nolan ignored the bitching. "Go on, son." He nodded, urging Nathanial to study the groove.

The boy walked a small circle, looking about all wide-eyed at the dead Indians. Nolan's gaze followed after the baby blues, studying a straight grooved line in the dirt. No...there were two lines about three or so feet apart. Nathanial touched the groove, then put his head down, ear to ground, looking to follow the rail-like markings. "A wagon?"

"That's right." There was pride in Nolan's grin at how quickly Nathanial was learning to read sign.

"The tracks are overlapping. The wagon came and headed back in the same direction. North." Nathanial pointed, and Nolan nodded.

There was one big difference in the two sets of tracks. Nolan wanted to make sure Nathanial saw it. "See how one set has cut deeper into the dirt?" He waited a minute while the boy studied the ground.

Nathanial poked a finger into each track to measure the depth. "Yes, sir. I see the difference, but how's it important?"

"They switched the ladies from riding horseback to a wagon. The weight of all the women together in the wagon bed is setting the track deeper. Traveling by wagon is slower than a single horse and rider. Why that switch was made, I don't know." Nolan nudged the bay to walk. There might be a less distinguishable clue that his sharp eye would pick up.

Nate kept looking about as Nolan was doing. The captain stepped his horse up close to Nate, and without warning, he gave him a shove with the toe of his boot. Nate stumbled back but didn't fall. That hurt, and he rubbed at his arm to stop the thumping. His sleeve was dirty from the captain's heel. Nate brushed it as clean as he could.

"School's over, so unless you want to be left behind, you git back on that horse."

What had Nate done to piss off Captain Farnsworth today? He couldn't think of anything. Surely the man wasn't still sore over stuff from before. Nate had been in Nolan's hip pocket all day and hadn't even been near the captain until now. He supposed he was just letting off steam. Other men Nate had ridden with had treated him far worse. A little shove was nothing.

"Don't touch him again!" Nolan's fierce tone startled Nate. It was no little warning. With a few jerks of the reins, the scout had the bay stepped between him and Captain Farnsworth. Nolan was faced off with the army commander … because of Nate.

He stood stock-still. Nolan's jawline was set in a hard way, his face red. A little kick wasn't worth getting angry about. It was okay for Nate to be mistreated. The captain hadn't called him any foul names that would have otherwise pissed him off.

Why was Nolan making big trouble with Captain Farnsworth for something so unimportant? Meanness had always been the affection he was most used to. Besides, he planned on just ignoring the captain and doing what he wanted anyway. Maybe Nolan didn't understand that what the captain had done was okay.

"There ain't no need to raise a fuss on account of me." Nate was just being honest.

Nolan's head swung around, and Nate's breath caught. Narrowed eyes glared at him. It reminded Nate of a deadly rattler about to strike. He was pissed off at Captain Farnsworth. That was unmistakable to all, but was Nolan mad at Nate too?

He shrank up and realized he was holding his breath. He wasn't able to keep his gaze on Nolan. Nate stared straight down at his feet.

"Son, look at me." The words weren't harsh, and there was something in Nolan's tone that gave meaning to being called son.

The term wasn't used casually. Nate was certain of it. Tears sprang to his eyes, though he wasn't afraid. He slowly shook his head and should have known Nolan wouldn't leave it at that. He expected Nate to do as he was told, no matter the size of what was being asked.

Nolan reached down from the saddle and lifted Nate's chin. He tried to sniff back his tears. His eyes were welled to the brim, and one escaped. The firm hand holding his chin wouldn't let him look away. There was no use in struggling, so Nate gave up. The effort had been puny anyway.

A gentle touch brushed the wetness from his cheek, and Nate looked up. "Nathanial, listen closely to me. Even if Captain Farnsworth or any other man has reason to be riled up 'cause of somethin' you done, I ain't gonna let anyone treat ya badly."

Straightening in the saddle, Nolan turned away from Nate and faced the captain once again. Pa had stood tall only with his gang of men. Captain Farnsworth had troops that could be ordered to back him up. There didn't seem to be anything or anyone that Nolan was afraid of.

The captain's glare was thrown past Nolan and hit Nate. He trusted Nolan to keep the captain from maybe beating on him. Captain Farnsworth hadn't raised a hand against Nate so far, but he wasn't going to get close enough to tease the man into catching hold of him.

"We have more pressing matters to concern ourselves with than that rotten kid." The captain barked the words at Nolan as if Nate weren't standing behind him to hear every word. "Where are the women? Who has them now? If they have switched into a wagon, have they been traded already?"

Nate turned and walked through the scattering of dead Indians as Nolan and Captain Farnsworth locked horns. He didn't want to hear their flaring argument. He was tired of everything in his life being a damn fight.

Nate figured the fancy man had done all that killing so he wouldn't have to pay more. Pa had done it a few times, and now there weren't enough people to keep the women from escaping. Rounded up cattle was easier to move than a loose bunch. Into the wagon the women folk went so they couldn't run away. Nate could see what had happened there pretty clearly. Though he wished he'd not seen any of it.

Strung out in a line of tired horses, the soldiers rode past him. All eyes were on the massacred. Would they all suffer the same fate? It'd been the very question Nate asked himself upon riding into that crimson valley of death.

His gaze met the girl's waterworks. She was pale, looking as if she might be sick. She wiped at her eyes as her horse stepped past him.

Nate hated every one of these dead savages for what they'd done to that poor girl and for killing Jenny. The stinking red pigs deserved each bullet they'd gotten. Nate was glad they were dead, that the buzzards would eat their rotten carcasses.

His feet stuck fast to the ground. Tears sprang to his eyes, and his mind whirled. The pound of his heart echoed loudly in his ears so he heard nothing else around him. *Breathe.* His gut twisted up so tight that what little air was in his lungs was choked out of him. Jenny's killer lay dead, gray-faced and dull-eyed. So why was Nate's fear taking over? His body shook so badly that he lost hold of his water. Not a step away lay the feathered devil whose arrow had stolen Jenny's life.

Tears ran down Nate's face, and his fists clenched. He stepped closer, unsure at first that his legs would hold up. He leaned over and spit in the rotten, dirty bastard's face. That wasn't enough to satisfy his raw hate. Nate's rage cut loose, and he kicked the devil in the ribs, then again and again. "I hate you!"

Nate dropped to his knees. His fists, at their own will, began to thunder on the hell-bound demon's chest. "Why did you have to kill Jenny? She didn't deserve to die!"

Nolan jumped down out of the saddle at a run toward Nathanial. He scooped up the kicking and screaming boy and threw him over his shoulder.

"Let me go!" Nathanial's small fists pounded on Nolan's back.

Twisting the youngster around in one quick swing, Nolan held Nathanial tight against him. With the other arm, he pulled the two of them onto his horse.

He quickly turned to the captain. "Follow those wagon tracks. We'll catch up." Nolan sank spurs into the bay, and the horse shot off at a run.

They raced out across the valley and away from all the death. The little boy howled in pain, the kind that tore at one's heart. Nolan held Nathanial tight and kept him from falling out of the saddle as he thrashed about. He slowed the gelding's pace as the youngster lost his fight more and more until Nathanial was nearly limp. His little head sagged, and the small body slumped forward. Nolan reined in, then loosened his hold on him. They sat quiet for a long spell.

"That hate you're feeling, I felt that once myself. It ain't no good, and it won't bring …" Nolan's words trailed off a minute, thinking of Mary and Matthew. "It won't bring Jenny back."

"I miss her." Nathanial's frail, choked-up voice was a mere whisper.

"Yeah, I know what that's like." Nolan nudged the gelding to walk. He knew too damn well the crippling pain of such a deep personal loss. He had been beaten down until the moment he'd decided to track the James brothers. They'd escaped the bank robbery that day when Mary and Matthew were killed in the crossfire.

The others who'd been involved in the killing had been shot, captured, and sent to prison. Nolan's motivation had never been to collect the bounty on the James brothers. Pure hate had spurred him toward revenge. He'd chased Frank and Jesse James for some time, without any luck. Then Nolan had switched tactics and pinned on a badge in hopes that it would lead him to the revenge he wanted. It never did work out for him.

Nathanial was following in the footsteps of revenge, going after Deegan Jones. Just the same as Nolan had. He was a man though. Nathanial was a wet-nosed pup that still had lots to learn about life. The half-pint didn't seem to see himself that way, always talking so tough. If the half-pint and Jones ever did come face-to-face, too quickly Jones would prove that the way Nathanial saw himself was wrong. He would end up with a bullet in him. Nolan did not want to see him die foolishly or any other way.

They made their own trail that day, and few words passed between them. Nathanial cried out all the grief that he'd locked inside himself. That night, they kept their distance from the soldiers' camp. Nolan wanted to give the half-pint time to fix his little mind right. If the boy wanted to talk, then Nolan would listen. He wouldn't push Nathanial to leave out any more grief than the boy felt the need to share. Nolan handed him a piece of jerky.

"I ain't hungry." The boy sniffed back tears.

"Well, I ain't askin', so eat."

They chewed their dried beef in silence. The crackling of the flickering fire was a small pleasantness that gave Nolan some comfort. Nathanial's glassy blue eyes stared far off into the flames. What was the boy thinking?

As if Nathanial had heard his thoughts, the boy began to speak. "I'm a coward."

Nathanial's eyes were blank, seeming to be lost somewhere, remembering another day. "I wanted to help Jenny. I wish I could've, but all those dead bodies scattered on the ground. I knew those people from the wagon train, and it scared me. All I'd been able to do was watch. Doing nothing that day proves that what I've always been told is true. I ain't no good, just like my pa." Nathanial raised his head and looked Nolan square in the eyes. "He told me all the time I weren't worth nothing. He was right."

Nolan had a hard time understanding why a father would beat down his son with such harsh words and so repeatedly that Nathanial actually believed he was worthless. His rough attitude painted a whole new picture for Nolan, given that it seemed his father hadn't really wanted him.

"You wanna know how bad I am? Jenny wasn't the only person I ever let die. There were two others."

Nolan stiffened. What was the boy talking about? Nolan had heard the whole story about Jenny dying. Nathanial must've been thinking he was responsible, but that just wasn't true. Besides her, who else was there? Surely the kid wasn't blaming himself for the deaths of Mrs. Harper and Nancy, the Harpers' daughter that Jones had hung.

"There was a stagecoach sitting not far from the bank that my pa and his gang had planned to rob. I quickly crawled inside to hide myself before the shooting started." The boy wiped tears across his sleeve. "I'd always gone first into the bank. My job had been to look for lawmen hiding themselves as customers or clerks. I have an eye for it. I'd falsely cry that I lost my mama, had she come into the bank, and a bunch of stuff like that. In truth, I don't even know what it's like to have a real mama."

So the kid's scumbag father had used him as a decoy. Nathanial could've been killed. Nolan shook his head in disgust.

"You're lookin' grouchy. I don't have to tell the rest of it if you don't wanna hear it." Nathanial rubbed his sleeve across his eyes again.

"Go on." Nolan wanted to know about the other two dead people Nathanial seemed to be carrying some guilt about. Being a decoy didn't explain anything about that, and the mention of the stagecoach had Nolan's heart pounding and the sweat pouring out of him.

"On that day, I should have known somethin' was up when a man hurried around the counter and shooed me out the door. He told me to run along home. Those townsfolk had known we were coming. Only, I hadn't realized it at first, and I went ahead and gave the signal. All clear. Maybe I hadn't cared if Pa or the others in the gang were caught. I hated that life." Nathanial paused for a long minute as if he couldn't bear to say what was coming next. "There'd been a pretty, dark-haired woman and a boy on that stage. He was maybe five years older than myself. They were just sittin' there, waiting to go on their way. I told them both they'd best get down. That's when the first rifle shot boomed. I should've told them to get out of there, to run as far as they could, but I didn't."

This story was beginning to sound very familiar to Nolan. Could Nathanial be talking about the attempted robbery in Northfield? He didn't want to believe that this boy had actually been a working member of the James–Younger gang. The same sons of bitches who had killed Mary and Matthew. How could that be?

It couldn't be true, but Nolan had been a lawman at that time, and he'd read the official report, which stated that a boy had been picked up as an accomplice in the attempted robbery. He'd thought that meant an older boy. The age hadn't been noted in the report. My God, Nathanial couldn't have been more than five years old, and Matthew had been ten. Five years older than Nathanial, just as the kid had described. Nolan's chest sank with a heavy sadness.

"The woman, she'd thrown her son to the floor, covering him with her body. Then she grabbed my wrist and yanked me down to hide in her bosom too. She'd held me as tight as her own son. We clung to her and cried, for different reasons though. Guns boomed everywhere around us. Her son was white-faced, and he shook with the fear of God. I cried at the touch of the loving arms wrapped tight around me. It made me quickly dream of having a mama. She soothed us both with kisses. I didn't want to let go. I'd planned to ask to go with that family when they pulled out on the stage."

Nolan didn't want to hear any more, but he couldn't stop listening. Clearly pictured in his mind were the frightened faces of both Mary and Matthew. Nathanial was right. It'd been in the report that the town had known what was coming, so why the hell hadn't the stage been warned? Nolan's wife and son might still be alive. He had put together wrongly from the report that the stagecoach had somehow ridden into the middle of it and got caught in a crossfire, but the stage had just been sitting there.

"The stage shook. The woman hushed our screams by holding us closer, if that were even possible. Our nostrils filled with gun smoke, and the stage rattled as bullets riddled the street. A volley of rifle fire echoed in our ears. I squeezed my eyes tight shut and wished for that moment in hell to pass quickly. The street got quiet, and I dared to open my eyes. Were we safe? Would the shooting start again?

"I looked into the woman's vacant eyes, then stared at her son's dull face. Luck hadn't been with either of them that day. Maybe if I had warned them or got 'em out of there, but I was too scared to do anything. It should've been me. Those folks were good people. I hadn't known them beyond those few minutes, but I could tell. She was kindhearted. Otherwise, she wouldn't have sheltered me with her body."

Nolan had only ever known the facts of how death had taken his family away. He'd never heard the story until now. It wasn't an easy thing to hear from this boy. Knowing that Nathanial's pa had been one of the killers involved shoved a wedge between Nolan and the boy.

"Hours later, the sheriff found me. He'd mistaken me at first for a passenger. After checking ticket sales, the lawman knew I was no good. A witness had stepped forward and confirmed that I'd ridden in on the back of Jim Younger's horse, the no-account I'd been born to. Can you believe I was dragged off and locked in the jailhouse? I hadn't fired any bullets at anyone, but I was sorry about that nice lady and her little boy. It took the tin star six days till he found someone to dump me with."

"Mr. and Mrs. Harper." Nolan wasn't truly asking. All the pieces were finally fitting together. Only, he didn't like the shape it'd taken.

The boy nodded, then wiped at his eyes.

"Jenny and I only pretended that we were brother and sister. That Indian in the field today was the one who pulled the bowstring, sending an arrow into Jenny, marking her for death. Then a few minutes later, the fancy man rode up and shot her down." Tears streaked Nathanial's face, dripping off his tiny chin.

Nolan just couldn't believe it. This little boy sitting across the fire from him had been there the day Mary and Matthew were killed. He stood and fetched his whiskey bottle. He pulled the cork. How would he ever forget who Nathanial's pa was?

"You think I'm a coward for not helping Jenny?" Nathanial watched Nolan drink from the bottle.

Slowly Nolan shook his head. Coward was the last word he would use to describe Nathanial. Unfortunate was what came to his mind. Taking another swallow of whiskey, he sat next to the fire.

Nathanial stared off into the flames. Nolan would have to break his unspoken promise to be a father to this boy. Without knowing it, they'd both been leaning on the hope of that promise for some time. The sight of the snowy-haired half-pint now stirred up old pain worse than ever.

Why had he let Mary and Matthew travel alone to visit her folks? He should've gone with them. He'd justified staying behind because two of their best brood mares were due to foal, and he and Mary had planned on having the largest horse ranch in the territory. Nolan's mind was flooded with memories of that hellish day the sheriff had ridden up to the ranch with a telegram in hand from the marshal in Northfield, which read that Mary and Matthew had been killed.

Nolan woke late, rolling to sit up. The sun was overhead, and his mind was still thinking over all the half-pint had told him. There was no question that Nathanial was innocent of any bloodshed, but the fact was still the same. The little boy had played a part, though unknowingly, in the deaths of Mary and Matthew.

Nolan looked across the burned-out fire to where the youngster had fallen asleep. Nathanial wasn't there. Only the blanket and the little wooden horse were left behind.

Nolan quickly got to his feet.

"Nathanial!"

He waited just a minute. No answer. He hurried to saddle his horse, and as he tossed the leather over the bay's back, his trained eye found where the grass was swayed. The half-pint had walked away, and not just from camp. Nolan shoved the horse figure in his pocket. It was a sign that Nathanial was walking away from everything.

He hadn't expected the child to run away. Yes, Nolan had been upset last night and drank too much after listening to the details of Mary's and Matthew's last moments on this earth. Maybe he had mumbled some things about Nathanial's father that he shouldn't have, or at least not in front of the kid. Nathanial was lucky to have made it out of that stagecoach alive.

Nolan stepped into the saddle and stared in the direction the kid had gone. That day in Northfield, Nolan wasn't the only one who lost his entire world. Mary and Matthew had been everything to him. Nathanial's father was no good, but that didn't mean the little boy wasn't suffering from some degree of loss. The kid couldn't help who he'd been born to, and Nolan couldn't stop worrying about Nathanial. Maybe somehow this would just work.

No longer was Nolan surprised at how much ground the little boy could quickly cover on foot, given the kind of men the kid had been raised around, always on the run from the law. Nolan rode miles across the grassy valleys and hadn't caught sight of the half-pint until the sun was setting low in the sky. He pulled up on the reins just outside the boy's little camp. Nathanial had a fire burning and was sitting quietly, warming his hands. The half-pint wouldn't look at him.

"Mind if I share your fire?" Nolan stepped down off the gelding.

Nathanial shrugged, keeping his gaze on the flames. Nolan left the bay grazing and sat down next to the boy. He leaned forward and looked Nathanial in the face. Their eyes held. "I should whup you for runnin' off. That was being a coward. Don't do it again."

Nathanial stared at him with wide, teary eyes. "You still wanna be my friend? Most folks run away like I have the pox after hearing my name." He reached without hesitation and took back the little horse figure that Nolan was holding out in the palm of his hand.

Nolan grinned. "I don't scare that easily."

CHAPTER 16

THEY BOTH SLEPT LATE, then together rode fast through the day to find the captain and his men. Shadows of the coming darkness were setting in as the bay trotted into the soldiers' camp. There was a fire, and Nolan could smell beans cooking. Tents were planted in a row, and one of the tents had two guards posted in front of it. Huh, that was odd. Most of the uniformed men sat around jawing and eating. One soldier cleaned his gun. A few others tended to the horses, all of which stood tethered to a single rope line.

Nolan lifted Nathanial from the saddle and set the boy's feet to the ground before stepping down himself. The half-pint was stuck to him, practically standing on Nolan's boots and getting his little fingers in the way, wanting to help unsaddle the bay.

He didn't growl at the boy for being underfoot, but he hoped Nathanial would go find something to do. Nolan needed space to think. It was hard for him to look at Nathanial and not think about what had happened inside that stagecoach. It wasn't just the loss of his wife and son that had him disturbed. Mary had a true mothering heart. If Nathanial would have shared his story with Mary and had asked to stay with her, she would've brought that stray pup home as quick as a wink, and Nolan's say wouldn't have mattered much. Fate had failed to bring him and Nathanial together the first time. The path they were on now was much rougher, and Nolan wasn't sure he could endure it.

He walked to find the captain. Jones was a somewhat needed distraction. Nathanial was on his heels until he saw Doc. Then the half-pint finally ran off for a spell. Nolan sighed deeply. What was he going to do about the kid?

Captain Farnsworth appeared out of the guarded tent. "It's about damn time you showed up. I suppose you brought that brat back with ya."

Nolan grinned, but it wasn't friendly like. "Thought we understood one another where the boy is concerned."

"Never mind that. I have something of Jones's that I want to show you." The captain began to lead Nolan toward the guarded tent.

"Gotta piss first." Nolan walked off.

"Can't it wait?"

He ignored the captain's question and kept walking toward the edge of camp.

<hr>

Nate licked up the last of the bean smear on the tin plate and noticed that Captain Farnsworth had joined the other soldiers around the fire. He could feel the captain's glare. The man had no cause to be looking so mean. Nate had done nothing but eat beans. He stuck his tongue out so Captain Farnsworth knew he felt the same way.

"I was hoping Nolan might lose you out there somewhere … One less headache for me." The captain chuckled.

Nate didn't find the mean words funny at all. "I don't have to listen to this bull, you horse's ass."

"You little bastard. I promise the first chance I git, I'll dump you off somewhere. You can be someone else's trouble." The captain looked to be one snorting breath away from taking hold of him.

Only, Nate was pissed off and didn't care. He threw down his empty plate, then whipped out his water maker and sprayed piss all over the captain's saddle. The army commander's mouth fell open and his eyes widened. He seemed to be frozen in place with that profoundly dumbstruck look on his face.

Nate just got himself tucked away as the captain came to and reached out to grab hold of him. Nate laughed as he raced full strides from camp with the captain a few running steps behind. Captain Farnsworth stopped, doubled over, and gasped to suck air.

"Ha ha. You're too slow to catch me." It was obvious to him that the captain was far too used to being a horse soldier. Good thing they didn't have to march anywhere, or the army would never catch up with the bad guys. Nate, too, stopped running, but not because he was out of breath. It might be fun to taunt the captain a little more. As long as the man didn't get a second wind and get his hands on him. He would be in big trouble then. Nolan was nowhere around to correct Nate, and Captain Horse's Ass was still breathing heavy, so why not chance it?

Nate bent over and wiggled his bottom at the captain. "Come an' git me if you can." Laughter roared out of him. He couldn't recall ever smiling so much. No doubt, after this, the captain wouldn't call Nate any more names.

◆—◆　—◆

Nolan stood behind the tree. Nathanial hadn't seen him. He slipped his belt from his waist, folding the leather strap in his hand. When he stepped around the tree and took hold of Nathanial's arm, the boy looked up wide-eyed at Nolan, then at the belt in his hand. Tears sprang to life in the tomcat's eyes.

"He called me a bastard." The boy tried to defend himself, pointing at the captain.

"I heard you call yourself that once," Nolan reminded him.

His teary gaze fell to stare at his feet, and he stood still and quiet, not giving any fight.

"I don't always agree with what the captain says, but he deserves respect. He's leading these men. He don't need any trouble from you." Nolan kept a tight hold on Nathanial's arm, marching the boy back to stand and face the captain. "Now apologize." He wasn't asking.

The ornery little tomcat held his mouth shut, silently fighting what he'd been told to do. Nolan handed his belt to the captain. Nathanial's big teary blue eyes begged him not to let the captain whup his backside.

"I'm sorry." The boy looked at the ground as if something sad was going on there around his feet, and the little voice did not convey conviction.

Nolan jerked Nathanial's arm. The boy was smart and knew what was being asked of him.

Nathanial's head came up, and he met the eyes of the captain. "I'm sorry, Captain Farnsworth." This time he spoke strong and clear.

The captain handed the belt back to Nolan.

"Pull that grass an' wipe down the captain's saddle." Nolan felt it was a fair punishment.

"Yes, sir." The boy dropped to his knees next to the saddle and yanked a handful of grass up by the roots, then began rubbing the leather dry.

There would be no second warning. Nolan would spank Nathanial if the captain's saddle wasn't well cleaned. "I'll be back to check that you done a good job." He turned to the captain. "You wanna show me whatever it is you have of Jones's?"

The captain nodded, and they walked off toward the tents.

The captain pulled back the flap, letting Nolan step inside first. This was quite a surprise. A man dressed much like himself, in filthy clothing covered in trail dirt, was sitting on the ground. Both his hands and feet were bound. The cold hazel eyes were a sign that this fella had no remorse for the bloody trail left behind by him and the others that rode for Jones. During the time when Nolan had worn a badge, he'd come across many a man like this one.

"We rode up on him and a few others while they were staking one of the women to the ground. She would've been the next to be found dead along the trail. This one's horse got shot out from under him. He dropped his weapon and surrendered as quickly as the other two had ridden away. We haven't been able to get him to talk. Maybe if we knew Jones's path, we could get ahead him and stop him." The captain was in a sweat.

Nolan wasn't worried about getting information out of this fella. Thundercloud, an Apache scout for the army and a fierce warrior, had taught Nolan a thing or two about using a knife. He would get this hard, sneering man to talk.

"The woman, is she okay?" The answer would determine Nolan's level of push against the prisoner.

"Frightened nearly to death, but otherwise, yes, she's fine. Thank God." Captain Farnsworth's relief was evident.

Nolan pulled his knife, showing the sharp blade to the prisoner. Hunkered down in front of the tightlipped man, he was about to get all the information. "I'd rather take you outside and hang ya right now. First I need you to tell the captain where Jones is headed with those women."

The man's eyes narrowed in a hateful glare. Maybe Nolan needed to be a touch more persuasive with this trash. He pressed the blade under the man's chin until the tough woman killer was stretching his neck to pull away from the sharpness.

"Most of the men we buried while following the bunch of you were laid to rest without their scalps, thanks to your Indian friends. Did ya ever wonder what it would feel like to git your hair, just under your skin, sawed off by the sharp edge of a knife? If you don't speak up … you will know that pain, and then we're gonna hang ya."

"Nolan, this is not the way the army conducts business." If that was the captain's way of ordering Nolan to stand down, it wasn't going to work.

"Well, I guess it's a good thing I'm not wearing a uniform." Nolan grinned at Jones's hired gun, whose face paled.

"Are you Captain Nolan Crosson?" The prisoner's tongue seemed to have loosened up.

Good for him, or Nolan might have cut it out. "I ain't a captain no more."

"I fought with you in the war." The man had nothing left but desperation.

Nolan raised a brow. Was this some kind of fool trick to slip the justice that was coming to this no-account? "I don't remember you."

"The regiment I'd been part of joined with your men. Our captain wanted to fall back. The Rebs would have then gained the high ground. You wouldn't let us retreat. Instead, you ordered us all forward and led the charge. I was nearby when you took a bullet in the leg, fell, then pulled yourself up. You kept us all pushing the Rebs farther back. I heard later that you'd dug the lead out yourself."

Nolan grinned. He wasn't being friendly though, not in the least. As this man looked up, scared and about to piss himself, Nolan recognized the familiar gaze. "That's true, only you've missed the best part of the story. The next day, with my leg bandaged and bleeding, I marched my men twenty miles. We fought in another engagement. We won that one too. So you see, I don't lose very easily. I just wasn't born to naturally roll over."

"If I talk … then you set me free. Otherwise, you might as well git on with hanging me, 'cause I won't tell you nothin'."

What made this murdering trash believe he had any room to bargain?

Nolan pushed the blade a might harder so the tip sliced the delicate skin under the man's chin just a nip.

"Jones is planning on crossing the border. Where exactly, I ain't sure. He talked of an old trail that some pack Indians and trappers traveled to trade." Sweat beads glistened on the man's brow.

"See there. Ratting your boss out wasn't too hard, now was it?" Nolan slid his knife back into the leather sheath strapped to his belt. Then, as he straightened, he yanked the prisoner up to stand. They were eye to eye. "That day when I got shot in battle, I dropped my rifle when I grabbed for my leg. You picked it up and handed it back to me. You've changed. I wouldn't have known ya. I do hope you've made peace with what's coming to ya."

He shoved the prisoner to the ground, then turned to Captain Farnsworth. "He ain't of no use to us anymore."

"You ain't gonna hang me, you son of a bitch!" The prisoner sprang to his feet. The iron shackles around his ankles rattled loudly. That quick, the man threw himself at Nolan. Together, they stumbled back, falling into the captain. All three of them hit the ground inside the tent with a hard thud.

The prisoner was over Nolan and had the length of chain cuffed to each wrist stretched. He pressed it down around Nolan's throat. Nolan swung hard with a right hook. He hit the man square in the jaw. It'd been enough of a blow to loosen the man's choke hold. He threw a second punch that rattled the prisoner's teeth and rolled the turncoat off him.

Before Nolan could get to his feet. The man struck with a kick. The hard boot heel cracked him in the mouth. He instantly tasted blood from his busted lip and was half seeing stars. But this fight wasn't over yet. Nolan lunged up off the ground. This time the prisoner's kick missed. Nolan was able to grab the trash and hold to a fistful of crumpled-up shirt collar. In the same breath, he drew back with the other hand to strike a hard blow.

Captain Farnsworth stepped into the brawl, swinging the butt end of a pistol like a hammer. One swift pound to the side of the prisoner's head dropped him cold to the dirt. The captain's effort had saved Nolan's fists from doing that job, and he was glad of it. He sat back to catch his breath, wiping the blood from his mouth across his sleeve.

"Lieutenant, form a firing squad." Captain Farnsworth barked the order, then gave Nolan a hand up.

"Captain, I'm gonna ask a favor of ya. Nathanial and the women don't need to see anyone else shot down. Could your men take the prisoner from camp and hang him where the boy can't witness it? Hearing gunfire in or around camp might spook the youngster and the ladies. There won't be any questions from any of 'em if they don't see or hear what's going on." Nolan hoped Nathanial wouldn't get curious and want to know what happened when he saw Nolan's swollen lips. There was no hiding the ugliness; that was for sure.

"Your one soft spot … that ornery little cuss." The captain studied Nolan for a long minute. "But I agree about the women too. Lieutenant, get a rope. I'll join you shortly to take the prisoner from camp."

"Thank you, sir." Nolan walked from the tent, leaving the captain and the soldiers to their business. He spit blood, then wiped his mouth again.

He looked about. Hmm, the boy wasn't at the captain's saddle or at the fire. Was Nathanial with Doc? Nolan hunted about camp, seeing nothing of Nathanial. It took some close looking in the tents until he thought to check the horses and found the half-pint playing with the bay. The horse's lips nibbled at his hair, making the youngster giggle.

Nathanial was just small enough to duck a bit and walk through the horse's front legs and under the belly. He disappeared on the other side of the gelding. Nolan walked up, patted the bay's neck, then stepped around the horse. Nathanial was lying on the ground not two steps from the horse. He had scratched his name in the dirt with a pocketknife.

"Hey, that's real good." Nolan was impressed with the legibly etched penmanship. He hunkered down to have a good look. From what he'd come to know about Nathanial's upbringing, he doubted the boy had ever stayed in one spot long enough to attend school.

Nathanial smiled. "Jenny taught me to read and write." His gaze then focused on Nolan's busted-up face. "Holy shit! Who hit you?"

"Never you mind, and watch your mouth." It wasn't important for Nathanial to know about Jones's man being captured. Protection rather than exposure was what the half-pint needed.

Nathanial got on his knees, standing right smack dab in front of Nolan, and studied his throbbing lips from a nose length away. "That looks like it hurts real bad."

"I'm fine. Don't worry yourself." Nolan winked at Nathanial. He hadn't expected to see tears in the boy's eyes.

"I could go fetch Doc for ya." Nathanial jumped up to run off after his own idea.

Nolan caught him by the arm. "It's just a busted lip. I'll live."

"You sure?" Nathanial eyed him for a minute and didn't look convinced.

"Son, it'll take more than a fat lip to kill me."

Nathanial slowly began to grin, then sat down and carved Nolan's name into the dirt without being told how to spell it.

Nolan ruffled the snowy patch. "I bet you can't spell ... Captain Farnsworth." He was playfully testing the boy's smarts.

"That's easy." Too smooth the words came out. The little polecat was wearing an ornery grin that told of being up to no good.

"Horse's ass is not the captain's name." Nolan couldn't help but chuckle. He took the small pocketknife, then rolled Nathanial head over tin cup through the grass.

The pup bounced up and pounced on him. They playfully tussled through the grassy dirt. He tickled Nathanial's little belly and armpits.

"Uncle, uncle! I'm gonna piss my pants." Laughter roared from the boy. Nolan could hardly understand his plea for mercy.

For a short time, Nolan forgot who this boy was. Nathanial Younger would always be the son of the killer who had taken the lives of Mary and Matthew. The thought sobered him. He picked Nathanial off his back, then stood him on his feet.

Nolan brushed the dirt from Nathanial's trousers and gave him a playful swat. "You best go on and git some sleep."

"Yes, sir." The boy skipped along next to Nolan toward the fire. He needed to make his own camp tonight and do some thinking.

To say it wasn't fair that Matthew had been shot down was just plain foolish. Nathanial, too, could have been killed just as easily in that stagecoach. That wouldn't have been right either. To keep treating him as a son though, it was just ripping his heart open instead of putting it back together.

Nolan felt a small hand slip into his and looked down. Nathanial happily smiled. The boy was leaning on that unspoken promise again. It was hard not to return that affection. For him to reach out without pause showed that Nolan had indeed gained his full trust. It was something special that the half-pint didn't just give away to anyone. The question was…What would Nolan do with it?

Nathanial released the grip on him and lay down on the blanket. Nolan shucked his coat and dropped it over the boy.

The mountain air got chilly at night. "If you need anything tonight, you find Doc. I'm riding out of camp."

Nathanial popped up like a jack-in-the-box and grabbed hold of Nolan's sleeve.

"You won't forget me, will ya? You'll come back and git me in the morning, right? The captain would probably leave me here if you don't." Nathanial's eyes welled up.

Forget this boy? That feat couldn't be done. Not by Nolan anyway. He was still half leaning on that promise himself. Nathanial was all Nolan's mind would be thinking on through the wee hours. He doubted sleep would find him for even a few minutes, being that he was so mixed up. There was an ache in Nolan to give Nathanial the name of Crosson, but how could he overlook who the boy's pa was and forget what he'd done? Not that Nolan was holding a grudge against Nathanial for Jim Younger's crime. It was the picture in his mind of Mary and Matthew dying inside that stagecoach that he would see every time he looked on Nathanial. That kind of pain Nolan couldn't live with every day.

"Git some sleep. I'll see ya in the morning."

Nolan didn't sleep a wink and solved nothing in his mind where Nathanial was concerned. Day was breaking when he rode into the soldiers' camp. He was tired, and his mood was foul until Nathanial jumped up from where he'd been sitting next to the fire. Swallowed inside the big coat, he took off running toward Nolan, tripping twice from the coat waist hanging low down over his feet. The boy hit the dirt, bounced up, and kept on running. Nolan couldn't help but grin. All the while, Nathanial wore a smile on his little face.

"You came back for me."

Nolan reached down and grabbed Nathanial's wrist to swing the boy up to sit on the saddle in front of him. He ruffled the snowy patch. "Did you sleep well…stay warm enough?" The morning air was chilly. The ground held a mist just above the grass. He pulled the coat collar up around Nathanial's ears.

"Yes, sir."

Nolan stepped down, leaving the boy to sit astride the bay. Keeping the reins in his hand, he walked toward the fire in hopes of finding some hot coffee. Soldiers everywhere were pulling tent posts and packing up camp.

In the days that followed, Nathanial might as well have been in Nolan's back pocket. The half-pint had become his shadow, never leaving his side. Everyone around them treated them like father and son. Mostly, that didn't bother Nolan. Even Captain Farnsworth had eased up some. Nolan's mind wavered so damn much on adopting Jim Younger's son—if that were even possible, considering the outlaw was still alive and would have to sign over his rights to the child.

Hell, Nolan was about ready to flip a damn coin to settle the matter. He just needed to forget it for now and get his mind back on tracking down Jones. It wouldn't be easy.

Nathanial, who was lounging back against him in the saddle, sat up straight, gave a nudge to Nolan's gut, then pointed. Nolan grinned. There, lying in the grass, were several busted wagon spokes. It had only taken a glance to figure it all out.

The captain pulled up on the reins next to Nolan and Nathanial.

"Captain, all these different tracks coming and going…Jones had to have been here the better part of the day, fixing that busted wheel. The women ain't more than an hour or two in front of us at best." Nolan wasn't going to get too excited. They'd been this close before, and Jones had managed to slip away.

"We've gained a good bit of ground. Excellent." The captain grinned and slapped Nolan's shoulder.

"Captain Farnsworth, sir, do you need Nolan and me to scout farther ahead?" Nolan took note of Nathanial's respectful tone.

"It's Nolan and I, not Nolan and me." For whatever reason, Nolan thought he should correct Nathanial.

The half-pint rolled them baby blues, then turned back to waiting for orders from the captain.

"All right. Watch for ambush...Jones knows we're behind him."

Two days later, they were still following the wagon tracks. Judging by the hoof marks in the dirt, the stride length showed that Jones had been running the wagon to gain back the ground he'd lost. It was no surprise when they came across a burned-out homesteader and saw that the dirty bastard had switched horses. The run-down, lathered beasts were left standing on quivering legs in the yard.

A man was found dead by the barn, shot in the head. Two children, a boy and a girl, also had their lives taken from them. The little boy couldn't have been any older, maybe even younger, than Nathanial. There was no sign of the man's woman. She was gone like the other women had all been taken. This woman was probably a replacement for the ones Jones had lost. Dammit. They were always one step behind.

Nolan picked up the wagon's trail after the soldiers planted the family. They rode as a group with the sun fading in front of them.

After a few more days of following, both Nolan and the captain were in agreement. Jones seemed to be headed toward a little town about a week's ride away. This was pleasing news. They needed to rid themselves of the women and put the boy somewhere safe before they caught up to Mr. Jones and his crew.

Nolan looked down at Nathanial, resting back against him in the saddle, fast asleep. A clear decision hadn't come to him as of yet. He was growing too used to having the mischievous boy around. Though he still pictured Mary's and Matthew's faces in that stagecoach when he looked at Nathanial. Over time, could he honestly let it all go and be a good father to him? It was a question he might never be able to answer.

CHAPTER 17

THE TOWN was not unlike any other Nolan had ridden through. One muck-filled street lined with buildings, holding businesses from dressmaking to banking. A white church stood at the edge of town, along with a cemetery. It made him think about marrying Kate and what a difference having a loving mother could make in Nathanial's life.

Nolan stepped out of the saddle in front of the jailhouse, as did the captain. A few of the soldiers helped the women down off their mounts. Nolan's little shadow slid off the horse, walking fast to keep pace next to Nolan.

"You wait here." Nolan pointed the boy to sit on a long bench just outside the sheriff's door.

He thought it best the boy not hear firsthand what was said about his placement somewhere. Nathanial had tried to run off before when he'd thought Nolan was trying to leave him behind. It wasn't right to let him keep believing that he, too, would be riding out after Jones once the army was ready to leave this place. But Nolan didn't have the guts to tell him yet. A big part of him didn't want to let go of Nathanial, not even for just a bit while he trailed down Jones's gang.

Nolan closed the door behind him so Nathanial hopefully would not be able to overhear. He tipped his hat at a deputy sitting just inside the door at a small table, playing a game of solitaire.

The sheriff stood and came around his desk to greet both Nolan and the captain with a handshake. "What can I do for you gents?"

It wasn't Nolan's place to explain the army's business. He would let the captain do the talking, but he wanted to know for certain that Nathanial would not be forgotten to run the streets. His mind wouldn't be at ease until he knew for a fact that Nathanial would be looked after while he was gone and until he decided what to do with the boy.

"We're in need of passage on the stage for two women. I will telegraph ahead and arrange for next of kin to be ready to take them in. I would greatly appreciate if you or your deputy could escort them partway for safekeeping. The man who stole them might try to take them back again. Deegan Jones is capable of just about anything."

The sheriff nodded. "I'll send my deputy."

Nolan cleared his throat, interrupting the two. "There is also the matter of the boy."

"Boy?" The sheriff raised a brow and eyed Nolan.

"Is there a town orphanage?" The captain interjected.

Oliver Twist came to Nolan's mind. He'd never forgotten that sad story and could easily picture Nathanial in the lead role.

The sheriff rubbed his head. "The closest orphanage is in Three Springs, and that's two, three hundred miles away."

Nolan had figured that Nathanial's care wouldn't be as simply solved as it'd been for the women. No one would have to keep a close eye on two full-grown females until stage arrangements were made and the women boarded. The boy, on the other hand, required constant looking after. None of this was sitting well with Nolan.

The captain stepped behind the sheriff's desk and stood front and center before a tacked-up map of the territory.

"Sheriff, whatever you decide to do with the boy is fine with me. My concern is Jones. Let me show you our trail so far, and maybe you could point out where any homesteaders are settled that we might be able to place ourselves between them and Jones." Captain Farnsworth had just brushed Nathanial away like dirt off the man's boots.

What the hell was Nolan to do? The road to Three Springs passed straight through some mighty rough country. He could be sending Nathanial straight toward more trouble. What if he did take Nathanial with him? Even after being notched with an arrow, the half-pint was holding up well. Given his background, he was used to being on the run. The army's fight with Jones would end eventually. Hell, even Doc seemed glad to have the boy with him when he needed him. But after all that, if they survived, what would Nolan do with the kid?

He had half a damn headache. He didn't want to hear the captain rehash their encounters with Jones to the sheriff. Worrisome thoughts about Nathanial were stuck in his mind. The little tomcat was feisty and used to running free. No doubt, Nathanial would be miserable locked up inside an orphanage. Who would adopt him after hearing the dirty little mouth cocking off? Most folks were probably looking for an easy child or a strong farmhand. Nathanial was neither. The half-pint's attitude wasn't the only thing stacked against him. Nolan was guilty of pushing away from him because of the Younger name. It certainly wouldn't be a motive for a potential family to take a shine to the youngster. Quite the opposite.

The tightness of the small jailhouse seemed to be closing in on him. He needed to take a breather. Nolan left the sheriff and the captain talking in the stale air. He stood on the boardwalk. The breeze should have been refreshing.

What would happen if Nathanial ran off from the stage en route to Three Springs? Being a child wouldn't guarantee his life would be spared if he found himself caught by the redskins. Though Jones's men were just as savage. They wouldn't hesitate to put a bullet in the kid. No. The boy could not go with Nolan.

What if he were to send Nathanial on a stage to Kate in Gray Rock? When Nolan had first made his silent promise to be a good father to Nathanial, that was where he had intended to go with the child. Kate had spoken many times about them starting a family. This probably wasn't what she'd had in mind, but he could send a letter explaining it all. He knew Kate too well, and she would never turn away any child who was in need. Her ranch would be the best place for the little boy, if Nathanial would go. It'd taken Nolan a long time to gain the kid's trust. It was doubtful that the half-pint would cotton to the idea of being sent away to a stranger.

The bench was empty. Where was that boy? One look down the boardwalk, and Nathanial wasn't hard to find. The half-pint's face was pressed against the window of the general store. Jars of penny candy lined the inside of the glass panes and surely teased any child that might walk by.

"Come on." Nolan motioned with his hand for Nathanial to follow. The boy came running, then walked tall next to Nolan along the boardwalk. Opening the door to the bathhouse, he let Nathanial step inside first. The boy immediately turned to run back outside. Only, Nolan was quicker and grabbed him by the arm. The half-pint wasn't getting away.

"I'm hardly dirty at all. I don't need no scrubbing."

Nathanial could whine all he wanted. He looked as crusty as a ripe old mountain goat and smelled like a barnyard. Nolan shook a finger. He wasn't giving Nathanial a choice. "You'll git in that tub if I have to hog-tie ya to git ya there."

Nathanial stomped a foot and huffed. Nolan didn't care none about a little fit.

A China woman walked toward them after pouring more water in a steaming tub. She was about to earn her day's wage.

"Scrub this mop of hair good." Nolan ruffled Nathanial's white patch. The boy pushed Nolan's hand away but gave him no lip.

The heathen scowled at the bath attendant as she reached out in an effort to pull the filthy rag of a shirt over Nathanial's head. Instantly the boy dodged the woman's attempts. Nolan would have to give that poor woman a good tip for her patience.

"Git your clothes off and git into that tub." Nolan was stern, and Nathanial knew he meant it, because the boy had straightened up for the moment. The rest would be up to the China woman, and good luck to her.

An hour later, Nolan walked into the bathhouse, carrying a surprise for Nathanial. He was greeted by a smiling, squeaky-clean kid.

"Put these on." He handed Nathanial the stack of clothing. The boy's hands didn't move to take the store-bought pants, shirt, and coat from Nolan. His wide baby-blue eyes stared at the items as if they weren't real.

"Those must've cost you plenty. I don't got no money to pay ya back. I could groom the bay or clean your guns or something to earn them."

Nolan placed the clothing in Nathanial's hands. "Just put them on." Was this boy never truly provided for? The man that fathered the child sure as hell stole enough money that Nathanial shouldn't have been wearing worn-out rags.

The half-pint gently fingered each piece before setting the clothing carefully aside on a bench like a basket full of eggs. His little face slowly began to glow like it was Christmas morning. Nathanial quickly stripped off his old shirt, then reached for the new folded one. Seeing the growing excitement in his rosy smile made Nolan grin.

The boy turned, practically dancing on his tippy toes, when a broad white mark across the half-pint's back grabbed Nolan's eye. He caught Nathanial by the wrist and spun the youngster the rest of the way around. If he had to guess, someone had hit him with the buckle end of a belt. Mostly, he was covered in old scabs, little more than flakes of dried-up skin.

"Who put those marks on you?"

The boy's head dropped, and he stared at the floor. His face had flushed a deep red. Nathanial wasn't speaking up but shrank back inside himself.

"Answer me, son." Nolan wasn't harsh. However, he wanted those marks explained.

Nathanial sniffled. "I deserved it," he barely whispered without looking at Nolan.

It took a minute for Nolan to catch hold of what he had said. "I wouldn't beat a stubborn mule this bad." He gently traced his finger along a mix of new and old scars and over a few scabs that were about healed. The half-pint didn't shy away from Nolan's hand. "This one is old. You took this lick before that son of a bitch Harper got his hands on ya?"

Nathanial nodded. The sight of the marked-up little body was sickening and made Nolan see red. This hadn't been the result of a child getting spanked because he did something he shouldn't have. When first Nolan had found the boy, Nathanial's raggedy clothes and foul mouth had spoken of a rough life. He hadn't realized until just now why it was that the boy didn't give trust easily. It made sense after seeing the proof on his tiny body.

Nolan picked up the new shirt and held it open for Nathanial to put his arms through the sleeves. He backed off then and let the boy button the front.

"It's too big." Nathanial's pout told of his disappointment.

"It's the smallest the store clerk had ... You'll grow." Nolan turned and walked to the window while Nathanial finished dressing.

A mother with a baby on her hip and two other little ones hanging on her skirt passed along the boardwalk toward the store. Nolan quickly thought of Kate. She would be a good mother to Nathanial. The street was busy with all sorts of people coming and going, and he could picture Kate and Nathanial walking the street of Gray Rock as happy as the folks he was seeing right now.

A wagon rattled by, then another. A man dressed in working duds carried one end of a spool of wire out of the store. The older boy, who carried the other end, must have been the man's son. They both had the same broad nose and beady eyes. Everywhere Nolan looked, there were families. He couldn't stop thinking of Kate. He and Kate could give Nathanial a completely different kind of life than the boy had ever known.

"How do I look?"

Nolan turned and eyed Nathanial from head to toe. Every stitch of the new goods hung on the boy's small frame. Nathanial held the pants up around his narrow waist. Even the new belt was too big.

"Come here." Nolan hunkered down and pulled his knife. Taking Nathanial's belt, he poked the tip of the blade into the leather and twisted a new hole so it could be tightened further. "Try that."

Nathanial fed the belt through the loops, then snugged it tight. "It fits." The boy was all smiles.

"It sure does … You look good." Nolan pulled a small brown bag of candy from inside his vest pocket and handed it to the half-pint. "Go on while I soak." Nolan nodded toward the door for Nathanial to git.

Nate took the bag, went outside, and plopped down on a bench near the laundry door. Nolan had already given him too much. The clothes were a grand gift, and he wouldn't ever forget it. Two surprises in one day. All his birthdays put together hadn't been this wonderful.

He opened the brown bag and peered inside. "Candy." What a treasure he held in his hands, a full bag. There were red, green, yellow, and purple gumdrops and cherry-red licorice whips, and it was all his.

He looked over his shoulder at the door of the bathhouse. No man had ever treated him so fine. He wouldn't forget to say thank you.

Which color should he eat first? He picked a purple gumdrop out of the bag and popped the sweet, sugary treat into his mouth. "Aw, yeah." Never had he tasted anything better. Nate didn't believe any of the people going about their business all around him could possibly be as happy as he was right then. The only thing that could make this day better would be if Nolan decided to lay claim on him.

Maybe the two of them could live somewhere in a busy town like this one. Everyone looked to be smiling and talking friendly with one another. A group of boys kicked a tin can around the street, playing some sort of game. How hard could it be to fit in with others his age? They were kicking a damn can, for pity's sake. Surely Nate could do that. It did look like fun.

The same reasons popped into his head as to why no one would ever want to keep him. There was no sense in dreaming about a family. It was a lie to think he could ever have such a life as those kids. Nate did have one hope for his future. Maybe after the army caught the fancy man, he could stay on as a scout with Nolan. The fine gifts were proof that Nolan liked him well enough to spend a good amount of money on him. Pa had never done that.

A horse blew close by, and Nate looked across the street at the small herd in the corral at the livery. He shoved candy in his mouth. A roan drinking from the trough caught his eye. It couldn't be. Maybe this really was Nate's lucky day. He stood and hurried over to have a closer look. He stepped between the wooden fence rails. It sure did look like Mr. Harper's saddle horse. Nate patted the mare's neck, then rubbed his hand along the length of the animal. There was one way to find out. He squatted down, looked for the scar, and found it. He grinned. Mr. Harper was dead, so Nate would claim the roan.

"Horse thieves git hanged around here." That deep voice was Nolan's. Nate spun around to see him grinning as he walked toward him.

Nate slipped back through the fence rails. "Guess what?"

"You filled your belly with candy, an' now you ain't hungry for supper." Nolan eyed the little brown bag in Nate's hand.

"No, sir, I'm starving." Nate forgot about the horse because he couldn't wait to bite into something hot and juicy. He was sick of eating army beans.

They took their supper at the only restaurant in town. Nolan chuckled to himself at the half-pint's wide-eyed awe. Nathanial was sitting on his knees, spinning around on the chair seat, and taking in every inch of the hotel dining room. The rich-colored drapes hung beyond the length of the windows all the way to the floor. Each table was topped with a lace runner and centered with a small vase of fresh-smelling yellow flowers. A painted picture of fruit in a bowl hung on one wall. And all the wood trimmings looked to have been primly polished.

"Sit on your bottom before you fall off that chair." Nolan tapped a finger on the table, also motioning to sit. Nathanial quickly did as he was told and looked stiff trying to sit proper while still trying to look around.

The time was such that the dining room was stuffed full with noisy folks who all seemed to be talking at once while waiting for their meals. This wasn't the place for Nolan to spring the plan to be sent to Gray Rock on Nathanial. He could definitely foresee the hissy fit the little hellcat would throw down at being tomahawked from chasing after Jones.

A stocky woman with her hair pulled up in a tight bun came to the table. "What can I git for you boys?"

"I'll have the steak, eggs if you have them, pie, and coffee. Do you have milk for the boy?"

She nodded, then pleasantly smiled at Nathanial. "Aren't you as cute as a button? You want the same vittles as your pa?" Her buttery voice somehow matched the woman's round face.

Nolan didn't see the need to correct her. Hearing himself called Nathanial's father didn't feel all that strange to him. He looked at the boy, who hadn't answered. Nathanial's brow was raised, and he sat quiet, just staring at Nolan. Perhaps he was waiting for a contradiction.

"The lady asked you a question. Answer her."

Nathanial quickly smiled. "Do you have fried chicken?"

"I sure do, sweetheart. And I'll put some fried potatoes on the side. You look to need a little fat on your bones." She left them then. Not fifteen minutes later, she reappeared and set two steaming plates, one in front of each of them, on the table.

Nolan waited until the waitress walked away to another table. "Don't you eat like a pig. Use your fork and spoon, not your fingers. And chew with your mouth shut." Nolan began to cut a piece of steak.

Nathanial picked up the fork, all thumbs, as if he'd never held a utensil before this moment. Nolan was embarrassed for the half-pint.

They ate quietly while listening to all the different conversations muttered together from the surrounding tables. Maybe Nolan should just get it off his chest and tell Nathanial the truth about being sent away. So far, though, their meal had been enjoyable. It would be a damn shame to ruin that. Nolan looked over at the half-pint, who'd scarfed down all except a bite of potatoes that was left on his plate. He tore into the chicken like a dog that was thrown a scrap.

"Slow down before you choke. No one's gonna take it from ya." Nolan was only half done with his steak, and Nathanial was already licking his greasy fingers.

The boy would likely be more than disappointed after Nolan explained that the kid wouldn't be going with the army and would be shipped to live with a woman he didn't know in a strange town. How could Nolan look at that too-cute smiling face and even think about disappointing Nathanial? There was a small window of time left before he would have no choice except to tell him.

"Don't you lick that plate." Nolan pointed a finger at him.

The waitress appeared at the table with two pieces of pie. And that's when Nolan saw the ornery twinkle in Nathanial's baby blues. He sat back, wiped his mouth, and waited to see what Nathanial had up his sleeve. The half-pint was wearing a long pout aimed at the waitress.

"Darling, what has you looking so sad? Don't you like my chicken?" The woman smoothed Nathanial's hair, then lifted the little chin.

The little stinkpot dabbed at false tears with his napkin. Nolan thought it nearly looked real. "Your cookin' is so good. It reminds me of…Mama's…God rest her soul. I miss her so much."

Nolan couldn't help but grin. Oh, this boy was full of piss and vinegar.

"Pa won't let me lick the plate. Ma always let me lick up the chicken grease." The boy falsely wiped at his eyes again. Nolan burst out laughing.

The woman's fierce scowl sobered him right quick. She hugged the ornery little cuss tight to her skirt. "Hush now, sweet pea. No reason to cry. You lick that chicken grease off the plate. No one will say a word, or I'll take care of them. That includes your pa." She turned a wagging finger on Nolan. "If you want that coffee topped off, then I suggest you keep quiet and eat the rest of your steak."

"Yes, ma'am." It was all Nolan could do to keep from laughing as the little coyote batted his baby blues and sweetly smiled at the woman. Nathanial was buttering her up thick.

"You surely do remind me of Mama." The boy sniffed.

The woman patted his little hand in hers. "I'll bring you some more milk, you sweet little thing." The waitress walked away into the kitchen.

Nathanial picked up the plate and began licking.

Nolan laughed. "I see you know how to work the heartstrings of the ladies." The boy's smile stretched from ear to ear. Nolan shook his head. *Unbelievable.* "Could you at least wipe your mouth on your napkin and not your shirtsleeve?"

"Yes, sir."

Nolan had just finished his coffee when Captain Farnsworth and two of his men marched up to the table. "We're ready when you are, but please do finish your pie first."

Nolan didn't appreciate the captain's unfriendly tone. "I plan on it." He forked a big bite into his mouth directly in front of the captain.

"The women have to be close. The clerk at the store recognized Jones from a wanted poster. He bought supplies not two hours ago." Captain Farnsworth's fists hit the table, and he leaned across toward Nolan.

The captain's impatient glare didn't bother him none. There wasn't a man that drew breath that he had a fear of.

Nolan smirked. "I plan on eating every crumb … since it ain't beans. Then I'll pick up Jones's trail. You'll get your man."

The captain's angry stare then turned against Nathanial. "I hope you enjoy your time in Three Springs."

Nolan instantly dropped his fork, jumped to his feet, and was standing nose to nose across the table with Captain Farnsworth. "You best shut your mouth." Nolan felt a small tug on his sleeve but ignored Nathanial for the moment. The captain didn't know he had other plans for the boy, but that didn't matter.

"Where's Three Springs? We going there after the fancy man?" Nathanial's innocence tore at Nolan.

It was the captain's turn to smirk. "Don't choke." Captain Farnsworth turned and quickly marched out of the restaurant with his men on his heels.

"Nolan, what was the captain talking about? Why are you mad at him?" The boy stared up at him.

What a headache Nolan was brewing. "Forget it. Everything is fine. Just sit down an' eat your pie." He flopped down in the chair. The dining room had gotten quiet. Everywhere he looked, people stared questioningly at him. He didn't care about them. Time had run out, and still, Nolan couldn't seem to find the words.

Nathanial forked the last piece of pie into this mouth. He'd scooted his chair closer to Nolan. Captain Horse's Ass must have scared the child a little.

How was Nolan to tell Nathanial that he would be sent out on the next stage headed to Gray Rock, and in the meantime, he would be left in the care of the sheriff?

Nolan stood from his chair and tossed money on the table. His little shadow was on his heels out the door. Every step down the boardwalk and closer to Nolan's horse was getting harder to take. He hadn't ever seen Nathanial smile so much in one day. Damn. He was about to break that happy spirit. Knowing, too, that he was minutes away from leaving Nathanial ripped Nolan apart.

"You wait here." Nolan opened the door to the jailhouse and went in. He explained exactly what he wanted done with Nathanial and then handed the sheriff money for the boy's stage ticket and anything else he might need between now and arriving at Kate's. "You got any paper and something to write with?" He waited while the sheriff rooted in a drawer, then produced a sheet and a pencil.

Nolan turned his back and quickly scripted everything he thought he should say to Kate. He folded the paper, went back out, and found Nathanial waiting right where he had told him to stay.

They headed toward the bay. Nolan fiddled with the paper in his hand.

Nolan tightened the girth strap on his saddle, and the crinkle of the paper seemed too loud. He then picked up the reins from the hitch rail and thought he'd better check his stirrups. He also straightened his saddlebags and bedroll.

Nathanial stood right next to him. Half a licorice whip was hanging out of the boy's mouth. Part of being a good father meant sometimes saying no. Nolan knew the boy expected and wanted to go after Jones. Surely everything would smooth out once Nathanial got to Gray Rock and met Kate.

Nolan hunkered down and handed Nathanial the letter with Kate's name written on the front of it. "Sorry, son, you're staying here for now." Nolan straightened and stepped into the saddle. He could hardly look at the boy. Nathanial's glassy eyes cut straight through his heart. "The sheriff's gonna look after you till…" Nolan choked on what he still needed to say.

What the hell was he doing leaving Nathanial there, basically alone? If he rode fast, he could have Nathanial at Kate's ranch in a week's time. Then it would be another seven-day spell until he caught back up with the army, and Captain Farnsworth would never tolerate two weeks without a scout.

Nolan cleared his throat. "The sheriff will put you on the stage to Gray Rock. You'll be going to live with a friend of mine named Kate James. And I'll come there as soon as I can."

Nathanial's mean little temper exploded, and the boy kicked at the ground, firing dirt into Nolan's face. The bay spooked, but Nolan jerked the reins to calm the gelding. Nathanial spit the licorice at Nolan and crumpled the letter in his hand.

"The hell you say! I'm going after Jenny's killer!"

Nolan's eyes narrowed. "If I catch you following, I'll give you a whupping you won't forget." It was a harsh warning to give after seeing all those scars on Nathanial's back from being beaten. Nolan meant it though. Deegan Jones was a dangerous man. Nathanial didn't need that explained to him because he'd witnessed it.

"Why did you change your mind about me? I thought you liked me." Nathanial's eyes welled up with tears. "I told you I'd work off the clothes."

He wiped his sleeve across his face and sniffled. This little boy was much more fragile than he'd ever let on. It wasn't anger Nolan saw in his baby blues. A trusted someone had caused him to suffer. He had gained Nathanial's trust, and he'd just thrown it back in the boy's face by leaving him there. And God only knew how long Nolan would be chasing Jones. It might be months until he could ride to Kate's ranch and be with the boy.

"You lied! You promised you wouldn't leave me! I hate you!" Everyone on the street stopped and looked. Nathanial sobbed, and all the pitiful tears streaked his little face. Those words struck Nolan harder than any fist could have.

Leaving Nathanial behind was for his own good. A father didn't just say yes because his boy was upset. Nolan wiped at his eyes and then began to turn the bay.

Nathanial grabbed hold of Nolan's leg and wasn't letting loose. "Please, take me with you. I don't want to go nowhere else but with you."

The captain and his soldiers were up ahead, waiting for Nolan at the edge of town. He almost didn't care about tracking Jones. Nothing was worth the bond he'd already broken. Nathanial would probably never trust another soul. *Dammit.* Leaving the half-pint just didn't feel right, even if it was just for a spell. The little fella would be alone and probably scared.

Nolan had given his word to Captain Farnsworth's superiors that he'd stay on as scout for however long the captain needed him to help ensure Jones's capture. This was the only sure way of keeping Nathanial safe.

"Son, I won't put you in trouble's path, and I ain't leaving ya forever. Just till the army captures Jones. Then I'll ride to Gray Rock as fast I can." It caused Nolan hurt to have to shake Nathanial off. "You go on now and stay with the sheriff." He spurred the bay and trotted away from the sound of Nathanial pitifully crying after him.

Nolan glanced over his shoulder. His little shadow just stood in the street, longingly staring. He had made a decision, for now, to keep Nathanial away from Jones and his savage men. This was the right thing for the boy.

CHAPTER 18

NATE WIPED HIS SLEEVE across his eyes. Pretending to be someone's friend was heartless. He looked down over himself and realized again that these new clothes were evidence that Nolan did care. Nate would never ever forget a minute of his time with the scout.

After Jenny's death, Nolan had become his best friend. If he could capture the fancy man, that just might prove his worth to Nolan. He'd had to convince Pa lots of times that he shouldn't be thrown away. And Nate planned on catching Jenny's killer anyway.

He rubbed his eyes. He wasn't any worse off than any other time in his life. When he'd started out after the fancy man, he'd been alone. Within the hour, he'd be ready to ride after Mr. Deegan Jones. Nate shoved the balled-up letter into his pocket, spun on his heel, and went for his horse. He'd read the letter later and see what Nolan had promised to the woman whose name was on the paper. Pa always had to pay cash when he'd dumped Nate with someone.

Nate hightailed it toward the livery, which was at the other end of town. He slipped into the corral and aimed to take what he saw was rightly his. He'd slaved for Harper over a year and had nothing to show but the marks on his back that Nolan had gotten ticked off about. That roan filly that used to belong to Mr. Harper should belong to Nate.

"Boy, where do you think you're going with that horse?" A tall, thin man with a mean, leathery face charged out from inside the open doors of the livery. The lead rope was yanked from Nate's hand.

"What the hell, mister?"

Nate was ignored. The old goat walked the roan off the street back toward the corral.

"Mister, I own that horse." Nate ran and put himself between who he guessed was Leroy Green and the corral gate. The big letters painted above the livery doors stated the proprietor's name.

"Git, kid." The roan's lead rope was whipped around and struck.

Under Nate's shirt, a welt instantly began to grow across his chest. It barely missed his neck. Tears blurred his eyes. The roan sidestepped at the second strike of the rope and nearly trampled Nate. The mare threw its head and pranced nervously. Nate dodged another lash while trying to keep from being stepped on by the horse. His back stung like hell from yet another slash. He jumped back, tripped over his own damn feet, hitting the ground, and dirt puffed up around him.

Before he could move, he was clutched around the scruff of his neck. He kicked out like a mule and thumped the man's shin, which made him let go. Thank God. Nate could breathe again. A firm hand grabbed and yanked him off the ground. Nate quickly wished Nolan were there. Then this bastard wouldn't be putting a hand on him. Nate twisted wildly to get free. The man jerked him around, shaking him until Nate wasn't sure which way was straight. But he was positive that he was being dragged down the street toward the sheriff's office.

Leroy Green wasted no time in telling the sheriff all kinds of lies.

"I'm telling you that horse is mine!" Nate stood tall behind his words.

The sheriff tapped his pencil on the desk and seemed to consider it.

"Sheriff, this boy is a thief. I seen how the army dumped him here. That's probably why."

Who was this pickled-faced jackass to confidently accuse Nate of anything?

"The roan belonged to Mr. Harper." It had just blurted out. The sheriff had to know of Mr. Harper. Captain Farnsworth surely had told the lawman about the massacred wagon train.

"There's a bow-shaped scar." Nate touched around his ankle, though he was talking about the horse. "Fur won't grow in that spot anymore. The mare got tangled in some wire." It was all the explanation he could give. It had to be enough to prove he wasn't a liar.

"Let's go see this scar." The sheriff stood. Out the door they went, and the sheriff walked between Nate and his enemy. "Leroy, git the horse." The sheriff pushed the thin man toward the corral. A few minutes later, Leroy had a rope around the roan, leading the animal through the gate.

"I don't see a scar, you dirty little horse thief." The skinny old bastard smirked with the sweet satisfaction of thinking he'd won this battle.

Nate wasn't done fighting yet. The sheriff's eyes narrowed. It seemed he believed the old bony stick. Nate bent down, and then he brushed back the overgrown fur hiding the bow-shaped scar.

The stinky old fart spit a wad of tobacco juice at Nate. He'd just barely sprung out of the way. Leroy Green was damn lucky no spit had splattered his new clothes. He'd have told the livery man a thing or two and probably have gotten himself in big trouble.

"Leroy, give the boy his horse." The sheriff jerked his head toward Nate.

Nate smirked at the old goat.

"That'll be a dollar for the feed I've given that horse." Leroy held out his hand to collect what Nate didn't have. Golly geez, why wouldn't the stubborn mule just give up on this fight? They both had heard the sheriff.

"Shut up, Leroy." The sheriff grabbed the lead rope away, tossing it to Nate.

One item down and one to go before he could leave town.

He rubbed at his chest where the rope had stung him as he followed the sheriff back to the jailhouse. This wouldn't have happened if Nolan hadn't left him. Water came to his eyes, but he shook it off.

He looped the lead rope over the hitch rail, then tailed the sheriff inside. He eyed the jailhouse from a chair where he'd plopped down, then found what he was looking for.

"You need something kid? I have work to do, so why don't you git out of here?" The sheriff jerked a thumb toward the door.

This would be one of the easiest jobs Nate ever pulled. The window behind the potbellied stove was open a small crack. Outside that window was an alleyway. Nate would hide there until the sheriff went to supper. Then he'd slip in through the window, grab his rifle, and be quickly on his way. There would be plenty of daylight to put some miles between himself and this town before the sheriff noticed him missing. If the man gave Nate any thought at all.

The regiment of fresh tracks on the roadway were not hard for Nate to follow, but they were running their horses a lot, which made it hard to catch up. For three long days, he ran after memories that made him lonely for Nolan. Especially after Nate had read his letter, which was all about becoming a family with a woman named Kate. Sleep never seemed to want to comfort Nate at night. Jenny's ghost haunted him when he closed his eyes. Worse, when he'd jolted awake, Nolan wasn't there to make him feel safe.

There was no sense in feeling sorry for himself. It wouldn't get him any closer to catching the fancy man.

———✦———✦———

Nolan had sighted Jones and his caravan resting in the shade just off a coach road. Captain Farnsworth had then secretly led his army to station themselves in a way that Jones would ride right smack into them. Men were positioned in wait along both sides of the heavily tree-lined road. Nolan lay in the thick underbrush at the top of the hill to overlook the road where Jones and his men would have to come through with that wagon. It was the only path in the area. Nolan pressed his spyglass to his eye, his rifle within reach.

Trees sheltered the roadway and threw shadows every-where to obscure his view. A single someone was riding toward them. A small fella. Maybe Jones had sent a scout ahead. Nolan squinted to see a little more clearly. Looked like a kid. *Aw, not now.* He couldn't be seeing right. *Dammit.* This was partly his fault. He'd been the one who'd taught Nathanial how to read sign, to track.

Jones, with his army of gun hands, certainly would come riding down that road any minute now. Nolan didn't have much time to get Nathanial out of there. He slipped from his position, ran down the hillside, and stepped out onto the dusty lane not far behind Nathanial. The half-pint must not have been able to find any prints to follow because he was slowly circling the roan and studying the ground. Nathanial had learned well—that lesson anyway. Though he'd forgotten the one about keeping his ears open to what was going on around him.

Nolan stepped up next to the roan. Nathanial's gaze was still on the dirt, searching for tracks. Nolan grabbed the horse's bridle. Nate jumped out of his skin, his eyes widening at the sight of Nolan looking none too happy.

"I oughta whup ya, but you need to git out of here now." Nolan didn't have time for the youngster's nonsense. Plus Nathanial was smart enough to know it was too dangerous for him to be there.

The rattle of an approaching wagon struck Nolan's ears. He turned and looked. *Aw shit.* It was too late. There was no time to duck into the tree line. He and Nathanial were stuck in the open roadway. If they ran, Jones would surely know something wasn't right. His militia would quickly ready themselves to fight. If the captain carried out the plan of ambush, Nolan and Nathanial would be caught in the crossfire.

The kid jumped off his horse and stood tight against Nolan's side. "The fancy man had a good look at me the day he killed Jenny." Nathanial was all but crying, and a puddle grew between the boy's feet.

There was no color in the half-pint's face. Nolan reckoned Nathanial's upbringing had made him wise. A killer wouldn't leave a witness alive to talk, and while Nate might have new clothes and not be recognizable by that part, there was no disguising his snow-white hair.

Nolan grabbed Nathanial by the arm, pulling him to stand hidden behind him. "If I tell you to run, you best do as you're told." He'd kept his voice low so only Nathanial could hear as the wagon stopped directly in front of Nolan.

The half-pint clung, arms full circle, around Nolan's thigh. His little face was buried into the back of his pant leg. Nolan's eyes didn't stray from Jones though. That's where the danger was. Nathanial had been right. Deegan Jones was a frilly dressed man with a smooth curling mustache. No man that Nolan ever saw in these parts wore ruffles on the cuffs or neck of his shirt. The fancy style would have fit better on a woman. The short-brimmed hat, bright-blue dress coat, and matching pants were telling signs of a polished city dude. The killer was a slick, almost slimy-looking fellow. The dandy-painted portrait wasn't one that would easily be perceived as dangerous. It likely had fooled many into trusting him.

There was nothing friendly in Nolan's grin as he nodded to greet the dandy. Nathanial had quite a grip around his leg. He could feel the boy shaking from head to toe and heard him sniffle. Nolan didn't blame the half-pint for being scared. There was a ruthlessness in Jones's eyes that had probably put a fright into all his prey. That pissed Nolan off.

"I told my son he had to finish his chores before going hunting. Boys, they need to learn a lesson now and then." Nolan fiddled with his belt as if he'd just threaded the leather through the loops on his pants, and not once did he take his eyes off Jones.

It wasn't easy to read Jones's sober face. Maybe he wasn't swallowing the lie. If Jones did accept it, then Nolan and Nathanial would appear to be locals. Nathanial, then, shouldn't be recognized or suspected as part of the massacred wagon train.

Not a glance did Nolan make toward the wagon full of women or the personal cavalry of men escorting the goods for safekeeping. He felt the weight of their heavy stares though. There were more than twenty guns to Nolan's one. Hell, he'd take on every one of those hard cases to keep Nathanial safe, and he would start by putting a bullet between Jones's eyes.

The holstered pistol strapped to Nolan's side seemed to be where Jones's distrustful gaze had drifted to.

"Is there a problem?" Nolan's hand came up easy and rested on the butt of his revolver. The fancy son of a bitch stretched his neck a bit to look around Nolan at Nathanial. "My boy is shy. I don't much take to strangers either, so why don't you be on your way?"

A meanness had stirred up inside Nolan, seeing the way Jones was studying the half-pint. His tolerance of Deegan

Jones was done. It'd only take one wrong twitch, and he'd blow Jones off that wagon seat.

"I'll leave you to your business." Jones's voice was too smooth for Nolan's liking.

Had Jones recognized the boy from the wagon train? If so, Nathanial was now a target.

The wagon lurched forward and rolled away. Nolan never turned his back until the buckboard rattled around a bend and Jones, along with his twenty armed horsemen, were no longer in sight.

Nolan pulled the boy off him. "What in the hell were you thinking coming after that man? You could have gotten yourself killed." Before Nathanial could utter a word to argue, Nolan unbuckled his belt, pulled the leather from his pant loops, and folded it in his hand. "I warned you what would happen if you followed me."

Nolan threw the brat, who was already bawling, over his knee. The leather cracked across Nathanial's backside three hefty licks. Nolan jerked the boy up from his bent-over position to stand and face him.

"You steal that horse?" Nolan pointed to the roan with the folded belt strap.

"No, sir." Nathanial whimpered through his sobs while rubbing at his backside.

Nolan hosed Nathanial up and flopped him onto the roan's back. "Git the hell back to that town where I know you're safe. You're supposed to be on the stage, an' Gray Rock is where I better find you."

Nolan slapped the horse's rump. It shot off at a run. The half-pint whiplashed back, almost falling off.

Nolan turned in the direction that the wagon full of stolen women had just gone. The roadway was empty, but he could hear a single rider coming. Jones was showing himself to be a cautious man by sending one of his paid guns back to kill both

Nolan and the boy. There was no other sensible explanation for why one of those men would return this way so soon.

Nolan stood in the open and waited. A black horse with a white blaze, carrying who could have been any man with a tied-down gun, came riding around the bend. Only, this wasn't just any hired gun. Nolan knew Tucker Brown's ugly face from a wanted poster he'd seen. He'd forgotten about seeing Tucker a few weeks ago at Jones's river camp, and since Nolan hadn't chanced taking his eye off Jones at all, he hadn't been able to see who all was riding with the filthy man.

Tucker slowed his horse to a walk, then pulled up on the reins. He stayed seated in the saddle. The leather creaked as he shifted his weight and leaned forward on the horn as if to casually talk. Nolan knew from rumors that Tucker was a lefty. That hand was still on the reins, not even close to his pistol.

"Nolan Crosson. How the hell are ya? It's been a long time." By Tucker's sneer, Nolan knew the words weren't meant as friendly. And he had no reason to think they should be.

"I don't recall that we've met." Nolan's mind would not be distracted with idle chat. That could get him killed.

"Well, that is true in the formal sense. We've not been introduced. See, I had a bead on the back of you once. My rifle jammed, or I would've blown your head off. You and your posse had just hanged my little brother, Toby." Tucker spit.

"So you were afraid to face me." The story had been told to rattle Nolan's nerve. This smart-ass little prick was doing nothing except pissing him off.

Tucker laughed. What an overconfident dumbass. Nolan might not be as fast on the draw as Tucker Brown, but he wasn't slow with a gun.

"No. It was nothing like that. Shit, I ain't afraid of you. The fellas I was with didn't wanna tangle with ya."

That day rushed to Nolan's mind. It had been completely accidental that the posse had ridden up on the stagecoach

robbery. Thank God they had, or who knows how many innocent folks would've gotten killed? The stage had been packed
full that day.

"Tucker, am I hearing you right? You've just admitted that
you ain't as smart as your friends." Nolan grinned. "I should
have taken time, trailed ya down, then hung the whole bunch
of ya. My mistake. I didn't 'cause I was due to guard a payroll
on the next stage out of town. And I'd lost my taste for little
fish after listening to your stupid shit brother blubbering like
a coward while I slipped a noose around his neck. I guess the
horse-size hole he'd blown through that passenger for not
handing over his gold watch wasn't so funny at that moment.
I suppose you didn't see Toby meet his end, tucking tail and
running the way you did."

Tucker slowly stepped down out of the saddle and then
squared off to face Nolan. Less than ten feet of open dirt and
grassy roadway lay between them. Tucker's left hand was
posed naturally close to the butt of the .38 in the holster. Their
narrowed eyes were locked on one another. Two mean bulls
and neither one of them was going to budge. "Where's the
towhead?"

"I sent him home." Dammit. Nolan should have resigned
for a short time, taken Nathanial to Kate's, then rejoined the
captain. His hand, too, was just grazing the handle of his pistol.

Chances were shooting it out with the slick gun wouldn't
go well for Nolan. Tucker likely would then track Nathanial
down and finish the job Jones wanted done. Nathanial best be
hightailing it miles from there.

Nolan's trigger hand was itching for Tucker to make his
move. One of them would not be getting back on his horse
today. A slight twitch of the gunslinger's hand gave him away
a second before he drew. Nolan's pistol cracked in his palm as
he threw himself into the tree line. Tucker's gun fired without
aim into the air.

Nolan squeezed the trigger a second and third time, keeping his aim on Tucker's chest. Tucker twisted one direction, then the other. He dropped to his knees, then fell over dead, eating dirt.

Nolan quickly reloaded. When Tucker didn't return, Jones might send out others to hunt and kill Nathanial. If anything happened to the boy, Nolan would never forgive himself. Now that he was really thinking about it, he probably shouldn't have sent Nathanial off. Chances were good that the boy wouldn't go back to that town. He might just run away, and would Nolan ever find him again?

Captain Farnsworth and a few of his men hurried from their positions hidden among the thick, leafy trees and rock clusters and joined Nolan. They eyed the dead Tucker Brown, and then the captain confoundedly studied Nolan for a long time.

"After the way Jones had eyed the kid, I'd hoped his whole ramble of men would turn around and come back. He had to know my troop was here somewhere. He'd seen us all in the field that day when he lured us out into the middle. Maybe not well, but good enough to know the kid was with us that day. That's why I waited instead of attacking after he'd gone on. I thought he was trying to get us to chase him again. Instead, he sent one man back. Do you know who that was? We don't have a choice now, thanks to you. Jones might have heard the gunfire. In short time, he'll know there's someone on his heels that is fast enough with a gun to kill Tucker Brown. I believe he'll then run with the women. We'll have to rush the wagon from behind."

"Captain, that strategy is awfully risky. The women could all git killed." Nolan understood though. This was the closest they'd been to possibly taking back the ladies.

"We must charge. If we lose a few of the women in the crossfire...well, I'll take responsibility for that risk." Captain Farnsworth nodded in agreement with his own answer.

They ran their horses. Nolan figured Jones would hear the thundering of the hooves and undoubtedly know the army was coming fast for him. God willing, maybe Jones wouldn't have enough time to ready his men for battle.

The soldiers rounded the bend, Nolan and the captain out front. They hadn't ridden but a hundred yards when a ricochet of gunfire opened on them. Uniformed men dropped from their saddles.

"Ambush!" a soldier yelled out before a bullet ripped open his throat.

Nolan swung his horse into the tree line, then jumped out of the saddle. He hit the ground, rolled, and propped up on his elbows with gun aimed. He squeezed off a shot and missed. A bullet tore through the brush past him.

Jones's men had the advantage of the high ground on the far side of the coach road.

The captain's horse had been killed, and Captain Farnsworth smartly used the dead animal as a barrier to protect himself from the rifle assault. Repeating booms echoed through the valley. The air quickly became clouded with smoke, and the smell of powder burned Nolan's nose.

He fired back at Jones's men, giving cover to those blue boys who were still alive but pinned down on the roadway. Over half the captain's men were dead, their bodies scattered about the ground. By God, it was a damn bloody mess.

Nolan knew better than to think that Jones and the women were there among the fight. No, sir, he was too strategically clever for that. Holding the position of the high ground, Jones's band of thieves could fend off the bluecoats for a long while. Jones, undoubtedly, was fast-pacing the wagon and miles up the road by now.

A bullet zinged past Nolan, and he aimed and squeezed the trigger. He reloaded, then returned cover fire as a soldier ran out of the exposed roadway and toward the trees.

A quick flash of a roan-colored horse caught Nolan's eye. He eased off from firing a shot. There was another glimpse of the running horse. He squinted to see better. A break in the tree line gave him a clear view.

Un-damn-believable.

Maybe it was the glaring sun making him see the little someone that was not meant to be there. He wouldn't sit for a week once Nolan got his hands on that boy. Nathanial fired the Henry into the air. Then a few seconds later, he squeezed the trigger again. What in the hell was the kid doing? Was he trying to get Jones's cutthroats to take a shot at him?

It hit Nolan then. Sporadic gunfire sounding from behind the line of fire might allude that some of the cavalry had flanked Jones's men to the rear. Nolan had seen men panic in battle when they believed themselves surrounded. The fear of dying was a powerful leveler. If Jones's men fell for the boy's trick, it would be just the distraction needed for the cavalry to quickly charge the hillside.

Nolan ran for Captain Farnsworth and quickly shouldered some of the man's weight to stand. They ran from the road into the trees. Now Nolan needed to get Nathanial, that gutsy, brazen little fool, out of there before he got killed. He thumbed shells into his rifle. Captain Farnsworth and his soldiers were already charging the ridge side.

Nate's rifle chamber clicked empty. He quickly shoved his hand into his pants pocket. No more bullets. *Aw shit.* What was he going to do now, and where was Nolan? There were lots of dead soldiers scattered everywhere. Was Nolan one of them? Tears spilled from Nate's eyes, and he almost forgot he was sitting in the middle of battle.

A gun boomed.

Nate grabbed his side and screamed. He'd dropped his rifle, nearly falling off the roan. Something had bitten into him hard along his ribs. The skin under his shirt had instantly become wet. Blood ran through his fingers where he grabbed himself. The deafening boom of guns reverberated between the hills all around him. The growing red stain on his shirt quickly crawled down onto his pants. Another burn bit into the top of his shoulder and sent him spinning backward. He toppled over the roan's rump, hitting the hard ground with a thud.

He gasped, attempting to suck some air back into his lungs. Red streaked from his shoulder and down the chest of his shirt. Something kicked up dirt not an inch from his boot. The roan reared and then shot off running.

Pain overtook Nate's attempt to crawl away. He curled up in the dirt. A bullet smacked the tree trunk next to his head, but all he could do was bawl. The burning inside him was unlike anything he'd ever felt before.

I don't wanna die. The fancy man's gonna win.

Nate's breathing grew ragged, and he could barely choke in air through his sobs. But he couldn't let go of the promise he'd made at Jenny's grave. He needed to stay alive and see that the fancy man got what he deserved.

As he scrambled up the hill to Nathanial, Nolan randomly fired his pistol. One look and his stomach turned. He scooped the boy out of the dirt, tossed him over his shoulder, and then ran. A bullet zinged past them. Still on the run, Nolan turned and squeezed the trigger.

As soon as the gunfire faded behind them, he stopped and then gently laid Nathanial out behind the cover of a thick tree. He frantically tore open the small shirt to see what chance the half-pint had. Nathanial withered in pain and hadn't let up from wailing. It was a strong sign that he had life left in him.

No longer did Nolan hear gunfire. He threw a glance over his shoulder but saw no one retreating. Was the battle over? Had Jones's men fled the high ground?

Nolan needed Doc now. Nathanial's wounds were far worse than he knew what to do with.

"Doc!"

What if he had gotten himself killed? The town where he'd left the boy was four days behind them. Was there even a doctor there?

Nathanial's eyes rolled in his head, and his tiny body fell limp. Nolan put his ear to the boy's mouth. He was breathing, thank God.

Doc came crashing through the trees toward him. Just seeing the medic brought relief. Maybe Nathanial would have a chance now.

Doc dropped to his knees next to Nathanial. "Aw shit." He immediately began looking over the boy's bloody wounds. When he glanced up, Nolan saw tears swimming in his eyes. Doc quickly got to his feet, hurried a few long steps, and yanked a hair from the tail of a stray horse that stood riderless. "This'll have to do. It's all I have."

Doc rooted in his bag, then handed a needle to Nolan.

He shook his head. "What the hell do you expect me to do with that?"

Doc held up his surgical hand wrapped in a blood-soaked bandaged. "I'll hold him down and talk you through where to place each stitch. If they ain't one on top of the other, real tight together, he'll bleed out."

With a shaky hand, Nolan threaded the coarse hair through the needle's eye. Nathanial woke, and his teary stare focused on what was about to jab through his skin. The boy let out a scream to high heaven, and Nolan hadn't even touched him yet. But he had to save Nathanial before he could console him.

Nathanial fiercely shook his head no, but Doc wasn't letting the half-pint squirm away. He forced the boy's shoulders to the ground, then shoved a stick into his mouth to bite down on. This was a living hell. There was blood everywhere, and the more Nathanial fought against the needle, the more he bled.

Nolan took a deep breath, then pushed the needle through Nathanial's skin. The boy certainly had a set of lungs. Nolan's ears were damn near ringing. He didn't care though. Mercifully, after the fourth stitch, Nathanial blacked out.

Doc flopped back and sat against the tree, wiping the sweat from under his hat. "I'm sure glad of that. I don't think I could've taken much more of that pitiful screaming." Then he rolled onto all fours, losing what had been left in his stomach from breakfast.

Nolan understood. Seeing a grown man, another soldier, hurt in battle was never pleasant. Though it was something a fighting man grew used to. In comparison, a bloody child on the verge of dying wasn't easy for anyone to witness. Nolan, too, fought to swallow down an awful sick feeling that had been creeping up from his gut since laying eyes on the deathly pale child.

He stitched as fast and carefully as his unsteady hands would allow. Surely Doc would speak up if he wasn't tugging the skin tight enough. While his hands worked, he glanced up. Doc was closely watching. That made him feel a little bit better.

"I need help over here!"

Both he and Doc looked in the direction of the needful cry. It'd sounded like Captain Farnsworth, but the thick evergreens obscured any view.

Doc hurried to stand. "You done yet?"

Nolan nodded and yanked the strand of horsehair tight before he tied it off.

Doc ran toward a second cry for help and quickly disappeared among the trees.

Nolan sat back on his heels and stared at his hands covered in Nathanial's blood. Nolan's shirt was all red too. He couldn't lose this child the same way he'd lost Matthew. There had to be some other way he could help, but nothing sprang to mind. He needed to breathe.

His mind spun in many directions. Most of the captain's men were killed or injured, and now Nolan was saddled with a half-dead child while Deegan Jones was able, for the time being, to keep all the stolen women. This wasn't just bad luck. It was an act of God.

Nolan scooped Nathanial off the ground. He might not know what to do, but he knew where he needed to be.

Nate's baby blues fluttered open as Nolan carried him toward his bay. "It hurts." He grimaced and squeezed his eyes shut tight. Tears streamed down the youngster's face. The strike of pain must have passed, and Nathanial slowly opened the baby blues again. Tears dripped off his small chin.

"I know it does, son." Next time Nolan saw Jones, the man would eat a bullet.

He stepped into the saddle, holding the limp body across his lap. Nathanial had passed out again, just that quick.

"Nolan, where are you going?"

He wheeled the bay to see Captain Farnsworth getting his arm wrapped by Doc.

"I need you here." With unfettered disgust, the captain eyed the gray-faced little boy cradled in Nolan's arms. "Leave him. He'll most likely bleed out by day's end."

Captain Farnsworth certainly knew how to piss Nolan off. Nathanial wasn't a grown man that chose to put on a uniform and fight.

"This boy just saved your life and mine too. You know he did. If he hadn't drawn their gunfire, where we were on the low ground, Jones's men would have kept shooting till they killed us all."

Captain Farnsworth yanked his hand away from Doc. He tied off the bloodstained bandage while glaring at Nolan. "You agreed to the position of army scout. I will consider you a deserter."

Nolan had his fill of Captain Farnsworth. If the son of a bitch didn't shut his damn mouth, he was going to get his teeth knocked down his throat. Nolan had already lost one son. He would do whatever he could to give Nathanial a chance at living. So be it if that meant leaving the army in the hellish mess they'd found themselves in. The captain was capable of getting reorganized without him.

"I work *with* you, not *for* you. I'll be back soon as I can." As a scout, Nolan had the freedom to leave the ranks when he wanted. Captain Farnsworth knew it too.

Nolan yanked the reins, wheeled the bay, and sank his spurs.

CHAPTER 19

NOLAN STOPPED only to force the boy to sip water. Nathanial fussed on and off when he came to, and his baby blues were never without glassiness. Nolan rode cradling him until darkness began to fall. He'd thought of riding through the night but decided instead that solid rest might do the boy good. And if his horse went lame from running him too hard, then that wouldn't get him anywhere they needed to be either.

The fire crackled, though it did nothing to soothe Nolan's raw nerves. He'd laid Nathanial out close to the flames for warmth, but the heavy coat and saddle blanket hadn't stopped his shivering. Sweat beaded Nathanial's brow, so he knew it wasn't simply the cold. There was no way of nursing a fever from the saddle.

Dammit. They were still three days from Kate's ranch.

Stars twinkled in the sky, but they held no wonder for Nolan on this night. There wasn't so much as a slight wind blowing down from the mountains to move the stale June air. But still a chill seemed to have settled around him and the boy.

Why hadn't Nathanial stayed in that little town?

Nolan's ears caught hold of a slight fussing, and he looked

over. It had been hours since Nathanial's eyes were open. Nolan grabbed the canteen, lifted the boy's head, and touched the rim to his lips.

"Where am I?" The small voice was so weak. Nathanial must have forgotten about his wounds, because he tried to sit up and yelped out in pain. Tears began to run down his little face.

"Lie still. You don't wanna start bleeding again." At Nolan's say-so, Nathanial settled himself, then swallowed a sip from the canteen. Nolan rested the boy's head back against the blanket.

"Am I dying?" Nathanial choked on the words.

Nolan didn't know if he would live or not. There was nothing he could say to give the boy hope.

"You're quiet, so I guess I'm purdy bad off. It's okay. I ain't got no one that'll miss me. I'm glad you're here with me though. Then I won't be so scared when my time comes."

Nolan didn't want to listen to the half-pint's pitiful, frail voice anymore. Nathanial was too much like a son. The thought of burying the pup was damn near killing him. "Shut up and save your strength. I'm takin' ya to someone who can help." But he honestly wasn't sure if Nathanial would make it as far as Kate's.

They were in the saddle before first light. Nolan had wrapped Nathanial tight inside the bedroll, and he slept across Nolan's lap. The shallow rise and fall of the boy's chest was barely noticeable. Time was against them.

When the sun dipped behind the mountain, Nolan chose to ride through the night and took the chance of laming the bay. He'd dozed a little in the saddle only when he needed to. When the sun was overhead, he was still pushing the gelding to cover precious miles. Nathanial had grown a worrisome ashen color, and Nolan hadn't seen those baby blues all day. Once, Nolan had gotten him to drink, but he'd choked up every drop.

Nolan woke in the saddle with the gray of early morning streaking the sky. He felt something warm and wet soaking through his shirt just above his belt buckle. He shifted Nathanial's weight real easylike to reach for the growing wet spot. He dabbed his fingers to his waist, under the boy, but the somewhat awkward position didn't allow for Nolan to see what it was. When he pulled his hand out from his shirt, he stared at the bright red blood on his hand.

Aw no.

Yanking the bay to a stop, he unwrapped Nathanial. The wound where the bullet had split through the ribs had come open.

"Shit!" He'd been real careful not to shuffle Nathanial around much. But it didn't matter how the stitches had come loose. This, Nolan couldn't fix. He was going to lose the boy if he didn't get to Kate's fast.

He madly spurred the bay to run, riding through the day, watching Nathanial grow paler by the hour. Other than a soft moan now and then, Nolan wouldn't have known Nathanial was even alive. He stopped long enough to dig his extra shirt from his saddlebags. A few slices with his knife and the material was cut into strips to use as a bandage. Why hadn't he thought of that earlier?

Nathanial grimaced and fussed a little as Nolan tightened the dressing, which slowed the bleeding. The boy still hadn't opened his eyes though. The fear of burying another child seemed to be coming to fruition.

Nolan cradled Nathanial tighter and kicked the bay.

The sun hung low, fading in the sky, when he rode into the ranch yard. The tidy house with the white picket fence and flowers in the window boxes was just as he'd last seen it. None of that mattered though. He looked down at Nathanial's wan face.

The door of the house swung open. Kate was more handsome than he'd remembered. Her light strawberry hair was pulled up loosely. She wore an apron smeared with evidence of her baking, and the scent of fresh apple pie wafted through the open doorway. Her smile said she was pleased to see him.

Nolan couldn't have been any happier to finally see her. Especially now, with Nathanial being in such a bad way. Kate, a woman, would know how to nurse his wounds in ways Nolan could never live up to. Matthew had always wanted mothering when he'd been sick or hurt.

Nolan stepped with care off his horse, letting the reins fall to the ground. That quick, Kate was standing next to him. As he cradled Nathanial in his arms, she smoothed the boy's fair hair. Without knowing it, she'd given Nolan a new hope that Nathanial would live.

Kate looked at Nolan, her watery eyes searching his face for answers. "What happened? Who is he?"

"Nathanial. And he's bleeding again." Nolan hustled to get him inside the house.

Kate was a step ahead of him. She threw open the door. "Put him there." With one swipe of her arm, she cleared the tabletop. Dishes crashed to the floor.

Nolan laid Nathanial out on the surface. He'd foolishly overlooked Kate's big heart. She'd been aching for another child. He'd known it since they'd met. So what did he do but show up with a dying little boy in his arms? Bringing Nathanial there wasn't fair to her. This was Nolan's concern, not hers. It was too late now though. They both might witness Nathanial drawing his last breath.

Kate swatted his hand away from the front of Nathanial's shirt. Her fingers worked quickly to unbutton the torn and bloody rag. "Git my sewing scissors and needle." She nodded Nolan toward the bottom drawer of a tall standing cupboard as she looked over the ugly half-stitched and seeping wound. "Did you think you were darning a sock? I can't say I've ever seen sewing that bad."

She grabbed the needle and thread from his hands. Just for a moment, Kate stopped and studied Nolan. She'd laid blame on the right person. Tears filled his eyes, and he turned away. He was guilty for not doing more to keep Nathanial safe.

Over and over, the thought of leaving his scouting position to bring Nathanial there had felt so right. But no, Nolan had thrown away that chance after he'd heard the name Younger. Now this little boy who'd put his trust in Nolan was dying.

"Nolan, I'm sorry. I didn't mean to upset you further."

He met Kate's stare. "Just git him stitched up."

She nodded. "Fetch some fresh water. Set it to boil for me. I'll cut some clean bandages before I stitch him."

When Nolan returned from the kitchen, Kate had Nathanial stripped down to nothing and was threading the needle. She glanced up, and there were tears on her face. Nathanial's bruised and bloody body was an awful sight.

Nolan wiped at his eyes. If Nathanial lived, he wanted to give the boy the Crosson name.

"Nolan, you ready?"

He nodded. Kate quickly but gently sponged the wounds clean. Nolan stood over Nathanial where, if needed, he could best hold the boy down from fighting the needle. His gut twisted with each tug of Kate's stitching. Nathanial didn't make a sound or twitch a muscle at the stab of the needle through his skin. The usually foulmouthed, ornery little tomcat should have yelled out or cried, maybe flailed or fought the pain in some way, but the boy showed no sign of health.

Kate began to cry. Nathanial just lay there flat on the slat wood table, looking like death. His lips were gray, the same color as the rest of him, and he was cold to the touch.

Kate hurried off upstairs while Nolan waited over Nathanial for a miracle. He put his ear to the boy's mouth, straining to hear something. Barely he felt a touch of frail breath kiss his skin.

Kate carried a man-size nightshirt in her hands when she returned. "Help me bathe the rest of him."

Nolan's hands were big and clumsy. He did his best though, to turn Nathanial real easylike while Kate sponged off the child. They eased the nightshirt over his head and down over the tiny shoulders.

"Carry him upstairs." Kate's eyes were fixed on Nathanial, her voice like a soft caress.

Nolan carefully lifted Nathanial and cradled the boy. He followed Kate up the steps and then into what had been the room used by her two children. A small desk and chair sat in one corner. Over the desk hung a shelf that held about six children's books. The title on the end facing Nolan was *Goldilocks and the Three Bears*.

The fireplace was cold. He would fetch wood. Nathanial should be kept good and warm.

Kate pulled the blankets back for Nolan to lay him in the full-size bed. It looked as if it would swallow the half-pint. Nolan didn't want to let go and held Nathanial closer.

Kate saw his pause. "Nolan?" She gently laid her hand to his arm where Nathanial's head rested. "I know that sorrow of wanting to keep someone you love wrapped in your arms. We tell ourselves that maybe God won't take that precious life away. This may sound harsh, but there isn't a thing you can do to save Nathanial. He needs rest to let his body heal. And if he loses this battle, then we'll bury him next to my children. I won't lie. I've nursed some bad wounds, but... it's a slim chance this little boy has of surviving. With whatever time you have left with Nathanial, make him comfortable. Let him know you're with him."

In Nolan's mind, he knew all what Kate had said was true. Somehow though, holding Nathanial close made him feel like he was doing something to help the boy get better. Really, it was just a comfort to himself. He bowed his head and touched it against Nathanial's, and he squeezed his eyes tight shut.

Dear God, let this boy live.

Kate rubbed across Nolan's shoulders. He let out a deep, troubled sigh.

His hands shook as he placed Nathanial in the bed, then gently tucked the blankets up around the boy's neck and shoulders. He sat at the edge of the bed, staring at the little wan face. Tears stung Nolan's eyes. Would he be digging Nathanial's grave tomorrow?

Kate sat next to Nolan and slipped her arms around his middle. "If you'd like, I can fix you some supper."

It was kind of her to offer. "I ain't holding much of an appetite."

"Tell me about him." She kissed Nolan's face. His mind flashed to the day he'd ridden up on the feisty pup digging the grave for the Harper woman. The ornery little cuss had been hell-bent on revenge. Nathanial was too tough to die.

"Nolan?" Kate's voice roused him.

"Wagon train. Everyone was killed except Nathanial." Nolan didn't tell Kate that the women had been stolen. She was a strong, brave woman but also a widow who lived alone on her ranch nearly two miles outside of town.

This wasn't Jones's territory. There was no need to scare Kate. She might get trigger happy, hearing the wind, and shoot her damn foot off. She'd had the chance to sell once and move closer to town. He'd pressed her to do so because he worried when he was away from her. She'd somehow turned that talk around to marriage. It had grown into a hell of an argument. Despite that, Nolan could picture him, Kate, and Nathanial becoming a family.

"Does Nathanial have kin somewhere?" Kate nearly had to smack Nolan from his thoughts until he shook his head, giving her an answer.

He touched his hand to the half-pint's clammy brow to check the strength of the fever. "Stay with him."

It wouldn't take him long to get a fire going.

The flames danced, and the room was hot when Nolan pulled a chair up and sat next to Nathanial's bed. He dropped his hat on the bedside table, then shucked his vest. The hour was late. The days of riding to get Nathanial there were catching up to him.

Before he took off his boots, maybe he should ride for a doctor.

He looked at Kate. "Does Gray Rock have a doc?"

"Yes, but Dr. Martin isn't due back from Birch Creek for another few days." She sat down at the edge of the bed with a bowl of hot broth in one hand. "Nathanial." She coaxed the boy sweetly.

Nathanial wasn't waking. Kate rubbed gently at the snowy hair and little face until the baby blues slowly fluttered open. Nolan quickly came to his feet and hovered over the child. The half-pint gave him a faint smile. It hit him like a beam of sunshine on a dark, rainy day.

Kate slowly guided the spoon of broth toward Nathanial's mouth. It was no surprise to Nolan when he shrank away. Kate was a strange face to the distrusting little runt. If they were to be a family though, Nathanial would need to learn that she wouldn't hurt him.

"You let her feed ya. She's a good woman." Nolan smoothed Nathanial's hair.

Nathanial weakly opened his mouth just enough that Kate was able to get the spoon between his lips. It wasn't long before the baby blues drifted shut. Getting five or six bites of nourishment into him, in Nolan's mind, was better than nothing.

Kate set aside the broth, and she smiled at Nolan. "I've missed you."

He'd missed her too. Nolan sat back in the chair and pulled Kate onto his lap. They kissed. Her taste was as sweet as honey. Lord Almighty, how many times had he longed to feel her soft, slender body wrapped in his arms? The fresh new blooms of spring after a long, cold winter weren't as beautiful as she was. How could he have stayed away so long?

He glanced past Kate at Nathanial neck deep under a pile of quilts. There was now a touch of pink in the boy's cheeks. Maybe it was just the blazing-hot room, but it gave Nolan a small hope. This was the family he'd been aching for. Only, now it might be too late.

Kate kissed Nolan. The tender affection pulled his mind straight back to her lovely face. He swept her up into his arms as he stood, pushing back the chair. Then he carried her to the bedroom they shared each time he visited.

◆——————◆

Nolan stretched sleepily across the bed and felt for Kate. The blankets were still warm where she'd been lying. It was no great effort to figure out she must be in Nathanial's room. She was the mothering type. Surely if Nathanial had gotten worse or—he hated to think it—passed on, Kate would have woken him.

Nolan threw back the blankets and sat straight up at the edge of the bed. Outside the window, the dark of night still covered the land. He rubbed at his tired eyes. Had he even slept an hour? Judging by the weariness in his bones, he doubted it. He stretched, then stood to go check on Nathanial.

The house was too quiet for Nolan's liking. What he wouldn't give to hear Nathanial's smart mouth going off about something or other. He leaned against the doorframe and listened. Kate was sitting in a way that her back was facing him.

"Don't you worry none. Nolan didn't leave you. He's resting, the same as you should be doing." Kate tucked the blankets in around Nathanial. She then turned and smiled, seeing Nolan standing there. He knew the boy must have been showing some good signs of life. Otherwise, Kate wouldn't have been beaming like a new mother. "I heard Nathanial crying out for you. Just trying to say a few words tuckered him out. He's asleep already."

Kate smoothed the boy's snowy hair, then softly kissed the little head good night.

Besides Nolan's late wife, he'd never known a woman with such a big, loving heart. He then took notice of her Bible sitting on the night table next to his hat. Prayer certainly couldn't hurt the boy. Kate had always been a believer in the word. Mary too.

Once upon a time, Nolan had read about mercy and forgiveness in the Gospels, and he'd lived it. The blisters on his hands from digging graves had taught him a different way of looking at life. Hell had become a certainty, like the rising of the sun. Nolan had witnessed it each day since chasing that rotten son of a bitch Deegan Jones. If Nathanial died, there would be no prayer strong enough to save Jones from getting a bullet drilled right between his eyes.

"Nolan, you look tired. Why don't you go on back to bed? I'll sit here with Nathanial." Kate fussed over the blankets, tucking them in tight around him. Then she looked up at Nolan a second time. "I mean it, Nolan. There isn't any sense in both of us going without sleep."

The sun was bright overhead when Nolan finally rolled out of bed. What time was it? The hour had to be past noon. He quickly dressed, then hurried into Nathanial's room. To his relief, he found the boy sleeping like a baby. And that was exactly what Nathanial looked like in the full-size bed. But where the hell was Kate? She was supposed to be watching over him.

Nolan quickly fed a few logs to the fire, glanced once more at Nathanial's pale face, then took the steps by two downstairs to find Kate. She'd better have a damn good excuse for leaving Nathanial alone.

The smell of fresh-brewed coffee led him marching into the kitchen to find her cracking eggs into a skillet. A slab of bacon sat on a butcher-block table, ready to be sliced to fry up for breakfast. What the hell was wrong with him? Nolan swallowed down his temper, full from eating crow. How much more of a weary fool could he be? There wasn't an unthoughtful or cruel bone in Kate's body. She would never have left the boy without trusting that Nathanial's well-being would not be compromised.

Kate poured Nolan a cup of coffee and then handed it to him. He took a sip. "Damn, that's hot." His tongue instantly burned.

"Well, I guess you're awake now." Kate chuckled. "You just watched me take the coffeepot off the cookstove."

He wasn't in the mood for jokes. Nathanial's poor condition had Nolan's nerves on edge. And it would be a crying shame if he couldn't taste the bacon and eggs. Maybe he should just go back to bed and start this day over.

"Nate was awake not long ago." What had Kate just called the boy?

Nolan raised a brow. Nate? The half-pint had been in Kate's care less than a day, and already she was calling Nathanial by a motherly nickname. It shouldn't have surprised Nolan. Truthfully, he liked it.

"Go sit down. Your breakfast is nearly ready." Kate shooed him out of the kitchen.

He went into the dining room, pulled out a seat at the table, and relaxed himself. The greasy smell of the sizzling bacon stirred his hunger.

Kate set a heaping plate of steaming food in front of him. "Nolan, dear, please wait a few minutes for everything to cool before you shovel it into your mouth." She winked at him, her grin one of amusement. Oh sure, she might have thought that him burning his tongue had been funny. It wasn't. His mouth was still stinging.

"I'm going to take some chicken broth up to Nate." Kate went back through the open door of the kitchen.

Nolan crunched a bite of bacon while she poured hot broth into a cup then disappeared up the stairs. If Nathanial woke up to eat, then Nolan wanted to be there to look into those baby blues. Would he see defeat or the fighting spirit the boy was so fond of? He hoped to find Nathanial with an appetite and a hankering for life in his eyes.

Nolan pushed aside the plate. The eggs were delicious, but his hunger could wait. In twos, he took the steps. As Nolan walked in, Kate was gently raising Nathanial's head from the pillow to drink.

Nathanial's gaze shifted and held on Nolan. The boy looked peaked and as weak as a newborn kitten. But Nolan's morning had just been made brighter by seeing that his eyes were focused. They were glassy with fever, but Nathanial was staring straight into his face with recognition. It was a small sign of healing.

Nathanial grimaced and whimpered faintly as he weakly reached out for Nolan. He clasped the little hand and gave a slight squeeze. The boy's teary eyes hadn't left Nolan's. Nathanial looked pitiful enough without the gut-wrenching sight of him trying to speak. His lips had hardly moved. The little voice was far too weak to be heard. Nolan leaned in closer so his ear almost touched Nathanial's mouth.

Kate wiped at her eyes and seemed to be taking in the sight of him and Nathanial.

"Thank you."

Nolan barely heard the faint whisper. But the meaning hit him. Instantly he straightened and nearly dropped his hold on Nathanial's sickly grip. Water had sprung to his eyes, and his stare clung to the boy's. What he saw there was years of pain beyond what a youngster that age should know. Nathanial, a rough-and-tumble little tomcat, didn't rub affectionately up against just anyone. The boy had said much more than thank you to Nolan. For a first, he had been taken care of without the price of being a thief or farmhand attached. As sickly as Nathanial was, he seemed to have appreciated that Nolan cared.

He shouldn't have ridden off and left Nathanial behind in that no-name town to get on a stagecoach alone and go where he wouldn't have known anyone. Had he kept Nathanial close, perhaps the little fella wouldn't be at death's door.

Nolan tucked his little arm under the quilt and then smoothed the snowy hair. "You eat, then git some rest." He couldn't bear to look at the grateful little half-pint swallowed in the big bed.

He'd no sooner turned to walk from the room before Nathanial began to fuss. It was understandable. Honestly, Nolan was all the boy had in this life. Kate was an exceptionally wonderful woman, but she wasn't the boy's mama. She was mostly unfamiliar to him. This was a strange house, and the boy was lying helpless in a bed that wasn't his own.

Nolan stopped midstep, then went back to Nathanial and sat at the edge of the bed. Just that quick, the half-pint quit his crying. Kate handed Nolan the bowl of soup to spoon-feed Nathanial. The tears in her eyes told that she'd been touched by his and Nathanial's bond, and her grin could only mean one thing. Kate was already carrying love for the child.

Nolan blew on the broth to make sure it wasn't too hot before he spooned Nathanial a swallow. It took a while, but he swallowed every bite. Kate then shooed Nolan and sat herself. She had a pan of water on her lap. She squeezed the sponge, then dabbed lightly at the sweaty little brow. Nathanial was already sleeping.

Nolan needed fresh air. His boots clomped down the stairs with the heavy load that was on his mind. He opened the door, stepped onto the porch, and breathed in the warm summer wind. The sprawling mountains were a lush green. Under the thick canvas of leaves was hidden an abundance of life. There he could hunt and find plenty of game for the table. Water was not in short supply. Creeks flowed down out of the hills, nourishing the ground on the flat land. The grass there grew tall for the deer and the many cattle that were raised in the area. A bluer sky he'd never looked upon. Kate owned plenty of good acres. Together as man and wife, they could build up her herd of horses for selling. This would be a fine place to raise Nathanial.

It was exactly what he wanted. He was finally willing to chance having a life there with the two people he cared about most in this awful world. So what the hell was that pang in Nolan's gut?

There was really no guesswork in the answer. He had made a commitment to the army and needed to fulfill that and return to Captain Farnsworth and his men. Hunting down Deegan Jones would give Nolan a chance at having justice served for the boy. Killing Jones would give him a deep satisfaction. Unfortunately, Jones's fate would make no difference in saving Nathanial's life.

There was another gnawing in Nolan's gut. As much as he wouldn't have minded getting his hands on Jones, he didn't want to leave Nathanial and Kate.

It was a lot to think over. Plus each of the three of them brought complications from their pasts. Could becoming a family work out in their favor? He supposed that would depend on whether Nathanial lived.

Pondering about it all had produced a tightness across his shoulders. There was nothing like some hard, backbreaking work to rid a man of his frustrations. Nolan went to the barn and picked up an ax.

Over and over, he swung until he'd split enough wood to keep Kate's fire going into the next change of season. Nolan straightened and wiped the sweat from under the brim of his hat.

"Supper's on the table." Kate waved to him from the porch.

Nolan sank the ax and then rubbed his sore hands. The hours had passed without him looking up from chopping wood to notice that he'd worked through lunch. The sun was now fading to the west. If his stomach had grumbled, he hadn't taken notice. His tired muscles actually felt good. He walked toward the house, dreaming of the day that he and Nathanial would do such chores together.

Nolan sat down to a hot plate of fried chicken, potatoes, and greens. "Smells good."

Kate sat across from him. He dug in, but she didn't touch her fork. There were tears in her eyes. Nolan didn't have to ask. Most likely, her memories of losing her children were being stirred by the failing half-pint. Nolan's mind, too, had thought of Matthew quite a lot when he and Nathanial had first come together. That had been different though. Nathanial hadn't been a breath away from dying.

Kate began to softly cry. Nolan put down his fork. His hunger vanished, and the food in his mouth became nearly tasteless as he thought of the pain he must have caused Kate by bringing Nathanial there.

"Nate hasn't opened his eyes since this morning." Kate wiped at her eyes.

Nolan let the words fully sink into his mind. The thankyou Nathanial had whispered before closing his eyes, Nolan had mistaken the words to mean I love you. In truth, the boy had meant goodbye.

Nolan quickly stood, pushing back his chair. Three running strides was all it took and he was at the bottom of the stairs.

Up the steps by twos he flew, hit the landing, and ran fast into Nathanial's room. His gaze fell on the seemingly lifeless little child. *Dear God, no.*

"Nathanial." Nolan hurried and sat at the edge of the bed. He put his ear to the boy's nose and mouth. His breathing was barely noticeable. No, he wouldn't let the half-pint give in to death this easily. Where was that spirited pup that never gave up?

Nolan began to rub with some force at Nathanial's arms and chest with the hope of stimulating his senses to come alive.

The pup's eyes rolled aimlessly open. A low, gargled moan choked up out of Nathanial's throat. Nolan had seen many men fall in battle. They'd gasp on their own blood until grace chose the moment to save them from their suffering. That gargled noise sounded much like the death rattle Nolan had heard on the battlefield. If Nathanial was bleeding on the inside, then all he and Kate could do would be to watch this little boy die.

Nolan cupped Nathanial's face in one hand and squeezed the boy's cheeks together to break the seal of the wan lips. With his finger, Nolan quickly swabbed the inside of Nathanial's mouth. No blood, thank God.

Kate sniffled. "Nolan, I'm scared."

He nodded, his heart pounding. Nothing came to his mind that would comfort her or himself.

"Bring me some broth." It was the only thing he could figure to do for Nathanial. The boy needed to eat to gain strength.

Kate hurried from the room, wiping at her eyes. She was back in no time at all. Nolan held Nathanial's head up and slowly spoon-fed the boy sips of the hot chicken broth. Nathanial weakly lifted an arm and tried to push away the spoon. The little piss pot let his head roll to one side to keep the broth-filled spoon from touching his lips. Nolan half grinned. This was the fighting spirit he had longed to see.

"Start eatin'." He spooned a sip of broth into Nathanial while holding his little head from turning away. Nathanial closed his eyes. His frail little arm dropped away from fighting the spoon. "Open your eyes, Nathanial. You got more to eat."

Nolan practically force-fed him until the broth was gone. Nathanial had just stared blankly the whole time. That vacantness in the half-pint's eyes spooked him.

Again, he recalled the battlefield. His men had been engaged with the Confederates for two days. There were dead everywhere. The number of casualties had been staggering. He'd carried wounded men into a tent to wait for a doc to patch them up or saw them to pieces. The groans and shrieks of the wounded had filled Nolan's ears, then turned his stomach. Most of those that had been lying about, bleeding all over the ground, waiting their turn to have the doc look at them, they'd worn the same faraway stare that Nathanial had when he had fed him. It was an unmistakable sign of a fading life. Some of those soldiers' lives had passed on quicker than others.

Nolan fought back the water in his eyes. He gently rested Nathanial's little head down to the pillow.

There would be no leaving Nathanial's side.

Through the window, the orange glow of the evening sun faded behind the mountain. Nolan sat in a chair next to the bed and occasionally sponged at the boy's fever. Hours slowly passed through what was the longest night of Nolan's life. He swore he could actually hear each minute of Nathanial's life ticking away. If the boy woke for even a breath, Nolan wanted to be right there so Nathanial might see he wasn't alone.

Sometime during the night, an achy, restless moan roused Nolan, so he sat up straighter. *Come on, boy, open your eyes and come back to me.* His quick, wishful thinking had done no good. The pale-faced child stayed asleep. At least he could see a shallow rise and fall of Nathanial's chest.

Morning light streaked the sky. Kate was asleep under a blanket, sitting in a rocker next to the warm fire. Nolan glanced between her and the boy. As awful as their situation was at the moment, he could foresee happiness further down the road. Nathanial would play in the yard while Kate hung the day's wash on the line to dry in the sun. The sweet smell of pie would waft out through the open kitchen window and reach Nolan's nose as he worked around the corral and barn. There was a school in Gray Rock. That would be a good first for Nathanial.

Kate stirred a bit, then opened her eyes. "How is he?"

Nolan looked over at her. Worry had left her eyes rimmed with darkness. He probably looked the same. "No worse. Now that you're awake, I'll go make Nathanial some broth."

Nolan stood to go to the kitchen. A stiffness had set into his tired muscles from a long night of sitting up in a hard wooden chair, and his legs could use some stretching.

"I'll do that. You stay with Nate." Kate hurried from the room before Nolan could argue against her will.

He walked over and looked out the window. The sky was a clear blue, not a cloud in sight. It looked like it was going to be a fine sunny day. He glanced over his shoulder. Nathanial would be out there playing real soon. Nolan took his seat next to the bed just as Kate came in carrying a steaming bowl of chicken broth.

He spooned Nathanial hot liquid until the bowl was empty and then did the same at midday. Days passed in the same way. He'd stepped away from Nathanial only when Kate forced him to sleep. So far, nothing that they'd tried had made any difference as far as Nathanial's health.

"He ain't gaining strength, but he don't seem to be weakening either." Nolan didn't know what else to do, and he was worried.

Kate situated the pillow under Nathanial's head, then tucked the quilt in around the small shoulders. Her eyes were teary. "Nolan, if you'll hitch the wagon, I'll fetch Dr. Martin from town. He should have been back from Birch Creek days ago. I don't know what could be holding him up. If we're lucky, he'll have arrived in town today."

"All right." Nolan agreed but had pause about it. As the man of the house, fetching the doc seemed like his duty, and the mothering should've been left to Kate. Nathanial needed to get used to her tending to him and understand that he would be okay without Nolan sitting right next to his bed.

But the few times Nolan had allowed Kate to shoo him from Nathanial's bedside to lie down and rest himself, he had no sooner laid his head to the pillow before Nathanial fussed. It seemed somehow that the child had been able to sense when Nolan wasn't there. The crying hadn't stopped even once until Nolan had sat close to the boy. He'd then talked of all the things they would do together as soon as Nathanial got better.

Nolan stood to go hitch the team, and he hoped Kate would find Doc Martin in Gray Rock.

"I love him, Nolan." Tears welled up in her eyes. Her gaze was resting on Nathanial.

Nolan turned Kate to look at him. "I know you do."

They kissed. Then he left for the barn.

———

Kate's trip to town and back had been much faster than Nolan had ever expected. Nate's fever had spiked while she had been gone, and Nolan was relieved to see the doc with her. The boy was now burning up.

Kate's arm was tightly wrapped around Nolan's as they stood close together and Doc Martin examined Nathanial's wounds. The half-pint never once opened his eyes or made a single sound. He was soggy, limp. Nolan's gut squeezed tight while waiting to hear what the doc had to say. The man wore a poker face that gave away nothing.

"Other than the fever, there's no sign of infection." Doc Martin turned from the boy to face Nolan and Kate. "The wounds are clean and slowly healing. The boy has lost a lot of blood though. His body is fighting to recover. As far as nursing his health…well, you're doing everything right. Nathanial needs rest. Push as much fluid into him as you can and keep sponging him off to get the fever to break. I'll come by again tomorrow to check in on him."

Kate began to softly cry into her hands. It wasn't the news Nolan wanted to hear either, but the doc could have said there was no chance of Nathanial pulling through this. No infection—that was a big blessing. Kate usually had been the one to see the good side of things. She'd always enjoyed playfully pointing it out to Nolan. Was she losing all hope for Nathanial? To lose faith wasn't like her. Nolan knew her to be a stronger woman than she was showing herself to be. Maybe it wasn't just Nathanial that had broken her down to sobs.

For some time, Nolan had constantly ridden in and out of her life. It had been selfish of him to play husband to her for a few weeks or however long he decided to stay. Their union usually had lasted until his angry thoughts of what he'd lost had blown him like a strong wind in another direction. Hunting down the wanted was where that path had always led him. Maybe he'd never really find peace with what happened to Mary and Matthew. And now this mess with Nathanial piled on top of Kate's already aching heart had Nolan truly turned into that much of a son of a bitch.

He gently pulled Kate into his arms. She buried her face into his collar, crying harder than he'd ever heard anyone sob. Doc Martin patted Nolan's shoulder. The doc's gaze, though, held on Kate and her grief. Nolan had been so lost in his thoughts of her that he'd almost forgotten that the doc was standing in the room with them.

"Nolan, will you walk with me to the porch?" His face was as sober as a judge. Nolan didn't want to leave Kate in such a state. The doc seemed to have something on his mind, and maybe he didn't want her to directly hear.

"Will you be okay till I get back?" Nolan still held Kate close.

She slowly pulled away from him. She wiped her eyes, then nodded.

Nolan followed the doc down the stairs and out onto the porch. He closed the door behind them. Doc Martin stood quiet at the top of the porch steps for a minute and stared out over the dark land. It seemed like a long time until he finally turned and faced Nolan.

"I'm glad you're here with Kate. I didn't want to say in front of her, but the boy will most likely only last a day or two more. The little fella has lost far too much blood for me to give you any hope of a full recovery. If Nathanial lives, it will be a true miracle." The doc turned, walked down the stairs, then stepped up into his carriage. He smacked the reins to the single horse. The black buggy rolled out of the yard and then turned onto the coach road.

Nolan just stood staring off into nothing for a long time. He wiped at his eyes. How would he find the words to tell Kate that Nathanial would not see the summer pass and the autumn leaves paint the trees?

Did either of them have the strength to bury another child?

No, Nolan wasn't ready to give up on Nathanial. Doc Martin could be wrong. The boy was in a poor way; that was for sure. But the ornery pup had bite. He'd shown that after the wagon train attack. What seven-year-old goes alone to take revenge on a killer and his mob? Most boys would have been curled up, sucking their thumbs. Not the half-pint.

Nolan wasn't going to tell Kate about the doc's hopeless prognosis, not unless he had to. Nathanial was still breathing. Nolan had to believe there was a chance that wouldn't change.

Doc Martin was true to his word. He stopped each day for several weeks to check in on Nathanial. There were no improvements to report today, like most days.

Nathanial would open his eyes for a short time to sip broth or hot tea from a spoon. The boy was still too weak to even hold a cup. On any given day, the little milk or water they coaxed him to swallow amounted to nearly nothing. Nathanial was shrinking up in front of them.

Now and then, the half-pint had given Nolan and Kate a weak sort of grin. It was a small encouragement to them. Though the very second that either one of them finished feeding him, Nathanial would fall back to sleep as quick as a wink. How long could this suffering go on? Nolan couldn't take too much more. All he wanted was for Nathanial to grow in strength, to become a healthy little boy.

Nolan dimmed the lamp, then made himself comfortable in the rocking chair.

He woke stiff in the chair next to Nathanial's bed. He stretched and felt a little handhold tug free from his loose shirttail. Sometime during the night, Nathanial had reached out to him.

The boy's eyes were open but staring off and dull. Nolan had seen that glazed-over look on the battlefield right before many a fallen soldier had drawn his last breath. During the war, Nolan had fought on for the greater good as those soldiers closed their eyes for the last time. This fight of Nathanial's was a battle Nolan could do nothing to win, and there would be no good that came from it. Nathanial was fading.

Nolan wept. He could barely breathe.

"Nathanial." He clutched the boy's little hand. If only he could will that strength would come to Nathanial. The wee, limp hand was just there in Nolan's. There wasn't even a little effort from the half-pint to hold to him. Nathanial's eye's shifted slowly to meet Nolan's grieving stare.

"Nolan." Nathanial's voice was a faint whisper. What Nolan heard was goodbye. The half-pint's baby blues drifted shut.

Nolan stood, pushing back from the bed, knocking over the chair.

Kate must have heard the crash and ran into the room. "What is it?" She was out of breath from hustling up the stairs. Her gaze darted between him and Nathanial.

Nolan went to march past her and out the door. She grabbed his arm and stopped him, but he jerked away from her grip. He couldn't sit by, doing nothing, and watch the half-pint die. A meanness crept up inside Nolan. He hated Deegan Jones with every ounce of strength he owned.

Tears sprang to Kate's eyes. "Is he...?" She choked and couldn't spit out the dreaded word. That was all right with Nolan because he didn't want to hear the truth of the coming reality.

He glanced away from Kate and over his shoulder at Nathanial. "Not yet. It won't be long though." Nolan marched away down the stairs and out of the house, slamming the door behind him. As true as the sky was blue, Jones would be a sorry son of a bitch. Hell was about to rise up against him.

"Nolan, wait! Where are you going?" Kate rushed out the door, leaving it standing wide open. She stopped at the edge of the porch and shielded her eyes from the sun. Nolan could see the tears running down her face. "That little boy upstairs needs you. Anytime his eyes open, he searches the doorway for you." She wiped at her eyes with the corner of her apron.

Nolan swung a leg over the saddle. He pictured Nathanial's pale face and dull eyes. "I can't bury another child, Kate!"

"Oh, but I can? Why do you think dumping a dying little boy in my lap is okay? You're a coward and the very essence of ignorant."

Kate was right. There was nothing Nolan could say to defend himself. He wasn't a good enough man to do right by her or Nathanial. Watching the boy slowly wilt had been a harsh reminder of why the family kind of life had ended for Nolan long ago. He was no father or husband, not anymore. He was a man with a fast gun who wanted to kill Deegan Jones.

Kate smacked her fists to her hips. "Nolan, don't you see? We need you here with us. Nathanial is still alive. What if, by some miracle, he recovers? Don't you want to have a hand in helping him through this battle? Nathanial needs both you and me, a father and a mother. You already treat him like a son."

Kate unfolded a crinkled piece of paper that Nolan recognized as the letter he'd written weeks ago when Nate was supposed to have gotten on a stagecoach and come there. Kate waved it at him. "There is a bond there that you cannot deny. You love Nathanial and me both, so why are you running away? You wanted this family more than anything just a few weeks ago, and them are your words, not mine." The red of her face nearly matched her hair. He'd never seen her so pissed off.

"The boy is dying, Kate. The three of us ain't ever gonna be a family." Nolan was ready to sink spurs into the bay and ride the hell out of there.

"Fine, then go. Yellow never was a color I favored on a man. Oh, and one last thing. Don't ever think of coming back to us. You're no longer welcome here." Kate turned on her heel, marched into the house, and slammed the door behind her.

All Nolan could do was stare after her, dumbfounded. He was being a damn fool. Maybe he should go after her. He loved her, but how could she love him, knowing it was his poor choices that put Nathanial in the bad way he was? He was going to die, and there was nothing Nolan could do for that, but he could make Jones pay. The sooner, the better.

Out there, Nolan could see to it that Deegan Jones never got another chance at hurting anyone else.

Nolan spurred his horse.

CHAPTER 20

NATE'S EYES SLOWLY OPENED. The rocking chair next to his bed was empty. He wanted Nolan. The lady with red hair wasn't there either. She, too, always seemed to be close by, tucking the blankets in around him or sweetly encouraging him to eat. He was neither hungry nor thirsty. When he breathed, his ribs hurt awful bad. He didn't want to be alone. Nate began to cry.

A little fuss usually brought Nolan running. This time it was his lady friend who hurried into the room first. He looked past her to the doorway. Nate didn't hear the quick steps of boots on the stairs or in the hall. He cried harder.

The teary-eyed woman pulled back the quilts, gently scooped Nate out of the bed, and sat down in the rocker, cradling him. She'd never done that before. The easy rocking soothed his cries. Her arms wrapped around him felt warm and soft. His head rested in the crook of her arm, and he stared up into her face. Her eyes were red as if she'd been crying hard. She must not have been sad, because she smiled. Nate felt safe tucked into her bosom. She began to hum a soft, sweet tune. Nate's eyes drifted shut to the melody, and he forgot all about his pain.

Nate woke. The fire crackled and dimly lit the dark room. He could see stars through the window. It wasn't overly hot in the room, but for once, his mouth felt dry. He wanted a drink of water. He didn't see Nolan and began to fuss.

Nolan's lady friend came to life, kicking off her blanket, and sprang from the rocker. She quickly hovered over him and smoothed his hair. "Nate, what's wrong?" She looked as if she might start to cry.

"Water." The word croaked out of him.

She picked up a cup from the bedside table, lifted Nate's head, then brought the cup to his lips. He drank every drop. She fetched more, and he swallowed that down too.

"Amen." Her praise, or whatever it was that made her seem so thankful, had come out of nowhere. Her eyes were teary, though she seemed to be beaming. She kissed Nate's forehead and then his cheeks. It all scared him a little, and he shrank away. Why would she be so happy that he'd drunk two cups of water?

He wanted Nolan. Nate looked toward the door.

She gently turned Nate's face to look at her. "Nolan isn't here, Nathanial. He left to go help Captain Farnsworth. Do you remember him?"

Nate weakly nodded, and she tucked a tuft of hair behind his ear. "I do believe scouting is a means by which Nolan is protecting us."

Nate cried until he fell asleep.

⟶———⟶

The pink of morning was streaming in through the window when Nate woke. Nolan's lady friend carried in a tray with a bowl of broth and a slice of bread on it. Tears sprang to Nate's eyes. She was real nice, but that wasn't who Nate wanted. She fed him small pieces of bread sopped in broth, and he was able to hold it down.

"While you're awake, I'm going to give you a bath. Before I do, I suppose I should properly introduce myself. My name is Kathrine James. You may call me Miss Kate." She smiled, then left him. A few minutes later, she returned with a basin of steaming water. She gently pulled the long nightshirt off over Nate's head, then sponged every inch of him clean.

It tickled when she washed between his toes. He giggled, and she smiled. She tickled his toes again. He'd never felt a gentler touch. She scrubbed his hair and brushed it. After she dressed him in a nightshirt that fit, she leaned over the bed, tucking fresh blankets in around him. Nate felt snug and safe there. He was tired and wanted to close his eyes. Though she'd done all the work of bathing and dressing him.

There was something he needed to know first. "Miss Kate, why do you smell like a flapjack?"

Miss Kate laughed. "A lot of my time is spent in the kitchen, so naturally, the aromas of butter and syrup might stick to me." She smiled sweetly.

"You smell good." Nate remembered that Nolan always smelled like fresh air and trail dust. He missed the scout. "When do you think Nolan will come back for me?"

"Nathanial, sweetheart, I have no idea. You just worry about getting better."

Days turned into weeks as Miss Kate nursed him toward health. Before Nate knew it, July had passed, and the mid-August heat was blistering everything. Miss Kate grumbled to Nate that her garden was shriveling up. They needed rain, or she would have nothing to can to eat in the winter months.

He'd never known anyone so full of compliments. She'd congratulated him each day for growing a little stronger. He liked it when she called him sweetheart. She'd also softly scolded him a few times when his appetite wasn't what she thought it should be. Nate's ribs could be counted, and Miss Kate didn't like it.

Doc Martin, who was still a daily visitor, had told Miss Kate to stop worrying. Nate would eat when he was hungry. He'd overheard Miss Kate mumbling to herself after the doc had left. What she muttered seemed strange to him. What connection was there between Nate not being the doc's child and it being easy for him to say that Nate could eat when he wanted to? He didn't belong to Miss Kate either. Grown-ups didn't make sense sometimes.

Time seemed to fly by. Nate was sitting up on his own and feeding himself. Miss Kate was always busy doing something, mostly for him. She'd scolded him more than once throughout the weeks that she would break him from eating with his fingers. For now though, she just wanted him to take in nourishment.

The doc's visits stretched out to every three or four days. Nate was feeling much better except for when he got to missing Nolan. Then he'd cry. Nate had lied to Miss Kate about it every time. His excuse for crying was always either his ribs or his shoulder pained him. She'd rock him until he felt better.

Nate smiled at Miss Kate as she walked into the room with Dr. Martin following behind her. He was itching to climb out of bed and get outside to breathe in the fresh air. According to Miss Kate, Doc Martin was the man to give that freedom.

Miss Kate helped Nate strip off his nightshirt so the doc could look over the ugly wounds. The breeze flowing through the open window tickled Nate's cheeks and smelled of honeysuckle. What a tease. He wanted to roll in the green grass.

This was the most time he'd ever spent in a home. He just wasn't used to it. The sun and stars had always been his roof. From the confines of the window, Nate had seen a fish jump in the pond near Miss Kate's orchard. He couldn't wait to splash in that water. Maybe it was the spot that Nolan had spoken of taking him fishing. He wished he could be with Nolan. Though living there with Miss Kate wouldn't exactly be that hard for Nate to get used to.

He shouldn't even jinx his luck by thinking it. Life was good with Miss Kate taking care of him. She never called him bad names, and her hands were always gentle. No one had ever combed his hair before or washed his clothes. Given his experiences with the Harpers and others, Nate didn't doubt that once he was feeling all better, Miss Kate would most likely throw him out the door.

"Nathanial, are you listening, boy? I said Saturday." Doc Martin grinned right in front of Nate's nose. He was roused from his thoughts. The doc wagged a finger at Nate. "You do as Miss Kate says. If she thinks you're able, then Saturday is when you can get out of bed and stretch those legs, but not for too long."

"That's five days from now." Nate reckoned he knew what was best for himself. Who was this sawbones to say that Miss Kate was the boss of him? She wasn't Nate's mama. Couldn't they see he was his own man and could do as he wanted?

Miss Kate smoothed Nate's hair, then kissed his head. "Don't pout. Saturday will be here before you know it." She stood from where she'd sat on the edge of the bed. "I'll be back with our lunch after I walk Dr. Martin out."

The doc packed his little black bag to leave.

Nate didn't call Miss Kate a liar to her face. Saturday was nearly a week away. There was nothing quick about that. The bright side was, during those long days of waiting, he would be lying in a soft bed and fed the best food he'd ever eaten. That wasn't exactly suffering. If it weren't for the pain in his side now and then, he might start believing he was in heaven.

It made him think. Why was Miss Kate so nice to him? Not only did she serve him all the meals, but she sat next to his bed with her plate and ate with him. The Harpers had fed Nate in the barn like an animal. Pa, too, had treated him like a dog. He'd lapped up scraps when he could get them. He kind of liked how Miss Kate fussed over him to eat every bite on his plate as if she cared. How could he be sure that she wasn't just tending to him as a favor to Nolan?

Nate reckoned it wasn't worth worrying over. Nolan would be back for him.

———————

The next two days, it drizzled rain. Logs burned in the fire-place and warmed Nate's room. He mostly stayed snuggled under the quilts, cozy and dry. There was only one person he was thinking about. Nolan, likely, was outside braving the wet weather to scout for the captain.

"Miss Kate… can I ask a big favor?"

She was standing at the end of the bed, folding linens and then placing them neatly into a basket. She looked up from her work. The worst she could say was no, and Nolan was worth the try.

"I lost Nolan's rain slicker in the mud. He's probably gittin' soaked to the bone. What if he gets sick? It would be all my fault. I'll pay ya back somehow if you'd order a new raincoat for him." Nate crossed his fingers.

Miss Kate slowly began to smile. He saw that as a good sign of her saying yes. He dared to bait her in a little more.

"Nolan has a nice smile. Don't ya think so?"

Miss Kate raised a brow. "Yes. He does have a handsome smile. Why do you ask?"

"Picture this, Miss Kate. We find out what town Nolan and the army will be headed to next. We could send the slicker ahead so the package will be waiting for Nolan. I just know he'll smile when he opens it. I can see it as if it's happening right this minute. It'd probably make me feel better too." Nate's idea sounded grand to him.

Miss Kate chuckled. "You're a little snake oil salesman."

"Huh?" Nate wrinkled his nose.

"Never mind that. Your concern about the slicker is sweet. I'm afraid though that a package would never find Nolan. As a scout, he's not in one place too long. How about this? When you feel up to a buggy ride, I'll take you to town. You can buy Nolan a new slicker and then keep it till you see him again. That way you can hand deliver the surprise."

Wow, Miss Kate was smart. Her idea was much better than Nate's. But what would it cost him? "So what do I have to do to earn enough money to pay for the coat?"

"Eat all the supper that I put on your plate, and we'll call it even."

That's all Miss Kate wanted from him?

"Are you shittin' me?"

This woman's mind didn't work like anyone else's that Nate had ever come across. She was softheaded; that was for sure. She could have asked for his right arm, and he would have chewed it off and dropped it at her feet. Nolan was all he had, and he planned to hold on tight for as long as he could.

"Nathanial, I'm going to pepper your mouth if you don't stop talking that way." She was shaking a finger at him.

"Sorry, ma'am." It was just that her asking price didn't make sense to him. She had him cornered. Why not take advantage of his penniless pockets and force him to work for Nolan's gift? Pa had never handed anything over without Nate clawing for it. Nolan was different than that, and it seemed like Miss Kate was too.

Nate kept his end of the bargain and ate every crumb. His gut was about to burst wide open. Had she heaped the food on his plate so she didn't have to make good on their deal? She wasn't getting off the hook. He was going to make sure of it.

"Put your right hand up and swear that you'll buy the rain slicker."

She smiled, then put up her hand. Nate saw nothing amusing. This was business. Not that there was much he could do if she changed her mind. He wanted to hear her give her word too. Nolan had always been good to his word.

"Say it." Nate was serious, so why was she chuckling?

"I promise. Now you get some rest. I'm going downstairs to do the dishes. I'll check on you in a little while." Miss Kate took his plate with her own and left.

It was two days until Saturday. Nate didn't think he could take being stuck in bed much longer. He thought his ribs were done hurting until he coughed. Holy Lord, he thought the stabbing pain was going to kill him. He'd hacked hard and was sure he'd busted more ribs. He hoped to high heaven he didn't sneeze until they were fully healed. Though none of that was enough to stop him from wanting to walk out the front door and feel the breeze touch his skin.

"It's close enough to Saturday. I wanna go outside." Nate was tired of waiting.

Miss Kate scowled. "You're not getting out of that bed a day early."

Nate wrinkled up his face real mean and figured on having a damn fit. Fine, he'd just keep pestering her until she gave in. He had already asked her once before this. He could keep this up all day.

Miss Kate turned a narrowed eye on him, and before his mouth opened to spit out another arguing word, her hands fisted and smacked to her hips. "Nathanial, I said no. Now that's twice that I've had to tell you in the past five minutes. I'm tired of repeating myself. Your stitches could pull, and you could start to bleed again. You're going to listen to Dr. Martin and give your wounds a couple more days to heal." Miss Kate huffed out of the room with a tray of dirty dishes in her hands.

How did she know what he'd been thinking? Lousy bad luck. She was a meanie. Why did she get to make the rules and he didn't? It wasn't fair. She wasn't his boss. But he needed Miss Kate to nurse his wounds. So he would have to keep his mouth shut…for now.

It wasn't long before she brought him a cup of hot mint tea to sip. She was too nice, and he couldn't stay mad at her. She went to a shelf and picked up a book. How had Nate not noticed the books before? Maybe it would have pictures of far-off lands or animals.

Miss Kate sat on the bed, propped herself up with pillows, then opened the pages and began to read. At first Nate hadn't even truly heard the words, struck dumb as he was. Miss Kate was treating him too good. He wasn't kin to her. This was time she didn't have to spend with him and could have been doing something that made her happy. But he wasn't going to question the kind gesture and have her stop reading.

Mostly, all they did to pass the time until Saturday decided to get there was read more and more often. It wasn't a complaint. Nate loved it. Miss Kate made faces with different voices. He had jumped out of his skin every time she'd read about the three bears startling Goldilocks awake.

"I can read." Nate was shy to say it because he knew what she would ask next.

"How many years of schooling did you have?"

A warm redness rushed to his cheeks. "I ain't ever been to school." He sadly thought of Jenny and what a good teacher she had been.

Miss Kate fetched a tablet of writing paper and a pencil from the desk drawer. "Can you write your name?" She was testing Nate.

He didn't mind. He wanted to show off a bit. Besides writing his name, he scripted all twenty-six letters of the alphabet plus his numbers one to twenty.

Miss Kate held the paper in her hands. "Your penmanship is very good. Jenny must have been an excellent teacher."

"How do you know about Jenny?"

"Nolan told me about your friendship with the girl and what happened to her."

Nate looked away and out the window. Tears filled his eyes. It had been some time since he really thought of Jenny or even going after the fancy man. Nate would be strong enough to ride soon. Hopefully, Nolan would come back for him. Nate wanted to be part of capturing Jones. If the killer hadn't already been strung up by Nolan and the captain.

"It's your turn to read to me." Miss Kate handed Nate a book.

He wiped at his eyes and then opened the book. "Once upon a time..." He easily read the words across the pages. In no time at all, he'd finished the story. "Can I read you another book?"

"It's may I, not can I, and yes, you may. Don't roll your eyes at me, young man." Miss Kate pulled each book off the shelf one at a time and held them up for Nate to see the covers. Together, they chose a title.

CHAPTER 21

HALLELUJAH. AMEN. Praise the Lord. Saturday had finally come. Nate was ready to get out of bed. To prove it, he let Miss Kate help pull a shirt over his head without giving her any sass.

"Don't stand too quickly after being mostly flat on your back for so long." Here she was, bossing Nate again.

Only, he didn't much care to listen. He hopped up from the bed. Pain shot through his side. "Ouch!"

His head spun, and Miss Kate caught hold of him to steady his wobbly legs before he crumpled and hit the floor. Okay, so in this matter, she knew what was best for him. Taking it slow might be the smart thing to do. Nate wasn't going to cry about his ribs though. Then Miss Kate might make him crawl back into bed for another long week.

She held Nate up some as he took that first step. Slowly they walked from the room to the top of the stairs. His breath was already coming heavy. He wasn't going to run anywhere; that was for sure.

"Hold on to the rail. We'll take it one step at a time." Miss Kate smiled in a way that Nate believed he could make it up and down those stairs ten times.

And she would be at his side, helping every minute until he made it. Nate was plumb tuckered out until they sat down together on the porch swing. To see the sunshine from outside was great. Nate could hardly believe how run-down he felt from just a short walk. He fought to keep his droopy eyes from closing. Would he ever get better and feel like his old self again?

———◆———————◆———

Nate woke in bed. How had he gotten there?

Pale moonlight faintly lit the room. Stars twinkled through the window. Miss Kate was asleep in the rocker next to the bed, with an afghan pulled over her. The last Nate remembered, it'd been light outside. Now it was as black as midnight.

"Nathanial?" Miss Kate's voice whispered inside the dark room. Why did she sound choked up while saying his name, like she might start to cry? "Are you feeling okay?" Miss Kate brought to life a low flame under the lamp globe.

Nate nodded but wasn't entirely sure of himself. "I don't recall walking upstairs to come to bed or changing into my nightshirt."

She wiped at her eyes and sniffled. "You fell asleep so quickly in the fresh air. It was like you passed out. I was afraid that maybe ya started to bleed inside where I couldn't see. Doc Martin looked ya over. He said the small amount of moving about had simply been too much for you."

What? Nate could hardly believe it. Miss Kate had been so scared for him that she'd saddled a horse, rode into Gray Rock, and fetched Doc Martin. It would have been a lot of trouble for someone to do all that, unless that someone cared. Then it wouldn't have been a bother at all. And so far, Miss Kate had done so much more than just tend to his wounds. She was Nate's dream of what a good mother would be. Had Nolan brought him to her because she was a kindly enough woman to overlook the no-good name he wore? Nolan had shaken it off and proved he cared when he'd brought Nate there to get better.

Miss Kate laid a hand to his head as she had plenty of times to feel for fever. "You slept all day till just now." She kissed the end of his nose. "I'm glad you're awake."

He could see the truth of what she'd said in her watery eyes and happy smile. Should he tell her that he liked her too? He was glad to be with her.

"I'm thirsty." It was all he could think to say. His throat was dry.

Miss Kate stood. "I'll fix you a little something to eat."

"I ain't hungry. I just wanna drink."

"Don't sass me, Nathanial." Her voice was firm but in a way that it didn't so much bother Nate. "You'll eat even if it's only a few bites. I'll bring you a glass of milk first." She walked from the room.

Nate shifted his weight to pull himself slowly up to sit in bed. Miss Kate was already back with his glass of milk. He took the cup from her hand, lifted it to his parched lips, and drank every drop. He was tired, so he closed his eyes to wait until she came back with the food.

It felt as if he'd just shut his eyes when he felt a slight rub at his arm to wake him. He yawned.

Miss Kate placed a tray of food across his lap. "Would you like me to read ya a story while you eat?"

They'd read and reread all the books on the shelf. They were kids' books, and he hadn't seen any kids besides himself. "Do them books belong to your children?"

Miss Kate's eyes got sad. "They did, but not anymore. They're yours now. My son and daughter..." She dabbed at her eyes with her apron. "They're in heaven with their father."

Nate felt sad that this nice lady's children had died. "How'd it happen that you lost your whole family?"

"I lost my daughter to fever when she was four. My son was a few years older. He'd been working in the pasture with his pa when something spooked the herd of horses. He'd been up on the wagon, but it got flipped in the stampede and he was trapped underneath. My husband tried to save our little boy and got trampled."

"I'm sorry." Nate recalled how hard he'd cried when he had to bury Jenny, and poor Miss Kate had planted three loved ones. Life was mean sometimes. He knew that lesson all too well.

"No need to be sorry. It happened a long time ago." Miss Kate patted Nate's hand and seemed to comfort him, though they'd been talking about her loss. "Why don't you pick out a book?"

What Nate wondered about wasn't *The Swiss Family Robinson*. "Where do you think Nolan is?" He missed the scout and couldn't wait to see him again.

Miss Kate smoothed Nate's snowy hair. "I honestly don't know."

There was something else he'd been curious about. Maybe now was the time to ask. "How did you meet Nolan?"

Miss Kate's eyes widened. It was easy to see that he had caught her off guard. Why was she getting teary? Nate was happy when he thought of Nolan.

"You don't have to tell me. I didn't mean to make ya cry."

"It's okay, sweetheart. I just haven't thought about it in a long time." Miss Kate was quiet then and stared off. Nate would bet she was picturing that day. "I'd been traveling after the death of my family. I couldn't bear spending time alone on the ranch. Everything around me was a reminder of a way of life that wouldn't be returning to me. The most important part of my life had been buried." She curled up next to Nate on the bed and then gave him a little peck on the cheek.

"That day had been just one of my many trips to nowhere to escape being alone in an empty house that no longer felt like a home. I had to do something to keep my mind from going crazy." Miss Kate's pain seemed different than what Nate had suffered in his past. Though he understood the want to run away from what hurt. Many times he'd thought about escaping from Pa and then Mr. Harper's cruel hands.

"I'd stepped onto the stage, and there sat Nolan. He was covered with dust and wore a deputy badge pinned to his vest. He'd tipped his hat, and his smile began to immediately win my heart. I hadn't known it then, but he'd been protecting a payroll. I'd asked where he was headed in hopes to gain his attention. I honestly hadn't cared where Nolan was going." Miss Kate's mushy talk was funny.

"Nolan had studied me for a moment, then finally answered. The bank in Newton. After I'd come to know his purpose on the stage, the thought had crossed my mind that maybe he'd wondered if I was a decoy bandit to distract him from his duty."

Nate burst out laughing. It made his side hurt. Who would be so addlebrained to mistake sweet Miss Kate for an outlaw? This story was good.

"What happened next was quite a surprise. Nolan came right out and said what he'd been thinking. That I was the loveliest woman he'd ever set his eyes on, besides his late wife. I'd felt highly complimented. I'd known from the hard-set jaw that this wasn't a man to share such sentiments so easily. We then talked of our earlier lives as the miles rolled by. We were the only two passengers, so it hadn't been hard to get to know one another better."

Miss Kate put an arm around Nate's shoulders and snugged him a little closer. He'd been stuck to her every word thus far and couldn't wait to hear more.

"What did Nolan do next?"

"The stage had rounded a bend in the road, and out of nowhere, gunfire rang in my ears. Men, with their faces covered, charged the coach on horseback. Nolan threw me to the floor of the stage and ordered me to stay down. I'd never been so scared, not only for myself, but for Nolan. I didn't want to see him get hurt or, worse, maybe killed. I was already in love with him."

"Eww, yuck, that's sappy. What happened then?" Nate scooted to sit closer yet to Miss Kate. He could hardly keep himself still. "I bet Nolan blasted them, didn't he?" His ears were aching to hear how Nolan had saved Miss Kate from the bad men, like Pa.

"He did." Miss Kate drew a fast finger up from her waist like a pistol. "Bang, bang." Nate jumped, then giggled, and Miss Kate chuckled. "The gunfire had stopped. The driver pulled up on the reins."

Nate's eyes widened, and he bit down on his lip, waiting to hear. Miss Kate had him on pins and needles. Surely Nolan just had to get the bad guys.

"Nolan told me to stay where I was, facedown on the dirty floor of that stage. He swung the door open, then stepped down out of the coach. He'd left me. I was frightened nearly to death without him. My only comfort was that I'd been able to hear his boot steps and then his deep voice curse that the shotgun rider had been shot and killed. The driver groaned that a bullet had gone through his shoulder. He was bleeding badly.

"Looking back now, I'd known better. I should have listened to Nolan and stayed inside the coach. I'd thought maybe I could be of some help to the wounded man. So I foolishly stepped down out of the stage. My feet had no sooner touched the dirt when one of the outlaws, thought to be dead, jumped up off the ground and grabbed me."

Nate jumped nearly out of his skin as Miss Kate's hands playfully shot out and took hold of him. His gut was so tight. If she didn't soon tell it all, he might just burst. He knew the ending was good, or Miss Kate wouldn't be sitting right next to him. But golly geez, how did Nolan get her out of such trouble? Nate was in half a sweat, biting at his thumbnail, and his heart was thumping.

"I'd been forced to stand as a shield between Nolan's gun and the scum who had his pistol aimed at me. It was a coward's way of escaping justice. I was crying, and I shook all over with fright. I'd believed I was going to die. Nolan's steely blues grew cold, and something told me he wasn't a man to be challenged for what he saw as his. Then just that quick—" Miss Kate snapped her fingers. Nate's eyes stretched wider. "I was pitched to the dirt. The outlaw gambled on his edge of having his pistol already drawn. The fool lost his bet and his life. Nolan's gun had slid so fast from the holster that I'd never seen his hand move. Both guns boomed, and the sound rang in my ears and nearly deafened me before I hit the ground."

"Holy cow." Nate was sure there wasn't a braver man alive than Nolan. "Is there more?" He curled up snug against Miss Kate. She seemed to like it and smiled.

"Oh yeah. The no-account dropped to his knees, then fell forward on his face … dead at my feet. Blood everywhere. The whole sight had been just horrible … except for the love that bloomed between Nolan and me."

Nate wrinkled up his nose and didn't want to hear about mushy love stuff. He didn't know anything of that anyway, so who cared? He wanted to hear that his hero had saved the payroll.

"That can't be the end."

"It's not." Miss Kate grinned. "Nolan walked over and lifted me gently out of the dirt. He'd held me in his arms, closer than he should have. We'd just met. I wasn't his woman, and our behavior wasn't exactly proper. I'd been a crying mess though. I just couldn't stop staring at the dead man. I hadn't ever seen anyone shot down before. Nolan's hand gently tilted my chin. Our eyes held for a long moment before he kissed me, ever so softly."

"Yuck. He kissed you? On the lips? I like your story till the kissing part. My stomach is gonna turn if you say another word about smooching." Nate had never even kissed Jenny or wanted to. Miss Kate sometimes kissed Nate's face. That was different though. It wasn't mushy, on the lips. Ugh. Nothing in the world sounded more awful to him.

"Girls have bugs. Everyone knows that." Nate couldn't believe his hero had gotten caught up in such sap.

Miss Kate ruffled Nate's snowy hair and chuckled. "Well, I liked it. And there were no complaints from Nolan." She kissed Nate's face. "There is one more thing. I can't believe I almost forgot. Nolan had been shot. He has a scar in the very same spot as you'll have." She touched at Nate's ribs.

He couldn't help but smile from ear to ear. "I wanna be just like Nolan someday. He'll come back for me. I'm sure of it."

Miss Kate stood from the bed, then tucked Nate under the quilts.

"Miss Kate, don't tell anyone, but sometimes I wish Nolan were my pa. His name would be a good one to wear."

Tears welled up in Miss Kate's eyes. "I hope for your sake, sweetheart, that wish comes true. Good night."

Nate woke, and there was pinkness in the sky through the window.

"Miss Kate!"

Running footsteps echoed in the hallway. The door was thrown open, and she stumbled inside, all sleepy-eyed. Her hair looked as if she'd just fought her way through a hell of a windstorm. He'd never before seen her in her nightgown. She wasn't all put together like he usually saw her. She looked absolutely plumb crazy.

"What is it? What's wrong, Nathanial?" She was breathing heavy from the short run into his room.

Nate felt sorry for obviously startling her awake. There wasn't anything he absolutely needed at the moment. There was no trouble to speak of. He wasn't sick or anything like that. He just felt better when she was close. Was there a way of saying all that without sounding like a baby?

"I just didn't know where you were. I'm sorry... You can go back to bed. I swear I'm okay." He hoped she wasn't mad at him for waking her for no reason.

Miss Kate picked up a blanket that lay folded at the end of his bed and wrapped it around her shoulders. "I think I'll sit here for a while."

She grinned knowingly at him, then went to the rocking chair and made herself comfortable. How was it that she seemed to always be able to read how he was feeling?

She rested her head back and closed her eyes. Nate slowly pushed the quilt off from over him. His ribs were still sore as he scooted to the edge of the bed. It didn't take much to wind him. He sat a minute to slow his breathing. His feet dangled inches off the floor. All the good cooking Miss Kate had been feeding him and still he wasn't growing any.

Nate glanced over at Miss Kate sleeping. He wouldn't wake her. He could do this. He would just take his time. The night table next to the bed could be his crutch. The wooden horse figure gifted to him by the army doc was posed at attention, waiting for Nate to play. Only, he didn't feel much like playing. The wood figure made him miss Nolan. Nate wondered where the scout was right then. Maybe this would be the day he came home. Nate pictured himself running to Nolan and being scooped up to sit on the bay. He slowly stood and waited for his sea legs to steady.

Nate braved a step. He let go of the tight grip he'd had on the table and took another step on his own. One after another, he slowly walked across the room toward the bright sunlight that warmed the room. He made it. It'd been nothing short of a miracle.

What a glorious day. He pressed his face to the panes, trying to feel the freshness of a new morning through the glass. It wasn't enough. Nate felt greedy and tried to heave open the window to let the sun touch his skin, and his shoulder pinched. *Aw, damn.* He'd felt that. That arm where the bullet had cut into the shoulder hadn't yet gained its full strength. It was stiff this morning, and now it hurt like hell. Maybe Miss Kate would rub his shoulder down with whatever liniment she'd used before to make his aches feel better.

"Let me get that for you." Miss Kate yawned, then tossed aside the lap blanket. She came to his side and lifted the window open. "You shouldn't have gotten out of bed without my help."

The scolding was softly given. Didn't Miss Kate know how to yell or curse? Nate couldn't ever tell if she was really angry with him. Not that he was griping about it. Her way of correcting him was definitely much better than Pa's or Mr. Harper's.

"Here, now sit." Miss Kate pulled the rocker over next to the window for Nate to have a seat, and he was thankful for it. Weakness seemed to overtake him with any little effort. He'd walked across the room, a good ten to twelve feet, and was tuckered out.

"I'll go make breakfast." Miss Kate walked from the room.

Nate turned to the window. He leaned forward, resting against the wide sill. The touch of warm sun on his face and arms was a comfort.

Horses ran in the pasture, and green mountains stretched as far as he could see. There were lots of pretty flowering blooms in Miss Kate's yard. She walked from the house, closed the white picket gate behind her, and headed toward the chicken coop.

Nate was hungry this morning.

She reappeared, holding a basket full of eggs, then gave Nate a wave. He put a hand up. She turned and walked to the barn. He figured she was going to milk the cow. The rooster crowed.

The dumb bird was late. Didn't it know the sun was up? But the cock-a-doodle-do wasn't what perked Nate ears. Hoof beats of a single trotting horse approached the house. Was it Nolan? An excitement started Nate's heart pounding, and he was already smiling. He squinted to see the rider coming at a distance off the coach road.

The creak of the barn door closing turned Nate's eyes for a brief minute. Miss Kate carried the bucket of milk. She stopped, set it down, then shaded her eyes to see who it was riding up to the house. She gave a friendly wave to the horseman.

The horse wasn't a bay. That man was not Nolan. There was no missing that whoever the man was, he wore a tin star pinned to his vest that glistened against the sun.

Not twice. This couldn't be happening again. Was Miss Kate turning Nate over to the law as Nolan had tried to do back in that dumb little town? He scratched his head. Stuck in bed with fever and weak for so long, he couldn't recall the reason Nolan had done that. But Nate had been locked up for a short time before he'd been thrown to the Harpers, and he remembered that all too clearly. No way, he wouldn't be tossed in a cage again.

Nate hunched down and kept himself mostly hidden behind the curtain so he could still spy out the window. The sheriff pulled up on the reins in front of Miss Kate. How could she have sold him out? Jail or maybe being given away again to some jackass like Mr. Harper...Was that truly to be Nate's reward for trusting her? The gentle touches, sweet words, and kisses to his head...Had they all been lies? Tears stung his eyes. Was he really that much trouble that no one wanted him?

Nolan hadn't come back yet. Maybe the scout had thrown Nate aside too.

No, something in his gut sensed that couldn't be true. Or Nolan wouldn't have brought Nate there to be tended to by Miss Kate. She'd shown herself to be a good person in all the little ways that she'd cared for him, until this. He'd been convinced, from everything he knew of her, that she was better than most people. He did trust that, but he was still scared of what that lawman might do to him. What if somehow the lawman had found out that Nate was a Younger? He'd been with Miss Kate for a while now and Doc Martin had been spending lots of time there, so people were bound to ask questions and wonder who exactly he was. The lawman might have done some digging into Nate's past.

Miss Kate still shaded her eyes while looking up and talking with the sheriff, who was sitting his horse. Maybe Nate was being a scaredy-cat for no reason. Miss Kate knew his past. If she cared about him at all, then she would send the lawman away.

The sheriff stepped down from the saddle.

Dammit. Tears slid down Nate's cheeks. He wasn't in any condition to run away.

Miss Kate was smiling, seeming happy with the company. Nolan had worn a badge for a while, but that didn't convince Nate to trust every tin star. He didn't know that man who was grinning at Miss Kate as though she were the stars and moon, and her wide grin conveyed that she wasn't exactly displeased by the attention. The lawman picked up and was carrying the bucket of milk toward the house. Miss Kate hooked her arm around that of the sheriff.

Nate rubbed at his eyes, then looked again. Surely his baby blues were lying to him. This was just getting worse. Miss Kate had two good arms. There was no reason she couldn't carry both the milk bucket and the basket of eggs. She did it every morning. Nate's longing for someone to love him had made him a fool. He'd honestly believed her to be a friend.

He needed to get out of there before the tin star caught hold of him. He'd never be locked behind iron bars again, ever. He wouldn't just peacefully go with the sheriff. He'd do whatever he could to get away. Damn Nolan for leaving.

Nate hurried as fast as he was able to the top of the stairs. He was out of breath, and his legs shook something awful. He'd crawl if need be. Most houses had a back way out. He would find it, slip outside to the barn, and steal a horse. Would he even be able to crawl onto a horse with the way his ribs were now paining?

The front door opened. *Aw shit.* It was too late for that plan. The sheriff and Miss Kate were both laughing at something as they stepped inside together.

Nate hadn't been seen. He quickly stumbled back into his room, frantically looking about for another path to flee. Sweat beaded his head. His sight became a little fuzzy. He wiped the sleeve of his nightshirt across the wetness on his brow and then looked down at himself. He couldn't worry about changing his clothes.

His head was swimming, but he had to chance another step. The floor rushed up and smacked his face. *Aw damn.* He tasted blood in his mouth. Well … he was lucky he hadn't blacked out.

Tears streamed down his cheeks. Head-to-toe pain made his breathing ragged, but he wasn't giving up. Nate pushed himself up on all fours, then let his arms and legs steady for a deep breath or two. Okay, this was going to hurt, but he couldn't waste any more time to let himself feel better. It was the only means he could see of staying free from a jail cell.

He crawled like a crying baby to the window, then pulled himself up on the ledge. If he stopped to rest, he might not find the strength to get his throbbing body moving again. *One, two, three …* He rolled himself out through the window, dropping onto the porch roof. Flat on his back, Nate sucked air. It was all he could muster at the moment. The bright rays of sun beat down and blinded him so he had to squint his eyes tight. How much time did he have until Miss Kate brought the lawman upstairs looking for him? Nate needed to get moving.

He forced himself to roll over onto his hands and knees, then crawled to the edge of the shingled roof. The thought that he was going to make it out of there put a weary grin on his face.

"Nathanial!" Miss Kate screamed from behind him.

Nate twisted around fast. A pain tore along his ribs, and he grabbed his side. Miss Kate hung half out the window, reaching for him. Then Nate saw the badge.

"Dear Lord, don't let me break my neck." Nate whispered the prayer to himself, then rolled off the porch roof. His fingers dug into the ledge, and he swung himself down.

Miss Kate shrieked.

A stab of pain cut through Nate's sore shoulder, and he nearly lost his grip on the roof. The muscles that ran the length of his ribs hurt as if they'd been ripped in half. He gasped and had to focus to not let go. His grasp was slipping, and Nate hung by his fingertips on the edge.

The front door was thrown open. Miss Kate ran at him with her arms outstretched as he dangled from the porch roof. The sheriff was a running step behind her. Nate swung himself and made a wild grab for the porch post. His hands caught hold of the wood. It wasn't a tight grip, but Miss Kate was nearly on top of him.

Nate began to slide down the wood post toward the boarded floor. It would be only a jump to the ground, and he could run away maybe.

"Ahh!" Nate lost his grip on the post. He fell and hit the hard sod. Eating dirt was no fun, and it hurt something god-awful. He curled up on the ground, held himself, and cried like a baby.

Miss Kate dropped to her knees beside him. She was crying too.

"That lawman ain't taking me away!" Nate pushed away Miss Kate's hands. The badge stepped closer. Nate squirmed and clawed through the grass to get away. "Don't you touch me!"

He glanced over his shoulder as he dragged himself farther from the lawman.

"Nolan won't let you hurt me. You'll be in big trouble when he comes back and finds out you locked me away." Nate wiped quickly at his eyes and kept crawling.

"Nathanial, Sheriff Fuller is here to visit me." Miss Kate was crying hard. "Sweetheart, Wade and I are friends. I promise I wouldn't let anyone separate you and me, not even Nolan. Now please let me help you." She slowly stepped toward Nate, and her tender words made it easy for him to give in. He had no fight left in him to crawl another inch. He lay down in the grass and sobbed.

"I want Nolan." Nate couldn't stop saying it.

Miss Kate scooped him out of the dirt and hurried with him toward the house. "Wade, please fetch Dr. Martin."

CHAPTER 22

FLUFFY WHITE CLOUDS dotted the blue sky, and a cool breeze flowed down out of the mountains. Nolan put up a silent hand, and all the bluecoats behind him, including Captain Farnsworth, pulled up on the reins inside the tree line where Nolan could scope out the roadway that lay not far ahead of them without being spotted if Jones and his bunch were anywhere along that long, straight section. Nolan didn't believe that bunch had had enough time to come quite this far yet, but they couldn't be too far from it.

Water splashed from somewhere behind the thick brush along the other side, and laughter filled the roadway. Sounded like some kids having a good time. Nolan would've grinned, but he was too worried. The high-pitched squeals made him wonder if Nate had lived. That day he'd up and left Kate and Nathanial, he'd been sure the boy was going to die that very hour. Since then, Nolan had lots of time to think, and he wasn't so sure anymore. He hoped his son had somehow pulled through and wished he had stayed and nursed the child.

Not knowing was eating at him, and he wasn't about to let Jones or his saddle trash have a chance at shooting more kids.

Nolan looked both ways as he stepped the bay into the roadway.

The long path was empty from one end to the other except for the silly giggles.

Nolan circled the bay, searching the ground. This road was the only one within seventy-five miles that Nolan knew of that was wide enough for a wagon. Maybe some deer paths in the vicinity, like the one he'd just led the army on, but nothing feasible for a wagon full of women to be easily toted over. Ground was too rocky in these woods. Jones would have no choice but to travel this roadway, and he didn't leave witnesses, not even ones that crossed his path by chance like those kids might.

"Captain." Nolan gave a quick wave for Farnsworth to join him. The captain stepped his horse up next to the bay. A wide, satisfied grin spread across Nolan's face. "Tell me what you don't see pressed into the dirt on this road."

The captain spit a string of tobacco. "I don't care to be schooled in your craft. I ain't no kid or your pet project. Now what is it?" Captain Farnsworth looked down at the ground.

One of these days, Nolan was going to have his fill of Captain Horse's Ass and knock those pearly whites right down his damn throat. Today, though, he was feeling somewhat forgiving because cutting through the woods had paid off and they were now ahead of Jones. God willing, they'd stop him.

"There ain't no wagon tracks, nor is there a mess of horse prints. Meaning Jones and his bunch haven't passed by yet. We're in front of them, just as we'd planned. However, instead of us turning back and charging straight at Jones, consider setting up an ambush. Them kids that we can hear having fun, they likely belong to the next homestead, which probably ain't too far away. A homestead way out here in the middle of nowhere... We both know how greedy Jones is. He won't pass by a possible profit, not when we've managed to take back a few more of the women. Jones will want to replace them. Plus we can keep these and any other kids there safe."

Farnsworth beamed, probably at the thought of getting his hands on that slimy bastard. More giggles floated up from behind the bushes. The captain sobered, and Nolan could rightly guess why. Three days back and an hour too late, the army had come across a young girl who'd been stabbed in the gut and left for dead. She couldn't have been any older than Nathanial. Doc had hurried and done his best to save her, and the whole time, she'd cried for her mama, who wasn't around because Jones had taken her.

Nolan might not ever stop hearing those pitiful cries, and he certainly couldn't forget the sad sight of that little girl withering and clinging to the captain's arm as he'd tried to keep her still while Doc worked.

There hadn't been a dry eye among them when they buried her. With every shovelful of dirt that'd been pitched while digging that six-foot hole, Nolan had ached with too many thoughts about Nathanial.

"Let's git them kids out of there." Nolan turned the bay and trotted his horse into the tree line where the giddy voices were coming from, and the captain followed.

He had gone no more than fifteen feet, and there stood a horse tied to a limb alongside the creek. A rifle had been left in the scabbard on that side of the saddle, and two small shirts, pairs of pants, and boots littered the ground nearby. Nolan looked toward the hoots and hollers as he walked the bay right up to the edge of the creek in time to see a boy of about ten years of age let go of a rope swing and fall into the middle of the creek with a big splash. A younger boy climbed up the bank and grabbed at the swaying rope.

"You boys keeping cool?" Nolan stepped down and let the bay drink. The boys, who were in nothing more than their drawers, stopped their play and stared at him all wide-eyed for a few seconds. His appearance out of nowhere must've startled them a little.

The older of the two boys nodded as his gaze floated past Nolan. Captain Farnsworth reined in next to Nolan, and both boys stared at the captain's sword with awe. Soldiers filed in behind Farnsworth, and the boys were both smiling.

Nolan squatted, scooped up some water, and drank. "You boys live close by?"

"Yes, sir. A mile thataway." The older boy pointed.

Nolan stood and flicked the wet off his hand. "I'd like to talk to your pa. I think the army could use his help."

"He was working in the barn when we left. We can show ya the way." The boys seemed eager to help and hurried through the water toward their clothing and horse.

Captain Farnsworth stepped down and also let his horse drink. "Maybe we can get some provisions for our horses if we have time. They're starting to look as sorry as we are."

Nolan nodded. That was a good idea, but the captain was right about time maybe not being on their side. They had no way of knowing for certain when Jones and his caravan might come down that road. Could be anytime now. The trail through the woods that Nolan had led the soldiers on in an effort to slip around in front of Jones had been rougher than he had first thought and had slowed their pace when it got too rocky. And most of the time, Jones had been pushing the wagon horses at a fair pace to cover lots of ground.

"Make haste, boys. Daylight's a-burning, and the army's got business to attend to." Nolan clapped his hands a few times to get them moving faster. Setting up an ambush wouldn't take too long if the layout of the farm was right for it, but they didn't need Jones accidentally sneaking up on them in the middle of getting themselves prepared.

"Yes, sir." The boys both hustled and yanked on clothing.

The two kids led the way into the yard. A skinny, dark-haired woman hung wash on the line. A baby sat at her feet inside a basket of linens. Two little girls ran from the chicken coop toward the house with a basket full of eggs, and a dog barked from somewhere near the barn. The woman turned, shaded her eyes, and watched the army kick up dust as they rode toward her.

Captain Farnsworth stepped down, pulled off a glove, and offered a hand. Nolan didn't care much about introductions. The trees of the surrounding mountains circled the yard so it formed a natural corral. This was a perfect spot to lure Jones into if the folks who lived there would oblige the army.

The two boys ran off toward the barn, and a few minutes later, a shaggy-looking fella that was not too tall walked toward the captain. The fella was carrying a rifle, and the boys had made themselves scarce. Nolan didn't blame the man for being protective.

"Bertha, git in the house." The sodbuster jerked his head toward that direction and stood in front of the captain. The woman picked up the baby and walked fast.

Nolan stayed on his horse and let Captain Farnsworth do all the explaining, and he must've done a good job because the farmer nodded as he eyed the captain's men. The man of the house probably figured that facing Jones with an army of guns was much smarter than gambling his family's lives. Jones wouldn't just ride on past, and Nolan would make sure of that.

The captain gave a quick wave for Nolan to join them. He introduced Nolan, and he shook Mr. Murphy's hand.

The man turned toward the house. "Boys, git out here." The older boy came running with the younger on his heels. "Take these men out back of the barn so they can hide their horses. Then you both get your rifles and get up in the hayloft. Hurry now."

"Not them." Nolan didn't like the idea of the boys being part of the fight. "They hide with your woman. The army will do the fighting."

Mr. Murphy's brow furrowed. "Both my boys can shoot straight."

"I don't give a damn." Nolan wasn't going to say how many kids he'd dug graves for while chasing Jones. It might rattle the boys even more, and they were already pale. Their pa might've been blind to their fear, but Nolan wasn't. "I ain't asking." His eyes narrowed, and his cold stare must have been convincing.

Mr. Murphy thumbed the boys toward the house. "Go on, boys."

Nolan followed them inside. A few minutes later, Captain Farnsworth came in through the back door and positioned himself next to a front window overlooking the lane into the yard. Nolan didn't have to ask. If the captain was there, then his men outside were in place and ready to fight.

Mrs. Murphy and all the kids were in the root cellar, and the boys had their guns just in case. Now the army just had to wait until Jones showed up, and guaranteed, he would. Nolan tossed more logs onto the fire.

Farnsworth huffed. "Good God, man, are you trying to roast us all out? I thought you were on the side of the army." The captain wiped the sweat from his head.

Nolan's shirt stuck to his wet back. "I wanna make sure Jones sees this place. It ain't far off the road, but that thick smoke for sure will be seen above the treetops. A signal can't hurt."

They didn't have to wait too long. Nolan stayed to the side of the window. Two men, neither of them Jones, trotted their horses all friendly like into the yard.

Dammit. Where the hell was Jones and what was that snake up to? Maybe he'd seen the smoke and sent a couple of men ahead to do the killing while the rest of them took their time getting there, but one of the women had been sent along. Why? She rode in the saddle behind one of the men.

Nolan looked over at Captain Farnsworth, who shook his head and shrugged. He looked back out and did some fast studying of the three, and Jones's slick plan came to him.

He turned and waved two fingers for Mr. Murphy to switch places. He went and stood next to the door. Oh, that son of a bitch Jones was sneaky. Who wouldn't open the door and welcome in a travel-weary couple and their companion? Most folks were hospitable, and a visit was how lots of people who lived out away from town got news. It wasn't uncommon to invite a stranger in. It was, however, unfortunate that Jones had stayed behind with the wagon. Nolan had been looking forward to feeding him a piece of lead.

"They're getting down off their horses." Captain Farnsworth quietly led Nolan through each step right up to the door.

The Colt was fully loaded and in Nolan's hand.

There was a pounding at the door. Nolan glanced at the captain, who nodded. Nolan threw open the door and shoved the barrel of the Colt into that bastard's face. A high-pitched scream jumped out of the woman, who then froze. Soldiers rushed from all sides, and Jones's men held their hands high. A couple of the blue boys grabbed the pistols out of the holsters of the two men.

Doc quickly led the crying woman inside by the arm, and she clung to him. Other than filthy, she looked to be okay.

A wagon wheel creaked, and Nolan looked up. Jones was out in front of the wagon on his white horse, and following behind the ladies were all the other fighting men. There was a brief pause as that fancy prick's stare turned cold, realizing his plan hadn't gone right. A terrible thought struck Nolan. Jones must've been so used to hearing a woman scream in fear that it never dawned on him to think of it as a warning.

Guns were palmed, and Jones's henchmen charged toward the house. Captain Farnsworth's regiment opened fire. Jones's man that Nolan held at gunpoint lunged, and Nolan's pistol flew out of his hand. Together they flipped back over a table and hit the floor, knocking over a chair. Fists were swinging. Nolan was burning with punches, but so were his knuckles as he landed shots of his own.

They were on their feet, and gunfire boomed from everywhere. Nolan grabbed the fire poker and swung, but that fella was quick and ducked. Nolan got a swift boot in the gut. Oh God, he couldn't breathe. Jones's man swung a chair up in the air, about to burst Nolan's head wide open. With both hands and all his might, he stabbed with the iron poker, and the sharp tip speared through the gut of that trash. The fella grabbed the metal shaft while blood poured out of him, and he dropped to the floor on his knees.

Nolan stepped forward and wrenched the iron. "That's for the bullet that one of you scumbags put in my son." His voice was an unforgiving deep growl. He twisted the shaft again. "And that's for them women. Enjoy hell, you bastard." He yanked out the bloody poker and tossed it aside.

Gun smoke clouded the room, and shots echoed in through the busted windows. Mr. Murphy lay on the floor, holding his bleeding arm. Doc was next to him, and the woman cowered in the corner with her hands covering her face. The captain wasn't there. He must've rushed out after Jones had appeared and Nolan had gotten knocked back through the doorway.

Nolan gave a stomp on the floor. "Open up, boys."

The cellar door squeaked. He quickly aided the lady down, then shut the door.

He grabbed his pistol off the floor and went to a window, the scattered glass crunching under his boots. He aimed and squeezed the trigger. The wagon wasn't in the yard anymore. Nowhere did Nolan see a white horse or too-frilly blue suit. Where was that slimy bastard?

He slipped outside and hunkered down behind a stack of wood not far from the house. Several cavalrymen lay dead in the grass, but they weren't the only ones. At least five of Jones's men were dead.

The gunfire ceased, and Captain Farnsworth came running. "We can catch him. Let's go."

Nolan grabbed the reins of a stray army mount and swung into the saddle. He sank spurs and charged out of the yard with the captain and some of his men. The wagon was up ahead about half a mile, and it was going too fast, weaving back and forth all over the damn road.

A boom rang out and dirt kicked up in the roadway. Nolan grabbed the rifle left in its sheath, aimed, and fired.

There was a sharp corner coming up in front of the wagon. It would never make that turn at such a wild speed. Both wheels on the right side lifted, and the women inside all screamed. The wheels didn't touch back down. They rose higher, and the wagon rolled three or four times before the canvas top smashed into the ground and halted it.

Jones's men quickly took position around the wagon, and some of them ran into the tree line. Rifle blasts echoed, and several of the captain's men fell dead out of their saddles. Nolan spotted the fancy man getting off his horse, and he squeezed the trigger, just missing. The lucky bastard had bent over as he grabbed one of the women who'd been crawling out from under the wrecked wagon.

Jones stood on the far side of his horse so Nolan couldn't get a clear shot as he threw the lady up onto the saddle, then swung a leg up while holding tight to her. Nolan still could not get a bead on Jones. If he chanced pulling the trigger, he might hit her instead.

Men everywhere snatched up the women who stumbled out and took off following Jones.

A bullet zinged past Nolan's head, and he ducked in his saddle. Jones was still in sight, and Nolan was closing the distance between them fast. A rifle cracked, and the horse Nolan was riding buckled underneath him, slamming him into the hard dirt.

His eyes fluttered open, and he blinked to clear his vision. Oh, his head hurt. He didn't move a muscle but just lay there not far from the dead horse.

Doc hunkered down next to him and held up two fingers, wiggling his pointer and middle. "How many do ya see?"

"Git your hand out of my face." Nolan sat up, pushing away Doc's arm. His head spun, and he rubbed at the knot on his crown. "Did the captain catch Jones?"

Now that he was seeing straight, Nolan looked all over the place. Soldiers worked around the busted wagon, pulling a woman out from under, who was crying and holding her leg. There were three dead women laid out in a row on the roadway.

Doc shook his head. "The captain and most of the troops are still chasing Jones. I was ordered to stay behind and tend to the women who were hurt and bury the dead." Doc handed Nolan his hat and then gave him a pull up onto his feet. "Per Captain Farnsworth, if you're not dead, then I'm supposed to tell ya to get your ass following and catch up." Doc pointed to where the bay was tied and waiting.

Nolan smacked the brim against his leg, releasing a puff of dust. He pushed his hat down onto his aching head and walked toward the bay with a heavy disappointment weighing his shoulders. Jones was still alive.

Nolan stepped into the saddle, thinking about Nathanial.

CHAPTER 23

TOGETHER, Nate and Miss Kate hitched the team to the buckboard. This was the first time since coming to be with her that Nate would set eyes on the town of Gray Rock. He crawled up onto the seat and plopped down next to her. She slapped leather to the pair of horses, and the wagon lurched forward.

Nate sat quiet the whole two-mile ride to town. The only thing stirring was the butterflies in his stomach. If he opened his mouth for any reason, his breakfast might fly out. Miss Kate must have sensed his nervousness and patted his hand. The wagon creaked along, and the blue sky overhead was speckled with puffy clouds. There was a cool breeze, and the sun was shining. How could anything bad happen on a pretty day like today? They rounded a bend, and Nate saw a wooden bridge up ahead and lots of buildings beyond that.

Wow-wee, the town sure was bigger than he'd pictured.

The buckboard rattled over the plank bridge and into the one long street. An old lady sat in a rocker on the porch of a boarding house with a wooden bowl of snap beans on her lap. The sign above the door read: NETTY'S. ROOMS 25¢ A NIGHT, MEAL INCLUDED. They passed a white-painted church with a picket fence that surrounded a small cemetery. The farther they went, the more Nate twisted around on the seat to take it all in.

There was a general store, a bank, a livery stable, and next to that was a round corral. The blacksmith, who banged away on a horseshoe, had a wiry gray beard and was not too tall. Gunsmith was painted in yellow on the window of a small shopfront. A gathering of ladies talked outside a dressmaker's shop. Henry's Hotel was made of bricks, by far the biggest building in Gray Rock. Nate waved to Doc Martin, who was sweeping the boardwalk in front of his medical office, or so the swinging sign read. There was even a telegraph office and a place to buy saddles and other fine leather goods. Nate snickered. Leather was spelled wrong on the painted window.

Houses lined the rest of the street, and everywhere he looked, there were people. Everyone seemed happy, shaking hands and greeting one another all neighborly. No one seemed to be wearing a frown. This might become Nate's hometown. Miss Kate had asked him about registering for school, and he'd always wanted to attend one. Jenny would like that he was getting an education. He hadn't thought about catching her killer in a long time, but he hadn't forgotten his promise to do so.

The jailhouse sat just off the square about the middle of town. Sheriff Fuller and his deputy were both lounging out front. Wade was tipped back in a chair next to the door, his hat pulled down over his face. The deputy played a game of checkers with another man, who was covered in dust and wearing chaps.

Nate hated when Sheriff Fuller came to the ranch and ate supper with him and Miss Kate. Oftentimes, Wade and Miss Kate would sit on the porch swing afterward and talk privately, and Nate didn't like that either.

He needed to get the sheriff out of his head. Thoughts of Wade Fuller were not going to ruin his first day of attending a real school. This was a special day. Even Miss Kate had said so at breakfast. The wagon stopped in front of a white-painted building that closely matched the church in shape and size. It didn't have a steeple, but it had a bell that hung to one side of the double doors at the top of the stairs.

"Here we are." Miss Kate grinned sweetly, and a flood of noises from many children running and playing took Nate's attention.

Oh boy, his stomach fluttered. There were a lot of kids, and Nate hadn't really ever been around more than just Jenny. Several boys tossed an apple like a ball back and forth to one another in a small orchard that grew at one end of the long schoolyard. A row of three swings had been fastened to tree branches along the wood line that skirted the backside of the playground. There were boys and girls spinning about everywhere.

"Are you ready to go inside?" Miss Kate patted Nate's leg, then stepped down off the wagon.

What if no one liked him? He might say or do something by accident that would cause him not to have any friends. Did Nate even know how to be a kid? He'd been raised by the worst sort of men until Nolan came along. The others had taught him skills like how to pick a lock and how much dynamite was needed and where best to place it to blow a safe. Nate didn't know how to throw a ball for fun.

"Nathanial, come on." Miss Kate waited.

He slowly crawled down and stood close to her side. The butterflies inside him were going crazy, and his heart raced. What if the teacher didn't like him? It wasn't out of line to think a curse might slip off his tongue. It had happened more than once in front of Miss Kate. She hadn't yet washed his mouth out with soap or peppered his tongue, but she'd threatened it a few times. What would the teacher do to him? She might be real mean.

No…this was silly. Going to school shouldn't scare Nate. Now, did he have time to convince himself before the bell rang? He'd run from posses of badged men who were throwing lead his way. School, for some dumb reason, scared him more.

Nolan wasn't afraid of anything. Nate could be brave too. To sit in a classroom was a wish he'd made many times, and it was about to come true. The first thing he would ask the teacher… Why was it that a person's hands took to sweating when, indeed, he was about to get something he wanted?

Miss Kate took his hand in hers and gave him a little squeeze. He needed her strength; that was for sure.

Miss Kate took the first step toward the stairs, and Nate followed. They stood before the door, and she reached out for the knob. His heart pounded. Could he fit in there? Would the other kids see that he'd been raised differently? He'd bet none of them had ever held up a stagecoach or robbed a bank.

Even if the other kids didn't like him, he had Miss Kate. She cared about him, and that was all he needed for now.

She opened the door, and Nate looked down at the patched-up clothing he wore. She'd done a fine job of scrubbing the bloodstains out of his pants. And she'd been kind enough to cut down a shirt that Nolan had left behind. The fit wasn't perfect, but he liked the reminder of Nolan. Maybe it would bring him good luck on this special day and all would go well. Miss Kate had offered him other clothes that would fit him, but he liked the idea of feeling like a part of Nolan was with him.

"Don't be nervous. You look fine." Miss Kate smoothed his snowy hair. "Mrs. McKay is a sensible and friendly lady."

Nate would just have to trust that she knew what she was talking about. There wasn't one worry line on her face. That made him feel a little confident. Miss Kate put an arm around his shoulders, gave a squeeze, and together they stepped inside.

A primly dressed dark-haired woman looked up from where she sat behind a big desk. Rows of bench seats were situated to center the room in front of her, and a blackboard lined the entire wall behind her. There was a small bookcase filled from top to bottom with things that Nate couldn't wait to learn. A small table stood next to the back door. Several glue bottles, some rulers, and a pair of scissors sat atop.

Mrs. McKay smiled as if they were all old friends. This was a good start, but Nate still had to remind himself to breathe. Miss Kate gently pushed him along to walk toward a promising but, at the same time, scary future. Except for the time he'd ridden with Nolan, Nate wasn't at all familiar with how life worked on the honest side of things. Getting an education to better himself hadn't been in his raising. That was the honest-to-God truth.

At first glance, the big broach Mrs. McKay wore on her lacy blouse had brought dollar signs to Nate's head. How to survive had been all he'd ever learned. Sticky fingers had at times kept food in his belly. But he couldn't let himself think like that anymore. Miss Kate had done this good thing for him. He wouldn't reward her by doing bad.

They stood together smack dab in front of Mrs. McKay's desk. Nate wanted to hide behind Miss Kate's skirt. Her soft ways were turning him into a baby. Where was Nolan when he needed him?

"Hello, Nathanial." Mrs. McKay's voice was nice, friendly.

Did Mrs. McKay know his last name? Nate's gaze fell to the floor. If Miss Kate shared who Nate's pa was with the sheriff or anyone and that word got out, it could mean trouble for both Nate and Miss Kate. Folks were never friendly when they heard the name Younger.

"He's shy around new people." On behalf of him not properly greeting his teacher, Miss Kate had spoken up.

Nate did manage to squeak out a grin.

What was he doing there? This wasn't who Pa had taught him to be. Nate had an angry past that always seemed to shadow him. Could Jim Younger's son just be a normal kid?

He'd bet everything that Nolan would be proud that he was starting school.

A troubled thought jumped into his head then, and Nate felt himself shrink up. How much learning could he do without books? He didn't have money to buy any. And it wouldn't be right to expect Miss Kate to bear the expense since she'd just a few days ago asked him to become her son and he hadn't given his answer yet. Wade was one reason Nate had paused, and the other was his promise to Jenny. But he needed to not think about those things right now.

His shoulders slumped, and water filled his eyes for more than he was about to mention. "I don't own a pencil, paper, or a slate." Nate felt a rush of heat to his face. Maybe school was a bad idea. He should have taken up Miss Kate on her offer to teach him one-on-one at the ranch. She'd said she would if he didn't feel ready to be introduced into the community.

Miss Kate lifted his chin. "I'll take you after school and we'll buy all the supplies you need." She gave him a wink.

"Nathanial." He looked over at Mrs. McKay. "Why don't you go ring the bell for me? School is about to start."

"Yes, ma'am." Nate's voice had been so timid he barely recognized himself. What was wrong with him? The teacher had done nothing more than smile at him, and he'd turned to mush. Maybe other kids, too, had felt like this on their first day of school. He started toward the door to ring the bell.

"Oh, Nathanial, what is your last name? I need it for my register." Mrs. McKay had a ledger open on her desk, pencil in hand. She waited for his answer, but he wasn't about to give one.

To tell the truth of his bloodline would be to number his days in Gray Rock. Good folks wouldn't want Nate's kind around to muck up the reputation of their peaceful town. He glanced between Mrs. McKay and Miss Kate. If Gray Rock were to be his home, then no one could link Pa's bad doings with him. His first day of school looked like it might also be his last.

"He will be using my name, James," Miss Kate stated as a matter of fact.

Nate's gaze settled on her loving grin, and he knew all would be okay, at least on this day. He ran, threw his arms around Miss Kate, and gave her a big, happy squeeze. She was definitely looking out for him. A nod from her ushered him toward the door to ring the bell as the teacher had asked.

"He'll be fine." Mrs. McKay assured Miss Kate, and Nate turned to signal the start of the school day.

He believed what Mrs. McKay said. He would be okay. What could the other kids do to hurt him? Poke fun at his poor clothes or maybe laugh if he was asked a question and gave a dumb answer. Those things would shame him a little, but... sticks and stones. He'd already lived through much worse.

Nate pulled the rope, and the bell clanged. All the kids came running and filed in the door past him.

Miss Kate waded out through the stampede of boys and girls to hand Nate his lunch pail. "Have a great day. I can't wait to hear all about it." She made her way down the steps and then waved goodbye from the wagon seat.

"Children, settle down and take your places. I would like to introduce our new student. This is Nathanial James. Please welcome him into our class."

Standing at the front of the classroom next to the teacher, Nate could feel every eye on him. There were probably thirty faces staring into his. No doubt, they could see his uneasiness by his quivering legs. Could they hear his heart pounding as well?

The student body as a whole bid him good morning.

"Nathanial, you may take the seat right there." Mrs. McKay pointed, and Nate sat down next to a boy he guessed to be his own age.

Jenny had been right. There was nothing about school he didn't like, and most of what they were learning came real easy to him. At recess, the other kids were friendlier than he'd thought they might be. Tag was the first game he learned to play. It wasn't so hard to fit in. He watched, then simply did what he saw the other kids doing. So this was what it felt like to be a seven-year-old boy. The ear-to-ear smile might never come off his face.

He sat under a tree for the shade at lunchtime. Before Nate even unwrapped his sandwich, a kid named Johnny and a few other boys plopped down around him, all with their lunches. "You mind if we eat with ya?"

In Nate's mind, he thought, *Hell yes, this is great!* He wanted friends. But he wasn't going to let that slip out of his mouth. Instead, he nodded. He took a bite of his lunch and felt the stares from the other boys, making him self-conscious of his chewing.

"Is it true that you got shot by outlaws? That's what my ma said she heard from Mrs. Jacobs the dressmaker." Johnny Filson seemed to be the leader of this gang, or maybe he just had the biggest mouth. The other boys all huddled closer to one another and nodded as if they, too, had heard the rumors from their folks.

"I overheard about the shooting from Doc Martin." A boy named Phillip did the talking this time.

Nate chuckled while the others all chimed in with their version of how he'd been shot, as if he wasn't sitting right there among them.

"I don't believe it." A sour-faced boy snipped at the others.

The schoolyard gang all turned and faced Nate. Every ear waited to hear an answer. Boy oh boy, did Nate have a story for them. He lifted his shirt. The boys all awed at his nasty-looking scar.

Nate cleared his throat. He wanted them all to hear him clearly. "It was a larger than normal bullet that I took while assisting the US Cavalry to fight off a gang of at least fifty vicious outlaws."

"Can I touch it?" Johnny asked first. Then the others all wanted turns. One by one, each boy traced his fingers over Nate's ugly, rough, patched-together skin.

"I was one of two scouts that helped the army save some defenseless females." The wide-eyed boys hung on Nate's every word. He added a cannon or two to the story and liked the way it sounded better. And when Nate had them all drooling for another bite, he shucked his shirt off his shoulder and displayed another deep, ugly pink scar. The boys all shook their heads in utter disbelief. Only, the proof was branded into Nate's hide. He could see by the dumbstruck awe on their faces that he was quickly becoming a hero among them.

"Oh yeah, I almost forgot. My leg nearly got taken off by an arrow from a renegade Indian, but I can't show ya where that scar is 'cause I'd have to drop my drawers." The boys all laughed along with Nate.

By the time the bell rang to sound the end of the school day, Nate had become one of the class. He'd been surprised and pleased at how fast he'd gone from being a stranger among the other kids to building friendships.

He ran from the schoolhouse to meet Miss Kate. She waved to him from the porch of the general store. His feet slapped the dirt as he fast-stepped it across the street straight toward her. What exactly it was that came over Nate, he couldn't say. Maybe it was just pure happiness. All he could think about was how badly he wanted to share his whole day with her. Miss Kate beamed, and Nate knew she couldn't wait to hear each and every word he had to say.

"I can't wait to go back to school tomorrow." He jumped up onto the boardwalk and skidded to a halt in front of Miss Kate, nearly plowing her over. "Mrs. McKay is the nicest teacher ever. I'm thinking Johnny Filson will probably be my best friend. All the kids like me."

"Well, what's not to like?" She leaned down and kissed his face.

They headed into the store. Shelving lined every wall from floor to ceiling. Tobacco tins, fry pans, stacks of clothing—everything imaginable had been stuffed on those shelves. There was also a long, waist-high counter with shelving underneath that centered the store. It, too, had every nook packed with merchandise. The cash register sat on another long countertop that displayed candy jars at one end.

Miss Kate bought Nate a slate, paper, pencils, and the reader that Mrs. McKay had said he should start with. This was his chance to brag a little to Miss Kate. Hopefully, she would be proud of him.

"After hearing me read and testing me some, Mrs. McKay said I was advanced in my comprehension of what she called the three Rs. Do you know what that is?" Nate was testing Miss Kate.

"Reading, writing, and arithmetic." She grinned. "Nathanial, that is wonderful. I'm so happy that your first day went well. Now, which material do you like better?" She held up a length of plain white yard goods, then pointed to a checkered pattern.

Hm. He picked the checks with a touch of his finger. She ended up having Mr. Henderson, the store owner, cut a length of both materials. He rolled his eyes. Why ask which he wanted?

"I think I'll use the white to make you a shirt for church, and the patterned material will be for an everyday school shirt." Miss Kate had spoken aloud to herself more than Nate. "Mr. Henderson, I need to see the catalog. Nathanial, I want you to pick out a coat for when the weather turns cold."

The storekeeper set a thick book on the counter for Miss Kate to browse. What a surprise. Books and paper, yeah, that expense Nate understood. Those items couldn't wait. He needed them for tomorrow. Fitting him with new clothes hadn't been part of the deal. Store-bought duds were pricey. Could Miss Kate afford it? It wasn't necessary for her to take on the burden of such an added cost. The other kids hadn't even eyed what he'd been wearing.

Should Nate argue in front of the storekeeper and his wife that he didn't need the clothes? There were other townsfolk doing their shopping too. The place was crowded. Maybe Miss Kate could return the clothes later. Nate flipped through the pages and made his selection with Miss Kate's help. It was kind of fun. He pulled on new boots before they left the store, and she bought him new trousers to wear for school tomorrow. They left the store, carrying all the packages.

This was all wonderful, and he was grateful and smiled. But it was too much. "Thank you, but you didn't have to do this for me."

Miss Kate grinned sweetly. "It's not that much, and I want you to understand it's not a bribe so you'll say yes to becoming my son. I wanted to buy these things for you."

Nate hadn't even thought of the gifts as bribery until she'd said it. His old self would have been immediately suspicious. Could one day of being Nathanial James have made that big of a change in him? She was the real reason, not the name.

"Miss Kate." He handed her the packages, and she placed them in the wagon bed.

"Yes, sweetheart, what is it?" She crawled up onto the wagon seat, then offered him a hand.

This was it. Nate was going to say it. The words would not get stuck on his tongue this time. "I love you."

Tears welled up in her eyes. She pulled him up onto the seat and into her arms. "I love you too, Nathanial."

With each passing day, Nate became more familiar with all the townsfolk. Everyone always greeted him and Miss Kate with kindness. Even Pete, the ever-grouchy-looking saloon owner, put on a smile and nodded when he'd passed them on the boardwalk. It was something how Nate had been accepted as one of them, a person of the community of Gray Rock.

All the praise went to Miss Kate for that. She was a gem, and everyone, not just Nate, recognized it. He grew fonder of her as days passed into many weeks. He'd also made a tight-knit group of friends at school and was a straight-A student. Somehow, with all the nice things Miss Kate had done for him, his daily chores seemed a lot less like work. Nate finally had a home.

But he was still troubled now and then by a little tug in his heart. That pull was Jenny. Someday Nate would have to face down the fancy man. That was all there was to it.

CHAPTER 24

NATE TIRED OF HEARING his friends try to goad him into skipping school. "Come on, chicken." Johnny scratched the dirt with his boot toe, and a few of their buddies clucked at Nate.

They were ribbing him hard to go with them. Their promise: a day of unsupervised, no-work fun. Nate didn't want to play hooky. He liked school but wasn't going to admit it to his pals.

"If Miss Kate finds out, she'll chew my ears for at least a week."

His buddies either shrugged or waved him off. Yeah, that was right. It was nothing to them if Nate got in trouble. Why couldn't his friends see that it wouldn't just be his hide nailed to the wall if they all got caught?

"Don't you guys think Mrs. McKay will be suspicious if none of the five of us show up for school? Collectively, I do believe our absences would be hard to miss in the classroom."

"Stop being a crybaby." If Johnny hadn't been better than twice Nate's size, he would have slugged the big mouth.

"Yeah, Nate, why don't ya pull up your skirt and quit being a girl?" Phillip taunted.

"He's yellow." Johnny spit out the insult.

Thomas and Curtis both flapped their chicken wings and

nodded in agreement. They were all ready to go. Nate seemed to be the only one worried about getting caught. Punishment followed crime.

Guaranteed, he'd only get a tongue lashing if Miss Kate found out. They'd better not get caught. "All right. Let's go."

The five of them ran from the schoolyard.

They ate their lunches as they walked up through the trees and deeper into the mountain. Sweat ran down his back from the long, hot walk uphill, and his hair was nearly soaked. Nate had never been to the meadow at Blue Sky Lake. He couldn't wait to feel the cool water of the mountain lake hugging his sticky, hot skin.

"How much farther till we're there?" The blasted heavy heat made Nate's feet drag.

They crested the peak, and his friends all took off at a run. In a beeline, they flew and stripped off their shirts as they went. Nate took off following, and tossed clothing fell in every which direction, leaving a trail on the ground behind his friends. Nate yanked his shirt off over his head and dropped it where he stood at the water's edge.

Thomas took a hollering run off a jetting of rock and held tight, swinging on a thick vine out over the clear sky-blue water. He let go, dropped, and ... *splash.*

Nate's buddies had been right when they'd told him this was going to be great fun. He couldn't shuck his boots and throw off his socks fast enough. His fingers weren't working as quick as he wanted to unbuckle his belt. Finally he jerked his britches off over his feet, then shot off in full strides toward the vine.

In nothing more than their drawers, Nate and his buddies all huddled in line for a turn to swing.

"I'm next."

"No, I am."

"I'm older, so I should have the next turn."

It was a mixture of the whole gang arguing. Being outsized by the other four, Nate wasn't getting in on the shoving match. He'd wait his turn. All he needed was to go home with a busted lip or black eye and have to explain how he'd gotten it. The last in line still got to make a splash. That's the way he chose to look at it. The squabbling stopped, so the pecking order must have been decided. Phillip grabbed the vine. Curtis would be next, then Nate.

"Woo-hoo!" Nate soared over the water, and at the peak of the swing, he let go and stretched his arms into the air as he began to fall. He hit the water with a splash.

Hours passed, and their fun just went on and on as if it would never end.

A rattling of a wagon nearing them turned all their heads. Time stood still as they waited to see the cart roll into sight. It was Johnny's pa. Oh hell no, this couldn't be good. Mr. Filson's face was fire red, and it wasn't a sunburn.

The big man jumped down from the wagon and grabbed Johnny by the scruff of the neck. Poor Johnny began to bawl, and Nate didn't blame him. He quickly looked between the others, and his mind screamed, *What should we do?* They all looked bewildered too. The whole stupid bunch of them just stood there frozen.

Poor Johnny was dragged back toward the wagon and thrown over Mr. Filson's knee. Nate's gut tightened. How could he have been such a fool? It had been four against one, but he should have tried harder to talk his friends out of skipping school.

Johnny wailed as his pa whipped him good and hard. Nate scrambled up the bank, hastily grabbed for his clothes, and ran. Everyone else scattered. Nate dropped his socks. No way would he take time to pick them up. Oh Lord, he could still hear poor Johnny getting leather slapped to his backside.

On the run, Nate quickly tugged his shirt over his head. In a flash, he remembered the sting of Nolan's belt across his bottom. Maybe it was a good thing Nolan wasn't around, or Nate likely would be getting the same punishment. He hit the ground and skinned a knee and his elbows. That's what he got for trying to run and push a foot through his pant leg.

There was no getting away from Johnny's cries fast enough. What was Miss Kate going to do to him when she found out?

A quarter down the mountainside, panic hit him. "Aw dammit!"

He'd forgotten his books and lunch pail. He knew right where they sat near the log by the lake where he'd first dropped his clothes. He couldn't go home without them. Miss Kate wasn't stupid. No doubt, she would notice right off if he walked through the door without those things. She packed his lunch every day, and there wasn't an evening that she didn't ask to see his homework. He'd have to go back. What if he was late getting home? Shit. How was he going to hide all this from her?

He hightailed it back up the mountain and was relieved to not see Johnny and his pa. Nate grabbed his stuff and hustled home. When he got there, it was later in the day than usual, so he went straight to doing his chores. To be honest, he was a little afraid to take one step into that house. What if Miss Kate already knew? She might not want him anymore for being bad. And somehow she always seemed to know when he'd been up to no good. Most of the time, she would call him out on whatever he'd been thinking of doing before he ever even had a chance to, as she called it, "push her buttons."

"Nathanial, supper is ready." She didn't sound angry.

Nate stood the pitchfork in the corner of the barn, then threw a weary glance at the star-faced mare inside its stall, chewing hay. "Wish me luck, girl. I have a sick feeling I'm gonna need it."

What if Miss Kate did know and had been holding back her temper until he got inside? He would soon find out. He closed the barn door and took a deep breath. Was fitting in worth the trouble he would be in once Miss Kate found him out? He seriously doubted it.

This was it. Nate faced the door. His heart thumped in his chest as he reached for the knob. There was no turning back. He needed to face her, but he wasn't about to confess unless she suspected something foul and questioned him. Nate opened the door and stood waiting for the hammer of judgment to fall.

"Nathanial, what are you doing?" Miss Kate's brow rose, and she stared. "Close the door and go wash your hands. Then come sit down at the table before supper gets cold."

She seemed none the wiser to his hooky playing. So why was Nate's gut so tight? Oh, he knew that answer. She'd told him once that she had eyes on the back of her head. He'd never heard of such a thing and would have liked to root through all that red hair to see for himself. But it must have been true because she always knew everything he did, even when her back was turned.

Nate hurried to do as he'd been told. He wasn't able to meet her gaze, but he could feel her suspicious stare and he got chills. This supper was going to be the longest hour of his life. He dried his hands on a towel, then quickly walked straight to his chair. He'd just plopped down in his seat and thought the roast smelled real good when he heard the haunting rattle of a familiar wagon roll into the ranch yard.

Miss Kate rose from the table and quickly went and peered out the window. "John Filson … What would he be coming out here for?"

Had there been a hole anywhere nearby, Nate would have surely crawled into it. Miss Kate turned from the window, and he could feel her studying him. He couldn't help but squirm and immediately stare at the floor.

"Nathanial, is there anything you'd like to tell me before I go outside to talk to Johnny's pa?"

He winced at her stern voice, afraid to speak up. He should have just spilled his guts, but instead, he stupidly shook his head. Maybe hearing the truth from him first would lessen the blow of what she was about to hear from Johnny's pa.

Nate looked up from staring at the floor as the door clicked shut behind Miss Kate. Why hadn't he said something to defend himself? Well, he was guilty. The roast lost its savory smell, and what little appetite he had was gone. There was nothing he could do now. What was done was done, and he definitely was going to pay for it.

He hurried to the window. Miss Kate was standing on the porch, and Mr. Filson talked through gritted teeth from the wagon seat. Nate couldn't hear every word being said, but the ones he did weren't so good. Bastard and outlaw were two of the troublesome names he was being called. It sounded as if Johnny had blamed Nate for talking the rest of them into playing hooky. That no-good, rotten—

Nate best stop himself right there. He was in enough trouble. The last thing he needed was to have Miss Kate catch him cussing. Johnny was no friend of Nate's, not anymore.

"Nathanial James, come out here!" The tone of Miss Kate's voice told him that she was one snorting breath away from killing him.

Nate was done for. He'd been an idiot for ever following along like an oaf after his so-called buddies. He should have just stayed behind at school even if his friends teased him about chickening out. Now Nate was standing neck deep in the shit of it.

He'd best not make Miss Kate wait. Nate opened the door. His legs were shaking, but he went and stood judgment before her. No lying, he could damn near see steam rolling out of her ears. Miss Kate's lips were pressed so tight together that they looked like one thin, straight line. No surprise, her fists were on her hips. He had to look away from her piercing glare.

"You want I should learn the boy a lesson for ya, Kate?" Mr. Filson's voice boomed.

Tears sprang to Nate's eyes, and he shrank back. Mr. Filson was a bigger-than-big man, the size of a bull. No way was that giant going to beat on him. Hell, he'd have no hide left, as strong as Mr. Filson looked to be. Nate would cut his ties there and run first. He sniffled, turned to Miss Kate, and pleaded with the welled-up tears in his eyes to be spared from feeling Mr. Filson's belt.

Miss Kate stepped forward and took Nate by the arm. "No. I believe I can handle it." She marched him down the stairs, through the gate, and off toward the barn. "Do you have your pocketknife?"

What would Miss Kate want his knife for? Steam was still rolling from her ears, so he wasn't about to ask. He pulled the small flip blade from his pocket and handed it to her.

She shook her head. "Cut a switch." Miss Kate pointed him toward a thin-branched bush. She crossed her arms and waited, foot tapping.

All Nate could do was stare, dumbfounded. Was Miss Kate really making him do this?

"Nathanial James, I am waiting." And by the tone of her voice, she didn't at all appreciate his slowness to grasp that he was about to get a licking from her.

Nate thought all the long, wiry branches looked like small whips. She probably wouldn't find him funny, but he was going to chance it. He cut the smallest, most flimsy limb. It was barely as big as his little finger was round. He half grinned and held out the wimpy, tender little baby switch for Miss Kate to take. She immediately snatched the knife out of his hand and sliced off a much larger, sturdier one. Yup, he'd been correct in thinking she wouldn't be amused. Again, she grabbed hold of his arm, and they finished their march into the barn.

After his punishment had been dealt, Nate was sent to bed without supper. He felt sorry for more than one reason. He lay under his quilt with his bottom smarting, thinking he'd never seen Miss Kate so mad. There'd been tears in her eyes when she'd told of how disappointed in him she was. And as if that weren't bad enough, Nate's best friend had betrayed him. Oh boy, he was pissed off at Johnny for pointing a finger in false blame.

That wasn't the worst of Nate's trouble. Where had Mr. Filson found out that Younger was Nate's true name? Gossip spread like warm butter. What he'd hoped to keep secret was now probably well known throughout Gray Rock. That rumor he couldn't blame on Johnny. Nate had never talked about his past with any of his friends, other than bragging about the months he'd ridden with Nolan. Once word got around that his name was Younger and not James, people would look down on Miss Kate for taking him in.

He'd heard it right from Mr. Filson. *Outlaw, bad news, trouble.* It was the definition of the Younger family name. What if all this difficulty made Miss Kate consider him too much of a pain in the ass and she wanted rid of him?

He didn't want to leave. This was his home. Why didn't he have the nerve to run downstairs and tell Miss Kate yes to being her son? He probably had screwed up that chance, and it was too late now. She deserved everything good, and that wasn't him. He supposed it was time to move on and hunt for the fancy man, but he had one thing to settle there first. The sun couldn't rise on tomorrow's school day soon enough.

Nate walked with a purpose into the schoolyard and stood tall in front of Johnny. The pudgy-faced backbiter was two years older and better than twice Nate's size. That didn't scare him a bit. He'd witnessed plenty of bar fights. Pa wasn't a big man, but he'd dropped a few giants. You just had to know where to hit a man to knock him to his knees. And Nate had seen too many brawls to forget where those tender spots were.

He'd bet, too, that in a peaceful town like Gray Rock, Johnny had never even seen a man-to-man, knuckle-to-knuckle fist-fight. Johnny's size might have been enough to bully others away from chancing a schoolyard scuffle, but Nate had been born with fight in his blood. Johnny was about to get the Younger name stamped all over his face by Nate's fist.

His and Johnny's friends grouped around the two of them. Nate wasn't going to bother saying why he was mad and felt mean. Johnny was smart enough to figure out that much on his own. If he even offered, Nate didn't want to hear any lame excuses for the blame of skipping school being pinned on him.

Nate swung with all his might and felt the bigger boy's lip split. Johnny dropped to his knees but quickly jumped to his feet and lunged at Nate. His tackle sent them both falling, and they hit the ground with a thud. *Aw shit.* Nate couldn't let himself get pinned under Johnny's weight. The fight would be over real quick.

A rush of feet surrounded them. Nate kicked his knee up into Johnny's gut, and instantly he rolled off him. Nate threw himself on top of Johnny and smashed his fist into his face. Blood splattered on Nate's shirt. He cracked Johnny a second blow to the teeth. Then he caught one up under his chin and bit his tongue. Tears sprang to his eyes, and he spit blood.

Johnny shoved Nate hard with both arms, and he flew and hit the dirt, tearing the sleeve of his shirt. The two of them rolled across the ground, hitting one another. A chant to fight rose in his ears. Both his and Johnny's names were called out and cheered on to win the battle. Nate had no intention of losing.

A big hand clamped down on Nate's shoulder and ripped him and Johnny apart. "The two of you, knock it off!" Sheriff

Fuller held them both at arm's length until the fight in each of them settled. Mrs. McKay hurried across the schoolyard, and the sheriff kept hold of their scruffs so they stood quiet.

Mrs. McKay shook a finger at one, then the other. "Boys, what is this all about?" She was steaming.

Neither Nate nor Johnny said a word to explain. Instead, they just glared at one another. Mrs. McKay looked between the two of them and waited for one of them to tattle. "I can only assume you both are at fault since neither of you are willing to speak up and tell me what happened. I will be sending notes home to your folks."

"That ain't fair. That bastard's pa is locked away in prison." Johnny sneered at Nate, and Mrs. McKay stiffened at the mention of Pa.

Why hadn't she said a word to correct Johnny's hatefulness? This was bullshit. Nate thought he'd finally found a place he fit in and could call home, but it had all been a lie. Being a Younger meant he'd never have friends, folks, or anything good. Nate wasn't wanted in this town any more than he'd been wanted any other place. The days of him being recognized in Gray Rock as Nathanial James were over. The faces all around him seemed to be looking down their noses at who he was. And if they wanted to see the meanness of a Younger, then Nate would give it to them.

With one twist of his body, combined with a yank of his arm, Nate slipped free from Sheriff Wade's grasp and swung with all his strength, smacking Johnny in the gut, knocking the wind straight out of him. Johnny dropped to his knees and gasped for air. Nate's second swing to strike up under Johnny's chin was a miss when the sheriff grabbed his arm. Only this time he was dragged off, kicking and fighting, toward the jailhouse.

"Git your hands off me! Let me go!"

"Shut your mouth!" The sheriff slammed Nate down to sit in a chair across the desk from where the deputy sat. Deputy Toller jumped to his feet real quick, and Sheriff Fuller threw himself down in the same seat.

Nate sat quiet and could taste the blood from his busted lip. Red dripped on the front of his checkered shirt, the one Miss Kate had taken the time to make special for him. She was going to be pissed, and he couldn't blame her. Nate rubbed at his sore knuckles.

"Ride out and bring Kate in to fetch the boy." Sheriff Fuller grunted at Deputy Toller, who nearly tripped over his own feet to hurry out the door.

"I have a name, and it ain't boy." Nate met the sheriff's glare with one of his own.

"Shut up, you little smart-ass brat, or I'm gonna lock you in that cell." Sheriff Fuller's eyes narrowed, and he pointed to an empty cage.

Nate didn't hesitate to quit squirming in his seat. There were few things that he was truly afraid of, but being stuck behind bars again was one of them. No doubt, Wade Fuller would do just what he'd said. That wasn't what worried Nate the most though. Miss Kate would probably make Nate cut his own switch again. She'd doted on his happiness, and he hated to think of how upset she would be at his fighting. Getting back at Johnny had seemed like a good idea up until now. When Miss Kate saw that the townsfolk didn't want him in their community anymore, she might just let go of him.

The pendulum on the clock ticked, and Nate waited out what would probably be the final minutes of his life with Miss Kate. His stomach twisted in knots. He didn't want to say goodbye to her. Sheriff Wade sure would be glad if she gave Nate the boot. There would be no more fighting over her attention.

A buckboard rattled out on the street in front of the jail-house. Both Nate and Sheriff Fuller looked toward the window.

Miss Kate jerked on the reins and slowed the team to a stop. The sheriff hurried outside, leaving the door hanging partly open, and Nate could hear the noise from the street real clear.

Miss Kate stood on the boardwalk, facing Sheriff Fuller.

"I told you before, Kate. That boy is trouble. He needs a strong hand to tame him. Let me contact the orphanage in Three Springs. He can go there."

"Wade, Nathanial is my son. Maybe not legally on paper, but I love him just the same. You don't just send your child away because he got into a little trouble," Miss Kate said with some fire in her tone.

After all Nate had done, Miss Kate still loved him, and it didn't sound like she would ever send him away, no matter what. Which meant he had a home forever, and that made him feel really bad about starting the fight with Johnny.

The sheriff chuckled. "I don't call starting a fight a little bit of trouble, Kate. I don't want his kind in my town."

Miss Kate's hands fisted and punched to her hips. Nate knew that look. Her dander was up. "*His kind.* Might I remind you, Sheriff Fuller, that Nathanial is a seven-year-old boy. So are you saying that children are not welcome in Gray Rock or just the son of Jim Younger?"

"Kate, I don't want to fight about this. You had your fun playing mama to that boy. Now it's done. What do you wanna keep some stray mutt for? It's downright embarrassing how you falsely gave that brat your name so he could go to school. You done shamed yourself, Kate, and me too. Do you see this badge on my chest?" Sheriff Fuller tapped the star on his shirt. "I won't have that boy looked at as mine. I'd be laughed at from four counties away. Whoever heard of a lawman taking in the son of an outlaw? Have you lost your damn mind, woman? If it's to work out between us, then that boy has to go."

Tears sprang to Nate's eyes. So Sheriff Fuller was making her pick between marriage, maybe more children, and Nate.

He'd leave on his own accord and make that choice easy for her. She'd told him herself that having a family would be everything to her. This was her chance. Nate wouldn't mess that up for her. He wiped at his eyes.

Miss Kate poked a finger at Sheriff Wade. "Wade, you listen up real close and try to understand, 'cause I'm not going to say it again. I will *never* give up Nathanial for you or any other man. Is that clear enough?" She stepped around Sheriff Fuller and swung open the door.

Her piercing, red-faced glare put shame on Nate. Only, he wasn't thinking about how pissed off she was. Had he heard right? She'd picked Nate, a no-good bastard, over Sheriff Fuller. Why? The sheriff could fulfill her wish of having a whole put-together family again, like the one she'd lost.

"Nathanial James, what were you thinking, starting a fight?" Oh boy, she was cross.

Miss Kate wouldn't know it from his teary straight face, but Nate was smiling on the inside. Not because he'd made her so darn angry. The reason for his happiness was it seemed no matter what his trouble, she never gave up caring about him. Not once had she even threatened to throw him away like dirty old trash. She must have seen some good in him, and everyone else was blind to it. It was a mother's love. She was his ma, and he hadn't even truly recognized what that love meant until this instant.

Nate jumped to his feet, fresh tears flooding his eyes. "I'm really sorry. I promise I won't ever git into another fight." He put his right hand up, and Miss Kate grinned forgivingly.

"Oh Kate, you ain't dumb enough to fall for what that little brat just said, are ya?" Sheriff Fuller flopped down in his chair and shook his head as if what Nate had said was so ridiculous it couldn't possibly be true.

Nate wanted to stick his tongue out at Wade Fuller, but that wouldn't help prove to Miss Kate that he could choose to be good. He bit his lip so his tongue wouldn't slip out on its own.

"Wade, I don't want to hear your opinion." Miss Kate's eyes narrowed, and Sheriff Fuller straightened in his chair. "I believe Nathanial will do his best to keep his word." She might not have realized what she'd done, but Nate was aware. She'd stepped just so that she'd placed herself between him and the sheriff.

Nate had once seen a mother bear tear into a cougar that had sprung out of the brush to make a meal of her cub. It had been a hell of a fight, but the mother bear just wouldn't give up and ran that cougar off. Nate keenly sensed that he was standing smack dab between a mother bear and a cougar. Only, he wasn't a defenseless cub.

"Sheriff Fuller said he was gonna lock me in a cell." Nate let his tears fall. The threat had scared him, but not as badly as he was letting on. He was just lending a hand in running off that cougar.

"Wade, how dare you?" Miss Kate's face steamed up mean, and she looked as if she might spit.

The sheriff sprang out of his chair onto his feet. "Now, Kate, I only said that to make the boy settle down. I wasn't gonna do it."

"He's lying." Nate pointed at the no-good tin star.

"You, shut up!" The sheriff slammed his fist on the desk, and both Nate and Miss Kate jumped. Sheriff Fuller had the look of wanting to kill him.

Nate shrank back and wished Nolan were there. Maybe this cougar was too big and mean for him to run off by himself.

"Wade, that is enough." Miss Kate turned from the sheriff, then knelt in front of Nate. She lifted his chin and studied his busted lip, then looked deep into his blue eyes. "I don't want to hear another word from you either. You are a master of pushing Wade's buttons and you know it, so stop."

Nate couldn't get away with jack shit. Not with Miss Kate anyway. There was one thing he did need to know and would brave opening his mouth one more time. "Does Sheriff Wade have the authority to take me away from you? I don't wanna go live in some orphanage." There would be no other choice. Nate would run away if Sheriff Fuller had the power to rip him from Ma. "Oh Ma, I wanna stay with you. I'm really sorry for being so much trouble."

Nate's breath caught when what he'd just said hit him. He'd never before called her ma. Should he say sorry for that? But it hadn't been a mistake.

Tears welled up in Miss Kate's eyes. What did that mean? Nate quickly looked down at the floor.

She cupped his face in her hands so he could only look at her. "Nathanial, sweetheart, no one is sending you anywhere. I do want you to tell me honestly. Do you want me to be your mother?" Her smile was warm, and the hope in her eyes told of what she felt in her heart.

There wasn't another soul Nate would rather be with. Except maybe Nolan, but he hadn't been around in a long time. "I sure do." He threw his arms around her neck and hugged her tight. Nothing would make him happier than to call Miss Kate mama. They squeezed each other for a long minute while happy tears flowed.

Ma stood, straightened her skirt, and then wiped the tears from her red eyes. "Wade." She faced Sheriff Fuller and took Nate's hand in hers. "I would appreciate it if you would send word to the courthouse in Birch Creek and request the paperwork for me to adopt Nathanial. The circuit judge can officiate over the signing when he passes through in another week or two. I'll be waiting to hear from you."

They left the jailhouse together without a word from Sheriff Wade. The man's steamy red face had told of sore unhappiness. Nate was smiling though, from ear to ear, when he crawled up on the wagon seat next to Ma. He had a mother, and the cougar was gone for now.

"Young man, don't think you're getting off the hook for fighting. I'm not pleased about that." Ma was still wearing a happy grin, so Nate figured he couldn't be in that much trouble. "You will do extra chores, including washing dishes for a month."

That sweet grin of hers had been pure deceit. She knew he downright hated doing dishes. There wasn't a worse punishment, besides maybe being locked in the jailhouse with Sheriff Fuller. Oh well, he wasn't going to let the thought of shriveled-up fingertips sour his good mood. He had a mama who truly loved him.

CHAPTER 25

NOLAN SPURRED the bay and trotted out of the clearing and onto the old mule trail. It was just wide enough that a wagon full of women would narrowly fit. Unless there was another path that the old-time trappers used to travel by, this was the spot where Deegan Jones would try to cross the border. Now it was a waiting game for Captain Farnsworth and his army. They were ready for the fight that would come.

Jones was a slick son of a bitch and had slipped past the rank of bluecoats more than once during this leg of the chase. It had cost two more women their lives, and somehow Jones had managed to gain five more women to the good. Those settler families had been completely blindsided. Jones's attacks had been different from the first victims who were killed months ago. The homesteads themselves had been left standing, not burned. Recent incidents seemed similar to the attempted assault at the Murphy farm, when the army had tried to ambush Jones.

From the tracks Nolan had read, Jones had been invited right up to each house, nice and easy, like a wolf in sheep's cloth-ing. At least once, it looked like Jones had been asked inside to take a meal while his men with the captives all hid in wait. The man of that house was found dead, facedown in his plate of stew. His brains had been blown out, scattered across the table.

It must have put an awful fright into the three children to have seen their pa killed. They'd tried to run, it seemed, and were gunned down around the supper table. Tipped-over chairs and where they'd fallen was evidence of it. Stuck in the high-seated chair, the baby girl had been spared a bullet, her neck slit. Jones, that sick bastard, gave a whole damn new meaning to being hospitable. Nolan wouldn't stop until his hands squeezed around Jones's throat. The poor women, after all this time, likely had given up any hope of ever being rescued.

Nolan reined in. This was the best place he'd seen to set up an ambush. The trees were thick along the hills on both sides of the road, and there were lots of rocks they could use as cover. They could not fail or let Jones outsmart them this time. It would be the army's last chance to stop Jones before he slipped across the border. Then the women would be gone.

Captain Farnsworth joined Nolan.

"Right there." Nolan pointed to the ridge side. "If you put a few sharpshooters behind that thick clumping of dead falls, Jones won't know what hit him. We can drop a tree across the trail just around that bend so Jones's men won't see it at first. It would take some time to turn a wagon on this narrow patch of path. I doubt it could be done under fire unless the man at the reins don't care if he gits plugged full of lead."

The captain nodded in agreement with Nolan's plan.

"To cover that side of the road, I would place some men among those rocks and trees. They'll be well hidden and covered when the fight starts. The rest of the men, I say we send back yonder that way. Once Jones passes through to this spot, they can form a rifle barricade to the rear. Jones will be boxed in. Retreat won't be an option. Straight to hell is where we'll send Mr. Jones, and I will enjoy seeing it."

The captain grinned and clapped Nolan's shoulder. "You and me both, my friend. I'll even buy the first two rounds of drinks after we git that son of a bitch." They both had a good chuckle. This war with the Jones gang was about to finally end. Captain Farnsworth turned his horse, trotted off, and shouted orders to his men.

Nolan hoped when the sun set on this day, there would still be breath in his lungs. For good or bad, none of them knew for sure how this battle would play out. Jones had been a savvy fighter thus far. Nolan pulled his rifle, then nudged the bay trotting into the tree line. Missing a chance to take a shot at Jones wasn't something he intended to do.

Pushing a branch out of his way, he hunkered down among the trees on the hillside. From there, Nolan could rush the wagon and get the women to safety if able, instead of them being stuck in a crossfire. He stretched his eyeglass, pressed the lens to his eye, and closely watched the mule trail.

It wasn't long until his mind drifted to Kate, and he wondered again if Nathanial had lived. It was a question he'd asked himself every day. Too many times, he'd felt cross for not turning the bay around and hightailing it straight back to Kate and the half-pint.

The farther away he rode from where they were and the more death he saw, the more the pain of their absence grew. Every mile was torture, and each shovelful of dirt thrown to make a fresh grave had stirred his mind to picture their faces.

Nolan was glad that for some reason, Jones seemed to let the area of Gray Rock alone. Not to say he couldn't work his way in that direction, but the killer hadn't so far, and that was good. What mattered to Nolan most was that Kate and Nathanial, if he'd lived, were safe. Today, if all went his way, Jones would soon be dead and Nathanial would no longer be a target on his witness list.

The rattle of a wagon filled Nolan's ears, and his mind sharply focused. He squinted an eye, and what he saw through the lens brought a pleased grin to his face. This was it. The final showdown was about to begin.

Five men rode a few yards in front of the wagon. There was a line on each side of four more riflemen. The team of horses was sorry-looking. The animals' heads hung low and their hip bones stuck up and showed the pace in which they'd been pushed to cover ground. The driver and shotgun rider made two more fighting men. Where was Jones? *Dammit.* There were more hired guns on horseback behind the wagon, but none of them wore a fancy blue suit. Nolan tallied the figures. The odds were in the captain's favor as far as the number of guns and the element of surprise.

The four riflemen behind the wagon were maybe two or three horse lengths off the pace, but the group as a whole was packed fairly tight into the narrow trail. It was just what Nolan and the captain wanted, with the exception that Jones wasn't there with his army.

A shot rang out. The driver toppled off the wagon. The battle had begun.

The half-dead nags reared. Some of the women screamed. Dropping his rifle, the shotgun rider grabbed for the reins. Jones's men opened fire, and just that fast, guns boomed everywhere. The wagon lurched forward to round the bend, and the horses stopped before they even began to run. Blocking their path was the downed tree.

Nolan squeezed the trigger. A hole was blown through the gut of the man holding the reins. Twisting, he grabbed at his wound. A second bullet tore into him just above his belt, and he fell backward off the wagon, hitting the dirt. The next man who picked up the reins of the wagon got a hole blown through his chest, and he flipped off the wagon and hit the ground.

Nolan rushed the carriage, and a few of the bluecoats followed his lead. Gun smoke loomed heavy in the air. Some of Jones's men turned their mounts to run. As planned, the captain's forces had the retreat blocked. In a salute of gunfire, Jones's men dropped from their saddles.

Nolan gripped the flap closing in the back of the wagon. Jones was still nowhere to be seen, and this could be a trap. He and the army men circled the back end, and all at once, Nolan pulled open the canvas and simultaneously trained his gun into the back. Upon seeing it was all women, he lowered and gave the all clear.

Every one of the women cowered and was crying. Their faces were all drained of color.

"Let's git them out of the open and into the tree line," Nolan ordered.

A young soldier immediately began to aid the ladies down out of the wagon. Another bluecoat ushered them at a fast pace to safety while Nolan and two other soldiers gave cover fire from around the wagon. Nolan thumbed cartridges into his rifle. The gunfire stopped, leaving the scene eerily quiet. Then a horse blew, and some of the women began to openly sob.

It was over.

A mass of dead, bloody bodies, including some of the blue boys, were scattered along the patch of trail. Captain Farnsworth rode out of the trees and up to the wagon. Reaching from his horse, the captain shook Nolan's hand. This day had been a longtime coming. The women were all finally safe.

"I'm gonna hold you to that drink." Nolan grinned.

Captain Farnsworth tipped his hat, dismounted, and then walked past to where all the women were huddled together.

Nolan was sorry that Jones hadn't been there to catch a bullet. Another time maybe. Here and now, he needed to assist in getting these ladies loaded up. Hopefully, most of them had some kin waiting.

Nolan stepped up onto the wagon seat, and with the help of a corporal, they got the rickety buckboard turned around. Others helped the sniffling women and girls up into the wagon bed. Blankets were given out to those who were shivering, likely from fright, because the sun was hot and there wasn't a breeze. Nolan handed the reins over to a corporal, then jumped down and went to mount his horse.

Soldiers filed into a line of doubles in front of and behind the wagon. Nolan walked the bay up next to the buckboard and looked over the raggedy lot. The canvas cover that had been torn up badly during the gunfight had been ripped the rest of the way off, so Nolan could see all the ladies pretty closely. Nathanial jumped into his mind…and the Harpers. Curiosity stirred him. Mr. and Mrs. Harper might have had more than the two daughters that had been killed. If that were true, then there was a chance that one of these girls might want to know what had become of Nathanial.

"Any of you go by the name of Harper?" His keen eyes caught the questioning glance between two girls near the back of the wagon. It was easy to understand why they would be frightened to speak up, given all they'd suffered through.

Nolan dropped back to ride beside them and studied the dirty-faced, frightened girls before speaking. Maybe he shouldn't say anything. From what Nathanial had told him, Jenny had been the only Harper that paid him any mind.

"I found Nathanial." Nolan wished he could say for sure that the boy was alive but couldn't with certainty, so he held his tongue. Their stares were blank, as if they had lost their minds and weren't able to comprehend what he'd just said. The one who appeared to be the oldest slowly began to laugh, becoming almost hysterical.

"Our farmhand?" Her stupid stare turned into a haughty look, and Nolan knew right then that this bitch didn't care even a small peck about Nathanial.

"Should we rejoice that you found our little bastard farm-hand…? What's his name again? Let me tell you something. Our pa was shot down not two feet from where I stood that day, and our mother was gutted in front of us. Nancy, our sister, was hanged before our eyes. Our baby sister, we don't even know what happened to Jenny. And you think we care for one minute that you found that no-good Younger boy?"

"Jenny's dead. Nathanial buried her real fine." Nolan spurred his horse.

The young woman had a lot of hurt eating at her and deserved to get some of it out even if it had been aimed at Nolan. But there was no excuse good enough to justify the heartless attitude toward the boy. Nathanial hadn't chosen to be a Younger, and there was no fault in being born to a name.

It took a few weeks until the army finally got the women to the nearest town, which also happened to be an army fort. Nowhere along the way had Nolan picked up any sign of Deegan Jones sneaking around to take back his loot. Besides, the number in Jones's army had shrunk considerably. That indeed was a big wound. It would take some time to heal from such a loss. To recruit more gunmen meant Jones would need cash, lots of it. After the failed deal involving the women, he had to have lost every penny.

Nolan walked outside the captain's quarters at the fort and squinted against the bright sun. He looked over at Captain Farnsworth, who was standing next to him. "Captain, it's been a long, rough trail, and we ain't always seen eye to eye, but you led your men well. And I would serve again at your side." Nolan stepped up and swung a leg over the saddle, then leaned down and shook Captain Farnsworth's hand.

"Travel safe… and for whatever it's worth, I'm sorry for the poor way I treated Nathanial. I do hope you find the boy well." The captain tipped his hat, then turned and walked back inside. The door closed behind him.

Nolan spurred the bay, and he couldn't wait to get to Kate's ranch.

He was making good time and figured to be enjoying some time with Kate and, hopefully, Nate by week's end. That was if she would still have him. Nolan didn't fully believe she'd meant what she'd said about not coming back. Enough time had passed that she should have simmered down. Though she'd been awful angry that day he rode out and left her.

Nolan rode through another night and rested some in the saddle as the pink of day lit the sky. He stopped only to rest the bay while the sun worked its way west. His coffee was gone, and since leaving the fort, he'd been living on jerky. Taking time to hunt meant losing minutes that he could be spending with Kate and discovering what happened to Nathanial. Riding straight through the days to get to the ranch was his plan.

Nolan skirted Blue Sky Mountain Lake and grinned with the hope that within the hour, he'd be sitting down at the supper table to have a good hot meal with the woman he wanted to marry and the boy he thought of as a son. The only thing that would kill his mood would be to find that Nathanial had passed on. No sooner did the thought finish than Nolan saw something that turned his day in an instant.

He jerked up the reins. There was one other thing that could destroy his happiness, and that trouble had been marked out in the shape of a fresh horseshoe print in the dirt. He circled the bay, studying the tracks. They were maybe an hour old. One print in particular he recognized as that of Deegan Jones's gelding. The horse must've had an injury to its hind leg at some time, which caused the horseshoe to sit slightly pigeon-toed on the hoof. It couldn't be mistaken for another. Nolan could easily guess who the other tracks belonged to, not individually, but as a group. More troubled men recruited by Jones.

"Dammit all to hell."

Jones was too close to Gray Rock for Nolan to feel comfortable. There was no riding away from the killer's trail. On sight, he would put a bullet in Jones. He backtracked and found where Jones and three others had camped for a night, but no clue had been left behind as to what Jones was up to.

An hour later and riding away from where Nolan wanted to be, he found the spot where two others had joined Jones. Only, these two hadn't stayed with him. They'd ridden in from and then back toward Gray Rock. Why? Jones had never attacked a town to get a woman. He preyed on single farms that were separated from any law. Fewer women but easier pickings. Was Gray Rock being targeted for some reason? Maybe Nathanial was the target.

No…Jones had no way of knowing that the boy was brought there. Being that this wasn't usually Jones's territory, he shouldn't have any awareness of who was in Gray Rock and who wasn't. Unless Jones had an accomplice. But who?

Looking back on the past months, the men hired by Jones didn't seem to make a move on their own. Nolan's best bet on taking down the boss would be to keep trailing him. Then the whole operation would fall apart. Slipping his arms around Kate and maybe seeing Nathanial would have to wait. He needed to know that Jones was riding on past Gray Rock. The friendly town wasn't Nolan's home yet, but it was where the two people he cared about most were settled.

He followed Jones's trail until dark, and the miles between him and Kate and the boy were growing. All he had thought about for days, weeks even, was marrying Kate and starting a family. Jones had stolen enough of his time. Tracking the killer again so soon after rescuing the women was the last damn thing Nolan hoped to be doing.

CHAPTER 26

NATE LET OUT a deep sigh and was awfully glad to finally hear the preacher say "amen," at last ending the long-winded sermon. The only thing he thought was evil about this day was the blasted heat and the smell reeking from the stinky buffalo hide of a man sitting next to him on the bench seat. *Phew.* Nate could practically taste the thick onion stench of the man. It was enough to make any sinner pray for mercy. He would have bet washing dishes for a month that the hairy, wet-looking fellow had forgotten to take his Saturday-night bath and that he'd crawled on his belly to Sunday meeting straight from Pete's saloon after a night of bathing in too much cheap whiskey. The horrible odor practically choked Nate.

What was taking so long for the pastor to announce the last song? *Come on already.*

As a congregation, it was routine that they would sing one more hymn before being dismissed. Nate could only pray it was a song that didn't have four or five verses. "Jesus Loves Me." Now there was a quick song, easy and directly to the point. For once, why couldn't they sing a quickie like that? Nate couldn't be the only one baking in the stickiness of the single room, crammed shoulder to shoulder.

Buffalo Hide coughed without covering his mouth, and the rancid breath spewed all over Nate. Water came to his eyes, and as if that weren't bad enough, in the same instant, the foul man had broken wind. Ma nudged Nate to stop his snickering. What did she expect? Stinkers were funny.

Nate hadn't thought it possible for the stink inside the room to get any worse, but rotten eggs seemed to have seeped out of Buffalo Hide and it wasn't funny anymore. For goodness' sake, this was the house of the Lord. Ma had scolded Nate once that he had to hold such vapors until he was outside. No one must have ever explained the rules to the foul beast sitting next to him.

"Please rise. We will sing 'Amazing Grace.'" Pastor Hicks cleared his throat to lead off.

Nate jumped to his feet, the first one standing. Why couldn't there be even a small breeze flowing through the open windows to push out the foul smell? This had to be punishment for something Nate had done. Then he remembered the picnic social after the service. It was his saving grace. The distraction he was in need of to forget the odor of sin standing packed tight in next to him while bellowing out the wrong words to "Amazing Grace." Fried chicken, slaw, red beet eggs, and a cherry pie for dessert. Ma had slaved to make it all.

"God bless you all. You are now dismissed." Preacher closed his Bible, and Nate pushed past Buffalo Hide and ran for the door, as did a few of his friends. A step into the fresh air and he shucked his boots to run to the creek. It would take Ma and the other ladies some time to set up the food tables. The water sparkled in the sun, and just hearing it trickle refreshed him. Some of his friends were already wading into the coolness. Nate couldn't wait to stick his toes in.

"Nathanial!" What did Ma want?

Nate kept running.

"Don't you run holes in those socks, young man!"

Nate grinned to himself and recognized the ornery streak in him that needed to cut loose at times. He stopped, yanked off his socks, and balled and pitched the smelly wad right at her.

Ma showed herself to be a good sport and caught the sock ball with a grin on her face. Then she waved Nate away to go have fun with his friends. He ran past Sheriff Fuller and stuck his tongue out at the tin star. It was always good fun to taunt the sheriff. The fool hadn't given up on Ma and still came around pestering for her affection.

As soon as Nate stepped foot into the shallow ripple of cool water, the soggy, sweaty feeling left him. He waded in up to his ankles, and the creek water felt oh so good against his bare skin. This was a little piece of heaven. A water battle erupted between some of his friends. He wanted in the worst way to partake in the splashing. But Johnny was in the middle of it, having fun getting soaked. Ma had warned Nate to stay away from the troublemaker. He would have to be satisfied just watching.

"Children, come along. It's time to say the blessing." Preacher waved them all to come.

Barefoot and hungry, Nate raced to where Ma had unpacked a checkered linen and placed two settings. Sheriff Fuller wandered over from where he'd been standing under a tree, watching everyone, and now stood in front of Ma. "May I join ya for lunch?"

After Wade and Ma's bickering match at the jailhouse. Sheriff Fuller had brought her flowers every day for a week, but he still hadn't won her over. And Nate was just fine with that.

"We don't have enough plates, so go away." Nate interjected on Ma's behalf, and he got a tap on the head for it.

"Nathanial, don't be rude. You know I always pack extra. I would never turn down anyone who was hungry," Ma softly scolded. "Yes, you may eat with us." She looked at Nate then and gave him a funny look, and he recalled that she said to be nice while waiting on Wade to get the adoption papers. But he was afraid she was starting to go soft on the mean son of a bitch.

Why did that man have to be mooning over his ma? Couldn't Sheriff Fuller go bother someone else? Nate plopped down on the blanket after the blessing had been said. Ma opened the basket. One sniff and he breathed in all the wonderful smells. It wasn't enough to make him overlook the sheriff, who'd just sat down and was making himself comfortable.

"Nate, sweetheart, would you please hand Wade a plate?"

Nate rolled his eyes and groaned as if it caused him pain to be nice.

Ma frowned. It was enough to straighten him up. Two nights ago, she had asked him to tend to the sheriff's horse during a visit to win Ma's favor. He'd waited until she and Wade went into the house. Then he'd untied the sheriff's gelding, slapped its rump, and sent it running home. Sheriff Fuller had walked the two miles back to Gray Rock, and Nate got a licking.

How could Ma look past all the teeth-gnashing and narrow-eyed glares thrown down between him and the sheriff? Pigs would sprout wings and fly before he and Wade Fuller became friends, if that's what Ma was still hoping for. She was friendly with the sheriff but not overly so, which made Nate wonder if she and Wade were really friends anymore or if she was just putting up with him like she'd told Nate to do until they got the paperwork. Her advice to him when he'd lost Johnny's friendship was to look for the positive when bad circumstances seemed to have wrecked his life. In that case, Phillip, Thomas, and Curtis all remained Nate's friends and played with him as much as they did Johnny. So Nate was going to find the good in serving Sheriff Wade as Ma had asked.

Nate picked up the plate and pictured himself throwing the tin at the sheriff's head. That was definitely a good thought. It made him smile cheerfully. Sheriff Fuller's brow rose as Nate peacefully offered the plate. Too bad he couldn't spit in Wade's food. And with that thought, he chuckled, and Sheriff Fuller turned the empty plate over then back, looking for something that wasn't there.

Ma served the food, and Nate dug right in. Yum, he'd never tasted finer. She was a true talent in the kitchen. His plate was empty in no time. Nate licked the chicken grease off his fingers and felt it his duty to interrupt the sheriff's blah-blah-blahing about tracking horse thieves. Ma was staring off into her half-eaten plate of food and looking bored anyway.

"Ma, you're the best cook ever."

"Thank you, darling."

The sheriff dropped his plate at her praising of Nate's compliment. Sheriff Fuller cleared his throat. "As I was saying to ya, Kate…"

Nate didn't want to hear the rest of Sheriff Fuller's story. They'd heard a similar one about a week ago. So what? The tin badge had lost the trail, but he was sure he'd run the cattle thieves clean out of the territory. How many times in one meal could Nate be made to roll his eyes because Sheriff Wade had said something stupid.

"I bet Nolan wouldn't have lost the cattle thieves' trail. He's the best tracker that ever lived," Nate bragged and was sure he was right.

Ma's eyes looked sad, and she smoothed his snowy hair. She only did that when she was upset or thought he was.

"Is that so?" Sheriff Fuller grinned with the viciousness of a rattler. "If that's true, then why has it taken him so long to track down that man for the army? Or maybe you're right… It ain't Nolan's work that's keeping him away. He has probably caught that man…It's you that's keeping that saddle tramp from coming back."

Tears sprang to Nate's eyes. This round went to the sheriff. Nate wouldn't believe it. Sheriff Fuller had to be lying. Nolan just couldn't be purposely staying away because of him.

Ma threw down her plate. "What an awful thing to say! I think you owe Nathanial an apology." She looked as if she might just slap Wade's mouth right off his face.

"Aw, did I make the little baby cry?" Sheriff Fuller shrugged, then forked a hunk of pie into his mouth. "The truth hurts sometimes, son."

"I ain't your son!" Nate hated Wade Fuller.

"Thank God for that." The sheriff's gleaming smirk seemed to show that he enjoyed Nate's pain.

"Nathanial is right, Wade. He isn't your son, but he is mine." Ma's dander was up so much that other folks around them all stopped their talk and were listening. "I wasn't sure how to bring it up till now. So I'm just gonna say it. Where are the adoption papers that I asked you to send for? The circuit judge has come and gone through Gray Rock twice. It only takes a week to get mail from Birch Creek. Or maybe you just never sent for the papers."

Ma didn't seem to care who was watching. Sheriff Wade, on the other hand, was looking about at the faces staring him down. No one in their right mind would believe for one iota that Ma was the bad guy in this story. Nate was sure of that.

"It must have gotten lost in the mail, Kate. I'll send for it again." Sheriff Fuller reached to take her hand in his. Ma wouldn't have any affection and pushed away his hand. The whole town saw it.

Nate should maybe do something to protect her. "Don't touch my ma."

Sheriff Fuller sprang to his feet, his face wrinkled up mean. Nate instantly shrank back, but not quick enough. A big fist grabbed him by the front of the shirt and yanked him up. His teeth rattled as he was given a hard shake. Tears spilled from his eyes. The exact moment when Pastor Hicks stepped up close to Sheriff Fuller and grabbed his arm was a blur to Nate. Phillip's pa and Johnny's pa were on their feet as well. All eyes were on Sheriff Fuller. Ma was crying. It was Wade's move, and he still had quite a mean grip on Nate.

Preacher placed a firm hand on the sheriff's shoulder. Nate wanted to reach for Ma, but he didn't know what was going to happen.

Pastor Hicks and the sheriff eyed one another for a long minute. "Sheriff, I haven't seen your deputy around. Perhaps you should go and check on him."

The sheriff shoved Nate away, and he fell to the ground, scuffing his knee. Ma bawled and hugged all over him. Those that had seen it all slowly came forward and kindly checked on him and Ma. They clung to each other until Nate felt safe enough to pull away and wipe his eyes. Damn Nolan for not being around. This time they'd been lucky there were men there to protect them from Sheriff Fuller. That might not always be so.

CHAPTER 27

"DO WE HAVE EVERYTHING?"

Nate shrugged at Ma. She'd packed way more than he thought they'd ever need. Birch Creek was only a week away. How much flour and sugar could they possible use? He didn't even drink coffee, but she'd packed all of what was left in the tin. There was a stack of extra blankets tucked in the wagon bed. She'd also insisted on packing their fair-weather coats in case of rain. It was September. The days were still hot, and the evenings weren't all that cool. Most nights, they slept with the windows open for air.

But Ma wasn't going to be happy until she had the whole house packed into the wagon, and going to Birch Creek had been her idea. She could have just sent for the adoption papers herself, but she said a certain someone they both knew might tamper with or delay the paperwork somehow. She didn't want to take any chances. Nate had heard her mumbling to herself that Sheriff Fuller had fouled up the air in Gray Rock and she needed to get away and breathe.

"We ready yet?" Nate crawled up onto the wagon seat and waited while she took one more look around inside. They couldn't have possibly forgotten anything because they had everything except the potbellied stove crammed in the wagon. It seemed like forever until she at last locked the door behind her.

"Come on. Let's go," Nate hollered and waved at her to hurry up. He'd never been to Birch Creek. From what some of his friends had told him, the town was bigger than Gray Rock.

Ma finally stepped up into the wagon. Leather was slapped to the team, and the buckboard lurched forward. In a week, he would officially be Kate James's son.

They passed though Gray Rock, and Nate waved goodbye to some of his friends playing in the schoolyard. Everyone knew where they were headed. All their friends and neighbors had at some recent time shared caring thoughts for their journey.

Sheriff Fuller hadn't come around the ranch since the picnic. Not that Nate cared.

There wasn't a cloud in the sky. The team was holding up well, and they'd made some miles before stopping for lunch, though they didn't dawdle. As soon as they were done eating, they were packed up and putting more miles behind them. This would be their routine for the coming days.

At night they slept under the stars. The air this evening was warm, but Ma, being Ma, tucked him in the blankets anyway. Nate didn't mind so much because he knew what always came next. A good-night kiss to the tip of his nose. Ma went to her blankets then, and he stared up at the twinkling stars. The fire crackled, and his mind came to rest on one person.

"Nathanial, what's wrong?" Maybe Ma saw the shine of tears in his eyes glistening against the dancing orange and yellow flames. She picked up her ground blanket, then came and laid it out next to him. It took her a minute to make herself comfortable, and all the while, she was eying him, waiting for an answer.

There was a long moment of silence. It was the same ache that troubled him every night and had for months. "I miss Nolan." Nate looked over.

Ma lay flat on her back, staring up at the many shiny little lights in the sky, the same as he had been doing.

"I know you do. I miss him too sometimes." Ma's own heartache was the only comfort she had to offer him. It was nice to know they were in it together.

The sounds of the night hummed around them like a soothing lullaby.

"I used to think Nolan cared about me." Nate was just talking to let out his hurt, and he sighed. He didn't expect an answer from Ma.

"Sweetheart, I don't want you to think for a minute that Nolan doesn't love you." She went to the wagon and came back with her Bible in her hands. She pulled a dirty-looking piece of crinkled paper out from between the pages. "I found this in your pants pocket the day Nolan brought you to me."

Ma sat down on the blankets next to Nate. He didn't know what that paper was. It looked like a letter, but it had Ma's name on the outside, so why would he have had it? He hadn't known her before Nolan had taken him to her ranch.

Ma unfolded the letter. *"Dearest Kate, what I'm about to say will come as quite a surprise, I'm sure. The little boy, Nathanial, who is attached with this letter is my son. Not in the way you might be thinking, but he is mine just the same. I would be obliged if you would care for him till I can join the two of you at your ranch. This ain't a proper way to ask, but I picture the three of us as a family. Duty takes me elsewhere, but as soon as I can, I will ask you proper. Take good care of my boy. Nolan. Postscript: I don't know for certain how long I might be away with the army. If Nathanial gets to missing me too badly, nail his boots to the floor to keep him from running after me. He can be spirited at times, but I like that about him."* Ma smoothed Nate's hair, and he wiped at his eyes. "So you see, sweetheart, Nolan loves you."

Nate had completely forgotten about that letter after being shot, losing all that blood, and being in a weakened state for so long. The words he had read months ago, after leaving that stupid little town where Nolan had left him to get on the stage, had slipped his mind entirely. He was glad Ma had shared it with him, and he smiled. "Do you think Nolan will make good on that promise for all of us to be a family?"

"You know what I would rather think about?" Ma had a sad look in her eyes, so she must not have believed so.

"What?" Nate was curious. It would have to be a strong thought to pull his mind away from wondering about Nolan.

"Tomorrow we reach Birch Creek. Oh Nathanial, I can't wait to see your name penned on the adoption papers."

Ma was right. That thought was pretty cheery. Nate smiled up at the moon and didn't think he would sleep a wink.

Breakfast came and went. And soon after that, Nate handed over the reins as they neared the edge of town. Holy smokes. There were a lot of big buildings and people everywhere. Ma steered the wagon down the main street. Getting to see the sights of what was a big city to Nate was far better than if they had signed the papers in front of the circuit judge. That was for sure.

The hustle of folks coming and going excited Nate. At least twenty wagons sat along the street. Horses dotted the hitch rails from one end of town to the other. Buildings lined either side of the road. They passed every business a person could ever think of and then some. Gray Rock didn't have a bakery or a theater. Ma pulled up on the reins in front of a three-story hotel. Henry's hotel back home only had a second floor. Nate hopped down from the seat and followed her inside.

Geez. The fancy lobby furnishings sure were something to see. He'd better not touch anything. All the wood trim was polished so it shone. Nate waited with Ma at the desk until she signed the registry, and the clerk handed her a key.

"You're in room seven, top of the stairs on the right. I will have a porter bring up your bags shortly." The bald clerk wore what Nate thought was a funny little visor.

Happiness emanated through Nate's smile as he skipped up the steps next to Ma. They weren't inside the big fluffy room but a minute when there was a knock on the door. Ma answered it. A man in a striped shirt carried their bags in and placed them carefully next to a chest of drawers.

"Thank you." Ma handed the fella a few coins, then closed the door as he left.

Nate flopped and sat on the brass bed, and he despised that Ma had unclasped the carpetbag, beginning to unpack. He wanted to go out and breathe in the city air. Who was to say when they might find themselves in Birch Creek again, if ever?

"Let's go look around town." He hopped off the bed and headed for the door.

"Wait a minute, young man. I want to freshen up a little. Then first thing, we are going to the courthouse." Ma picked up a small bottle and spritzed herself. She hadn't stunk, so why bother covering up with perfume? Who cared if she smelled like a flower?

"You smell good enough to pick. Can we go now?"

Maybe all mamas were fussy about how they kept themselves. Nate looked down over himself. There were a few wrinkles in his shirt and a stain of dippy from his eggs at breakfast, but it was buttoned straight. Good enough. He was ready to be set free to explore Birch Creek.

Ma was still fussing over herself in the mirror.

"Ma, your hair looks fine. Daylight's a-burnin'." How much whining would he have to do before he got his own way? He wanted to go outside.

"Here, change your shirt. Then we can go." Ma handed him the starched white shirt he wore to church each Sunday. If he moaned about dressing up, he'd just be wasting time.

She'd always won that battle. At least she hadn't packed his tie … that he knew of.

He quickly ripped off his dirty shirt, then yanked the other down over his head lickety-split. "I'm ready."

"Tuck in your shirttail and then brush your hair." Ma handed Nate the brush, and in two swipes, his white duck fluff was smoothed down enough to satisfy him, but Ma was frowning, of course.

She took the brush from his hand, then slicked each strand so it lay just so. This was worse than getting ready for church.

Finally, after five minutes that felt like twenty, they left the room.

They stepped out onto the boardwalk. Nate wanted to run and see everything. There was a man with a peddler's carriage, selling elixir right in the street. Another fella loudly advertised fortunes for a dime. Mysteriously, he could tell one's future by reading the lines on that person's hands. Amazing.

"Ma!" Nate nearly tripped himself as he pointed. "That bay right there. It's Nolan's horse. I know it." Outside the saloon stood a saddled gelding that Nate recognized from riding its back for months.

"Sweetheart, I know you want him to be here with us, but I think that's just wishful thinking. There are lots of bay horses, and the chance of that one being Nolan's … I'm afraid aren't very good. Come on. Let's get to the courthouse." Ma took Nate's hand and led him away as he twisted around and stared at the horse.

Likely, she was right. Maybe it was time he stopped believing Nolan was coming back to them. What Nate should have been thinking about was standing before the judge who would decide Nate's future with Ma.

He couldn't have felt any smaller as he and Ma walked between the tall columns up to the courthouse, and his legs weakened. Tears welled up in his eyes. It was a good thing

Ma was holding tight to his hand and took the first step in the door. Otherwise, he would have retreated awful fast from this battle. Hiding behind her skirt wasn't something he'd admit to his friends when he got back home. Though he was just fine with it right this minute. What if the judge was mean and wouldn't let Miss Kate adopt him? Nate's rotten, no-good pa was still alive to claim him.

"Nathanial, come on." Ma coaxed him sweetly.

He shook his head. Tucking tail and running was what he was thinking of doing. Couldn't he and Ma just keep on living as mother and son without the official paperwork? What if the judge threw Nate in jail for all the bad things he'd done with Pa? This was either going to be the best or worst day of his life.

A slight tug from Ma, and Nate took a deep breath and followed close on her heels. Not ten feet inside the door, they were met by a man who sat quietly at a desk. The paper pusher had a long beaklike nose, and after a minute, he looked up over the rim of his spectacles at them.

"We're here to see Judge Prescott."

The steadiness of Ma's voice convinced Nate she was a brave woman. His legs were quivering, and he doubted his voice would have worked other than to maybe let out screaming if he were to be dragged off to jail. That was if the judge decided to sentence Nate for his crimes with Pa.

Not one worry line wrinkled Ma's face. She was wearing a sweet, loving smile, like always.

"Judge Prescott's chambers are upstairs to the right. It will be the fourth door on the left." The man pointed them to a full flight of steps.

Which would give out first, Nate's mushy legs or his pounding heart? Somehow Ma had managed to drag him to the bottom of the staircase. Nate would be much braver if Nolan were there. Encouragingly, Ma squeezed his hand, and he knew she would be helping him along every step of the way.

He just had to face Judge Prescott. If he was lucky, after today, he would never again have to admit his ties to Jim Younger. Sweat poured out of Nate as if he were actually climbing a mountain.

Okay, he was still breathing, and the summit had been reached. His heart hadn't slowed any, but it hadn't exploded either. If it was a jail sentence he was walking toward, then he would do his time without crying like a baby. It was easy to think that way while holding tight to Ma's hand. Would she adopt a jailbird? What if she didn't want him when he got out? They should have never come to Birch Creek. Why couldn't stinking Sheriff Fuller have sent for the papers? Then Nate wouldn't have to stand before Judge Prescott. It was the exact opposite of what he'd thought upon arriving in town. Nate wiped at his eyes.

They stood before a door with a rich gold plaque that read Judge Prescott. Ma squeezed Nate's hand, and he looked up at her. "It'll be okay, Nathanial."

Sure it would. She would soon be visiting him in jail. He was no good like Pa, and as soon as the judge heard Nate's name, he would be done for. No happy life with Miss Kate as his mama.

Tears teetered on the rims of his eyes as they stepped inside a waiting room. Nate's lip quivered. Could he be any more of a sissy? The plump-faced secretary, sitting behind a desk, looked up from her work and smiled. Yup. The friendly gesture was all it took, and like a scared rabbit, Nate jumped quickly behind Ma to hide himself. The soft folds of her skirt were a safe place, and there was about a snowball's chance in hell of him letting go to show his face.

"I'm Ms. Kathrine James. I'm here to speak with Judge Prescott."

"Please have a seat. I'll let the judge know you're here." The woman's kind, soft voice did nothing to soothe Nate's fear of what he was minutes away from facing. For all he knew, Judge Prescott had horns and carried a pitchfork.

Ma smoothed his hair and then kissed his head. Gently she pulled him off from clinging to her. "I love you, Nathanial." Her honesty got him to smile.

"Judge Prescott will see you now." The secretary held the door open for them.

A tall, lean man walked around from behind a desk and shook Ma's hand, greeting them both with a smile. "What is it that I can do for you folks?"

"I would like to file for adoption."

The judge eyed Ma, studying her for a minute, then turned and looked at Nate. "I see. First I need to ask some questions." Judge Prescott offered a chair to Ma.

Nate took a seat as the judge made himself comfortable behind the big desk. This was it. The end of what was the best life Nate had ever known. His luck had never been any good. Why should this work out for him? He'd wanted Nolan to come back for him, and that never happened.

"State your name for me, young man." The judge held his hand ready to write. Maybe this would be the last time Nate ever had to be embarrassed to tell who he was. No shame had ever been attached to Ma's name. But he was scared of the trouble he might be in once Judge Prescott heard who his pa was. He'd faced wrath before. Miss Kate was worth the risk.

"Nathanial James Hardin Younger."

The judge raised a brow and studied him. Nate shrank back in the chair.

"Is your father presently in prison?"

"Yes, sir." A flush rushed to Nate's face, and his gaze dropped to his boots.

Ma's tender hand lifted his chin.

"I ain't ashamed of you." She had a knack of saying words that warmed him inside. "You don't hide your face from anyone. Nathanial, you are an intelligent, witty, and wonderful little boy. I will be proud to be your mother." Ma kissed his face.

Two hours later, they walked outside the courthouse with Judge Prescott's best wishes. The adoption papers had been signed and were tucked safely away inside Ma's purse. They'd been assured by the judge that Jim Younger would sign away all rights to Nate. The judge did have his ways, all legal of course, of leaning on the inmate to get what was absolutely best for Nate.

The greatest news was that he'd been pardoned from any guilt he might be carrying around for those crimes committed by Pa. Judge Prescott had called Nate a minor and stated he wasn't responsible for the robberies during the years he'd ridden with Pa. That part of his life was over and could be forgotten. There was simply nothing he could think of that could possibly make this day any better. He might not ever stop smiling.

Well, he wished Nolan were there with them.

The air outside the courthouse pillars seemed fresher somehow, and he breathed in deep. It was a great day. The town was bustling with folks. Wagons rolled along the street, and people were coming and going along the boardwalk. The clang of the smithy's hammer rang in his ears from across the way. It was as if Nate were seeing it all again for the first time.

To shout his newly granted freedom from the middle of the busy dirt roadway would give him pure joy. No one that hadn't walked a day in his troubles would understand the heaviness of the chains that had broken the very minute Judge Prescott signed the papers and pardoned Nate. His past with Pa was now dead. God willing, it would never come alive to haunt him.

"We have the whole day to celebrate. What would you like to do first?" Ma was smiling.

Nate wanted a special treat. "Gumdrops." They walked into the store, and both he and Ma were still smiling wide.

"You may pick out a full bag of candy." Ma was surely letting Nate feed his sweet tooth, and that was important to him, absolutely. But he was more interested in evangelizing the good news that had descended from heaven upon him. It was a gift of grace to be shared, so why not tell it?

"I got adopted today," Nate announced to all the shoppers, though he was smiling across the counter at the apron-wearing clerk with the beady dark eyes and brown hair to match.

"Is that so?" The man stared dumbly at him.

"Well shit, mister, I ain't lying to ya." Every eye turned on him, including Ma's, whose face flamed red.

"Nathanial James." Ma had darn near dropped the length of material in her hands. "You apologize, and don't ever let me hear you using such language again."

"Sorry." Nate quickly offered the apology, and the clerk nodded his acceptance. He hadn't meant to piss off Ma. He was just so happy that he couldn't hold it in. Fine, if the clerk was too dim to appreciate the bold headline, then Nate would advertise it to others.

He turned to face the door creaking open. "Hey, lady and you, the fella with her. I got me a mama. Judge Prescott signed the papers less than an hour ago."

They must have been related to the store clerk because they were both wearing the same stupid openmouthed stare.

Ma's hand clamped over Nate's mouth. "Nathanial, why don't you pick out your candy and let these folks go on with their shopping?"

He nodded that he would, and she let go of him. He skipped off to the jars of sweet treats. Seeing the colorful gumdrops made him think of Nolan.

Nolan sat alone and poured himself another drink from the bottle on the table. He'd pursued Deegan to the outskirts of

Birch Creek, then lost the killer's trail. Jones must have gotten smart to potentially being followed and covered his tracks well. Considering that Nolan's mind had also drifted miles behind to Gray Rock, it hadn't been hard to lose his hound dog skills.

The plain truth of it was he wanted nothing more than to get on his horse and ride back to Kate and hopefully Nathanial. Why couldn't he just get lucky first and find Deegan Jones? Then this matter could be laid to rest.

Hitting the trails again didn't appeal to him, and shit, there was no chance of encountering Jones just down the street. Nolan chuckled to himself. Birch Creek was the home of his friend and famed lawman US Marshal Joseph Huckabee and Deputy Tate Horn. If a man rode on the far side of the law, that man would be a fool to gamble being caught by either lawman. Nolan had ridden posse and done the tracking for Marshal Huckabee dozens of times. Pinning on a badge had been easy when he worked with men that upheld justice the way the marshal and his deputy did. They were honorable men, and Nolan had always been glad to lend a hand. Never once had they missed bringing in the lawless to face sentencing.

Nolan would have to warn the marshal about Jones. Maybe he'd do that now. He stood, pushing his chair back, and wavered on his feet for a minute. Plumb drunk he wasn't, but damn, he was feeling the nearly whole bottle of red-eye he'd guzzled down.

His shoulder slammed off the doorframe, but he somehow made his way outside onto the boardwalk. The beaming sunlight hit him hard, and he stumbled back a step or two, then swayed in place while his eyes adjusted to the brightness.

Shit, it was a good thing that public drunkenness wasn't a crime. Otherwise, his old pal the marshal might have to toss Nolan's saturated carcass in the hoosegow to sleep it off.

It had to be the whiskey. Was he seeing things? Because it sure as hell looked like Kate and Nathanial walking out of the general store and up the street. When Nolan had lit a shuck from Kate's ranch that day, he'd all but given Nathanial up for dead. What a fool he'd been. He never should have ridden away from them. They'd consumed his thoughts every day and night since he'd left them to go after Jones.

They were walking Nolan's way but hadn't seen him yet. How lucky. He quickly ducked into the alleyway between the saloon and another building. Looking around, he saw a water barrel, splashed his face a few good times, and then brushed the stink off his clothing the best he could. Kate would be pissed about the smell of hard liquor on him. Maybe she would see he was at least an ounce sober. Well, he'd just have to beg her forgiveness. One more splash of water and that should make him a little more presentable.

Waiting was making him sweat. To stumble upon gold wouldn't be as good as seeing them up close. A side-by-side pair of footsteps walked closer along the boardwalk. Nolan's heart pounded. He could already taste Kate's lips. She stepped past him. It was true. There she was, right before his eyes.

His back was flat to the saloon wall, behind Kate, so neither she nor Nathanial was facing Nolan to see him. Kate's head was turned down, smiling at the boy. Nathanial hadn't grown any but looked to be in good health. The half-pint was walking tall for his size, like always, and there was a pink bubbly glow to his face. All seemed to be well with the two of them. With that thought, Nolan couldn't help but smile. Kate was pretty as ever, and to see Nathanial so chipper and full of himself, water came to Nolan's eyes.

He lunged from the shadows and grabbed Nathanial up, swinging the youngster around in the air. The boy let out with a scream. None of it helped Nolan's already spinning head, but he was a truly happy man.

"Nolan!" Nathanial's eyes lit up bright and glassy. He and the boy just smiled at one another until he brought Nathanial closer. And then the half-pint threw his twiggy little arms around Nolan's neck and held tight. This was honestly a moment he would never forget, ever.

"I've missed you, son." Dear God, had he missed this boy.

"Did you come here to find me and Ma?"

To hear Nathanial's squeaky little voice was pure joy. He wasn't going to tell the truth of who had led him to Birch Creek and maybe stir up forgotten ideas in the boy's head about chasing after Jones.

It sank in then what Nathanial had just said.

"Ma?" Nolan looked at Kate for an answer and let Nathanial slide down off his hip and stand.

"Miss Kate adopted me." The proud half-pint puffed out his little chest before Kate could say a word.

There was no restraining Nolan's happiness at the fine news. He pulled Kate into his arms and kissed her. What she'd done for the boy was wonderful. He kissed her again. The two people he cared about most in this world were now connected as kin. If Kate would have him, Nolan wanted to be the missing piece in that family. She and Nathanial could both be wearing the Crosson name before leaving Birch Creek. The thought put an even bigger smile on his face.

"You stink like whiskey." She slightly pushed him away.

But the liquor was making Nolan ornery, and he wasn't letting her step past him. The curve of her waist fit his hands perfectly, and he kept her held close. The feel of her pressed tight against him was steamier than noonday on the Fourth of July in the Texas panhandle. It was all he could do to keep his hands from roaming over the length of her.

"Nolan, you're making a public spectacle of us." Her huffiness made him chuckle, though he doubted she was trying to be cute.

For the first time, Nolan looked about with recognition and saw the town at its busiest. Fine, he wanted her to himself anyway. He scooped up Kate and carried her a few steps into the alleyway. No more were there unwanted eyes on them.

"Put me down." That redheaded temper made him want her more.

"It'll cost ya a kiss." Nolan smiled. A giggle sprang from Nathanial, who was standing at Nolan's side. He looked down and winked.

"You're not behaving proper. My son doesn't need your bad influence." Whew, Kate knew how to sober a man and right quick, but his joy hadn't been killed by her anger. He did put her down to stand. This was no way to get her to say yes.

"You're drunk... Let's go, Nathanial." Kate grabbed him by the hand to leave.

Something inside Nolan just felt alive upon seeing Kate and Nathanial standing side by side as mother and son. He plain as day heard the testiness in her voice, but he was just so damn happy to see them. "Kate, wait."

She stepped around him as he reached for her arm.

"Leave my ma alone." Nathanial playfully pounced on Nolan. He pretended that the tough little tomcat had tackled him. They tussled through the dirt in the alleyway, and the sound of the boy's hardy laughter was truly wonderful.

"Oh my Lord, the two of you, please stop. Nathanial, look how dirty your clothes are getting. Nolan, how old are you?" They quieted their play, and the stern mother hen's lips were pursed in a way that Nolan thought she might peck at them again for not behaving.

They just lay in a heap of fun on the ground, grinning at her. The half-pint held Nolan's head locked in the crook of his tiny arm as they caught their breath. Neither of them moved to get up out of the dirt.

"We're just having a little fun." Batting the baby blues wasn't working on her as far as the boy begging for more time.

It would have worked to soften up Nolan. Besides, he was feeling like a youngster himself, and who were they hurting? With one twist of Nolan's arm, he held the little tomcat in a headlock as well. Nathanial squirmed to get free, and Nolan chuckled. "I got ya ... You ain't gittin' loose." He tormented the wiggly, squealing little varmint.

Nolan looked up to see Kate standing with hands fisted on her hips and frowning.

"Oh Ma," Nate whined but kept going with the fun.

A half-forgiving grin slowly began to spread across Kate's face, which pleased Nolan. He rolled Nate head over tin cup, and once again, they scuffled through the dirt.

"Is there a problem, ma'am?"

Nolan rolled onto his back and looked up, and there was his good friend. Kate stared wide-eyed at the tin star on the marshal's vest. For the moment, it seemed she'd lost her feisty words. It would just be unkind of Nolan to let her sweat the sudden appearance of the lawman.

"Marshal Huckabee." Nolan stood while pulling Nathanial off him. He dusted Nathanial's britches off, then his own pants, before he shook the marshal's hand.

"Nolan, good to see ya." The marshal clapped Nolan's back, and he did likewise. "It's been a while. Do you remember my wife, Constance?" Nolan tipped his hat, greeting the woman round with child.

"I believe we were expecting the last time you seen us. After three boys, we're hoping for a girl this time." The marshal's laughter was lighthearted. It was obvious the man was proud to be a father.

"This is my ... um ... lady friend ... Kate James ... and my sparring partner is ... uh ... her son, Nathanial." Nolan hadn't been sure how to introduce Kate. He would have liked to have said his soon-to-be wife. And he'd wanted to say "our" son but couldn't. He'd barely gotten his fumbled words spit out. What was wrong with him? Other than he was half-drunk, but that wasn't it.

Marshal Huckabee grinned at Nolan with the knowing look of a lovesick fool. The marshal leaned close so only he could hear what was about to be said. "I once had a lady friend. She's now wearing my name."

Was Nolan being smitten truly that obvious? "You caught me. Marrying Kate is all I've been thinking about."

It wasn't that Nolan had to admit the truth. His friend was a smart fella and had seen right through his blubbering introduction. So there was no denying his affection, not that he would have.

"Then wise up and ask her before some other fella does. I have a good sense about people. She seems to measure up to be a fine woman, and I've only known her about a minute."

They both chuckled. "She is a fine woman." Nolan stated the fact.

He'd never heard a word spoken that could tarnish Kate's upright reputation. Coming and going from her life, and most of the townsfolk in Gray Rock knowing it, he was the only blemish she wore. He aimed to amend that and make them both honest. She just needed to say yes.

Marshal Huckabee pulled his pocket watch from inside his vest and glanced at the time. "We really must be going. Nolan, why don't you come by the house later? We'll have a drink and talk a spell. I'll have Constance ready the spare room for ya."

"Thanks, I'll do that."

The marshal tipped his hat at Kate. "Ma'am, have a good day." The Huckabees walked on to the general store.

Kate's smile quickly faded, and her gaze walked up and down both Nolan and Nathanial. "Look at the two of you. Filthy from head to toe. What am I to do with ya?"

Kate shook her head. Nolan couldn't deny that he and the boy were both a dusty mess. Speaking for himself, he could easily think of a few things he would like Kate to do to him...that weren't proper to say in front of Nathanial. His urges would have to wait until he and Kate were alone.

"You, come with me." Kate pointed one straight finger at Nathanial, who was standing tight next to Nolan. "You." She wore a lovely scowl. "If you want to come to supper with us, then you need to sober up, take a bath, and shave...and put on a clean shirt."

Nolan reckoned that was Kate's invitation for him to dine with them. No way would he turn it down. He could not have been happier and couldn't seem to take his eyes off Kate and Nathanial. She'd taken the boy by the arm and marched the two of them off toward the hotel. She was fiercely shaking her finger at Nathanial. He couldn't hear what she was griping about but could rightly guess by her eying the dirty child from head to toe.

A chuckle came over him. Poor Nathanial was getting the ear chewing that should have been Nolan's. The boy's not-so-clean clothing had been Nolan's fault. With one hand, Kate brushed away the dirt that dusted Nathanial's fair-colored hair, and the frown hadn't left her face.

Twisted around in her grasp, the half-pint waved. This wasn't goodbye. Nolan gave a wave. Life was about to change for the three of them, but first he needed to hear that one accepting word from Kate. Should he ask for her hand at supper?

<hr/>

Nolan strolled into the dining room, clean-shaven and wearing a fresh shirt. Nathanial waved wildly at him to hurry and join them at the table. Maybe a crowded, noisy hotel dining room wasn't the place to get down on his knee and propose.

He'd no sooner sat before Nathanial was bending Nolan's ear. "I've made lots of friends at school. I'm a straight-A student. I played hooky once, and Ma made me cut a switch."

Nolan grinned at the boy tattling on Kate for the punishment. He had deserved a tanning for skipping out on learning. Education was important.

"I like my teacher. I don't like Sheriff Wade and how he's always riding out to the ranch to be friendly with Ma."

"You best slow down from all that jawing, or you'll tire yourself out before ya eat." Nolan forced a grin at Nathanial, who was smiling. And then he shot a glaring look at Kate. Wade Fuller, was it? That sack of horse—

Nathanial cut off Nolan's strangling thoughts toward the sheriff.

"Ma gave me a mare. She's all shiny black except one little white star between her eyes. I can jump her over the corral fence," the half-pint bragged.

"Don't let me catch ya doing that, or you're in trouble. You could break your neck." Nathanial took to instantly pouting, and Nolan ruffled the snowy patch to let the boy know he wasn't angry.

"Nathanial, it isn't polite to rattle on in front of our guest."

Guest…, Nolan thought and almost spit the word across the table at Kate. Should he remind her of their lovemaking the first night they'd met? Never once had she treated him as just an acquaintance. He couldn't begin to count the nights they'd shared a bed. She'd always been much more than just a common companion to him.

A waitress stepped up to the table to take their orders.

"Steak and potatoes." Nolan hadn't meant to sound so gruff. Swallowing down his temper was what he needed to do before he choked on it. He wasn't going to ruin this evening by arguing.

Was this honestly where he stood with her? Were they now no more than old friends?

Kate smiled at the waitress. "I will also have the steak. Nathanial, would you like fried chicken?" She talked as if there were nothing for Nolan to be riled about. The fact that his irritation didn't seem to bother her irked him even more.

"Yes, ma'am." Nathanial had sat quiet in his chair and waited for his turn to order. The boy's manners had been genuinely polite. Nolan was well impressed. Now wasn't the time for him and Kate to talk out the matter of Sheriff Fuller. It wouldn't be a conversation for the young ears at the table.

"Guess what?" The old Nathanial that Nolan had come to know so well was smiling devilishly, as if holding back from tattling a big secret.

"Ya sprouted a sixth toe on your left foot." Why that had come to Nolan's mind, he didn't know, but Nathanial giggled at his stupid joke. This was exactly the distraction he needed to stop thinking of Sheriff Fuller and Kate.

"No, silly goose. Ma and I went back to the general store today after we seen ya, but first I had to get cleaned up. She let me buy you something. It's a surprise." The boy turned to Kate. "Ma, can I run upstairs to the room and fetch Nolan's gift?"

Nolan truly felt touched by the kind little gesture. It was probably gumdrops, which Nathanial would eat most of. Nolan chuckled to himself.

"Here come our meals. It will have to wait till after supper." Kate wasn't being harsh. Their plates were placed on the table before them.

Nathanial was wearing a little pout at being told no, and he scooted his chair and sat closer to Nolan.

Nolan leaned and whispered into the boy's ear, "I can't wait to see what it is."

Nathanial grinned and looked happy again. Nolan ruffled the boy's hair.

"Everything smells good," he remarked to the waitress as she poured him coffee. He was ready to fill his stomach.

Kate had worked some miracles. Nathanial actually used both the fork and spoon and wiped his mouth on the napkin without being told to. He wasn't gulping it down like a pig either.

"I got in a fight with a big blabbermouth at school. Knocked him in the teeth good and hard." The half-pint slowly played out the jab toward Nolan's face.

"Nathanial, settle yourself and eat." Kate threw down a stern look. Nolan was impressed that he quickly straightened in the chair and went back to eating what greens were left on the plate.

"Did your ma make you cut a switch?" Nolan wanted to know about Kate and Nathanial's lives those past months when he'd been chasing Jones.

"Nope." The half-pint beamed a bright smile.

Nolan raised a brow. "I doubt she let you git away with throwing punches."

"I had to scrub dishes … for a month." The boy rolled his eyes and huffed.

Nolan chuckled. "So she sentenced you to hard labor?"

"Yes, sir. It was awful. My hands got all dried out." The half-pint was wide-eyed serious, making the matter all the more amusing.

A light and easy happy mood now surrounded the three of them. Nolan wouldn't ruin it by mentioning that the Harper girls had been found and reminding Nathanial of Jenny … and Jones. That could all wait for another day. He cut a piece of steak, and Nathanial forked a potato. It was good to see the boy's appetite. He'd hardly been holding down broth the last time Nolan had seen him.

The waitress came and topped off his coffee, then a few minutes later served them each a piece of apple pie. Nolan was enjoying the evening and very much liked the fit of the three of them together. Family felt good to him.

Nathanial yawned sleepily. The dining room began to thin out. The hour was not all that late, but Nolan could imagine the boy's exhaustion. To shed an old way of life and start over—it couldn't have been easy on the youngster.

Nolan should have been there for that moment of change. Instead of becoming Nathanial James, well, he did have some hope that Kate would see fit to take the Crosson name for both her and Nathanial.

"Kate, I'm sorry that I didn't stay those months and help nurse Nathanial. I really should have."

The half-pint's head hung chin to chest, and he dozed in the chair. Nolan's gaze went to Kate, and what he saw was a not-so-friendly smirk. That day when he'd taken off from her and the boy, had she honestly meant those horrible words? Was he no longer welcome in their lives? Had his chance come and gone to be her husband and a father to Nathanial?

"I understand it was important for you to hunt down the man that hurt Nathanial. I don't fault you for that. Tracking down the lawless… that is really who you are. I had thought once that we wanted the same things in life. But I was clearly wrong. That was proved the day you left me and knew that I might have to bear the heartbreaking labor of burying Nathanial." Tears welled up in her eyes.

Nolan was guilty. Saying he was sorry a second time wasn't going to help. It seemed she had indeed made up her mind about him. Lowdown and skunk were the two words that came to mind. The hard set of Kate's jaw told him that getting her forgiveness wasn't going to be easy. Otherwise, he would have begged. There was a fierceness to her that he'd never before seen. Her glare was a definite sign that he wasn't getting a second chance.

Maybe she would allow him to come to the ranch now and then to visit with Nathanial. Could Nolan honestly make himself even do that much, knowing that one day he might ride up and see her with another man? He'd find himself on a wanted poster real damn quick.

Kate stood from the table. Nolan didn't want her to go. Her eyes were all over Nathanial, who slept with his snowy head resting on the table. That's where her true concern was. What could be said to convince her that he honestly did want to be a husband and father? Nothing that came to his mind seemed like the right words. He was going to lose her, dammit. He needed to say something.

He wiped the sweat from his brow. "Kate…"

"Nolan, please don't." She shot him down from giving another apology and pointed a fierce finger at him. "Let me tell you something." At that moment, Nolan would have much rather been facing the pussycat Deegan Jones.

"I will get over the heartache of not having you around. I might even someday begin to look for the affection of another man to perhaps marry again. But none of that worries me. What's ripped my heart to pieces has been to hear that little boy praise your name every day over the months while he got better. Would you like to guess how many times Nathanial has asked me when I thought you were coming back for him?"

She wiped at her eyes. Nolan could hardly look at her.

"I wasn't able to look into those big, loving blue eyes and tell Nathanial you left 'cause you're a coward. So I made a liar out of myself for your sake. I told Nathanial that scouting was a means by which you were protecting us. What a mistake I made. The truth is you're a selfish man. So imagine my overwhelming joy when you stumbled into us here…drunk. If it weren't for Nathanial's happiness, I could have turned my head and pretended not to know you."

All Nolan could do was sit there utterly dumbstruck. Kate had faked that beautiful smile for Nathanial's sake, and Nolan had kissed her. It had all been done to not upset Nathanial on his big day. She turned her back, and with loving hands, she gently shook Nathanial to wake so they could head upstairs to their room. The youngster began to fuss and squirm to be left alone to sleep.

"Here, let me." Nolan stood, pushed in his chair, then picked up Nathanial. The half-pint's head rested against his shoulder. He got lucky that the little sleepyhead hadn't stirred awake at being jostled. A tired, grumpy child would be no fun, and Nolan wasn't trying to make Kate's job of mothering any harder.

She eyed him and the boy for a minute, then nodded and led the way up the stairs. Nolan waited as she unlocked the door. The silence between them was thickly awkward. He stepped inside the room behind her. Kate lit the lamp, then went to the bed and pulled back the blankets for him to lay Nathanial down.

Was this really goodbye? Nolan's heart pounded. He laid Nathanial's head to the pillow, then pulled off the boy's boots and tucked the blankets up around the tiny shoulders.

Nathanial's eyes fluttered open and clung with hope to Nolan's. "Are you gonna marry Mama? You would make a real good pa."

"You go on to sleep. I'll see ya in the morning." Oh, how Nolan wished he had a happy answer to that question. He smoothed the snowy hair, and Nathanial closed his baby blues.

"I think it's time for you to leave." Kate hadn't ever been so firm with Nolan.

He straightened from the edge of the bed. "Kate, you might not want to hear it, but... I love this boy."

She grinned. Did she think he was trying to be funny?

"I know you do. I didn't think you sat at Nathanial's bedside every minute of the day when he was hurt because you despised him... That was up until you ran away from us."

Damn. Kate was riding roughshod over him, but he was owed it. "Kate, I'm sorry. I love you."

Surely she knew those words didn't roll easy off his tongue. Until this very minute, Mary had been the only woman he'd ever whispered affection toward. For some reason he hadn't thought about Kate needing to hear those three words. He'd felt them since first laying eyes on her. Why hadn't he told her before now, when it might be too late?

She seemed to have not heard him, then pointedly looked at him. "Your invitation to drift in and out of my life is over. I will not have that for Nathanial."

Kate's love had been something he'd just figured would always be waiting for him. Nolan stepped closer, and he hesitantly slipped his arms around her waist to pull her against him, but she held him at arm's length.

He maintained persistence so she'd know how he felt. "I ain't fooling around, Kate. I want ya as my wife."

"That's quite a proposal." She pushed away from his attempt at a kiss. "I'm not sure about us anymore, Nolan. I won't deny my love for you, but I have pause. Let me think for a while." Kate walked toward the window and stood facing the street.

Nolan owned the reputation of being one of a handful of unshakable trackers. Not everyone could take bits and pieces of a man's trail, put them together, then look down a straight path into what was to come. But he'd failed to read Kate's sign. She was a mother now, not Nolan's personal whore. Not that he'd ever thought of her that way, but that was exactly how he'd treated her. Only, he hadn't seen it until now. She had every right to be pissed at him. Hell, he was angry with himself.

"Good night, ma'am." Nolan glanced at Nathanial, then walked toward the door.

"Oh, here, don't forget this." Kate's hurried footsteps were behind him. Nolan turned and faced her, and she carried a package in her hands. "I'll tell Nathanial I gave it to you." She handed him the gift from the boy.

"Thank you." Nolan tipped his hat and turned to go.

"Don't thank me. Make your peace with that heartsick little boy who cries himself to sleep each night, waiting for his almighty hero to come home to him. Nathanial doesn't know it, but when I'm lying in bed, I can hear him in the next room, aching over you. I'm not even sure that letting you around Nathanial as much as I have today is good for him. You're not the man I once believed you to be."

Nolan was glad he wasn't facing her. Kate was right, and there was nothing he could do tonight to fix what he'd broken. He walked out and closed the door behind him. What a damn mess he'd made. Good advice was what he needed.

He left the hotel, standing a moment on the boardwalk. He drew in a deep breath and let out a troubled sigh. The town was quieting down. Only the music and hoots and hollers from the saloon polluted the street. The sun hung low over the mountain, and the sky was a brilliant pink. A sailor's delight, or so the old saying went. Good for the damn seamen. Nolan, too, could use some good fortune.

He looked down at the package in his hand. It wasn't a small brown bag of candy like he'd thought when Nathanial had first mentioned the gift. *Let's see what the boy was so excited to give me.* Nolan pulled open the paper wrapping and stared. A rain slicker. What Nolan held in his hands was honest and pure thoughtfulness.

He stepped into the street and headed for Marshal Huckabee's house at the edge of town. That drink sounded good right about now. He wasn't going to give up on marrying Kate and adopting Nathanial. He would hash out his troubles over a whiskey with his friend. They had until sunup to think of something to make her see Nolan not just differently but in a way that would win her heart and she would throw her arms around his neck, kiss him, and say yes.

———

A touch of morning gray faintly lit the sky when Nolan took a seat in the lobby, waiting for Kate and Nathanial to come downstairs for breakfast. Fiddling with his hat in his hands was only setting his nerves further on edge. The clerk had looked at him strangely at least a dozen times.

Nolan pushed his hat down on his head, then wiped the sweat from his hands on his pant legs. It was nearly eight o'clock now. The sun had been up for over an hour. Were Kate and the boy going to sleep the day away?

Syrupy smells drifted out from the dining room and into his nose. It was driving him about half mad. Constance Huckabee had offered him breakfast, but he'd politely declined. That had been a foolish decision. He hadn't slept a wink. All he'd wanted with the rise of the sun was to hurry to the hotel. His fingers were crossed that Kate, too, had been up all night, thinking about the possible future they could have together as a family.

He could picture her standing in front of a mirror, pinning her hair just so. It might be lunchtime before she and Nathanial walked downstairs from room number seven. Maybe Nolan should go knock on the door. No, hurrying Kate wouldn't help his cause any.

"I told Ma you'd be here!" Nathanial took off running down the steps and threw himself around Nolan's waist. It was a relief to see Kate smile, and he knew it was genuine. The boy's face was buried in the front of Nolan's shirt, hugging him tight, so Nathanial couldn't see her face, meaning she didn't have to fake a smile for his sake. Nolan hadn't been so sure of how he might be greeted this morning. She didn't say a word about him leaving, so he reckoned she was okay with him being there.

Nathanial took Nolan by the hand and led him to a table. Kate followed, and he could feel her gaze on him. He pulled out a chair, and she sat.

"What are you doing?" The boy's nose wrinkled up. "Ma ain't no weakling. She can scoot in her own chair." He studied Nolan with a raised brow, and Kate chuckled.

"It's called being a gentleman."

Nathanial shrugged, then took a seat.

They ate steak and eggs for breakfast. To look at the three of them together, no one would have known how badly Nolan was sweating in wait. Kate might shoo him off any minute. So far, everything seemed to be fine. Not one harsh look from her, not even when the boy was focused on other things and wasn't looking at them. Kate's eyes were mostly on Nathanial as he ate. Nolan looked about the place. There weren't too many people there. This was it. He was going to do it. He wiped his mouth, then dropped the napkin on his empty plate.

"Kate." Nolan reached for her hand, and his throat went dry. He choked on the proposal as he looked between her and the boy. He was a fool with his mouth hanging open.

"Are you all right?" Kate's brow rose, and she stared.

"Here." Nathanial got up from his chair, hurried, and brought Nolan a glass of water.

Maybe asking Kate to marry him in front of the boy wasn't such a good idea. If she said no, Nolan could picture the hellish fit Nathanial would throw. What he needed was a few minutes alone with her. He swallowed down a gulp of water.

"We're leaving this morning… Would you like to come home with us?" The youngster knew what he wanted and was not afraid to go after it.

Nolan outright laughed. He looked at Kate for the answer, and his gut tightened. If she didn't want him, then he wouldn't go. It was her happiness that mattered to him.

"I suppose you could travel along with us to Gray Rock, and we can see how it goes." So there it was. She'd punched Nolan's ticket to ride only as far as Gray Rock.

That's where he would get off the train. Unless Kate's eyes were opened to truly see that he was a changed man. Being alone had been his solace after Mary and Matthew were killed. Now, being without Kate and Nathanial was pure misery.

"You look pretty this morning."

Kate blushed a little. Nolan hoped she knew he was being honest and not just trying to win her over with a compliment.

"Sure she does. She fussed over her hair for twenty damn minutes before we could come downstairs," Nathanial tattled.

Nolan chuckled, and Kate's cheeks grew a deep red.

"You watch your mouth," Nolan warned but wasn't angry with Nathanial. "Excuse me. I have some business to talk over with the marshal. I'll meet ya both at the livery in an hour or so?"

Kate nodded, and Nolan swallowed down the last drop of coffee in his cup, then stood from the table.

"Can I go?" Nathanial jumped up from the chair and tugged impatiently on Nolan's sleeve for permission.

"It's fine by me, but your ma has to give her okay." Until Kate said yes, Nolan figured it wasn't his place to tell Nathanial what he could do.

"Please, Ma." The little stinker was batting those baby blues ever so sweetly.

"Oh, you're awful. The two of you get out of here." Kate winked at Nathanial, then turned a serious eye on Nolan.

He reckoned he could guess her worrisome thoughts. Given Nathanial's great happiness and with all the time Nolan would spend with the boy between there and Gray Rock, how hurt would Nathanial be if he rode away again? Couldn't Kate see that his intention was to be the head of this family, to raise Nathanial together as theirs? For a first, Nolan could picture their future filling up with more children. Nathanial could have brothers and sisters.

"Come on." He tugged on Nolan's arm and brought him back to thinking of his business with the marshal.

"All right." Nolan pushed in his chair.

Nathanial copied him.

They left the hotel. Nathanial walked tall next to Nolan along the boardwalk. There was no doubt he had just gotten his little shadow back. That, indeed, was a great feeling, and he believed his grin showed it.

Nolan opened the door. Nathanial went first into the marshal's office. Marshal Huckabee sat at his desk, shuffling papers. A towhead boy was sitting on the corner of the desk, happily swinging his feet. Damn. That boy was the spitting image of the marshal. Nolan had forgotten how strong a resemblance there was between Joseph and little Joseph, or Deputy, as the boy had been nicknamed for as long as Nolan could remember.

"There ain't no denying who fathered that child." Nolan and the marshal both chuckled. Then the marshal greeted him with a friendly handshake.

"Something I can do for ya?" The marshal leaned back in his chair and seemed to be waiting to hear Nolan out.

Nolan tossed a quick glance between the two youngsters, who were eying one another all friendly like. He would guess them to be the same age. And he'd seen for himself that Deputy could be just as ornery as Nathanial at times. The two little yahoos could be real trouble without having a close eye kept on them.

"Deputy, you and Nathanial scat for a while."

Nolan hoped the marshal knew what he was doing sending those two off together. Deputy hopped down from the desk corner, and the two youngsters ran out the door. A fast friendship had been born.

"Don't git into any trouble!" Nolan hollered after the boys, but the warning was meant mainly for Nate's ears.

It pleased him to see that the clock had been reset for Nathanial. No longer did it seem that the boy was trying to act like a man. A childhood had been gained with his new life, and he finally was acting his age. There was, however, one person who could spoil that. Jones needed to be captured.

Nolan sat after pouring himself and the marshal a cup of coffee. "You ever hear of a killer by the name of Deegan Jones?"

"I never seen hair of the man, only a wanted poster that came across my desk. Why?" The marshal sat up straight behind his desk, and his full attention was aimed at Nolan.

"Well, I lost his trail a few miles from where we're sitting." This time the truth was something he didn't enjoy admitting. It was a hit to his reputation.

"You couldn't pick up his tracks again?" The marshal raised a disbelieving brow. "Who the hell is this man that he could throw the Hound Dog off his trail?"

An hour later, the marshal knew every godforsaken bloody detail of Nolan's time chasing after Jones to get the women back. And Nolan's friend now fully understood the bond between him and Nathanial.

"I'll ride out and see if I can find any sign of where this Deegan Jones might be headed. If I do pick up a good clue, I'll send word to Captain Farnsworth at the fort. And I'll telegraph you in Gray Rock." The marshal gave his word to Nolan.

He set down his coffee cup and stood to go. The marshal also got to his feet. One then the other walked out the door. It would be a fine day for traveling. The sun wasn't so hot, and there was a cool breeze.

"Where do you suppose them two little troublemakers are?" Birch Creek was the marshal's town, so Nolan hoped he would have some idea.

"I'd put money on the pond behind the house. Deputy ain't happy unless he's driving his ma plumb crazy with head-to-toe muddy clothes."

That wasn't what Nolan wanted to hear from the marshal. Kate would not only box Nathanial's ears for dirtying up his clean duds. She might just skin Nolan for letting him run loose to find trouble.

The marshal clapped Nolan on the shoulder as they walked to find the boys. "So I take it Kate's said yes. I doubt Nathanial would be with ya had she refused your proposal."

"Don't go congratulating me just yet. I rehearsed every word in my head on the way to the hotel this morning. But then at breakfast, it just didn't seem like the right time to spring it on her."

Apparently, the marshal thought the whole matter was funny because he was chuckling. "I ain't ever known you to be a coward."

"It ain't an easy thing to ask when the answer might be git out of my face. If I recall correctly, Marshal Huckabee, you stumbled over your tongue a few times before correctly spitting out those words to Constance. I was there once to hear your botched try, remember? It was at a church social here in Birch Creek." Nolan all but dared his friend to deny the truth.

The marshal grinned, then began to chuckle. "Nolan, I wish you the best of luck." He clapped Nolan's shoulder again.

They reached the edge of town and found both Nathanial and Deputy stuck knee-deep in mud, trying to catch frogs in the pond. Yup, Kate was going to kill Nolan. Nathanial was covered in thick, mucky slime from head to toe. Nolan had never thought for one minute that it was possible for him to get so damn dirty in only an hour.

He shook his head in disbelief and looked over at the marshal. "I'm about to have a steaming woman biting at my ears."

There was really nothing his friend could say. The marshal, too, was going to have some explaining to do. Constance Huckabee was maybe even more particular than Kate.

CHAPTER 28

NOLAN GAVE A WAVE to come on. Nathanial waded quickly from the water and came running. Deputy was on Nathanial's heels as the two little mud balls raced to where Nolan and the marshal stood. Nathanial skidded to a halt at Nolan's feet.

"You know your ma is gonna have a fit when she sees your filthy clothes." Nolan figured he had known the plan to leave Birch Creek within the hour. Wasn't that the same as saying stay clean? He should have thought better than to roll around like a pig in the mud.

Nathanial shrugged without worry.

"Yeah, we'll see if you feel that way when you're facing your ma." Nolan was sure the lecture would be aimed mostly at him. It was certain proof that he was rusty at being a responsible father.

"Say goodbye to Deputy. Let's not be late to meet your ma at the livery on top of this mess." Nolan then shook the marshal's hand. "See ya later, Deputy."

Nathanial turned and waved goodbye as he followed close behind Nolan.

Kate's gaze walked up and down Nathanial's muddy clothes, face, and hair. Nolan's ears were ready to hear it from her. He threw up his hands. It was true. He was guilty for not keeping a better eye on her son.

"Oh Nathanial, look at how dirty you are. You're not sitting on the wagon seat beside me. Crawl in the back and change before we go. I hope I can scrub those clothes clean and that they're not ruined."

The boy quickly did as his ma had told him.

"Sorry, Kate, it was really my fault." Nolan thought he should apologize. She didn't seem as angry as he'd expected, which was good.

"Fine, then you can scrub the clothes." Kate grinned from where she sat on the wagon seat.

Nolan chuckled, and just that quick, Nathanial reappeared out of the covered wagon bed. The boy was sporting clean clothes, but the naturally fair hair was still streaked brown with globs of mud. He plopped down next to his ma.

Nolan untied the bay from the wagon gate and brought the horse forward. It had been kind of Kate to see that the bay was saddled so they were all ready at once to leave.

An idea came to him, one that he thought Nathanial would like better than rolling along in the creaking wagon. "How about you try out the bay and see how the horse fits ya?"

Nathanial's answer was his bright smile.

Nolan lifted the half-pint off the wagon and onto the horse. "Be easy on the bit and don't run the horse. If you do, I'll tie the reins to the back of the wagon, and you'll have to plod along from behind."

"Yes, sir." Nathanial accepted the reins.

Nolan stepped up onto the wagon and sat next to Kate. Now he and the boy were both happy. Surprisingly, she threaded her arm through Nolan's. He slapped the reins to the team, and the wagon lurched forward, then steadied into a rattling roll.

The days traveling to Gray Rock passed quickly. The three of them were a good fit. Everything between Nolan and Kate seemed to be going well. The only small trouble so far was that he'd found some trampled-down smudges of horse prints while he and Nathanial had been hunting supper. The boy had seen him study the tracks. But thankfully, he hadn't asked what had happened to Jones.

Honestly, Nolan hadn't been sure whether it was a sign of the killer or maybe just a few men riding the country together. The tracks had been trodden over too many times for him to make out the detail that would have clued him to identify Jones's horse. He hadn't meant to scare Nathanial when he'd wheeled the bay and hightailed it back to Kate. The boy had seemed on high alert, though he said nothing of his fear.

That night, while Kate and Nathanial slept, Nolan stood guard.

He was tired when morning rose on a new day, but a cup of Kate's coffee would keep him going. As the sun moved overhead from east to west, his eyes searched every hill and clump of trees that could hide men on horseback. To see Jones and his men storm down on the wagon with guns blazing wouldn't surprise him a bit. Kate was a fine-looking woman. She would, no doubt, fetch a handsome price. Nolan kept his rifle close at hand.

They stopped for an early supper. Tomorrow by this time, they would be in Gray Rock, and Nolan hadn't yet found the right time to propose. He steered the wagon under a patch of trees for shade.

"Hey, look there." He pointed out a small stream to Nathanial. "Git the fishing poles, and let's see if we can catch some supper."

Nathanial quickly crawled under the canvas flap and into the bed of the wagon from where he'd been sitting on the seat between Nolan and Kate. It was but a minute and Nathanial was standing next to him at the side of the wagon with poles in hand, waiting. "I'll go dig some worms."

"Try to find some fat ones." Nolan stepped down off the wagon and took the poles before Nathanial dashed off to scratch in the dirt for bait.

He found a comfy mossy spot, propping himself lazily against a tree. His feet were crossed, and he was just about to tip his hat over his eyes when he caught sight of Nathanial running toward him from farther down the creek. Huffing and puffing from the short spurt, Nathanial stopped in front of Nolan and reached deep into his pants pocket.

"Don't tell me you put the worms in there." Nolan wasn't really asking, and he shook his head as Nathanial pulled five or six fat night crawlers out in his hand. "Those are good ones."

They each hooked their bait, then cast a line. They sat and watched closely for a flick or a snag on the line that would tell of a fish biting at the lure. Bubbles rose from the muck that lay deep within the water under some overhanging roots of a tall tree.

"Keep your line away from that spot. I would bet there's a big snapper hiding down in the mud under those roots."

Nathanial stretched his neck and looked deeper into the water and studied the spot. Quietly Nolan set down his pole so Nathanial wouldn't take notice. He grabbed the boy as if pushing him into the water but kept hold of him. Nathanial let out with a scream, and Nolan chuckled.

"That wasn't funny. My heart's pounding. I'm gonna tell Ma on you." The half-pint picked up the pole he'd dropped.

"So that's the thanks I git for trying to help you. Why, I was saving ya from falling in and maybe gittin' your toe bit off. You know, if you hook that snapper, then we'll have to eat turtle soup instead of fish, and I'm hungry for trout." Nolan nudged the half-pint.

"Yuck, I ain't eating no turtle." Nathanial wrinkled up his nose in disgust.

Nolan tried to keep a straight face. "Turtle tastes just like chicken. It's good. Fried chicken is your favorite, ain't it? I bet you couldn't tell the difference between that and fried turtle." He was pulling the boy's leg, but Nathanial wasn't catching on so well. The half-pint stared at Nolan all thoughtful like and seemed to be trying to decide if he was serious.

Before he made up his mind, Kate walked over to the edge of the water. She handed Nolan a cup of fresh steaming brew, then sat down and joined them. It smelled good but was too hot to sip.

"Ma, Nolan said turtle tastes like chicken. Is that true?" The half-pint had just tattled.

Kate smirked with amusement, as did Nolan. "Someone told you a tale. To me, turtle simply tastes like turtle, not chicken." She winked at the boy.

With Kate's answer, Nathanial dropped his pole, sprang to his feet, and playfully pounced on Nolan. "You're a no-good fib teller." The cup got knocked out of Nolan's hand, and coffee spilled down the front of his shirt.

Tears sprang to Nathanial's eyes, and he wiped feverishly with his bare hands at the wetness. "I'm sorry. Please don't be mad." He pulled up the waist of his shirt and scrubbed hard at the stain. Tears streamed down his face, and there appeared to be frantic craziness in his eyes. "I'm a clumsy good-for-nothing. I'll clean your shirt. I swear. Don't leave me and Ma. I don't want ya to go."

Nolan pulled the blubbering child off him, but Nate wouldn't stop pawing wildly at the coffee mark on his shirt. "Nathanial. Stop it. What in God's name has gotten into you? It's just a little spilled coffee, and my shirt ain't that important." He grabbed the boy's wrists to keep Nate from rubbing at him.

Nathanial wrenched away and backed off a step. What in the hell had just happened? One minute he and Nate were being silly, and the next, he was pale and shaking all over. Why?

Nolan glanced at Kate for some explanation. Tears made her eyes glassy. It gave him reason to believe she'd never before seen Nathanial react to anything in such a strong way.

"Son, I don't understand why you're so upset."

"Go ahead. Cuff me. Just git it over with. I deserve a good slap or two for being so damn dumb." Nathanial was still bawling. "Will you stay? Please."

Nolan didn't understand this at all, and judging by Kate's wide, teary eyes, she didn't have a clue either. Why would Nathanial believe he would just hit him or leave him because of spilled coffee?

The boy had his eyes squinted up tight and his chin slightly tucked into his chest, as if he were waiting for Nolan to belt him upside the head.

Kate grabbed up the hem of her skirt to hurry toward Nathanial. Tears now streaked down her face. Without a word, Nolan quickly shook his head. It was understandable that, as a mother, she wanted to give comfort to her child who was obviously upset about something. First Nolan needed to hear a reason for this fuss. If Kate was crying all over the boy, Nathanial might not speak up. She stopped midstep, wiped her eyes, and stood by Nolan's decision without knowing what would happen next.

Nathanial needed to learn that not all men hit.

"Nathanial, son, look at me." Nolan's command was firm but not uncaring. Even if Kate said no to marriage and Nathanial didn't become his son by name, he didn't want his hand to be feared by the little boy. What had set off the kid? Surely not just the spilled coffee, but nothing else had happened and Nathanial had never been afraid of him before.

He slowly opened his squinted eyes. Nolan knelt and gently pulled the youngster to him. Tears dripped off Nathanial's chin, and he once again stared at the stain on Nolan's shirt. The half-pint slowly reached out and lightly touched a finger against the wet, and his eyes were glazed over as though he were remembering another day maybe similar in a way to this one.

"Nathanial, tell me what happened." Nolan wiped at the tears on the boy's face, and Nate kept staring off.

"Pa barked at me to fetch him coffee. If I wasn't fast enough, I'd get slapped around 'cause it'd happened before. In my hurry, I had tripped and splashed Pa with the whole cup, right down the front of his shirt. I got beat with the buckle end of his belt till I could hardly breathe."

Nathanial slowly looked up, and his faraway stare now focused on Nolan's face. "Mr. Harper. It wasn't coffee but grain, and I'd only spilled a little. Jenny nursed me for two weeks to bring me back to health." The half-pint threw his arms around Nolan's neck and sobbed into his collar, and he held his son there.

Those scars that Nolan had seen on the boy's back cut far deeper than just through the skin. And the bad memories Nathanial had shared explained a lot about his overreaction to spilling a little coffee. Jim Younger was the one that deserved a damn good beating, not this boy. And if that no-good Harper son of a bitch wasn't already dead, Nolan would have liked to have gone a round with that piece of shit as well.

He needed to simmer down before Nathanial maybe got it into his little head that he was the cause of his anger. As a father, he would teach Nathanial a whole different kind of life. Kate just needed to say yes first.

"Dry your eyes. There ain't no cause to be all fussed up. My shirt, coffee, your old pa, and Mr. Harper—I don't think any of it's worth ruining our good day of fishing." Nolan wasn't trying to make light of Nathanial's awful past, but he didn't want the boy to stay focused on it.

Nathanial wiped his sleeve across his red eyes. Then he looked up at Nolan and hinted at a grin. "You ain't mad at me, even a little?"

The boy seemed to think he should be in trouble for something so unimportant, and there was only one way Nolan could think to explain otherwise. "Nathanial, when I was a little boy like you, my pa took a hand to my backside only when I needed to learn a lesson to grow up right. I will do the same to you if you disobey me. Just like when your ma took a switch to ya for skipping school. You did wrong and got punished for it." Nolan pulled the half-pint off so they could look at one another. "I know them other men from your past hit ya, but have I ever beaten on you?"

Nathanial raised his right hand. "Honest, I ain't afraid of you. I know you're not hateful like my old pa or Mr. Harper. But sometimes those bad things that happened to me…that fear, it creeps up and spooks me without me even realizing it. This was just one of them times."

The boy then began to slowly grin. "Does that mean you and Ma are getting married and you're gonna be my new pa?" Nathanial was too smart and had read between the lines of Nolan's story about his upbringing.

"Well, your ma and I have some talking to do. You just keep your fingers crossed."

The half-pint tore from Nolan's arms and in one running step was hugging around Kate's waist. "Please say yes, Ma." The boy brought out the big guns, and he was batting those baby blues like nothing Nolan had ever seen before. Only, Kate's gaze wasn't on Nathanial. She stared directly at Nolan. What he saw was a glassy shine.

"Nathanial, I want you to go wait for me at the wagon." Her eyes never left Nolan's.

"Yes, Ma." The half-pint lost his happy grin and walked backward while he kept a close eye on them.

Nolan hadn't planned on proposing this way, but it looked like his time was up. He would have his answer in another breath or two. Kate's face wasn't giving off the glow of an expectant bride to be, nor was she wearing an angry frown. This family wasn't Nolan's, but he valued it more than anything in this world. It would cost him nothing to ask for Kate's hand. But if he heard the word *no* come out of her mouth...then damn. Nolan would lose everything that was most important to him.

He hunkered down on one knee in front of her, then took her hands in his. From the corner of his eye, he could see Nathanial standing at the back of the wagon, waiting to see if this would be a celebration.

"Kate, I love ya. Do me the honor of becoming my wife."

She began to weep. Nolan wasn't sure if these were joyful tears. He understood the reason for her pause. She'd waited a long time for him to finally come to his senses, and he was now able to picture their happy future as she always had. Maybe Kate's silence was his answer. He somehow knew what was probably going through her mind. Could he be happy as the family man, no longer riding the trails to wherever he was called upon to help?

He waited and searched her teary eyes. They loved each other. He didn't doubt that. "Kate?" He roused her from her thoughts, and she finally wiped at her tears.

She studied him for a long minute, then glanced lovingly over her shoulder at Nathanial. "That little boy. He thinks you're taller than Blue Sky Mountain. I can't have you riding away from us. He needs you, and so do I."

Nolan knew exactly what Kate meant. The many times he'd come and gone from her life, leaving her empty without him. It wasn't right how he had hurt her all those times, and now it wasn't just her that would be hurt by his selfishness. They had Nathanial to think about now.

"What did she say?" Nathanial hollered from where he stood.

Kate chuckled through her tears, and Nolan couldn't help but smile. Obviously, Nathanial was as anxious as Nolan to get an answer.

"Nothing would make me happier than to share my name with both you and Nathanial. Marry me?" He held tight to Kate's hands. His heart was pounding, and the sweat poured out of him.

"Mrs. Crosson … I very much love the sound of that." She smiled, and Nolan now knew that her tears were happy ones.

He jumped to his feet, grabbed her up in his arms, and kissed her.

"Woo-hoo!" Nathanial celebrated. The half-pint made a beeline as fast as his feet would go straight at them.

Nolan caught him mid running leap and spun the happy little fella around in the air a few times. The three of them were simply enjoying the moment of becoming a family.

CHAPTER 29

"NOLAN, I NEED TO BUY a sack of flour before we head home."

Nolan pulled up on the reins, stopping the wagon in front of the store, then helped Kate down. The bell over the door rang as she went inside. Nolan rubbed his hand along the sorrel's legs, looking over the team. The animals were holding up fine. He turned from the horses to check on where Nathanial had gotten to. A few boys his age stood in the schoolyard close to the bay. Nathanial twisted around in the saddle and pointed at Nolan. He grinned and chuckled. He could rightly guess what he had said ... He'd gotten himself a pa.

Nolan turned, hearing the store bell ring. A huge fella carried several packages, probably for the dark-haired lady on his arm. They nodded as they strolled past. How long did it take to buy flour? He was tired of the thumping ride of the wagon and wanted something hot to eat.

"Mr. Crosson." A man hurried and crossed the street toward Nolan, waving a telegram.

He took the slip of paper and read as the man waited for his response. So the marshal had picked up Deegan's trail and followed the killer for some time, riding back this way. It wasn't certain that Gray Rock was where Jones was headed, but the wanted man was definitely in the territory.

"Dammit." Jones was too close for Nolan's liking. He'd promised Kate and Nathanial that he was done with that part of his life. Hunting Jones was no longer his priority. He wouldn't leave his family. What he could do was give this information to Sheriff Fuller and let him track down Jones.

Kate came out of the store, walking toward Nolan.

He helped her onto the wagon. At the same time, he felt the hard glare from across the street. "I'll be back in a minute."

Kate didn't question him but must have felt the tension too and glanced between Nolan and Wade Fuller. He walked to where the sheriff stood, leaning against the porch post of the jailhouse.

He handed the wire to the sheriff without a word of explanation and waited for a response to the information.

"I see you and Kate are friendly again. What does she see in a trail bum like you?" Fuller snarled, but Nolan chose to ignore it. What to do about Jones was more important at this moment.

Sheriff Fuller finally looked at the paper in his hand. Anytime Nolan's gut tightened, it usually meant trouble. Fuller hadn't flinched at reading that Jones was in the area. The man was no ten-cent thief. He was a wanted killer with a large bounty on his head.

"I've helped to bury a lot of families 'cause of that man's greed." Somehow what Nolan had just said didn't seem to bother the sheriff. What was it going to take to get under Fuller's skin? Did Jones need to prance his fancy ass into town and practically give himself up? Because hell would freeze over before that happened.

"You forming a posse? I'll ride with ya." For a minute Nolan had forgotten his promise to Kate and Nathanial. This town as a whole community was in danger. Was Fuller blind to what Jones was capable of, or was he just too much of a damn coward to go after the killer? He'd probably rather sit on the boardwalk in front of the jailhouse and play checkers with his deputy.

"Nope, I ain't gonna chase after Jones." Sheriff Fuller was too casual. Then he gave Nolan a hard stare. "Unless someone's missing that I don't know about."

So the sheriff did know of Jones's history of smuggling women.

"Jones has a price on his head. That's all the reason you need to go after him." Nolan wasn't finding the sheriff's smirk funny at all. There were plenty of ladies in the town of Gray Rock, and that wasn't including the surrounding areas. Nolan hated the thought of another woman being ripped from her home and loved ones. These were Fuller's people. What the hell was wrong with the man? Wearing a badge and having been sworn in to protect sure hadn't born in him a sense of loyalty.

"Listen up, Crosson. I'm the law here in Gray Rock, and I say this telegram is wrong. Deegan Jones has never bothered this town, and he ain't gonna start now."

Nolan thought Fuller was awfully confident. It was sort of odd. How did he know what Jones was planning on doing?

Nolan and Fuller stood nose to nose. If it weren't for the tin star pinned on Wade's shirt, he would have hit the coward square in the teeth. "I never realized how yellow you are."

"Kate's a fool if she thinks you're more man than I am. I'm done with her anyway. She went and adopted that damn Younger kid." Fuller looked over at his deputy and smirked.

It was the last smart-ass word Nolan would take from Sheriff Wade Fuller. A quickly thrown punch square to Wade's jaw dropped him to the ground.

Nolan hauled the good-for-nothing lawman up out of the dirt by a fistful of shirt collar. "She was never your woman. We aim to be married, and that is my son. You best keep them two things in mind when you're speaking to me."

Deputy Toller hurried from his seat and gave him a hard shove away from the sheriff. Nolan stepped back a pace or two into the street and remained facing the two.

Sheriff Fuller rubbed at his jaw. "I could arrest you."

Nolan held his hands out to be cuffed. It was true. Sheriff Fuller had the legal right to lock him behind bars. He'd go peacefully. Spending the night in jail wasn't where he wanted to be, but it wouldn't kill him. Kate and Nathanial would have to stay in town at the hotel. He wouldn't allow them to stay out on the ranch alone, not after reading the marshal's message.

Fuller's deputy stepped off the boardwalk toward Nolan, probably to lead him inside to a cell.

"Leave him."

Nolan caught the shifty look between the sheriff and his deputy. This was Fuller's chance to shove his badge in Nolan's face and lock him behind bars. So why wasn't he grabbing him and throwing him in a cell? It did make Fuller look like the bigger man in front of Kate and those who'd gathered on the street watching. None of them was close enough to see the hateful glint in the sheriff's eyes or the pulsing vein in his neck.

Fists balled up at his sides and lips pressed tight together, those things could be seen, and Fuller shook as if barely restraining himself from hammering on Nolan. He was the type who always liked to throw around the weight of his badge, so why not now when he had an audience? It wasn't like Wade Fuller to back down when he knew he had the upper hand. There had to be a reason for the sheriff to just set Nolan free.

Nolan smirked, then tipped his hat at Deputy Toller, who was now standing empty-handed. He turned and walked toward the wagon.

In Birch Creek, the marshal had said that he would also send word to the fort. Hopefully, Captain Farnsworth was already on his way. Nolan would send a second wire for urgency.

He gave a wave to the telegraph clerk. A message was quickly penned. "Send that right away."

"Yes, sir." The clerk hurried off.

Nolan stepped up onto the wagon.

Kate's eyes were still wide, and she placed her hand on his. "Do I need to be worried?"

"No, ma'am. Let's go home." He slapped the reins to the team, and the wagon began to roll. Nate trotted the bay up next to them, wearing a victorious smile. It wasn't hard to guess why. There was no love lost between Nathanial and Sheriff Fuller.

Nolan caught sight of Fuller's deputy hurrying into the telegraph office. Huh... There was nothing of importance in his telegram that the sheriff couldn't read it. Why would Fuller maybe think that Nolan was hiding something? It didn't matter though. Enough time had passed from when the clerk had gone inside to send the message and when Deputy Toller followed. The telegram couldn't be stopped. Maybe the coincidence of both Nolan and the sheriff having to send out wires after their confrontation was nothing. Sheriff Fuller had simply needed to send a message.

But Nolan didn't believe so.

CHAPTER 30

THEY'D SETTLED IN QUICKLY as a family. The preacher had been called away to tend to a sick relative, so Nolan and Kate couldn't be married until Pastor Hicks returned. Nolan worked around the ranch, fixing loose fence posts and nailing down lifted boards on the barn. He was sorry that he'd never before seen the many small things Kate needed mended. Most all of it would have been too much for a lone woman and little boy to fix. There were plenty of jobs to keep Nolan busy. None of it, though, distracted his mind from too often wondering of Jones's whereabouts. At no time had he received any word from the fort or Marshal Huckabee concerning Jones. Maybe the killer had just moved through the territory. That thought didn't make him feel any better.

The half-pint worked beside Nolan every day after school. It was nice to see that whatever the job, his little shadow was always there, wanting to be taught. If word of Jones did come from Captain Farnsworth or the marshal, Nolan didn't want Nathanial getting any half-cocked ideas about running after him. The boy was shedding that tough exterior and learning how to behave himself. Though he was still quite a handful at times and had an ornery streak that stretched from daybreak until dark. Even now, family life was a big change for Nathanial.

"That was a fine supper." Nolan rose from his seat to help Kate clear the dishes from the table.

"I'm going outside to play." Nathanial hopped up from the table and ran toward the door. He'd left his chair out and hadn't taken his plate to the kitchen. The door slammed.

Kate let out a deep sigh. "That boy has too much steam."

Nolan grinned. It was true. Though his mind wasn't on the boy's manners. He stole a quick kiss from Kate, then another. Before he knew it, his hands began to roam over her curves.

"Nathanial is outside," he whispered between kisses.

"I mean it, Nolan, not till we're married."

Shot down again.

"Fine." He would have to find pleasure in sitting on the porch and taking in the cool evening air.

He walked from the house, leaving Kate doing the dishes. He'd lost that battle a number of times. It slightly irked him. She'd never denied him before. Now, all of a sudden, they had to be man and wife, and until then he'd been banished to sleep in the spare room. He was sick and tired of going to bed without feeling the soft warmth of her body cuddled up next to him. He chuckled then, picturing that most mornings, he woke to find Nathanial draped over him instead.

Nolan flopped down and sat on the porch swing. The evening sky was a soft orange, and birds chirped. The moment was peaceful, and the three of them were real happy. At times he still worried about Nathanial maybe running off after Jones. Now and then, his son would bring up Jenny's name. Her death was a slow-healing wound that Nolan didn't want painfully torn back open if Nathanial happened to learn that Jones hadn't been captured.

Nolan looked about to see where he had run off to play. The little nincompoop swung on the bay's tail like a rope. "Git out of there before ya git your head kicked off!"

Where was the boy's sense? Nathanial set his feet to the ground at hearing the warning, then sneaked a glance over his shoulder at Nolan. He could almost read the boy's thoughts of chancing another swing. Nolan was sitting a good fifteen yards from the corral and wouldn't be able to catch hold of Nathanial to stop him.

"I said git!" It was the last warning.

The boy still held tight to the bay's tail, and he seemed to be weighing the risk of another swing. Nolan's irritation grew into anger. Nathanial turned his back as if he hadn't just been given two warnings to stop. Instead of taking a swing, the half-pint climbed up onto the bay's back.

He grabbed a fistful of black mane and kicked the horse into a run around the ring. "Watch this!"

Nolan jumped to his feet, felt the flaming red heat in his face, and marched toward his son. What popped into his mind was Nate bragging at supper in Birch Creek about how he'd jumped the mare over the corral fence. He ran the bay straight at the railing. *Aw shit.* If the bay caught a hoof on the rail and fell, Nathanial could be crushed.

The gelding jumped the fence, and sure enough, Nolan's fear came to life. One of the bay's back hooves nicked the top rail. The gelding stumbled as it landed, and Nathanial lost his grip and was pitched forward over the bay's shoulder. He hit the ground, and when he stopped rolling, he gasped for wind and, thank God, didn't hesitate to curl himself into a ball. The big horse stepped over him and just missed trampling him. Kate must have seen the near miss too and screamed from somewhere behind Nolan.

He grabbed his son up out of the dirt and stood Nathanial on his feet. Dusting the boy off, he looked him over good. Nathanial was only scraped up some that he could see. "What were you thinking? You could have been killed if that horse had fallen on ya."

Nolan wasn't taking pity at the sight of the tears streaking down the half-pint's face. Nathanial had been warned more than once not to jump that fence.

"Go to the barn. I'm gonna give ya a whuppin'."

Fresh tears sprang to Nathanial's eyes. Nolan unbuckled his belt, pulled the leather from his pant loops, and folded it in his hand. Nathanial ran to his mama, threw his arms around her waist, and was crying into her skirt.

"Your pa's right. You need to learn a lesson. You could've killed yourself." Kate agreed with Nolan's punishment, and he was glad to hear it.

Nolan stormed toward the barn, and Nathanial clung to his ma. "I'll do dishes till my next birthday."

Begging only served to irritate Nolan more. The boy should have done as he'd been told and left the bay alone. Then he wouldn't be trouble. "Nathanial, let's go."

Nolan stood outside the barn door, waiting. Kate pulled the boy off and pointed him toward the barn. He began to bawl even harder and shuffled his feet. Nolan was about to take hold of his son in the middle of the damn yard and give him something to cry about. Nathanial deserved to have a tanned bottom. He could've broken his neck.

Nolan bent him over his knee, and the boy wailed before even feeling the first stinging lick of the belt. He didn't like doing it, but Nathanial wouldn't forget the hard lesson. So maybe next time the boy would listen and do as he'd been told.

Nolan stood Nathanial upright. Tears dripped off his chin, and he whimpered and rubbed at his stinging backside.

"Look at me, Nathanial."

The boy raised his head and met Nolan's stern stare. He wasn't finished handing out punishment yet. "Since you don't know how to treat a good horse, you will walk to school till I tell ya otherwise."

Nathanial ran off and crawled up the ladder into the hayloft. It always seemed to be his place of retreat when he got in trouble. Nolan left the barn. Hopefully, the boy would think over what he'd done. That certainly wouldn't hurt him any. One of these times, he wouldn't be so lucky, and he would get hurt trying to jump the fence.

Nolan flopped down on the porch swing. A bullfrog croaked from the edge of the pond. Night bugs that were silhouetted orange in the light of dusk produced a soft hum.

Kate sat down next to him on the swing, and her gaze drifted to the barn. "Did you have to spank him? Wasn't falling off the horse and hitting the dirt punishment enough?"

Nolan laughed at her. "If I recall correctly, I heard you agree that Nathanial needed to learn a lesson. Kate, our son needs to understand that he can't ignore what either of us tells him and then do as he pleases. I'm sure that's how he lived before, but Nathanial is my son now. I won't tolerate disrespect."

"I know all that. I am worried. You and I both have seen the tantrums when Nathanial thinks he should be allowed to do something that we've said no to. I get scared sometimes that he'll run off. Having a mother and father to answer to is a big life change for a little boy who basically had no one looking out for him since the day he was born." Kate rested her head against Nolan's shoulder.

Nolan didn't say what he was thinking. Nathanial wouldn't run off because he'd gotten spanked. But the boy might light a shuck after Jenny's killer if he ever found out that Jones hadn't been captured. He slipped an arm around Kate and pulled her close. They kissed.

"Nate hasn't come in from the barn yet."

What Kate was really asking was for Nolan to get up, walk to the barn, and check on Nathanial. He'd give her what she wanted.

"Let's go git him." Nolan stood while gently pulling Kate up from the porch swing. Hand in hand, they walked toward the barn.

"Nathanial, come on down!" Nolan looked up at the loft from the floor below. No answer. He'd seen the boy climb up there. What if he'd been wrong about Nathanial running off?

He quickly stepped off the rungs of the wooden ladder to the hayloft. His gaze settled on Nathanial, who was fast asleep in the hay, and Nolan let out a deep sigh. For a minute there, he'd felt sick. He picked up the half-pint and then carried him into the house.

He gently laid Nathanial in bed, and something on the night table caught Nolan's eye. He hadn't ever noticed the wooden horse figure sitting there before this. It was the gift given to Nathanial months ago by the army doc. First toy that he had ever gotten, and unfortunately, it made Nolan think of Jones. As a witness, Nathanial would be in danger until Jones was captured.

He glanced at Kate. She'd stripped the sleeping child and was pulling a nightshirt over his head.

If Nolan told the boy about the marshal's message, that Jones was in the area, then Nathanial might feel the need to look over his shoulder every minute of the day to see who was there. That was no way to live. He'd already done that long enough in his short life.

There might come a day when Nolan would have to break his word and go after Jones.

He tucked the blankets that Kate had just straightened in around Nathanial, and she eyed him. "Nolan, is something wrong?"

"No." He'd answered too quick and felt Kate studying him. He walked out of the room to get away. She had accepted his proposal only after he'd sworn that his days of riding off to track down scum like Jones was done.

"Nolan." She hurried into the hallway a few steps behind him. He turned and faced her. She pulled a small slip of paper out of her apron pocket and handed it to him. "I forgot to give this to you. I found it earlier in one of Nathanial's books when I was checking his homework. Ned from the telegraph office must have given it to Nate to pass on to you, and I guess he forgot."

It was a telegram from Marshal Huckabee. "Important message on its way. Stop." Nolan flipped the paper over. There was nothing else said.

Message on its way ... What the hell did that mean? If the marshal needed to communicate important information to Nolan, then why hadn't Huckabee just sent all the facts in this message?

"Was this the only telegram you found?"

Kate nodded.

Dread settled in Nolan's gut. There had been a time or two when Huckabee had sent messages in parts like this. It was always to code them a bit because the places they were going had someone on the inside.

"Nolan, you have that look, and I don't like it." Tears welled up in Kate's eyes.

"What are you talking about?" He slipped the paper into his vest pocket. He would have to talk with Ned and find out if there had been another wire that had come through from Birch Creek.

"You have that far-off stare you always get before you ride off and leave."

"Kate ... you and Nathanial mean everything to me." Nolan pulled the telegram back out of his pocket and held it so she could clearly see the small slip of paper. "You might not see Jones's name on this message, but that's what it pertains to. There's a reason that Marshal Huckabee didn't wire all the information he has for me. I would guess that Jones has an ally in Gray Rock and the marshal didn't want the message leaked."

What Nolan had said made Kate's face lose color.

"So I'm gonna do whatever is necessary to protect this family." They stared at each other for a long moment, and she wiped at her eyes. "Kate, I don't want to have to break my promise." Nolan meant it.

Kate turned away and walked into the bedroom, shutting the door.

Nolan felt exhausted. He would bar the doors, then get some sleep himself.

———————

Nolan woke early. The sun wasn't up yet, and surprisingly, for once, Nathanial wasn't cuddled up at his side. He stood and stretched, then walked into the hallway from the spare room.

Nathanial's door hung open. Hm. The half-pint wasn't in bed. Surely the boy wasn't up this early spreading mischief. Nolan went and peered into the room that he and Kate would share as man and wife and found the little tomcat curled up there. What a sight the two were. Nolan couldn't help but smile.

Kate's strawberry hair was spread in a mess all over her pillow. Nathanial slept lying over her back like a saddle.

Nolan crawled into bed next to Kate, then slipped an arm around her shoulders. Her eyes fluttered open. Her smile was more beautiful than any sunrise. She didn't ask him to go back to the spare bed. Instead, she kissed him, then closed her eyes again.

Nolan and Kate both woke to Nathanial jumping up and down on the springing bed. Nolan needed coffee, and the blasted bouncing needed to stop. "Nathanial, go gather the eggs so Ma can make breakfast."

One energetic leap and Nathanial was off the bed and running out the door.

Nolan had just sat down at the table and Kate was pouring him coffee when Nathanial flung open the house door. A full basket of eggs was held in the half-pint's arms. Still dressed in his long nightshirt and no stockings, he wiped the chicken dirt off his feet on the rug.

"Oh Nathanial." Kate had washed the rug only yesterday. Nolan had seen her scrubbing away at a small stain. She'd always been a tidy housekeeper. More than that, she was a forgiving mother. She was already grinning sweetly at their son, who was batting those big baby blues at her.

"Sorry, Ma."

"Just try harder to remember not to track so much dirt in the house … Now go change for school."

Nathanial set the basket on the table, then tore off to do as Kate asked. It wasn't but a few minutes and he returned to take his seat just as Kate set plates of eggs and bacon in front of each of them. Nolan picked up his fork and dug in. It wasn't like Nathanial to not wolf down any bacon in sight. Something must have been eating at the boy. Nolan saw the signs of it in the fact that Nathanial was plowing the scrambled eggs around the plate and staring off at his milk glass.

"If you don't wanna go to school on an empty belly, then you best git eating."

Nathanial looked over at Nolan. There was a pause as the boy began to open his mouth to say something.

"Speak up, son. What is it?"

Nolan hoped that Nathanial hadn't somehow found out Jones was still at large and in the territory. He would sit on the boy or nail Nathanial's boots to the floor before he would let his son foolishly run off after the killer.

"Pa … I'm real sorry. I won't ever jump the bay over the fence again. It could have broken a leg."

Nolan was relieved to hear that it had been the horse matter causing Nathanial to look all troubled.

Sheriff Fuller and his damn deputy had been running their lying tongues about how the army had dismissed Nolan because he was unable to perform the duty he'd been hired for, and according to those two, it was all about his inability to trail down some two-bit thief. Plus everyone knew Fuller had his eyes on having Kate as his own.

Nolan didn't want Nathanial's head filled with the rumors floating around town. People were talking about Nolan and Sheriff Fuller's words in the middle of the street and patching together what had set each of them off based on what they thought they knew. He had figured if he'd tried to defend himself, Fuller might make up worse lies and maybe then involve Kate and Nathanial. No way in hell would he tolerate that.

Nolan squared around in his seat and directly faced Nathanial. "It wasn't worry over the horse that had put the fear of God in me. When I saw the bay fly over that fence with you hanging on tight... I thought you were gonna be killed. It ain't nice to scare the hell out of your pa." Nolan grinned and ruffled Nathanial's snowy patch.

"Ma...Pa said a bad word." Nathanial smiled playfully, then shoved a piece of bacon into his mouth.

Nolan knew that happiness wasn't from tattling on him for cussing. Nathanial's ear-to-ear grin was most likely from hearing that he was cared about. It seemed to need continually reinforced. Many times Nathanial had asked—and still sometimes wanted to know—if Nolan was mad at him for dumb little things that didn't matter. To hear the unsure small voice ticket himself as worthless in his efforts to do right, it wrenched Nolan. The half-pint questioned most everything he did as bad.

"How about after school, we do some fishing?"

"Yes, sir."

Nolan never tired of seeing that bright little smile.

Nate was sitting next to the window on the long bench seat. Johnny was beside him, doodling in a paper tablet while Mrs. McKay blah-blah-blahed about something Nate already knew. He doubted their teacher would be amused if she were to see the funny picture of herself with a mustache that Johnny was now adding fanged teeth to. Nate thought it was funny and would have whispered so to Johnny, but they hadn't ever made up after their fight.

Would the school day never end? He couldn't wait to go fishing with Pa.

He turned his attention to stare out the window, and a speck of blue had him squinting his eyes to see better.

What? It couldn't be. Surely Nate's eyes were lying to him. There was no damn way he could mistake who it was that wore a fancy blue suit with a short-brimmed hat. It had been just a glimpse. All he'd seen was the back of the dandy on his white horse, trotting out of town.

Nate had no doubt. That man was Deegan Jones.

"Nathanial, please sit down." Mrs. McKay spoke a second time and stared at him queerly.

When had he even jumped to his feet and clung to the window frame? He'd been staring a hole through the glass before forcing himself to look away and at his teacher.

His mouth blurted out the first thing that came to his mind. "I gotta use the outhouse real bad."

The classroom as a whole snickered as he danced around a bit to be convincing. He needed to go all right, to follow the blue velveteen-wearing devil. This was his chance to get Jenny's killer. His heart raced, and his mind flashed a picture of Ma and Pa. They wouldn't know where he had gone and would be worried sick. Maybe he should go fetch Pa first.

"Yes, you're excused." Mrs. McKay waved Nate off with both hands.

He ran out the door and down the steps. His thoughts were that Pa could handle the fancy man. Pa could take down anyone. But there wasn't time for Nate to run home to fetch his father. He didn't want to lose this chance at catching the fancy man. Months ago when Nate had been on Jones's trail with the army, the killer had slickly stayed ahead of Captain Farnsworth and being captured. Nate didn't want to give that fancy bastard any breathing room this time. He aimed to dog Jones just as Pa would.

Nate hightailed it across the schoolyard, through the street, and followed the road out of town, away from home. There were too many fresh hoof marks on the dusty coach road from folks coming and going in and out of town. He wasn't able to easily follow the fancy man. He had seen the killer come this way and then just *whoosh*. The fancy man, Deegan Jones, had vanished into thin air. A demon ghost.

It was eerie how silent the empty stretch of roadway that lay before Nate was. The hair on the back of his neck stood. He slowed his running pace until he stopped and just stood there, huffing to catch his wind from hoofing it so far. Was the fancy man watching him right this minute? Maybe the devil had a bead on him and was about to pull the trigger and splatter his brains everywhere. No, he wasn't going to let himself be scared.

He took a step and slowly began to walk forward down the road, farther away from town. His eyes focused on a hoofprint in the dirt. Hm … it was fresher than the others. Was it the fancy man's? If so, then Deegan Jones had changed direction and he was now headed up the mountainside. The trees were thickly clustered, and from where Nate stood, he could only see a short way into the hills. Nothing blue caught his eyes, and the bright suit would stand out against the earthy tones.

Nate's legs were tired, and his breathing was labored. No way could he keep up the pace of trailing Jones, who was on horseback. Dammit. It wasn't fair. He was so close to getting what he wanted, and that was to see Jenny's killer stopped. There was an end to everything. Just as time had caught up to Jim Younger and done away with his thieving ways, so too would Deegan Jones fall, and Nate couldn't wait to see it.

It was a long way from there to home, but the star-faced mare was fast and trail wise to these mountains. Pa could saddle up and help Nate hunt the fancy man. Hopefully, Ma didn't get pissed off. Pa had been made to swear that his days of tracking wanted men were over. Nate, though, hadn't given his word to that.

Nate ran back through town and toward home as fast as his feet would carry him. His head was wet with sweat. Mr. Henderson, Phillip's pa who owned the store, was the first to see him hoofing it with a purpose straight down the middle of the street. Mr. Scott, the banker, and old man Pike from the livery were among others who turned from what they were doing and stared at him. Sheriff Fuller and Deputy Toller stood from where they'd been sitting as Nate ran past. He ignored the lawmen and their questioning glances. If they only knew the danger. Jenny, Mr. and Mrs. Harper, Nancy, Sarah, and all the folks from the wagon train were dead because of the evil of one man. And Deegan Jones was here.

As quivery as Nate's legs were, he'd fallen off his hurried pace quite a bit. But he wasn't going to give up. Home was two miles from town. He would make it to the mare if it killed him. He could rest once he was on the horse and going after Jones.

Nate stumbled into the ranch yard and could hardly catch his breath. He hoped he didn't pass out. "Pa!"

He quickly looked about the yard. Where was Pa? He wasn't chopping wood or at the corral with the horses.

Ma left her basket of linens sitting on the ground and came running from where she'd been hanging sheets on the line to dry in the sun. "What's wrong?" She tried to catch hold of Nate.

He ducked past her and kept running toward the barn. "Pa!"

Nolan dropped the leather harness he'd been fixing and hurried from the barn. What was Nathanial doing home? It wasn't but noontime. School wasn't out for the day. The boy sounded worked up about something. The usual cheery little voice was pitched much higher.

Johnny Filson better not have been picking on Nathanial again, or this time Nolan would have a talk with the boy's pa.

He wasn't more than a long stride or two outside the barn door when Nathanial nearly plowed into him. He had been running like his tail was on fire. Nathanial's face was pale white and sweaty, as if he'd seen a ghost. This was no school-yard trouble.

"I seen him." Nathanial eyes shone wet. The youngster was so breathless that he'd hardly been able to choke it out.

"Who?" Nolan didn't understand what he was trying to tell him.

"In town … the fancy man." Nathanial's words hit him like a swift kick.

"You sure?" He stared down at his son and thought it was dumb that he even asked. There was no doubt in his mind that Nathanial was being truthful. Nolan didn't have to question if Jones had seen him. The boy would be dead had Jones recognized him.

"We need to go after him. I'll get my rifle." Nathanial turned quickly to run toward the house.

Kate gasped, and Nolan reached out, grabbing hold of their son and pulling the half-pint to him. Kate's eyes were filled with tears. This had been their fear.

Nolan hunkered down and looked Nathanial eye to eye while keeping him held by the shoulders. "We ain't going after Jones."

"What?" Nathanial tried once to jerk away from his grip.

He wasn't going to let loose of the boy, gripping him tighter.

There were blazing-hot tears in Nathanial's eyes. "That son of a bitch killed Jenny."

"Bite your tongue, boy." Nolan wasn't going to tolerate the foul little mouth for any reason. "It's Sheriff Fuller's job to hunt down those who trample on the law. We'll ride to town and tell the sheriff and his deputy what you saw. Then we're gonna come home. You will stay put on this ranch rather than going to school. Do you understand me?"

"Yes, sir, but...why don't you wanna go after that awful man? You seen what all he done." It was Nathanial's way of begging Nolan to bring justice for the boy's lost friend.

Yeah, Nolan wanted to put a bullet right between Jones's eyes for many reasons. But he wasn't going to teach his son vengeance. "You remember Captain Farnsworth?"

Nathanial nodded.

"Well, he and his men...we got the Harper girls. We fought Jones's men and rescued all the women. The captain had been fixin' to send them home before I met up with you and your ma in Birch Creek. Do I like the fact that Jones was smart enough to escape capture? No, I don't. But our mission was successful in that we saved the lives of nine women. I ain't under the army's order anymore. And you are a little boy who needs to understand that your ma and I know what's best for you. I'm forbidding you to run after Deegan Jones."

Nathanial was quiet for a long minute. Nolan could almost see the boy rolling all he had said around in his head. His face wasn't wrinkled up as if he were disgruntled and disagreed with Nolan. The half-pint was still learning what it meant to have a mother and father.

"Pa...I don't feel right about letting Jenny's killer just ride away, but I'll do as you say." Nathanial was showing trust, not just obedience. The boy could have nodded in agreement and then huffed off in angry silence to stew on it until he talked himself into big trouble. His face was soft, and his muscles were not standing tense.

Nolan truly believed that the youngster was no longer envisioning himself wholly as a man. Nathanial was in fact a child who had witnessed his best friend shot down by an outlaw's gun, and he was still aching badly inside because of it. That would take plenty of time to heal.

Nathanial followed Nolan into the barn where they saddled the bay. A few minutes later, they were on their way to Gray Rock.

Mrs. McKay hadn't questioned Nathanial's reaction to seeing someone from his recent past. Everyone in town had heard rumors of Nathanial's outlaw upbringing, and his teacher was no exception. The boy gathered his books, and they left.

"Nathanial, you play here in the schoolyard with Phillip and Curtis. I'm gonna go have a word with Sheriff Fuller." Nolan packed Nathanial's books in his saddlebag before crossing the street to the jailhouse.

He opened the door and walked inside. The sight of Wade Fuller was one he could hardly stand. If the lawman had tailed Jones after Nolan had first given him the marshal's message, Fuller might have had the killer behind bars by now. Better than three weeks had passed since Nolan had handed the no-account sheriff the first telegram. And Fuller had excused the second message from the marshal because of how vague it was. When Nolan explained that it might mean Jones had a man in Gray Rock working with him, sweat had broken out on Fuller and Deputy Toller had damn near dropped his coffee cup. Surely a sighting of the killer in town would get Wade jumping after Jones.

"I got word Deegan Jones was in town today."

The sheriff shuffled his cards, then dealt one to his deputy. There was barely a pause in tossing a card across the table to

Toller, but Nolan caught sight of the eye shift between the two badged men.

Fuller looked up from his two pair. "Who said Deegan was in town?"

Huh, that was an awfully casual way to address the killer, by his first name. It had rung in Nolan's ears as if the sheriff and Jones might be friends. Nolan was no fool. His son's name would never be mentioned.

"That don't much matter. Jones rode out to the north. I'm telling you so you can go after him." It wasn't given as a friendly suggestion.

"And why would I do that? Did you see him? No, that's right. This someone you won't identify told you that Deegan Jones was in town. Do you happen to know what he wanted?" Fuller laughed at his stupidity, and his fool-headed deputy chimed in with a chuckle.

Arguing wasn't going to get Nolan anywhere. Sheriff Fuller wasn't going after Jones. That was clear. The fool was too easygoing about the killer perhaps having business in Gray Rock. Wade Fuller put shame on the star he wore.

Nolan slammed the door on his way out of the jailhouse.

He stepped into the saddle, then gave Nathanial a wave to come on. They rode for home.

Nolan didn't like where his thoughts were going once again. Maybe he would have to go after the devil. Fuller was a coward, but what if it wasn't that the lawman was afraid to posse up and pursue Jones? Could Wade Fuller be working with the likes of Deegan Jones? Nolan hoped not, because if that were true, he would hang Fuller as quick as he would throw a rope around Jones's neck. Then Nolan might have a mob of townsfolk storming the ranch, ready to lynch him for doing away with their sheriff. Fuller wasn't much, but he did keep the ruckus down in town. Folks liked a peaceful street that they could walk without worry.

Instead of tracking down Jones, Nolan needed to stick near Kate and their son. If there was to be a fight, then he would welcome Jones to bring it, but Nolan would not push for it. He was not the law, and it seemed that Gray Rock was lacking a true badge.

"Pa … Pa?" Nathanial's hand waved about an inch in front of Nolan's nose, finally rousing him from his thoughts. "Should I git the fishing poles?"

The half-pint's mind was already miles from Jones. That was good. Nathanial likely believed that Sheriff Fuller was going after him.

"Sure, you go on, and I'll meet ya at the pond in a few minutes."

Nolan took Nathanial's arm, helping the boy slide down off the bay, then stepped down himself. He needed to talk to Kate before he did anything else.

Aw, the stubborn woman hadn't wanted to hear sense. When he'd asked, Kate's opinion had been such that she didn't believe Wade Fuller would take up sides with a known killer. Nolan's gut sensed otherwise.

He left Kate the pistol since she'd insisted on staying at the house to fix supper and mend a hole that Nathanial had torn in the knee of a pair of trousers. Thankfully, from where Nolan sat with his line in the water, he could see the house fairly well. The front door was visible, but he couldn't see the back door that led into the kitchen where Kate spent most of her time. If Jones struck, it would be without warning.

Nolan had the rifle. Nathanial said nothing of the Winchester lying close to his side. A soft tune was hummed while Nathanial stared at his line, waiting for a bite. The boy seemed oblivious to Nolan's worry.

Some time passed but not quick enough for Nolan. Kate being all alone was all he could concentrate on. "The fish ain't bitin' today. Come on. Let's go on home."

The house smelled of a good supper. Nathanial sat down with his McGuffey reader and opened the pages. "Pa, do you wanna listen to me read?"

"Uh, yeah, sure. I'll be right there." Nolan could feel Kate's gaze on him as she placed the settings on the table. Nolan went and poured himself some coffee.

Why would Jones risk riding into Gray Rock and maybe being recognized by the law? Surveying the outskirts, Nolan would understand. Jones and his army had attacked all settler families in outlying areas that had no protection of a town or law near to fight. It seemed the profiteer had maybe changed tactics. Why there in Gray Rock? Or maybe Jones wasn't worried about the law because Fuller was working with him.

"Pa, hurry up." Nathanial whined impatiently.

Nolan carried his cup into the dining room and sat down.

Kate placed a platter of fried chicken on the table. "Nathanial, put the book away. It's time for supper."

Their son huffed. "I don't want to. I ain't hungry."

Nolan wasn't in the mood to hear lip. "Nathanial, do as your mother says, or I'm gonna give you a good tanning."

Tears welled up in the boy's eyes.

"Nolan, you okay?" Kate took her seat.

Maybe the warning had been a little harsh. His nerves were raw, and it had soured his mood and shortened his temper. Kate softly cupped her hand over his, and they intertwined their fingers.

"I'll be fine."

She nodded, but the worry in her eyes caused him to think she didn't fully believe him.

They ate in silence, other than an occasional clink of a fork or spoon scraping a plate. Afterward, Kate cleared the table and washed up the dishes while Nathanial quietly finished his homework. Nolan stood by the window and kept watch over the land. His rifle was propped within reach, and the Colt was strapped to his hip like always.

How long would he have to guard his family until Jones was caught?

Shadows of the coming night spread across the valley like a dark blanket as the sun dipped and touched the mountaintop.

"Nathanial, it's time for bed." Kate spoke from behind Nolan. He glanced away from the window.

She picked up jacks off the floor, and Nathanial was half-asleep, sprawled out on the settee.

Nolan turned back to watching darkness settle in around them. A small hand tugged on his sleeve.

"Pa, are you still mad at me?" Nathanial's pout was the most pitiful thing ever.

"Son, it might have seemed like it, but I wasn't upset 'cause of you. I have some things on my mind, and occasionally my worry gits the best of me." It was a poor excuse, but it was the truth.

"Will you tuck me in?" Nathanial had ahold of Nolan's hand. Maybe he, too, was sensing the trouble that was coming.

"You bet I will."

Nolan and Kate tucked Nathanial into bed. Then as they quietly left the room, Nolan closed the door behind them. He went and stretched out on the settee in the sitting room. The Winchester was propped within easy reach. With the window slightly cracked open, he would hear any horse that might walk or rush into the yard toward the house. The front door was right in his line of vision. It would be a damn sorry man who opened it without being welcomed.

CHAPTER 31

"NATHANIAL!" Nolan sank the ax, then looked about the ranch yard.

The boy came running from the pasture where he must have been playing. Nolan didn't want him too far out of sight. He'd kept the boy home from school the past few days. He just hadn't felt comfortable sending Nathanial anywhere alone.

Nolan pulled the ax, then handed it to the half-pint. He set up a piece of wood on end to be split. Nathanial's face reddened with the effort of trying to heave the heavy ax overhead to swing. Nolan chuckled to himself. Nate had nearly tipped himself over backward. The half-pint had some growing to do.

"Here." Nolan took hold of the long handle, swung the ax around over his shoulder, and split the hunk of wood.

"I can carry the wood inside once you have the chunks split." Nathanial leaned down and picked up several hunks of wood off the ground.

Nolan looked up after swinging another chop. The sun glared in his eyes, so he had to squint. A rider was coming down the lane. It looked to be Tate Horn, Marshal Huckabee's deputy. Tate was the only man Nolan knew who rode a solid red horse.

"Tate." Nolan grinned, then wiped the sweat from under his hat across his sleeve.

"How the hell are ya, Nolan? It's been a while. I think the last time I saw you, we were both tying one on at the Dippery Saloon down in Texas near the border. We'd just captured Roscoe Ruck and his gang. Do you remember that sweet little dancing señorita? Whew… that was a good time."

Tate stepped down from his horse and then shook Nolan's hand. Nolan cleared his throat and nodded toward his son. Tate liked to talk, and Nathanial didn't need to hear anything more about that dancing señorita.

Tate ruffled Nathanial's snowy patch. "Howdy, boy. I heard all about you from little Deputy Huckabee."

"Did Deputy come with ya?" Nathanial looked past Tate toward the coach road.

"Not this time. I'm here on official business. I have to talk with your pa, so why don't you run along and play or go do chores or something?"

If Deputy Horn was dismissing Nathanial from the conversation that was about to take place, then Nolan knew it was serious. He recalled the telegram from the marshal. He would bet Tate was there to deliver whatever information the marshal had wanted to pass to him.

"Yes, sir." Nathanial skipped off toward the barn.

Tate pulled a telegram from his pocket and handed it to Nolan. "After Marshal Huckabee sent word to you about Deegan Jones heading back this way, we intercepted this telegram sent from Gray Rock. Someone here is definitely working with Mr. Jones. The marshal wants you to track that dirty bastard. I'm here to help you capture him. Marshal Huckabee would have come himself, but his wife is due to deliver any day now." Tate wasn't asking for Nolan to use his skills. Both the marshal and Deputy Horn were *expecting* Nolan to sniff out Jones's trail and tree the killer.

The truth was Nolan and Tate were a strong pair. Together, they wouldn't easily be shaken off. They'd ridden posse side by side many times and knew too well how the other worked. There was no doubt in Nolan's mind that they could end the trail of misery that Jones had left behind him.

Kate wasn't going to like it at all, but Nolan was about to break his promise. He needed to do this…not for the marshal or Tate or even himself. It was Nathanial that Nolan was thinking about. Maybe then the boy could truly lay Jenny to rest.

"I'll git my rifle." Nolan walked into the house.

Kate looked up from dusting near the window. "You're leaving, aren't ya?" There were tears in her eyes.

Nolan nodded as he walked by and fetched the Winchester from the study.

Kate was on his heels out the door and across the yard. "I can't believe you're leaving Nathanial and me. You're going to make me a widow before we're even married. You haven't slept all night in days because you're so worried about him coming to get Nathanial, and now you're leaving us on our own? Is this about our safety, or is this about you needing to run and play hero?" She just wasn't going to let up on him.

"Kate, I'm coming back." Nolan didn't want to argue with her. The last thing he needed right this minute was her nagging at him. He saw Jones differently than she did. "You have never seen the horrible things that man is capable of, and it don't matter—man, woman, or child. I've dug graves and laid to rest mothers, fathers, and babies all on account of that heartless son of a bitch. Not a one of us, especially Nathanial, is safe as long as Jones is running free, and I think you realize that. I ain't sitting up at night, cradling my rifle and babysitting over the house, 'cause I enjoy going without sleep. Till that man is caught, every day will be a gamble. When and where the killer will strike can't be guessed, and I ain't gonna play that game with this family."

Nolan wasn't going to fight with her anymore about what he felt he needed to put to rest. Jones would be ended on sight. Couldn't Kate see he was protecting them?

He walked the bay out of the stall, then grabbed his saddle and tossed it onto the horse's back.

"I'm asking you not to go. You gave your word that your days of riding away were over." Kate choked up on her tempered plea, and tears streaked down her face.

Nolan didn't know what else to say to make her see that riding after Jones was the best way of stopping him before Nathanial got recognized or even before Jones started stealing women from around Gray Rock, including Kate. Nolan and Tate needed to strike and take down Jones first.

He cinched his saddled, then slid his rifle into its scabbard, and he could feel the weight of Kate's sad stare. "I'm sorry, but I have to do this."

Kate sniffled and wiped at her eyes, and Nathanial stepped around the bay and stood next to Nolan. *Aw shit.* Nolan had forgotten that Nathanial was in the barn. Here, too, he was seeing tears, and lots of 'em. Dammit. This was a headache that he didn't need right now. His mind should be clear when riding after the likes of Deegan Jones, or he would perhaps make Kate a widow.

"Pa, I'm going with ya. I'll git my rifle." Nathanial turned to run for the house to fetch his gun.

Nolan quickly caught hold of the boy and turned him so they looked straight at one another. "You don't step a foot off this ranch. I promise I will git Deegan Jones. But I need to know you're here with your ma."

He and Nathanial eyed each other for a long minute. "Yes, sir."

Nathanial had been slow to answer. If the boy was lying and disobeyed, Nolan would tear the hide right off his backside.

Deegan Jones was no one to be fooled around with. Handling a rattler would be less dangerous.

Nolan led the bay from the barn. He couldn't meet Kate's glassy-eyed glare. Tate was sitting the roan, waiting. Nolan stepped up and swung a leg over the saddle, then took a quick last glance at Kate and Nathanial holding tight to one another. He sank spurs to the bay and rode out of the ranch yard with Deputy Horn at his side.

Tate chewed on a piece of jerky. "I say we ride into town and tell the local law first. Maybe we can git a posse together." Easygoing, that was Tate. Besides Marshal Huckabee, though, there wasn't another man Nolan would rather have fighting alongside him.

"I ain't so sure that Sheriff Fuller isn't the one who's working with Jones. Fuller didn't bat an eye when he saw the telegram from the marshal about Jones's vicinity to Gray Rock. His deputy hadn't seemed surprised either. It's never sat well with me. You're wearing a badge. We don't need Fuller. I say we hunt down Jones on our own." Nolan didn't have to wait long to hear Tate's thought on the plan.

"There are only two men I can say this about, and Marshal Huckabee is the other one. I trust your gut as much as I do my own. We'll go at Jones alone, then confront the sheriff."

They skirted Gray Rock and picked up Jones's cold trail where Nathanial had described the spot where the fancy man had turned his horse off the roadway and weaved up through the mountainside.

Nate wore a sulky pout while he finished his chores in silence. What if Pa or Tate got killed? He wiped at his eyes. Two against who knew how many armed men that the fancy man might have ready to fight. Nate shuffled his feet toward the house.

He wasn't hungry for supper, picking at his plate of food. Ma hadn't touched more than a bite. They were both miserable without Pa there.

"May I be excused?"

Ma looked up from her potatoes and meat. Worrisome tears made her eyes glisten.

It made Nate want to cry. "I want Pa." He was on the edge of bursting out in tears.

"Me too, sweetheart." Ma stood from her seat, came around the table, and hugged him tight in her arms. "Help me clear the table, please."

Nate did as Ma asked, and somehow it made him feel a little bit better. They stood together in front of the window at the dry sink in the kitchen. Ma washed each plate in the scrub bucket, then handed it to him. With a towel, he wiped the china spotless.

Ma sniffled, and Nate looked up. A steady flow of tears streamed down her cheeks.

"Pa will git that slick, dandy son of a gun." Nate believed Pa could do anything.

Ma grinned, then wiped at her eyes.

A thunder of rushing horses pounded in their ears. They both looked up from the dishwashing and out through the window at the same time. Nate's eyes widened, and he froze in fear and helplessly stared. They were there. Deegan Jones's men. Somehow Nate just knew by the mean look of them and all those guns.

"Nate, run!" Ma pushed him toward the back door.

"No!" He wouldn't go without her.

She yanked at his arms, trying to drag him to go. "Nathanial, please, they'll kill you. They only want to take me."

He knew what Ma said was true. At the wagon train, he'd buried all the children and men. Jenny was the only girl killed. The rest of the women had been kept alive and stolen.

Ma shoved at Nate to get out the back door before Jones's men burst into the house.

He didn't want to leave Ma to face the bastards alone. "I need to protect you."

What would they do to Ma? Sarah popped into Nate's head, and the girl whose leg had been broken. Jones had sold her to the mountain man, and poor Sarah had been killed. Nate started to cry, and for a first, it hit him. As much as Nate wanted to fight and keep Ma safe, he was just too young and couldn't step into Pa's boots. He wasn't a man yet. It would be too late for Nate if Jones's men saw him.

"Nathanial." Ma shook him to listen. "There's a hole under the chicken coop. Hide in it till dark. Then go tell Sheriff Fuller to find your pa. Go quick." With one big push from Ma, Nate stumbled out the back door and fell and hit the dirt. He scrambled to his feet.

Ma could have run and hidden too, but she was giving herself up so he would be safe. Jones's men wouldn't search around and find him if they easily got what they'd come for.

Nate crawled as fast as he could under the smelly coop. Lucky for him, he was just small enough to slip between the wooden floor and the dirt. He curled himself up tight inside the hole and felt himself shaking all over. Ma screamed from inside the house. Nate wanted to howl right along with her. From where he was hidden, he was able to peek out into the yard. Ma was dragged from the house, kicking and screaming. Nate wanted to run to her, wishing he could save her. But how could he when there was one, two, three … six of those assholes with guns?

Nate heard Pa's words in his mind. He was only a little boy. He needed Pa.

Ma was thrown to the ground.

"Hey, boy, come out from wherever you are, or I'm gonna kill your mama." A man, not the fancy man, cocked the trigger on his pistol, aiming at Ma's head. Nate could almost hear her silent plea for him to stay safe. Tears streamed down his face, dripping onto his shirt.

"I told you he's not here!" Ma snatched up a handful of dirt and threw it at the man holding the gun on her.

Nate covered his eyes. He couldn't watch her being killed like Jenny. But at the same time, he didn't want to take his eyes off her and forced himself to look.

A different man than the one holding the gun took hold of Ma's arm and ripped her upward to stand. She spit in his face. A hard backhanded slap across her cheek knocked her to the ground, and she held it, crying. That rotten pig then grabbed a fistful of Ma's red hair. She screamed as he yanked her to her feet.

Nate's breath caught. Ma was thrown on a horse, and as quick as Jones's men had ridden into the ranch yard, they were all gone and Ma with them. This just couldn't be real. First Jenny and now Ma. Nate wished Pa had been there. Jones's men wouldn't have gotten away with taking her. But Pa and Tate were in the mountains, hunting the rotten bastard that was responsible for this.

Nate wiped his eyes. It was up to him to get help to Ma.

He waited as long as he could. Ma had said not to move until dark. The time was close enough. The orange sun was fading low in the sky, not quite touching the mountaintop. Nate squeezed out from under the smelly chicken coop, then ran to the corral. Up and over the top rail of the fence he climbed. He quickly led the star-faced mare into the barn to be saddled. He put a foot in the stirrup and climbed up onto the horse.

Nate kicked the mare and hung on tight. The horse raced toward town. Sheriff Fuller would track down Pa. That's what Ma had said. Nate wasn't too sure about that. What if the sheriff wouldn't help? He never did like Nate and hadn't ever done one nice thing for him. The sheriff only ever tolerated him because he was in love with Ma.

Nate shouldn't run after Ma himself. Pa would skin him, and Ma wouldn't be too happy about him chasing down bad guys either. They were his mother and father. They knew best, and Nate needed to mind what he'd been told.

He jerked up the reins, skidding the horse to a halt in front of the jailhouse. Nate jumped down out of the saddle and ran toward the door. The glow of a lamp was beaming out from the window. A mix of voices came from inside. Through the window, he could see a man standing opposite Sheriff Fuller. Nate nearly tripped himself to a stop just before throwing open the jailhouse door.

What the hell? No. This had to be a lie. Standing right before Nate was the fancy man. He was grinning all friendly like and seemed to be talking peacefully with Sheriff Wade.

Nate backed up and forgot to watch his step off the boardwalk. A big hand caught him midfall before he landed on his bottom in the street. He looked up into the face of Johnny's pa.

"What's wrong with you, boy?"

Nate's tongue was stuck. All he could do was stare dumbly at Mr. Filson.

The jailhouse door creaked. Shit. Someone was coming out. If the fancy man saw Nate, then he would surely be dead and Ma and Pa would never know what happened to him. He was on his own. The sheriff was now the enemy.

With a hard jerk, Nate tore away from Mr. Filson's hold on him. And like a flash of lightning, he climbed back into his saddle. The big man's brow furrowed, and he stared in what looked to be confusion.

"They took my ma." The truth finally blurted out of Nate's mouth. Tears ran down his face. "I have to find my pa."

Nate kicked the mare into a run before Johnny's pa could grab the reins and stop him.

He ran the horse the whole way to where he'd told Pa and Tate to turn in to the mountains. Okay, he needed to calm his breathing. What had Pa taught him? The first thing to do when tracking was to study the fingerprint or horseshoe mark. Nate studied the prints of the two horses that had left the roadway right where Nate had said to, and he picked up Pa's trail real easy.

The sun would be setting within the hour. Time was against Nate, and he needed to find Pa quick. The dark of night wouldn't end his search, but it sure would make it a lot tougher. Knowing the country around him was an advantage. Nate and his friends played all through these woods. Also, the mare was a surefooted animal, and thankfully, his horse wasn't spooked at every little shadow or sound. Those were all good things that would help his effort to find Pa. Nate kicked the mare to go.

It was taking too damn long to follow each footstep that Pa's and Tate's horses set in the ground. Pa had explained to Nate once that to catch a man, he would read the sign, then look ahead at what that man's next step might be to get ahead of him. Nate had to chance it. He couldn't follow Pa and Tate in the dark, and the sun was almost down. Blue Sky Lake was a sensible route for Nate to search, and the large body of water wasn't far from there.

He gave the little mare her head. The horse weaved its way slowly but steadily up the mountainside as darkness began to fall all around them. What if he was going the wrong direction to find Pa and wasting time? If Nate had to start over where he'd left Pa's and Tate's trail, it might cost Ma her life.

Nate wiped at his eyes. Ma just had to be okay. Those dirty sons of guns better not hurt her.

The pale moonlight wasn't quite enough for him to see any tracks on the ground. A wolf howled in the distance, and the mare raised her head, ears perked. What if it was a different kind of wolf that had the mare's attention? Maybe a little sound had been heard by the horse that his ears weren't able to catch hold of. Was it one of Jones's men? Nate could be drawing his last breath.

He was grabbed off his horse and thumped hard to the flat of his back on the ground. He heard a gun cock in the darkness. Instantly piss warmed the crotch of his pants. He didn't want to die.

"Nate?"

He recognized Deputy Tate's voice. Oh thank God. Nate let out a deep sigh. Holy cow, his heart had been about ready to give out.

He lay there in the dirt, his muscles like mush. "Dammit, Tate. I'm all wet. You scared the hell out of me, and I pissed all over myself."

Tate chuckled.

"Boy, I'm gonna tear the hide right off you." Pa's stern voice thundered out of the dark.

Nate sat up quickly, and his eyes widened. Storming down on him in the pale moonlight was a tall, broad-shouldered silhouette. His ass was getting sore just thinking about Pa taking hold of him.

"It's Ma." Nate spit the trouble out as fast as he could. "Those dirty bastards came about an hour after you left and stole her."

Pa kicked the ground and said nothing about Nate's cursing. Deputy Tate holstered his pistol, then pulled Nate to his feet, helping brush the dirt off the back of Nate's pants.

He looked between Pa and Tate. "There were six of them. The fancy man wasn't one of them. But I did see Deegan Jones. I went to the jailhouse to fetch Sheriff Fuller, and the fancy man was there. And he weren't behind locked bars." Nate was scared for Ma and didn't want to cry in front of Deputy Horn or Pa. They were tough men, and he wanted to be just like them someday.

Nolan understood why Nathanial had trailed him. Sheriff Fuller for damn sure wouldn't have stopped Jones from putting a bullet in the boy. Dammit. Nolan should have called out Fuller for working with Jones when he first suspected it. It all made sense. Kate had been safe when Wade Fuller thought he could have her as his own. The intercepted telegram had read, *Come get her. Stop. Former army scout in Gray Rock. Stop. Meet me prior for details. Stop.*

The meeting must've been that day Nathanial had run home from school all riled up because he'd seen the fancy man. And before that, the day coming home from Birch Creek when Nolan and Fuller had exchanged unfriendly words in the middle of the street while practically the whole town watched, part of that confrontation had been about Kate. Shortly afterward, when Nolan and his family had been leaving town, that's when Fuller must have sent his deputy hurrying to the telegraph office and he'd sent the telegram that had been intercepted by the marshal.

The best Nolan and Tate could figure, Fuller had been warning Deegan as to where the law was looking for him just the same as Fuller had tipped off Jones that Nolan, ally to the army, was in Gray Rock. The sheriff must have gotten hotheaded when he'd seen Kate with Nolan, especially after he had spoken about marrying her. Then Sheriff Fuller had decided to rid himself of more than just her. Had Nolan been on the ranch when Kate was stolen, he and the boy might both be dead. He would have fought, and he figured that was exactly what the sheriff had hoped for, six guns against one.

Nolan looked over at his son, who was sitting quietly next to the fire. The hour was late, but the boy would probably have nightmares if he closed his glassy eyes. Nolan had been ready to ride for town and finish Jones wherever he stood. Deputy Horn talked him down from seeing red.

Nolan took a deep breath. He couldn't wait to get his hands on Mr. Jones. And with that murderous thought, Nolan felt a small weight snug up tight against his side. Nathanial had come and sat next to him. He was Nolan's other problem. When the fight with Jones did start, Nolan didn't want his son anywhere around. For a first, Nathanial looked like a teary-eyed and very frightened little boy who wanted his mama. Nolan didn't know how to comfort his son with soft words. Kate was best at that sort of thing.

"Try to git some sleep. We'll be riding after Jones at first light."

Nathanial laid his head to the ground blanket and closed his eyes.

Morning hadn't come quick enough for Nolan. There was barely light in the sky when the three of them took off back to the ranch where Nolan easily picked up the trail of six horses, and one of them was carrying two riders because that horse's print was set deeper than the other five, meaning that was the horse Kate was riding double on. They followed the trail of Jones's men through the mountain at a fair clip and put lots of miles behind them.

The sun was overhead. Nolan recognized the horse print in the dirt. He'd found the place where a single rider, Jones, had met his hired guns. Nathanial was showing his sand for being a half-pint. The boy was keeping pace on the mare, and it wasn't that Nolan or Tate was slowing theirs.

They reined in at a shallow creek to water the horses. Nolan twisted in the saddle and watched their back trail. There was dirt in the air and that rumbling noise about a hundred yards behind them. What he heard but couldn't see yet because of the fullness of the trees was a group of riders running up fast behind them. Nolan doubted it was Jones. In the past, the killer had attacked head on. Lately though, Jones had changed some strategies. Nolan didn't want to risk being wrong for Nathanial's sake.

"Hide yourself in that thick stand of trees and stay quiet no matter what." Nolan quickly slapped the rump of Nate's mare. Nathanial had just disappeared among the pines when Nolan felt the hair on the back of his neck rise at the sight of Sheriff Fuller.

"Easy." Tate warned Nolan quietly under his breath.

Nolan took quick account of who was in the posse. The sheriff, Deputy Toller, John Filson, Mr. Scott, and Mr. Henderson. Nolan would bet only Fuller and his deputy were working with Jones. The others were honest family men. So what was the sheriff doing way out there with a posse?

Tate must have been thinking the same thing as Nolan. "Are you looking for the woman?" He was blunt.

Sheriff Fuller nodded and pointed a thumb at John Filson. "John busted into my office last evening, hollering around that Kate's boy had been in town, crying that she'd been stolen. Deputy Toller and I rode out and looked around the ranch. We found that the door had been kicked in. The place was a hell of a mess."

Nolan didn't like Fuller's coy tone. It wasn't easy to fight down his temper. He wanted to jump off his horse, rip the sheriff out of the saddle, and beat the daylights out of the man.

Fuller rubbed his chin in a fretful way, and judging by his wrinkled brow, he didn't like what he was thinking. "You're Deputy Tate Horn, ain't ya? How did you know she was missing? Birch Creek, that's a long way from here." Fuller seemed to be sweating Tate's presence.

All friendly like, Tate nodded as he lifted one leg from the stirrup and crossed it casually in front of him over the saddle. It appeared natural. Only, now Tate's holster faced the sheriff. The fast hand rested on the butt of the pistol. If Tate had to draw, the position would quicken his aim. A second faster at squeezing the trigger might mean staying alive. Nolan had seen it before.

Without notice from the posse, Nolan's hand had drifted to rest on his Colt. They were ready if the sheriff or his deputy made one wrong move.

"Well, sheriff, this is how it is. Nolan and I are old pals. We go way back. He'd been out hunting and came home to the mess that you seen. He hadn't been able to find his boy. The youngster must have been hiding at the time. Nolan lit a shuck to report the thieving to you when, lo and behold, who should be coming down the road for a nice friendly visit but myself?" Tate had always been a gifted bullshitter.

The men in the posse all nodded. Even Fuller seemed to be swallowing Tate's lies. Or the man was just smart enough to know when to keep his mouth shut.

"I thought it best we set out to find Kate right away." Tate's tone spoke of having the backing of a tin star pinned to his shirt.

Nolan knew Fuller wouldn't question the official actions of Deputy Horn. Tate was a well-known and respected lawman. Not the kind of badge to be easily put aside by a tough-talking, spineless coward like Sheriff Fuller.

"We'll join your posse." Tate wasn't asking.

Fuller shifted uneasily in the saddle, as did Deputy Toller. "Fine by me." Fuller was lying. It could be heard in the pitch of his voice. The man's brow was glistening with sweat. "The trail seems to be going off this way." Fuller pointed west. The lawman was already trying to throw them off Jones's trail.

Nolan wasn't blind or green. "We ain't going that way. We're riding north. These tracks are less than an hour old."

He nodded toward the fresh tracks in the dirt. Any man there could see the truth of which way the prints were headed.

Sheriff Fuller couldn't twist his way out of the obvious and kept his mouth shut, though the man's face steamed red. No way would Nolan let the crooked lawman lead the posse around by the nose instead of actually tracking Jones to find Kate.

"Okay, army scout, then why don't you lead? And I'll be right behind ya." Fuller smirked.

Nolan could almost feel the lead ball plug his back. Nolan and Tate had ridden together too many times not to watch out for one another. It was an unspoken oath but one they both took particularly serious. Tate would shoot Fuller out of the saddle if the man raised a gun while Nolan had his back turned. That wasn't his worry.

Nathanial, at the moment, was hidden in the trees. Nolan couldn't leave his son behind, and once he fetched the boy, Nathanial would be a much easier target for a coward like Wade Fuller. He had no choice at this time. His son had to go forward with the posse to hunt Jones.

He gave a whistle. Slowly Nathanial and the mare appeared out of the tree line. The sheriff's eyes narrowed, and then he threw a quick glance at Deputy Toller. Nolan knew too damn well what Fuller was thinking. Nathanial was supposed to have been on the ranch, which meant he'd have been shot down by Jones's men. Nolan would have a piece of Wade Fuller before this fight was over.

Nolan took the half-pint's reins in his hand. The last thing he wanted was for Nathanial to get scared and lose control of the horse. He would string the boy's mare next to the bay, keeping him close.

"Why'd you run off last night?" Sheriff Fuller barked at Nathanial.

Nolan jerked the reins, wheeled the bay, and rammed Fuller's horse. They were nearly sitting nose to nose. "Don't raise your voice to my son. Nathanial, you don't have to answer the sheriff."

"It's okay, Pa."

Nolan stepped the bay back but kept himself firmly planted between Nathanial and Sheriff Fuller.

"I was afraid you wouldn't help me. That maybe you might still be mad that Ma is gonna marry Nolan and not you."

Stifled laughter came from the others in the posse, including Deputy Toller. Nolan reckoned that what Nathanial had said was, in part, the truth. The boy was smart not to have mentioned that he'd seen Jones and Fuller together.

Nolan turned the bay, and with it, Nate's mare followed.

It wasn't long before the sheriff's horse supposedly had a stone in its hoof. It took Fuller twenty damn minutes to falsely dig out the troublesome pebble before the posse could be on its way. Not an hour later, Deputy Toller's saddle had worked loose and they had to stop again. Then not long after that, the horses seemed tired, according to Fuller, and they should rest the animals for a spell.

Nolan was growing angry with these tactics to slow their efforts. He was about ready to shove Wade Fuller's excuses down his damn neck. The others in the posse, with the exception of Tate, didn't see what the sheriff was doing to assist Jones. Nolan could easily scout ahead, but now that he had Fuller under his nose, he didn't want to give the man any reason to escape, so he had to tolerate the sheriff's attempts to slow them.

Nolan stepped into the saddle. "Let's go. The horses are fine."

Evening was setting in when the posse stopped to make a fire for coffee. Nathanial chewed on a piece of jerky. The tough little pup hadn't complained even once about being tired or hungry. And if the boy was scared, he was hiding it well. Nathanial had every reason to be on edge.

Before making camp, Nolan had nodded just enough toward the prints in the dirt for Nathanial to take notice of how fresh Jones's tracks were. With Fuller riding on Nolan's back, he hadn't been able to outright warn his son of the danger they were closing in on. If he had, it would have tipped off Fuller. They were nearly on top of the gang that held Kate prisoner. Fuller might do something stupid to protect Jones.

Nolan needed to get his son out of trouble's path. Nathanial was sitting with Tate, playing a game of poker. Nolan poured himself a cup of hot mud, then stood and walked toward the horses. Fuller wasn't the only one who could play games.

Nolan rubbed his hand down over the leg of a horse wearing three white socks and a stocking. "John!" He called the big man over to join him.

He handed John the coffee cup, then picked up the horse's leg. He pulled his knife and then lifted the iron shoe from the hoof without looking up at Big John. Credit was given to the man for blindly showing his trust of Nolan by not blurting out what the hell was going on.

"Wait at the split pine that we passed a few miles back." Nolan had spoken in a low voice that only John could hear.

He dropped the hoof and straightened.

The others in the posse all sat around the fire, jawing.

"Looks like we have a problem." Nolan spoke to everyone. "John's horse threw a shoe. He'll have to ride back to town." Nolan hoped Fuller didn't catch on to what was happening.

Tate got quickly to his feet. A subdued wink and Nolan knew he was on board.

"John will need help to git that lame animal out of the mountains before dark. You, the banker, and, uh, Mr. Henderson saddle up." Tate fed right into what Nolan was trying to accomplish. The two townsmen tossed their coffee and hurried to follow through with Deputy Horn's order.

The sheriff showed no outward sign of knowing that in one play, Nolan had removed the others from the coming fight.

There was one important thing he needed to take care of yet. "John, I'd be obliged if you would take my son back with ya."

The big man glanced between Nolan and Nathanial. "Yes, sir, not a problem."

They shook hands. Nolan knew by John's raised brow that the big man had no idea as to what was about to happen.

"Nathanial, you mind what Mr. Filson tells ya." Nolan lifted Nathanial and sat him behind John in the saddle. He gave the boy's leg a pat, then walked away. He waited until they were out of sight, making their way back toward town. Nate was safe. That alone was most important to him.

He stood from where he was squatted next to the fire and walked a few steps to face Sheriff Fuller. From the corner of Nolan's eye, he could see that Tate had positioned himself to have a clear shot at Wade's deputy.

"Where's Kate? I know you're working with Jones."

Fuller had always been a fool and proved it the instant he reached for his gun. Nolan took a long step and swung his fist. Wade Fuller's nose popped.

"Damn you, Crosson!" Fuller grabbed for his face, dropped his gun, and blood gushed out of his nose.

Without warning, Wade lunged. Nolan hit with an uppercut and then another. The sheriff was knocked back against a tree. Pistol shots fired behind them. It distracted Nolan enough that Fuller landed a fist to his mouth. He tasted blood on his lips. A smashing blow just above Nolan's belt knocked the wind from him, and he stumbled back. Wade charged with a swing. His knuckles connected squarely, cracking Nolan's jaw. Somehow he was able to keep his bearings. His fist smashed into Wade's face. They fell to the ground, grappling as they rolled through the dirt, trading punches.

Nolan found himself on top of Fuller. Before he could throw a solid punch, Nolan's chest was slammed by a double kick from the sheriff's boots. It sent him rolling.

Nolan could barely breathe and lifted himself from the dirt in time to see Fuller scramble for his pistol. Wade swung around to fire. The Colt in Nolan's palm jerked. Instinctively he'd drawn and fired.

Fuller dropped to his knees. A red stain quickly began to spread across the chest of his shirt, and the man pulled the trigger of his gun. A bullet kicked up dirt near Nolan's boots. Fuller's second shot was that of a dying man, aimed wild into the air. It didn't take long until Wade Fuller bled out, face in the dirt.

CHAPTER 32

"THERE SURE WAS A LOT OF SHOOTING." Tears welled up in Nate's eyes.

Johnny's pa looked over his shoulder. "I'm sure everything is just fine."

Sweat drenched the man's brow, but the fading sun wasn't that hot. Nate didn't doubt that Sheriff Fuller and Deputy Toller were getting the worst of that fight, but that didn't mean Pa or Deputy Horn couldn't catch a bullet.

The posse waited at the split pine for what felt like hours. All eyes were on the trail when the bay came through the bushes.

"Pa!" Nate's smile stretched from ear to ear. He jumped from the back of the horse before Mr. Filson could grab hold of him, and he ran up the trail toward Pa. He reached down, took hold of Nate's wrist, and pulled him up into the saddle to sit. He stretched a little and peeked behind Pa. Sheriff Fuller was lying facedown over the saddle. It was a sad thing, but the sheriff had been a bad man. Deputy Toller was sitting slumped forward in the saddle, holding tight to his bleeding arm, while Deputy Tate rode next to him, holding Toller's reins.

Pa turned Nate around from the harshness of life that he'd been gawking at. A nudge from Pa and the bay trotted until they joined the others at the split pine. He pulled up on the reins, then tossed the reins of Sheriff Fuller's horse to Mr. Scott. "I don't care what you do with Fuller's body, but your former deputy…" Pa turned a thumb toward Jack Toller. "Lock him up till I return to Gray Rock, and that cell door don't git opened for any damn reason, not even to let Doc Martin dig the lead out of Toller's arm, or you'll answer to me."

The three townsmen nodded that they clearly understood Pa's orders.

"John, I have another favor to ask of ya."

Nate could guess what Pa was going to say, and he didn't want to go with Mr. Filson back to town. If Pa thought it best though, then he wouldn't get sassy about it.

Pa glanced once between Nate and Mr. Filson. "I need to know my boy is safe. I don't want Nathanial left to his own means while I hunt the man who has taken Kate."

Johnny's pa nodded. "Nathanial is welcome in my home for as long as it takes."

Wouldn't Johnny be happy about this? He and Nate weren't even on speaking terms.

Pa passed Nate to sit the horse behind Big John. It took a minute for him to settle himself comfortably, and he could feel Pa watching him. He looked up, and their eyes held.

"I don't know how long it will take, but I *will* be back with your ma."

Nate nodded, though he was a little bit scared and wished he could stay with Pa.

Pa and Deputy Tate turned their horses, riding back up the trail. They quickly disappeared out of sight, and Nate fought back his crying. What if neither his ma nor pa ever made it home to him? No. Nate couldn't let himself think like that.

The sun wasn't fully up, but there was enough light in the sky for Nolan and Tate to ride. They ran their horses through the wooded mountain pass, then turned north. Weaving a trail through the trees, their horses scrambled farther up into the rocky hills. They rode onto the flat, slowing their heavy-breathing mounts. This was the spot. It had to be.

Before they'd turned Toller over to the posse, Tate had squeezed at the former deputy's injured arm. To no surprise, the spineless Toller had been more than willing to rattle off Jones's plan. Nolan and Tate were indeed getting close to the cabin and hopefully closer to capturing Mr. Jones. If Toller hadn't lied, then the cabin should be no more than a mile from where they were.

Jones might have a guard posted. Nolan didn't have to tell Tate to be watchful. They were both cautious men.

It wasn't long before the filthy shack came into sight. It stood not a hundred yards directly in front of them. They left their horses and crept forward under the cover of the trees and scraggly underbrush. Was Jones really that overly confident in Sheriff Fuller's ability to throw the posse off that no lookout had been posted to watch his back trail? Maybe Mr. Jones wasn't as smart as Nolan had first thought.

He and Tate hunkered down behind a dead fall and silently watched the single room for a long time. No one came or went from the cabin. But now and then, raised voices from inside broke the quiet.

Nolan couldn't stop thinking about Kate. He would kill any man that laid a hand on her.

Tate nudged Nolan's arm, then nodded toward a string of horses. They both grinned. Six animals, plus one. All the men who'd taken Kate from the ranch and their leader were there. Most importantly, Deegan Jones was inside that cabin. He wouldn't escape justice this time.

"I say we make our stand just before dawn. We can scatter their horses first. I'll ask them to surrender before we use our guns." Tate's plan was good.

Only, Nolan had been chasing Jones too long and knew better than to think the killer would give himself up to Deputy Horn or anyone. Jones himself wasn't a fighter, but that fact didn't make him any less dangerous. The men he'd been known to hire, like the late Tucker Brown, were cutthroat. This time Nolan would see to it that Jones wouldn't slip away from the battle and leave his men behind to do the killing.

The morning mist floated high above the ground, making the mountain air damp and chilled. Nolan left Tate hidden in position among the trees, rocks, and underbrush to cover the front door. He stepped real carefully so as not to snap any twigs and alert them inside the cabin. Slowly he worked his way around to the rear of the building. The log shack sat too quiet, not a single sound coming from inside.

Nolan slipped the knot and dropped the rope rail that held the seven horses. If Jones ran, it would be on foot. Nolan swatted the rump of one horse to get them all running. It wouldn't be long now. The thundering hooves would be heard. He hunkered down behind a fallen dead tree and readied himself by aiming his rifle so he could easily throw lead at the back door or the rear window.

Tate should soon be calling out to the house. He'd been waiting for the horses to be gone.

"This is US Deputy Marshal Tate Horn. You boys are surrounded, so throw down your guns and come on out with your hands in the air."

The house came alive. Nolan could hear men quickly scrambling about inside. A backlash of gunfire thundered out from the cabin. The rear door swung open, and Nolan's rifle boomed. One of Jones's men dropped to the ground not a step outside the shack.

Kate's high-pitched scream filled Nolan's ears. A rifle broke through the window and fired. A bullet smacked the tree next to him. Nolan squeezed the trigger, returning fire. Hopefully, Kate was out of the way and kept her head down.

A ricochet of gunfire echoed through the air from the front of the cabin. Nolan fired on the run and kept himself in position to cover the back door. Tate had moved spots and was holding his own. Two of Jones's men had been killed and were flat out on the patch of ground near the front door.

A shot rang out from the open rear doorway. A bullet bit into the hardwood that covered Nolan. He stepped around the tree and squeezed the trigger. A man fell to his knees. Nolan's second shot tore through the man's chest, pitching him backward to the ground.

A Carbine was tossed out the door.

"I'm coming out!" It was one of Jones's men, surrendering with his hands in the air.

Nolan slowly walked forward. All the while, his rifle was aimed at the man's chest. The fella was no fool. He was taking it one slow step at a time toward Nolan. A pistol cracked off a round from the doorway. Jones's man hollered out in pain, grabbed his leg, and stumbled forward until he fell, hitting the ground with a thud.

"Damn you to hell, Jones." The man's teeth were gritted, and he held tight to the bleeding hole in his leg.

Nolan swung his rifle to the doorway and fired. Jones twisted, falling back into the darkness of the cabin. The dandy had shot his own man for backing out of the fight. What a son of a bitch.

There was no gunfire heard from the front of the cabin. All was eerily quiet. Was Kate alive?

"I got one prisoner! Jones is still inside!" Tate shouted from somewhere unseen.

"I have one of Jones's men down back here! He's bleeding!" It was important that both Nolan and Tate were aware of the odds. Jones was the only man left to fight, and Nolan aimed to end the killer.

He threw a glance at the groaning man bleeding all over himself. "You move, and I will shoot you." His stare then fixed on the cabin.

Kate was standing in the doorway, and her eyes were red, tears streaming down her face. Nolan could see her shaking with fear. Jones held her tight in front of him as a shield.

Nolan walked slowly closer. His eye squinted to see clearly down the barrel of the aimed Winchester. Jones's one arm was bleeding where Nolan had shot him. He stepped away from the cabin with Kate and glanced toward where the horses had been tied. The man's enterprise had fallen apart.

"I need your horse." Jones hatefully glared straight at Nolan. "Drop your gun. I don't think I have to tell you what will happen if you don't."

Had Jones not been holding Kate, Nolan would have laughed. "I can't put a bullet between your eyes if I drop my gun, so I reckon I'll just keep hold of it."

They stared down one another. Though Nolan kept his eyes locked on the killer, he could see Tate stepping quietly in behind Jones. Nolan was no glory hound, but he wanted to be the one to take down Jones.

"He's mine, Tate!"

In that split second, Jones twisted on his heels to see Tate.

Nolan dropped his rifle and palmed his pistol. The Colt cracked in his hand. One then two times he'd squeezed the trigger. Deegan Jones twisted away from Kate.

She ran toward Nolan.

"Git down!"

Nolan hadn't killed Jones. If the man still held breath, then he was a danger. Kate dropped to the ground and covered her head with her hands.

Nolan walked toward Jones, who was lying in the dirt, bleeding. He kicked the killer's pistol away from reach, Nolan's Colt aimed at his forehead.

So many lives had been destroyed by this man and his army of lowlifes. It wasn't just the families they'd buried. Would the rescued women ever really be free from what Jones had done to them? Anytime they heard a bump in the night or saw a strange horseman approach, Nolan would bet their hearts would race. Their minds probably would be flooded with the horror they'd been forced into.

Every time Nolan had seen Nathanial's scar from the gunshot wound, it was a reminder of those hellish days and nights of sitting at the boy's bedside, wishing for him not to die. Jones was responsible for all of it. The killer deserved a bullet.

"Don't do it, friend."

Nolan looked over at Tate while he kept his aim on Jones.

"That trash ain't worth cutting down your good reputation. We will see Mr. Jones's end come to him, but let the law judge him first. We'll take him back for trial. Then he'll be sentenced. I don't doubt for a minute that when the gavel falls, that man will git a rope thrown around his neck. We've got him, and he's lost his fight. I can't just let you kill him." Tate was right, and Nolan knew it.

He slowly lowered his pistol and slid the Colt into his holster. He grabbed Jones by the front of the shirt, yanking the filth to his feet. "I do find pleasure in knowing you'll hang."

Nolan shoved Jones toward Tate to bind the fancy man's hands behind his back. Nolan went to the downed man, whose leg was still bleeding. He jerked the fella up to stand.

"I can't walk on this leg." The man was pale and sweating.

"I don't wanna hear your damn bellyaching, so shut the hell up." Nolan gave the man a hard push in the direction to get his hands tied.

Kate's sobs finally took hold of Nolan's ears, and he turned his attention away from his work. She hadn't moved from where she'd thrown herself flat on the ground. He went, took her by the hand, and gently helped her to her feet.

Her eyes were bloodshot from crying. She brushed the dirt off herself, then straightened and looked him in the face. "I love you." She slid her arms around him, and he pulled her close before they kissed.

Nolan gave Kate a hand up to sit the saddle behind him.

The prisoners all would have a long walk out of the mountains. Tate led, with Jones and his two men tied up and strung out on a rope line. Jones had been warned that if he even thought about escape, he would be shot.

Nolan and Kate followed close behind the three prisoners. He wasn't going to take his eyes off Jones until the man was locked behind bars.

The hour was late the following day when they reached Gray Rock with their prisoners. Kate was half-asleep in the saddle behind him. He, too, was tired.

Tate pulled up on the reins in front of the jailhouse, and Nolan did the same. He stepped down and took his rifle. The prisoners were led onto the boardwalk. Nolan banged on the door twice, heard the jingle of keys, and then the door swung open.

John Filson stepped back out of the way as Nolan and Tate marched the prisoners inside. John just stood and gawked at the scraped-up and limping lot of them. Nolan grabbed the keys off the desk, then went and opened the cell door. There was great satisfaction in locking that cage behind the three guilty men.

He turned and tossed the ring of keys to Tate.

Deputy Horn was already tipped back in what used to be Wade Fuller's chair. His legs were crossed with his feet resting easy atop the desk.

Nolan put on some coffee, though all he really wanted was rest. He turned toward John. "Has there been any word from Captain Farnsworth?"

"Yes, sir. The army should be here sometime tomorrow or maybe the next day at the latest." John retrieved the wire from a desk drawer and handed it to Nolan to read himself.

"How's Nathanial?" Kate was at John's side.

"The boy is just fine, ma'am. In fact, he and Johnny have made up and are good friends again. Johnny told me the truth that it was his idea to play hooky that day. I'm sorry for the trouble, ma'am."

"Will you take me to see him?" Kate's eyes were glassy.

Nolan, too, would have liked more than anything to see their son, but that wasn't going to happen. He would stay with Deputy Horn until the captain showed up to transport Jones and the others to the fort for trial.

"Yes, ma'am, I will as long as I'm not needed here." John looked at Nolan, and he shook his head.

Kate followed John toward the door.

"Kate."

She turned.

"You and Nathanial don't go to the ranch alone. Git a room at the hotel for the night." They would go home as a family.

"That won't be necessary. The whole town is grateful for what you and Deputy Horn have done. Kate and Nathanial will stay the night with my family. It's the least I can do. You come fetch them when you're able." With that decided, both John and Kate disappeared out the door.

Nate dreamed that he heard Ma's voice whispering his name until his eyes fluttered opened. Was it a dream, or was she really staring into his face?

"Ma." Nate threw his arms around her neck. She hugged him tight right back, along with smearing his face with at least a dozen kisses. "Where's Pa?"

If Ma was there, then Pa was most likely just fine.

"He's at the jailhouse with Deputy Horn."

"Can I go see him?" Nate threw back the blankets and scooted toward the edge of the bed.

"Slow down, young man. It's the middle of the night. You can see your pa in the morning." Ma waited for Nate to crawl back into bed, then tucked the blanket up around him. "Mrs. Filson fixed me a room. I'll see you bright and early." Ma kissed his head one more time, then left and closed the door behind her.

He cozied up under the blanket and was happy that Ma was only a step or two away from being there if he needed her. It might have upset Ma if he'd asked what had happened to Jenny's killer. Causing Ma to shed more tears wasn't what he wished to do. A peek inside the jailhouse to see who was behind those bars would end his need to know. Captured or killed, Nate reckoned the dandy's fate would be the same. Hell would be plus one.

———◆————◆———

Nate woke early. A hint of pink morning light streaked through the window, and the house was quiet. He slipped out of bed, dropped his nightshirt where he stood, and pulled on his pants and shirt. Through a crack in the doorway, he peeked into the hall. No one seemed to be awake. He eased the door quietly open and glanced once more to his left then right before stepping real easy one at a time down the stairs.

Ma wouldn't like what Nate was about to do. He could almost hear her saying that a jailhouse was no place for a child. He needed to see for himself though. The sly devil had escaped justice before.

Nate quietly tugged on his boots, and he didn't smell coffee boiling. That meant neither Ma nor Mrs. Filson was in the kitchen and wouldn't see him leave the house.

The walk from the Filsons' home to the jailhouse was not far. Nate's heart pounded. If Deegan Jones was there, could Nate face Jenny's killer?

He peered through the window. The steam of his breath on the wavy glass blurred his vision so all he could see was the figures of four men in the two cells. Sweat poured from him. Had justice finally caught up to the man that put Jenny in her grave? Nate's hands shook as he touched the doorknob, and he slowly turned the latch. He nudged open the door, and his feet seemed to be planted in the entryway.

Breathe.

His eyes looked to each caged man. The former deputy was asleep on a cot. In the same cell, a man lay on the floor, snoring. Blood stained one leg of his pants where he'd been shot. The other cell held a sleeping man who sat at one end of a cot, slumped against the bars. Nate looked directly at the fourth man, also sitting on the cot but leaned back against the wall. Deegan Jones with his curled mustache. The dandy blue suit was torn, dirty, and stained with blood.

The fancy man's gaze met Nate's. Nate glanced away to Deputy Tate, who was tipped back in the desk chair, snoozing. Pa was asleep on a cot near the little potbellied stove.

Jenny's killer was less than ten feet from him. Nate's legs quivered, but he found the strength to slowly walk forward. The cell bars were the only thing separating him from the caged animal with the hateful eyes. Somehow Nate had fooled himself into believing that once justice had its grip around the fancy man, Jenny would come back to him. He'd known better. The truth was that Jenny was just as dead as the fancy man would soon be. Only, Jenny and the others hadn't deserved to die. Nate didn't care in the least that Deegan Jones would be hanged for his crimes.

"What are you staring at, kid?" The fancy man sneered.

Nate glanced over his shoulder at Pa still sleeping on the cot. He felt stronger than ever. No longer was he afraid of this dandy-dressed son of a bitch. His hands gripped the bars of the cell, his eyes narrowed, and he glared right back at Deegan Jones. The dandy would get his answer.

"I'm looking at the coward that killed my sister and tried to take my ma."

Jones smiled coyly.

Nate spit through the bars, hitting his target on the chin.

Jones jumped to his feet and charged. "Why, you little…" Jones madly wiped at his face and stopped midstep.

Nate didn't have to look to know who stood behind him. It was the one man who'd been watching out for him since the first day they'd met and always would be. A firm hand came to rest on his shoulder. He looked up, and Pa grinned.

Nate turned back to face Deegan Jones. "You ain't nothing that I can see. My pa, he stopped you from hurting anyone else's Jenny."

The troubled tug in Nate's heart was gone. He was going to be okay. He couldn't have Jenny, but he would always treasure his lovely memories of her. What he did have was a ma and pa who loved him. Without a doubt, Jenny was looking down and was happy for him.

The rattle of a heavy wagon turned their eyes toward the street. Nate, just that quick, forgot about Jones and ran to the window. "It's Captain Farnsworth, and Doc is with him."

Nate threw open the jailhouse door. Pa was right behind him, followed by Tate, who'd finally woke. The iron wagon was a cell on wheels. No way would the fancy man escape that thing, and besides, the captain must have had a dozen armed men with him.

It was starting out to be an all-around great day. The sun was shining. There was blue sky overhead, and the air Nate breathed seemed as fresh as spring.

"Hello there, son." Captain Farnsworth smiled and ruffled Nate's hair. It was surely going to snow in September.

Nate smiled. "Good morning, Captain. Hi, Doc." Nate waved. It was like a family reunion.

"Howdy, boy. I see you're still hanging around with this fella." Doc shook hands with Pa, and both men chuckled.

Nate walked next to Pa as Jones and the others were led from their cells, marched outside, then loaded into the barred army wagon. The town had come to life, and folks were gathered about, whispering. The iron door clanged shut, and the chain lock clicked behind the prisoners.

Captain Farnsworth turned to Pa and Tate. "Thank you, men, for what you've done. Do call on me personally if ever I can return the favor." The captain tipped his hat, then stepped up and swung a leg over the saddle. The wagon began to roll at the wave of Captain Farnsworth's hand to move out.

Nate was truly happy. Justice had finally caught up with Deegan Jones.

Tate leaned down from the saddle and shook Nolan's hand. "Well, Nolan, it's been a real good time, but I should be heading back to Birch Creek." Deputy Horn chuckled. "Next time we meet, let's make it at a saloon with some of those dancing señoritas." Tate grinned in that easygoing way of his.

"Here, I think you're the right man to wear this." Tate tossed the sheriff's badge that once belonged to Wade Fuller right to Nolan, and he caught it in one hand. "Gray Rock needs a good lawman, and I think these townsfolk will be happy to have ya. I have no doubt that Marshal Huckabee will support my decision and swear you in as soon as he gets a chance."

Nolan hardly believed that he was the new sheriff of Gray Rock.

"Get yourself married before starting that new job." Tate tipped his hat, spurred his horse, and was gone.

Nolan smiled down at Nathanial, who was standing next him. "Let's go git your ma."

They walked side by side to the Filson home. Nolan knocked once before the door was opened. Oh Lord, he had waited a long time for this. Pastor Hicks was back in town. He'd come to the jailhouse, preaching words of repentance to the prisoners.

Nolan swung Kate up into his arms and carried her toward the church. "I ain't sleeping in the spare room tonight."

They laughed between kisses, and Nathanial ran off as fast as he could to fetch the preacher.

ABOUT THE AUTHOR

J.B. Richard, author of the Western Promises series, resides in the Seven Mountain region of Central Pennsylvania, where her grandparents' farm is nestled, cultivating inspiration through her wild days-gone-by adventures with her many cousins. She is an avid outdoorsman who enjoys hiking and exploring Civil War battlefields. A highlight of her life was riding horseback on the same road that General Robert E. Lee had ridden into Gettysburg.

Visit J.B. Richard at www.jbrichard.com or
on Facebook at J.B. Richard.

CPSIA information can be obtained
at www.ICGtesting.com
Printed in the USA
LVHW091952021219
639194LV00001B/79/P

9 780999 155318